Praise fo

'Charles Lambert is
Owen King, au
and co-author ~~of Sleeping Beauties~~

'A writer who never ceases to surprise'
Jenny Offill, author of *Dept. of Speculation*

'A seriously good writer'
Dame Beryl Bainbridge

'Compulsively readable'
Kirkus Reviews

Praise for *The Children's Home*

'This disquieting novel is surely one of the year's most bizarre stories. Mr Lambert's subtle prose enhances the novel's creepiness, as does his refusal to fully resolve or explain its many mysteries'
New York Times

'Beautifully written and crafted, and more compelling than many thrillers'
Daily Mail

'A genre-defying dream of a novel'
Toronto Star

Charles Lambert is the author of several novels, short stories, and the memoir *With a Zero at its Heart*, which was voted one of the *Guardian* readers' Ten Best Books of the Year in 2014. His most recent novel was *The Children's Home*, described by the *Toronto Star* as a 'genre-defying dream of a novel'.

In 2007, he won an O. Henry Award for his short story *The Scent of Cinnamon*. His first novel, *Little Monsters*, was longlisted for the 2010 International IMPAC Dublin Literary Award.

Born in England, Charles Lambert has lived in central Italy since 1980.

PRODIGAL

AARDVARK
BUREAU

For my family

PRODIGAL

Charles Lambert

Aardvark Bureau
London

An Aardvark Bureau Book
An imprint of Gallic Books

Charles Lambert has asserted his moral right
to be identified as the author of the work.

First published in Great Britain in 2018 by Aardvark Bureau,
59 Ebury Street, London, SW1W 0NZ

A CIP record for this book is available from the British Library
ISBN 978-1-910709-498

Typeset in Garamond Pro by
Palimpsest Book Production Ltd, Falkirk, Stirlingshire
Printed and bound by CPI Group (UK) Ltd, Croydon CR0 4YY

And what's romance? Usually, a nice little tale where you have everything as you like it, here rain never wets your jacket and gnats never bite your nose, and it's always daisy time.

D.H. Lawrence

PART ONE

(2012)

1

JEREMY

The call comes when he least expects it. He's tidying away what's left of lunch – some cold meat wrappers, a crust of baguette – when the phone rings, in that short-tempered peremptory way machines have. He almost doesn't answer it; he's been fending off unwanted offers of insurance, unlimited broadband, crates of discount wine for months now. His name must be on some list somewhere – Jeremy Eldritch, sucker, with a five-star rating after it to indicate the extent of his gullibility. Or maybe four. Why be so hard on himself always, so unforgiving? These past few weeks he's found himself saying no with unexpected ease, behaving with a brusqueness he's superficially ashamed of, but deeply pleased, even smug, to find as part of his telephone repertoire. I'm getting bad, he's said to himself. Even my mother would be ashamed of me. I'm finding my teeth after all these years of pandering to people I've never met and would almost certainly hate to the deepest pit of my heart if I did, as they would me. He throws the paper and crust towards the bin two feet away, wipes his greasy hands on a tea towel hanging from the oven door and picks up the phone.

It's his older sister, Rachel. 'You'd better get back here,' she says. 'He's on his way out.'

Jeremy lives on the fourth floor of a building ten minutes' walk away from Place de Clichy in the seventeenth arrondissement, his favourite part of Paris. In the days when people read Henry Miller, long before he lived here himself, he'd use the man's *Quiet Days in Clichy* as a sort of cultural landmark. Not exactly my idea of quiet, he'd say, referring to the book, more like a movable fuck-fest of very little literary worth, and people would leap to Miller's defence, or not, depending on their age and sex and artistic pretension, or look at him with an anxious glance, surprised to hear such language from such an apparently mild and amenable man.

This is the smallest flat he's ever lived in, just under eighteen metres square, a truncated cupboard masquerading as a kitchen, an all-purpose living space not much larger than a decent walk-in wardrobe, a bathroom small enough to shower while crapping and still be able to rinse one's razor under the tap. It was sold to him as a studio and might even have had room for a desk or drawing board of some kind if he hadn't squeezed a double mattress in the space between the cooker and the door to the bathroom, now a sort of improvised futon Jean-Paul produced by lifting the mattress up with the sort of strength the adrenalin of rage produces and flinging it against the wall. It skulks there, a drunken observer, its back against the plaster, a sheet hanging rakishly down from one corner, while Jeremy eats and writes and reads at the round wooden table that takes up most of the rest of the room. Jeremy sleeps on the horizontal part of the mattress, a not quite rectangular rhomboid with a couple of pillows thrown at the wider end and a duvet gathered at the other. He waits for Jean-Paul to come back and sort things out. He has been waiting for just over two months.

What made him buy the flat, other than its price and the fact that he likes small places, prefers them even, was the honey-coloured parquet and the window, which reaches to the ground and gives onto a courtyard and blue-grey roofs of weathered zinc and is altogether too splendid for the room in which it finds itself; a situation, Jeremy feels, that has some affinity to his. His favourite position is to sit at one side of the table with his back to the mattress, looking out through the wide-open window, his feet on a small wooden box that once held a magnum of champagne and is now filled with letters from the time when people wrote them, his arms crossed loosely above his stomach in the restful position of a man on his own tomb. He'll have a book somewhere near his chair, or his laptop, or the manuscript he's working on, but will have abandoned it to watch the gently urban wind in the leaves of the courtyard's single tree, which may be a lime or may be something quite different, but which he continues to think of as a lime. He'll be watching the leaves as the wind turns them white and then dark again, and the movement of the young man in the window opposite, who has no time at all for Jeremy and who wanders around his slightly larger studio in pyjamas or less, a large bowl of coffee cupped in his elegant white hands, and whose presence contributed in no small measure to Jean-Paul's final fit of jealous rage.

Jeremy has been in this flat for the past seventeen years, in or near Batignolles for almost twenty-five, in Paris for thirty-four, give or take the odd few months elsewhere, for reasons of the heart or penury. He was dispatched here by his mother when no other solution seemed feasible, with the address in

5

his wallet of a girl she'd known at school, who'd married someone in publishing, the business card of a hotel she'd stayed in briefly before she married his father, in whose company she didn't say, some traveller's cheques for the first few months and a copy of a guide to the churches of Paris she'd claimed to have bought in a local jumble sale, trusting that some kind of solace might be gained from it. He studied the names as the ferry pitched its way towards Calais. Saint-Denys. Saint-Gervais-et-Saint-Protais. Saint-Germain-des-Prés. What a saintly city it must be, he mused. He'd read French at university but spent his year out in Montpellier and only passed through Paris twice. He was saving it for when he was in love, he told himself, which made it feel vast and hopeless; the depth and span of its stations dispirited him, the elegance of its men, each one of them single and aloof and self-sufficient. His mother's hotel, though, set him right within hours, when one of the kitchen hands followed him back to his poky, single-bedded room and gave him a lesson in a brusque and richly communicative sexual argot his three interrupted years at Exeter hadn't prepared him for at all. So this is Paris, he thought, his face in the pillow as a slim Algerian whose name he never caught left teeth marks in his shoulder.

His mother's friend's husband had turned out to own not a publishing house but a sizable printing works to the south of Paris. He caught the train out there one late autumn morning, enjoying the sense of being a foreigner these journeys within the larger journey always heightened. I don't belong here, he found himself repeating in mantric rapture, in time with the leafless poplars that lined the railway track as soon as the city and its suburbs were behind him. I don't belong here. And its counterpoint. And so I'll stay.

He was met at the station by a short man with a large

moustache who introduced himself as the general manager of the works, which impressed Jeremy, as it was no doubt meant to. The man drove him to a smallish factory on the outskirts of the town, with a row of sedately smoking chimneys, their off-white pads of vapour sloping away to the side in infantile chorus like something from an impressionist painting. The printing works were behind this, in a squat red-brick *manoir*-like building, from which came the sound of machinery, an arrhythmic thudding that nonetheless reminded Jeremy of his journey and gave him a sense of inevitability he realised he had been craving. He wondered what was being printed behind such mundane walls. What had seemed like a courtesy visit took on a new importance.

The manager walked him round the works, explaining each stage of the process, but Jeremy's French was barely up to it, and what he did understand made it all seem more mysterious. He watched a young man his age set type, his hands like birds after seed, and didn't want to know any more than that; that hands had made it. He heard the presses at work, glistening black giant looms weaving words, or text as he had learned to call it during supervisions with his teachers, always with the epithet *holy* in his head, as though the words were measured out by gods who wished both to remain secret and to be obeyed. The author was dead, but the printer survived, the actual artisan of the text, a man no older than he was, fine-featured, stooped like a heron over water, all of these images of birds tumbling one after the other; perhaps there was some sort of narcotic in the ink they used, he thought, as he stumbled behind his brisk, gesticulating guide until he was suddenly in an office, the distant thud of the printing attenuated by music he couldn't place. Something that reminded him of Satie, but wasn't.

A man unfolded himself from behind a desk and held out his hand. He announced, in rumbling, accented English, that he was Jeremy's mother's friend's husband, presumably to show off his grasp of the genitive. Jeremy sat down in the seat provided and let the man talk for a little until he could make up his mind about what he thought. The man was tall, large-boned, with long, slightly thinning hair and expressive hands he was clearly proud of; he'd catch sight of them suddenly and pause, as if surprised by such contingent elegance. His name, he said, was Armand. Jeremy wasn't sure which name this was, his first or second. He glanced above the man's head to what looked like a university degree, framed in gilt, and saw the name Armand Grenier in blood-red copperplate across its centre. The truth, thought Jeremy as he cautiously glanced around the rest of the room, its cabinets and glass-fronted bookcases, its telephones and in-trays, its general air of business being conducted, was that he knew nothing. He had a degree in a language he could read but barely speak without being aware of an anxious, even supercilious, look appearing on the other person's face. He would have to work harder, work faster, he told himself, if only to stay in the same place, wherever that was, let alone get out of it. He hated his hotel room. The kitchen hand was avoiding him or had simply left. He might have been traceable if only Jeremy had discovered his name. He might have been able to run him to ground, to leave for Algiers with his Berber love, to lose himself in the desert as whatever-his-name had done in *The Sheltering Sky*, a book he loved, except that the hero had died, which Jeremy would rather avoid.

While all this ran like water through his head, Grenier was explaining the workings of the printing industry in fluent, heavily accented English. Jeremy heard little, and would have understood less; he had an aversion to practical knowledge of any kind. He wondered why everyone should want him to know so much about the intricacies of book and magazine production, and commercial printing, and only later asked himself, as the train took him back to Paris, whether he might not have been the victim of a plan cooked up by his mother and Hilary, or whoever she was, to keep him busy until his father would have him back, assuming he would. Busy, and even, if it weren't too much to ask, involved in some sort of business, a money-making activity of some sort. Money. That would be the type of thing to win his father over: for Jeremy actually to be capable of making money. Slumped into his chair, he watched the Frenchman's floating hair and almost verbal hands in a wordless daze, until he was startled into attention.

'Your mother has told us you write,' said Grenier.

'Well, yes,' said Jeremy. 'I mean, not really.'

'Come, come, *mon ami*, no modesty, please.' Grenier stood up. 'You will accompany me now to my second office, where I have something I wish to show you.'

Jeremy followed him along a narrow corridor with a suspended quality about it; metal-framed windows overlooked a sloping zinc-covered roof at one side, the other side lined with advertisements for household goods of various types: detergents, domestic appliances, cosmetics for women, shampoos for men with prematurely greying hair. There was a house style – crude, slightly retro but knowing, a nod towards the nouvelle vague, but pop-arty as well, the style he recognised immediately when Grenier opened the door at the end of the corridor and, walking him to a tilted draughtsman's table in the middle of the room, pointed down to the sheet of paper on its surface.

'This is the front cover of a little publication we plan to export to your country,' said Grenier.

A woman has been stretched face down across what appears to be a stone altar. Her flimsy clothes have been torn away and her ankles and wrists attached to usefully placed metal loops by flimsy golden chains. What looks like a conquistador's helmet lies on the floor beside her. She's blonde, with high round buttocks that already appear to have been beaten a deepening rose. Behind her a man in a feathered headdress and bulging loincloth is holding a whip and smirking as he lifts it. Across the top third of the cover, in the sort of jagged font used for 1950s science-fiction movies, are two words: *Montezuma's Revenge*.

'It is only a working title, naturally,' said Grenier. 'Our private joke. Intestinal, yes? We would like to find something with a little more, how do you say, libido.'

Jeremy, mute with embarrassment, nodded as Grenier squeezed his arm above the elbow, almost tight enough to hurt.

'Perhaps you can help us?'

'With the title?'

Grenier shook his head, bared his large grey teeth in a grin. 'With the book.'

Jeremy puts the phone down and stares out of the window, his eyes misted over against every expectation. He sits there for what might be minutes, or tens of minutes, the leaves on the tree in the courtyard outside almost motionless, as though they were also waiting for some further change to take place, some further news to arrive. But the air is still. After however long it is, he reaches down and picks up the laptop beside the chair and reads what he has written that day.

Lady Mirabelle held back the curtain with her slim white hand so that her view into the formal garden was uninterrupted. Beds of pink and yellow roses meandered gracefully towards the lake below, but Lady Mirabelle's attention was less on the scented array of blooms than it was on the gardener, only recently employed, whose name she had still not discovered. Against regulations, he had taken off his shirt in an attempt to cool down from his exertions and was standing no more than thirty feet from the house, his lustrous hair tied back from his strong brown neck, his smooth skin glistening in the late morning sun as if waiting for the birch, the birch that would duly arrive if she decided to rebuke him for his shirtless state. Lady Mirabelle lifted her Spanish fan to her face and agitated it, her bosom rising and falling. She was about to sit down when a sound behind her caused her to turn.

'I have some bad news for you, my Lady,' said Grenier, the estate manager and her family's most trusted servant.

'Bad news?' Her voice was faint.

'Your father, my Lady, my Lord Clichy, he's . . . Oh, my Lady . . .'

Lady Mirabelle gave a gasp. Dropping the fan to the parquet floor, her delicate fingers grasped the heavy brocade of the drawing room curtain for strength.

'He's dead? My father's dead?'

'You must come with me, my Lady . . .'

Thus life imitates art, thinks Jeremy. That sentimental fool Oscar Wilde was right. He writes: *'Bloody good riddance,' said Lady Mirabelle, with a casual, but heartfelt, laugh. 'The selfish bastard deserves to die'*, then reads the words aloud in a trembling voice, a faint voice, and pauses for a moment before deleting them. Not yet, he thinks. Not now. It is early after-noon. He puts the laptop down and covers his face with both hands, shaking with unexpected grief.

2

RACHEL

Rachel is waiting at St Pancras International, by the branch of Marks and Spencer nearest the Eurostar exit. She's been shopping. Jeremy should have been here an hour ago but missed his train, and texted her when she was already on her own train to London, thereby wasting her morning in a way that was so typical of her brother and of his hopelessness she can hardly bring herself to feel angry about it. She's made use of the time to buy some stuff she can pop in the microwave, which will make it easier – a couple of curries, a steak and kidney pudding, fish cakes, various sorts of vegetables she doesn't even have to wash. How easy life is these days, she thinks, with a wriggle of resentment. If only it had always been so simple. At least she won't have to listen to his carping about her cooking and how they do things this way and that way in France, and how infinitely preferable it is to anything anyone does this side of the Channel. No wonder he's getting fatter by the visit, all that goose liver and fussed-about-with potatoes, although she hasn't seen him for almost three years, is it? That time he came with some boyfriend who didn't speak a word of English she could understand, with Jeremy swearing blind he was fluent and she was cloth-eared and just didn't *want* to understand.

She can't imagine how anyone might want to sleep with him, which, she feels, is a blessing. Their father asked her quite recently, before he retired to his bed, *You don't suppose lesbians always use dildos, do you?* as though she might be expected to know. It was one of his more lucid days, and they'd been watching *Loose Women* while she was gathering up the lunch plates to leave for Dhara. She told him to keep his dirty thoughts to himself, but she can't help wondering the same sort of thing about men. Men together, that is. Does Jeremy play the woman, she asks herself as people sweep out through the exit. Is that what they do? She has a sudden mental picture of Jeremy in a bra and knickers, his hair done up in a bun, like some awful vision of a sports mistress in her dismal privacy.

She glances at her watch. Sixty-five minutes late. She has a feeling there's another M&S just round the corner from here, which is bound to be where he'll go first, Murphy's Law being, as always, in operation. He's probably standing there now, with one of his silly hats in his hand and his canvas rucksack on his shoulders; absurdly, for a man of his age, he's been dragging the thing round for decades. Get yourself a trolley case, she's told him, no one cares any more, it isn't *feminine*, but he won't listen. He never does, not to her anyway. And now she's going to have to tell him that their father no longer knows who she, or anyone, is in any reliable way, and that in the three days that have passed since she called he has said no more than a handful of meaningless words, if words are what they were, none of which expressed the least desire to see his son, although God knows that's nothing new. He's expressed no desire to see Jeremy in the past three decades as far as she can remember, though he's mentioned him often enough. Jeremy this. Jeremy that. She wishes he hadn't. He's doubly incontinent as well, but she'll let that pass. Why put Jeremy off before he's even home?

And here he is, trailing along like some teddy bear in the hands of a child he's too dim-witted to see. 'Jeremy,' she calls out, and waves, and he gives her one of his half-hearted smiles and slopes across.

'Where did you pop out from?' she says, turning her head away from him as he kisses her cheek, so that what he gets is the patch of rough skin beside her ear, where she's plucked out the odd hair. He'll be diving in for a second one, she thinks, and steps back, giving his shoulders a brisk shake that will do as well as anything else to express her affection. She hates him when he gets too close. She expects him to smell of something French, like cheese.

'Oh, all very confusing here,' he says vaguely, readjusting his rucksack. 'I'm not sure it's entirely an improvement, this new station.'

'You'd better get used to things changing,' Rachel says, with grim satisfaction, because it will be amusing to see him befuddled and caught off guard. Apart from the sheer fun of it, his bemusement will give her the advantage she needs to make sure he doesn't take over at this point in the game, now that the old man is barely with them any longer. It would be too bad if Jeremy simply walked in and took control after decades of frittering his time away in Paris, of all places, like some alcoholic American novelist between the wars. She's been reading a lot of them recently – Faulkner, Hemingway, Fitzgerald – sitting beside the bed with the television headphones clipped onto her father's face like a bridle, looking up now and then to make sure he's still alive as one property show is succeeded by the next. She's working her way through a list of the hundred greatest novels from a book her neighbour gave her for Christmas, though she can't imagine what the criteria might have been that allowed some of them into the paddock, nor why her neighbour should have thought she'd want the book in the first place. She decided to regard it as a challenge. Most of the novels she's had to order, which makes her wonder exactly what purpose the public library is supposed to serve if it doesn't have a single work of classic fiction; if all it can dish up is horror, large-print P.D. James and Jeremy's latest offering, if you're prepared to deal with the looks you get.

'I suppose you've had something to eat on the train,' she says, nodding briskly before he can answer, 'so we'll be getting on, shall we? Don't want to keep Daddy waiting.'

'How is he?' says Jeremy. His voice sounds tired.

'Away with the fairies most of the time,' she says, not looking at him, staring at the flow of commuters that separates her from her goal with an angry, affronted glare. 'Still, you'll see soon enough.'

'You've left him alone?'

What she could say, what she wants to say, is, And what business is that of yours? You washed your hands of him years ago. You walked out on us both to lead your own selfish life in France. But there will be time for that later, when they're both at home and he can see the lie of the land himself, and it will hit home harder. For now, she shakes her head. 'There's Dhara with him.' He probably doesn't even remember who Dhara is. 'And we've got a sitter who comes in when she's needed. It's all provided by the government. Extraordinary, really. He'd probably hate it if he knew. You know what he thinks about nanny states.'

He nods. 'Yes,' he says, and from his tone she feels as though what he has heard is not what she has said but what she thought.

Later, on the train, he says, 'I didn't expect you to come up to London to meet me.' He's leaning forward, swinging his hat between his knees, his face crumpled with concern she can't help but see as mawkish. For a moment, he reminds her of their mother in one of her moods of wanting to know all about them, as though they would tell her everything, all their secrets, succumb to her simply because she wanted it, because the mood to want it had possessed her for a moment. She'd have had a magazine in her hand, or the receiver of the phone, and this whim would have distracted her from the call she was about to make, from the article about some person she didn't know from Adam, from the recipe she'd subject them to the following day. And then, like a puff of smoke, the moment would pass. Jeremy is like our mother, she thinks for the thousandth time. So what does that make me? What am I left with?

'You think I should have stayed with him, I suppose,' she says, bridling. She won't be criticised by someone who's given so little. The man sitting next to her turns his head in her direction; she must have raised her voice without meaning to. He fiddles with the volume on his mobile and the dull pumping sound of some dreadful pop music becomes audible to her left as she's cut out from his life again. His elbow is touching hers, as though she were part of the train itself, part of the fittings. If she were alone, she'd move. Jeremy is staring through the window at an industrial estate, low prefabricated buildings behind barbed wire, graffiti-daubed walls, waiting for her to carry on. She's caught him with his eyes on the man beside her more than once.

'No, no, not at all,' he says, finally, turning back to look at her. 'I'm just surprised. You don't usually.' He smiles. 'It's nice to be met. I'm hardly ever met.'

'He's perfectly well looked after,' she says.

'Honestly, Rachel, the last thing I want to do is upset you. I was trying to express my gratitude.'

'What makes you think I'm upset?'

He leans back in the seat and sighs quietly, which makes her feel it's all her fault. After a moment, he lifts his hat towards the window.

'Just look at it. We could be anywhere,' he says. 'Anywhere in the world. People making things nobody needs in the ugliest surroundings possible.'

'We'll be in Rochester in five minutes,' she says. 'You can look at the castle then. I imagine that's more to your taste.'

He smiles again. 'Medieval bloodshed? Oh yes.' His eyes flicker back to the man, who has started to agitate his leg in time to whatever he's hearing. 'I think you've been wonderful,' Jeremy says, and he reaches across to rest his hand for a second on her knee. 'I wouldn't have done what you've done.'

She sniffs. 'Yes, well, it's not over yet.' That will teach him, she thinks, as the train grinds to a halt outside the station. 'You'd better get your rucksack down ready. We don't want to miss our connection.'

They're on the next train when she says, 'You didn't need to go all the way to London, you know. You could have got off at Dartford. I'd have driven over. It would have been easier for everyone.'

'I didn't think,' he says, after a moment, and she isn't sure if he's heard her or is simply responding to sound and tone, the way her horses do. A vague sense of reproach, of the need to apologise. She's about to explain how typical this is of him, not to think, when she remembers how much she welcomed the chance to get away for the day, or half-day, to shop in a different M&S, to see a few different, citified faces. She settles the shopping more comfortably between her feet and looks across at him, hoping he'll say something else. But he's staring out of the window again, his face expressionless, passive, contained within its thoughts, excluding her. She's reminded suddenly of an afternoon when they were both children and their mother had told her to keep an eye on Jeremy. He couldn't have been more than five or six, which made her eight or nine, and they were in the garden of the house they lived in then, near Faversham. They'd been playing some kind of game when Jeremy had picked up a stone from one of the flower beds and put it into his mouth. It was a large stone and he'd had to open his mouth wide to get it in, and she can still remember a sense of horror, as though his bottom jaw might snap off under the strain. And then the stone was inside him, inside his mouth, and he was looking at her with a sort of smirk, as though he'd done something clever. She'd been so frightened. The oddest thing was that you couldn't tell the stone was there; his face just looked fuller somehow, heavier. She thought, he won't be able to breathe. Spit it out, she said, and he stared at her for a long time, or what felt like a long time, before shaking his head very slowly from side to side. She didn't know how to tell if he was teasing or couldn't speak. Spit it out, she said, and then she started to cry and pummel him with her fists and he'd let himself be hit, he'd gone all floppy apart from that hard, wet stone in his mouth, which he wouldn't give up, no matter what she did.

She doesn't remember what happened next, although she

half sees her mother running across the lawn and Jeremy being swept up and cuddled, covered with kisses. But that might have been some other day; her mother was always making a fuss over Jeremy. The stone must have fallen out of his mouth somehow, slick with his spit. Or perhaps he'd taken it out himself or had it wrenched out by Mummy; she'll have pushed her fingers in to shift it. Later that day, although even this may be nothing more than a false memory, her father slapped them both on their bottoms, and she had wondered what she'd done wrong. She'd only tried to help; it was Jeremy's fault, not hers. The next day she looked for the stone, but couldn't find it. She can still remember her father's hand on her bare skin.

'I don't feel as though I've ever really lived here,' he says, as they stand in the hall an hour later. 'Not properly. It's odd, isn't it, that I should think of it as home?'

'I've put you in the usual room,' she says. 'I've had to move most of your stuff out of it, because it's where I was going to put the night nurse. Not that that came to anything, and I can't say I'm sorry. Sharing the house with another woman at my age. Apart from Dhara, of course.' She's aware of talking and of not talking, to him, at least. Of talking in order to not talk, she supposes. It's what she's always done with Jeremy, as though she has to prevent him saying something that might hurt her by taking the silence out of the room, by replacing it with a sort of banter that's either irrelevant or spiteful. She knows herself well enough to know this; she doesn't need the inspiration of the world's greatest fiction to be able to step outside herself and see what she's up to, her little schemes, her little deceits. She can see them now, as if she were floating outside her body and standing at the top of the stairs, looking down into the cluttered, old-fashioned hall she's never considered changing in any way these past few years, most of which she has spent here and not in her own home, because neither has she lived here, not really, not with her heart. Not for years. Her heart is with her horses, fifteen miles to the east; her heart is with Denny, in Austria as far as she knows, or has been told.

She can see the two of them suddenly, brother and sister, in her mind's eye, in her floating body's eye, from the landing. Jeremy is lowering his rucksack to the ground and reaching into the pocket of his jacket for – what? A handkerchief? A packet of cigarettes? She doesn't know yet if he still smokes. She's heard that even France has banned it in bars and cafés, and about time too. And now she is doing it again, only this time she's silencing herself. Because there she is, foreshortened, a few feet away from her brother, her younger and only brother, although people often assume he's the older one, her M&S reusable bags at her feet, and she must get the perishables into the fridge before she does anything else, she thinks, and the thought unites her with her other self, all one again in the dimness of the hall, a late-middle-aged woman with her brother beside her and their father dying upstairs. She'll have to pop up in a minute, to check. There's no point in her calling; his hearing has almost gone by now, although not his voice. When she called the sitter from the station to say they were on their way, she was told he was dozing. 'Off you go,' she said. 'It's way past when you should have left. He'll be fine for ten minutes.' And for a moment she thought, her heart in her throat, what if he isn't dozing? What if he's dead?

She picks up the bags and leaves Jeremy standing there, looking round in his mole-like way, a crumpled piece of paper in his hand with something written on it, so she was wrong on both counts. How unpredictable life is, she thinks, and it doesn't make her happy, quite the contrary. It makes her anxious and frightened, and wishing everything were different.

Jeremy shakes his head and puts the piece of paper back in his pocket. 'I'll go up and say hello,' he says, not following as she goes into the kitchen, a trace of sound behind her, like someone calling from a train as it pulls away and you're left with your arm raised foolishly to wave.

'Yes,' she says, over her shoulder, 'you do that. I'll be up myself just as soon as I've sorted out the shopping. He's probably asleep. I wouldn't wake him unless you need to. He'll only want to be put on the commode.' She still hasn't mentioned the double incontinence. It's her trump card, she's decided. She opens the fridge door, noticing, as these days she rarely does, the postcard Denny sent her months ago of the Lipizzaner stallions, with their uniformed riders, standing in 'v' formation in a covered space that looks as though it's made of icing. *Hope you're well*, the back said. She isn't even sure it's his writing. How cruel men can be, she thinks.

'I can do that,' says Jeremy, but she can hear the trepidation in his voice.

'I doubt that very much,' she says. 'Fish cakes all right for you? I'm afraid we're out of fatted calves.'

'I'd much prefer you to be there,' he says.

3

JEREMY

The last time Rachel came to visit, Jeremy had already moved into the studio flat in Rue Nollet. He'd booked her into the hotel round the corner in Rue des Dames as soon as he knew. The thought of her squeezing beside him onto the mattress, which was still at that time entirely on the floor, was too awful to contemplate. He imagined her snoring and rolling towards him in her sleep, her breasts like seal pups trapped within a nylon nightgown. One morning, soon after he knew of her plan to visit, he woke in a sweat with the sense that he was suffocating in her, his sister transformed into some uncontrolled, viscous substance, unmistakably Rachel. Besides, there was always the chance that Jean-Paul would sniff out an opportunity for mischief and show up unexpectedly to embarrass them both. Jeremy booked her into a room that very day, a single room with shower overlooking the street. The hotel was cheap enough, and looked clean, and a sign by the door said *English spoken*. It would do, he thought. He still wasn't sure why she'd called to say she was coming, certainly not for pleasure, but he was sure that he'd be told soon enough. Rachel had no gift for secrets.

'I don't know how you can live like this,' she said when

he opened the flat door and ushered her in. He saw her shoulders set, heard her slow sigh as she put down her suitcase, a flimsy looking thing on wheels, ridiculous beside the bulk of her. His instinct was to place his hands on the small of her back and push her further in, as though they were trying to enter a carriage on the métro before the doors closed. But she took a step, and then another, and was already in the centre of the space he thought of as his living room, because all his living was conducted in it. He wanted to show her the view, the window, his beautiful window, and beyond it the roofs in the early afternoon light and the tree only now coming into leaf, because she was visiting him in spring, but she'd turned towards him and had her back to everything that was lovely; her squarely inexpressive form, in jeans and windcheater, blocked everything of value out. She stroked the empty surface of the table and, for a moment, he thought she was checking for dust and was reminded of a hotel they'd stayed in together, decades ago, when she'd done precisely that, and the owner of the hotel had taken their bags and, cursing the perfidious race of tourists, had thrown them out of the place before they'd had a chance to protest. 'Never do that again,' he'd told her, furious, as the door behind them slammed. When she glanced at the tip of her finger to see what it had gathered, he realised he'd been right. Either way, he thought, whether there's dust or not, I'll have disappointed her.

He'd met her at the Arc de Triomphe, where the shuttle buses stopped. He would have gone directly to the airport but she insisted she was more than capable of crossing Paris without him, and that was what she had done. They kissed each other's cheek. She refused to let him take her luggage as he led the way from the Air France bus to the métro entrance, preferring to stomp along in his wake. He could hear the rattle of her trolley-case wheels behind him, like time's wingèd chariot, until they reached the stairs and she was forced to pick the case up and carry it. And that, my dear, serves you right, he said to himself. Throughout the journey, from the platform at Charles-de-Gaulle-Étoile to the exit at Clichy, she'd stared around her with a look of intense critical dissatisfaction, while Jeremy imagined what she might be thinking and holding back, not to spare him but to render her company even more frustrating and intimidating than it need be, and felt his gorge rise. He caught her running an eye across the tiled walls of the station corridors, so reminiscent of school lavatories, at the posters of musical theatre performances, with faces that could belong to no other category of creative endeavour than musical theatre, faces so filled with ersatz joy they barely qualified as human. Spit it out, he wanted to say, spit it out. But she held her tongue. When she finally did speak, as they turned the corner from Place de Clichy and it started to rain, a soft grey drizzle, to comment sourly that she'd expected better weather, as though Paris were the Côte d'Azur, he snapped that people didn't come to Paris to sunbathe, and felt immediately at fault, as though she'd caught him out. And now here she was, examining her finger.

'It's exactly what I need,' he said before she could speak, taking off his jacket and hanging it on its peg behind the door. 'People only expand to fill what space they have.'

'I suppose they do,' she said. She sounded hurt. Had he been cruel, implying that someone of her bulk would obviously require more space than a Paris studio flat could offer? Had she seen herself, as he now did, slowly but steadily inflating like some grotesque balloon until he would be forced to leave for lack of air?

'Anyway, you won't be sleeping here,' he said quickly. 'It's all sorted out. I've booked you a room round the corner in a very comfortable little place. I'll take you round there as soon as you're ready.'

'I won't be sleeping here?' she said. And now she really did sound hurt. He would have told her on the métro but he'd thought that, once she'd seen the flat, she'd be only too happy to sleep elsewhere. Perhaps she was worried about the cost.

'Don't worry,' he said. 'It's all taken care of. I mean, the bill and so on.'

'Oh,' she said, as though she hadn't heard. 'I'm so sorry I won't be here. I was looking forward to spending some time with you.'

'Oh, we'll manage to do that, I'm sure,' he said, doing his best to sound enthused. 'Now, can I offer you something before we go round to the hotel? A cup of tea? A glass of wine?' He eased himself past her towards the fridge, the kettle.

She shook her head. 'No,' she said, 'let's get it over with.'

'I'm so sorry, Rachel,' he said, embarrassed, guilty, more than anything surprised. 'I thought you'd feel more comfortable somewhere else.' He filled the kettle, but she snatched it from his hand with surprising vigour and replaced it with a bottle of Bordeaux from the worktop. 'I can't remember the last time we shared a room, let alone a bed.'

'No, neither can I,' she said, watching him as he opened the bottle with his favourite corkscrew, the kind sommeliers carry in their front trouser pocket, opening the small curved blade like a penknife to remove the foil, running it around the neck, lifting it off in one neat move, aware that he was showing off, enjoying himself. He eased out the cork, raising it to his nose with a little flourish, to take a sniff, in control of the situation. Except that there she was, her eyes not leaving his, and he didn't believe her; she sounded as though she remembered perfectly well but wasn't prepared to tell him. He didn't deserve to be told. And now he did remember. That awful night. That awful hotel. And then their mother dead.

'The glasses are behind you,' he said.

Later that evening they were sitting in a Thai restaurant five minutes' walk from the hotel. He'd brought her there because the menu was pictorial and the food not French. He'd wanted neither to translate nor to defend the cuisine he most loved in the world from the attack he knew would come. Rachel hated food that had been *fussed about with*, as she put it. This evening she opted for spring rolls and chicken and cashew nuts, adding, as the waitress walked off with their orders, that her local Chinese had a much better choice and wasn't what she'd chosen Chinese food anyway, not Thai? Did they eat spring rolls in Thailand too? 'I've no idea,' he said, wishing the wine would arrive. When it did, he filled both their glasses and raised his in a toast.

'To a pleasant stay in Paris.'

She emptied her glass. 'Denny's walked out on me,' she said.

'Dennis has left you?' He had never been able to call the man Denny.

'I wasn't going to tell you, not this soon anyway.' She refilled her glass. 'I'm sorry.' She drank again, then gave a short laugh. 'I'd planned to lead into it gently.'

How many times have we told each other we're sorry these past few hours, he wondered. All we seem to do is apologise, as though constantly in debt in some way, some weird emotional economy he couldn't grasp. When did that start?

Had it always been like this or not? Had something changed, and if so, when? How did that happen? How do these things happen? Jean-Paul and he would do this sometimes, this litany of excuses, for no apparent reason. Was it something he did to people? How sad she must be, he thought, and all she can do is apologise for her timing. He wanted to take her hand in a show of comfort but the food was arriving, everything at once, already the surface of the table was covered; he would have had to reorganise the plates in some precarious fashion, dishes would have fallen to the floor, glasses been overturned. Besides, both of Rachel's hands were busy with a small black beaded bag he hadn't spotted before this moment, but now recognised as the one their mother would always use for special occasions, formal dinners, dances. Oh God, he thought, she's made an effort. And he noticed, also for the first time, that she'd dressed up, a dated floral print dress he'd never seen, cut low at the front, a pearl necklace and matching earrings that had also once belonged to their mother. Even her hair looked different, as though she'd backcombed parts of it and then changed her mind and tried to damp it down. She looks a wreck, he thought, and it was this, rather than the news that she'd been left by her appalling husband, that finally moved him, the sight of her fumbling for a handkerchief in a bag designed for dinner dances at the Savoy, in a dress she must have had run up from curtain material, or worse, her desperate stab at femininity and sophistication as sad and hopeless as a bunch of dying flowers in the hands of an eternal bridesmaid. They sat together, at either side of the table, overburdened by now with mediocre, rapidly cooling food, not looking at each other through their separate film of tears. She's made such an effort to look nice, he thought, her first evening in Paris, and I've brought her to a place that really isn't any better than her

28

local Chinese, she's absolutely right, the food's filthy here. It isn't even cheap. Or French.

'Why are the tables always so small?' she said, with a sort of irritated laugh, putting her handkerchief back in her bag. 'I hardly dare breathe out.'

'It's something you get used to,' he said.

She grimaced. 'I suppose one can get used to anything.'

'Where is he now?'

'Who? Denny? Oh, I don't know. With some new tart, I expect. He could be anywhere.'

'I see,' said Jeremy some moments later, when it was clear that Rachel had finished.

'I know you don't like him, Jeremy. You never did.'

'That's not entirely true,' said Jeremy, although it was. Dennis had always treated him with indulgent derision, as someone he'd once termed, although not in Jeremy's presence, the family's 'off-white sheep'. And because he didn't trust the effectiveness of his comment, he'd added, apparently, *Not quite naughty enough to be black, you see*. His father had found this amusing, according to Rachel, although this might have been his sister making things even worse in an attempt to excuse her husband, to somehow spread the responsibility. He didn't mean anything, she'd said, and he'd asked her how something that had clearly required a certain amount of mental effort on Dennis's part, that might even be said to contain a trace of wit, could possibly not mean anything. Everything means something, he'd said. Oh leave us alone, she'd said. You do go on.

'I think we're going to need some more wine,' said Rachel now, with what might have been a brave smile if the effort to produce it hadn't been so obvious. 'If we're actually going to eat any of all this.' She glanced at the waitress, who was sitting at the cash desk, bare legs crossed, watching what appeared to be a Japanese quiz show on a portable television, the sound turned off. No one else was in the restaurant. 'Can you catch her eye? She seems to be engrossed in her programme.'

'He just walked out, then? What about the stables? The house? I thought you'd sorted it all out after you got Mum's money out of Greece?'

'Look, Jeremy, I'm sorry I started. I really don't want to talk about this now.' She picked up a spring roll and took a bite. Hot fat spurted out. 'I'm here in Paris to enjoy myself. I want you to show me a good time, honestly.' She put the roll down. 'Damn it, I've burnt my mouth. Now where's that blasted wine?'

'I'm not sure this is really my sort of place,' Rachel said as Jeremy led her into a bar two blocks away from her hotel. She stumbled against a table, regained her balance by grabbing his hand, her evening bag slipping over her wrist and catching on his watch. They stood there, giggling, disentangling themselves while a large, heavy-featured woman in a tight white lurex top that barely covered her breasts hurried across from behind the counter to lead them to a table by the window. It was dark outside, but the front part of the bar was brightly lit. We've been put on show, thought Jeremy, ordering Calvados for them both. She's using us to raise the tone of her establishment. This made him smile. By the time the woman came back with the drinks and a bowl of salted peanuts on a tray in one hand and a damp cloth in the other, Rachel had had time to look around.

'Those women over there,' she said. She lifted her arm in a drunken way to point towards a group in the corner of the bar, while the woman wiped their table with the cloth. 'They aren't women at all, are they?'

Of course they aren't, Jeremy was about to say, they're transsexuals enjoying a well-earned rest between johns they've picked up on Avenue de Clichy and fucked in rented rooms, which would have led to Henry Miller, someone his sister would not have read, but that didn't matter. Jeremy, who was also drunk, knew enough about Henry Miller for the both of them. But before he could say this, his sister had knocked the bowl from the woman's hand, scattering its contents across the freshly wiped, still glistening table. Swiftly, the woman tucked the cloth into the waistband of her skirt and swept up the strewn nuts into her hand, her breasts almost spilling from her top, her smile almost glutinous with anxiety and the desire to please as she tipped them back into the bowl.

'They're men, aren't they?'

'Not entirely, not always,' said Jeremy, suddenly hungry, swilling down still-damp nuts from the bowl with mouthfuls of Calvados. 'They often have, well, what they're born with, so to speak, but they also have breasts. They're pretty ecumenical on the whole.'

'They're very dark-skinned,' said Rachel, glancing at him to check she'd heard correctly. You seem to know a lot about them, her expression said. I'll tell you what I do know one of these days, he thought. But not now, not yet. 'They don't look French to me.' She sipped her drink cautiously, and then less cautiously. She looked at the nuts, but didn't take one. Jeremy took a second handful, ordered two more Calvados.

'I wonder what people see in them,' she said. Jeremy had anticipated – and would have welcomed – outrage, and didn't know what to make of Rachel's mild, almost academic curiosity. He turned to look at the group behind him. There were three of them, their heads together, two blondes and one brunette, long gleaming legs tangled beneath the table, the low hum of their voices interrupted by occasional raucous laughter. One of them spotted him, or was tipped off that he'd been looking, and turned stiffly from the waist to size him up, her pockmarked cheeks plumping as she smiled his way. For a moment he thought it was Miriam and wished he hadn't come. He still wasn't ready for Miriam.

'I've heard they're considered the essence of femininity,' he said.

'Well, you ought to know,' she said. 'All those books you write. All those love-struck women and their randy servants.' He could hear, beneath her slurring, the usual tickle of contempt. 'You seem to know what men and women want.'

She's taking the piss, he thought, and it took him a moment to wonder if perhaps he'd been wrong, and a glance at her face to confirm this, that she meant what she was saying, that she saw him as an authority on love, on desire, on the whole bloody caboodle. Had she actually read his books, he thought, a sense of panic rising, as though he'd been caught with his trousers down between cars. Had she taken him seriously through all these years of intellectual debasement and humiliation? He felt sick. It was all her fault, he thought, that he should be so lousy at *people*; she'd always squashed him and stood in his way, preceded him somehow, told everyone what to expect. He's my brother, she'd say, lifting her eyes to the sky. Her father's daughter. And what was he? His mother's son? His dead mother's son. No wonder his emotional life was a tragic farce.

And then he really did feel sick.

'I think we should go,' he said. Rachel was fiddling in her bag as he pushed himself up from the table.

He'd just made the street when the first wave hit him. When Rachel caught up, complaining about the cost of alcohol in Paris, he was hunched over a bin, his hands on the metal ring, his guts in his throat.

4

RACHEL

She watches him cross the room to their father's bed, not sure if she should leave, yet knowing that she doesn't want to leave and faintly resentful of that inner voice that tells her, just now, just for a moment or two, that her rightful place is elsewhere, beyond the circle of intimacy her father and Jeremy might want, or need. But there is no intimacy, not as she understands it; there never has been. Her father is fast asleep, she was right, and she wonders, as she always does, if this will be the last time, if the final step has already been made and he will simply not be there at some point; he will have arrived. Wherever he might be going, and she wishes she could be sure, of that at least, he will have arrived. She sniffs the air; the usual scent of ointment and powder. No nasty surprises, thank God. Jeremy stands there, his back to her, almost as if he doesn't know what to do. She wants to say, *He won't bite, you know*, but their father has bitten so often, in one way or another, she's not even sure that's true, quite apart from its being uncalled-for. She's not a cruel woman, whatever Jeremy might think of her. He's bitten them both, and their mother, and a thousand other people, men who might have loved her chased away for her own good, and not only because a father has a right to be jealous. Isn't that what parents are for, in the end? To make sure their children are safe? He has always been good to her, in his way. She has always been more than a daughter to him, they've both known that.

Jeremy has taken his father's hand and is holding it while glancing around for a place to sit. Rachel could move the chair she normally uses a little closer – it's just off to Jeremy's left – but something stops her, some twinge of resentment she doesn't want to feel, and she moves back onto the landing, not quite ashamed but not wanting to be seen as covetous of her father's love. She stands outside the room, her fingers pressed to her wrist, counting her pulse as Vikram has told her to do, listening to the blood rush in her ears. She has taken her heart pill, she's almost sure of it. Jeremy's arrival has shaken her out of her routine. When she steps forward again, enters the bedroom, she sees Jeremy bent over the bed, his own ear against his father's mouth as if he is listening for the sound of breathing. She catches what seems to be a word. Her father is saying something. And Jeremy, his face hidden, his shoulders rounded and lump-like, is also speaking. His voice is louder than usual, and she can hear quite distinctly as he says two words. But what the words might mean she has no idea. All she knows is that her father's head falls back onto the pillow with what sounds – inexplicably – like a laugh. It's weeks since she heard her father laugh. Jeremy coughs, and turns away, and she does nothing. He's back, she tells herself. You mustn't be mean. Daddy wouldn't want it. It's his turn now.

Jeremy turns round and smiles at her, the first real smile she has seen all day.

'Yes,' he says, 'fish cakes will be fine.'

There is a baby monitor on the worktop beside the table. Jeremy doesn't notice it at first. When he does he picks it up and plays with the volume control in a distracted, lackadaisical way, turning it up and down, shaking it finally as though he expects it to respond to his attention. Rachel wants to snatch it from his hand, but knows better than to encourage him.

'Is this what he does?' he says. 'He cries?'

'He calls my name usually.'

'Usually?'

'Sometimes it's hard to understand,' she says, defensive without knowing why. She opens the oven door and takes out the tray of fish cakes. Jeremy has already concocted a salad, despite her best efforts, while she was making sure the sheet beneath their father was wrinkle-free and coaxing him to drink one of his special fruit juices through its little straw. He'll have found something to dress it with, no doubt, she thinks, some powdery Provençal herb she should have thrown out months ago.

Jeremy finally puts down the monitor and stares around the kitchen at the dressers, the stoneware sink, installed decades before such things became fashionable, the Aga she never uses because it's too much of a fag. The clutter and the bareness, all at once. Remnants of their mother after all these years have passed. Is that what he sees, she wonders?

'My whole flat would fit in here,' he says, in a tone she can't place, at the same time critical and amused, 'with space left over. Absurd, isn't it? What on earth made him stay on, do you think?'

She puts two fish cakes on each of their plates. 'After Mummy went, you mean? I suppose he saw no reason not to. All the business of moving house. What would have been the point?' And then there was Dhara to be taken into account, she thinks but doesn't say.

'I suppose you're right.' He pokes at one of the fishcakes

with his fork, probing and breaking it into two, watches the creamy filling ooze from the heart of it. 'Interesting,' he says. 'That's not what I expected.'

'What did you say to him upstairs?' Rachel says, despite herself. She'd sworn to herself she wouldn't ask. She doesn't want him to know he was being watched. She doesn't want him to think she cares.

'What?'

'You said something to him. You made him laugh.' It's the laugh that has annoyed her most. 'I couldn't make it out.' And now, as usual, she has given the game away.

'Oh, that.' He dips the tines of his fork into the filling and warily licks it off. 'Hmm. Better than I thought,' he says. 'Cheesy.' She watches this performance, trying to show neither impatience nor disappointment, as though she expects no better.

'You know Toulouse-Lautrec?' he says.

'Of course.'

'Well, yes, of course you do. I didn't mean to suggest you . . .' He pauses. 'His father never got over his son being a cripple, you know. He was a hunter, a bit of an eccentric, really. He wanted a son who would go hunting with him and when that didn't happen, well, he lacked understanding. He was a bully, an emotional bully.'

Rachel can see where this is going, the familiar lament, poor little Jem whom no one loves, but she waits for him to carry on, furtively checking the volume control on the monitor. She wouldn't put it past Jeremy to have turned it down on purpose.

'When Toulouse-Lautrec was dying, his father came to see him. It's not clear why, they'd had nothing to do with each other for years. Anyway, there are two versions of what happened. The first is that Lautrec said something like, I knew you'd be here for the kill. Which is bad enough, in its way. But I prefer the other version.'

'Which is?' says Rachel, when Jeremy stands up and crosses the kitchen to carry the salad bowl to the table.

'The one where he says "*Vieux con*".' Jeremy pauses until Rachel's impatience becomes apparent. 'He called his father an old cunt. They were the last words he said before he died. It's often translated as "old fool", I believe, but I don't think that's what he meant. I think he knew exactly what he wanted to say to his father.' He smiles to himself; she might as well not be there. But it's also for her, she can see that, the little curl of triumph. 'Old cunt,' he says again, as if trying the words out for size in his mouth.

'You mean you just called Daddy an old cunt? In French?' She tastes the corner of a rocket leaf from the salad, putting the rest of it back on her plate, which she then pushes away with a gesture of disgust. She doesn't know what else to do. It's not a word she ever uses. She's not sure when she last heard it said. At the stables perhaps, one of the hands. Even Denny – who always used to swear like a trooper – hated it. She wants to burst into laughter from embarrassment.

Jeremy nods, shamefaced, but smiling – she knows this face from when they were young – as though he's done something unexpected and clever. Her urge to laugh disappears. 'Yes, I'm afraid I did.'

'Well, it's a good thing he doesn't speak French,' says Rachel, thrusting her chair back from the table. Standing up to take away the plates, she pulls a face, disgusted. 'You've ruined this salad, Jeremy. It is garlic, isn't it? Where did you find it? You didn't bring it with you, I hope?'

'Oh, but he does.' Jeremy is insistent now, wriggling in his chair like an excited child. But what about? What matters, finally? 'He does speak French. Quite well. Well enough to read it anyway. Don't you remember? That letter he got? The one Mum always said was the final straw? She never said who it was from though, did she? You saw it, didn't you? All that time ago.' He smiles. 'I wouldn't have said it to him if I'd thought he wouldn't understand.' The smile grows broader. 'And he wouldn't have laughed, would he, if he hadn't understood?' He shakes his head. 'You've got to hand it to him,' he says.

Later, when Jeremy has gone to his bedroom and she has checked that their father is comfortable, as the district nurses say, and seems to be asleep, Rachel goes into her own room, places the baby monitor beside her bed and picks up the box of letters she has been going through these past few nights. They are letters her father received from various people when she was a child and later, after she left home, and she doesn't know what to do with them. Her first idea had been to find the ones she herself had written to him as a child from places she'd been sent on holiday, odd letters over the years, to see what kind of child she'd been, and then later letters, when everything got difficult, and she hadn't been able to keep it to herself. Letters she later wished she had never sent. But there were none to be found. He might have destroyed them; it wouldn't have surprised her. He has never been brave enough in the end to face up to things. He has always brushed truths off. Or maybe he has kept them in some other, more precious place. Yes, that was it, she decided. He would have kept her letters safe, somewhere only he would find them. She wondered where that might be and prayed to God she got to them first.

But thoughts of herself died away as she read what the box

contained. Now she would like to burn the lot of them, particularly the filthy ones, but knows she can't, not while her father is still alive. After that, she'll see. One of them might have been the letter Jeremy mentioned, the letter that sent their mother away; more than one is in French, which she doesn't read, and doesn't want to. They look as though they were written by a woman, but they would be, wouldn't they? She can't even bear to contemplate the idea of another man writing in French to her father. She would show them to Jeremy but she's anxious he'll laugh or find them useful in his war against his father, which she has witnessed all her life, the most wavering of allies, constantly shifting sides for reasons she has never quite understood. She should have protected him, she knows that – her little brother, hopeless at sport, the natural victim of bullies at school and at home too, she won't deny it. How can she? She's had a hand in it. She'd like to think it's her nature to defend the underdog, but that hasn't always been the case with Jeremy. There have been times when her father has held all the cards and she has exulted. Yes, she has said, beneath her breath, her barely heard voice an echo of her father's, his contempt hers, his fury hers. *Why don't you go and live in Cuba, if that's what you think? Who's kept you in luxury up to now?* Adding, to herself: *You're spoiling everything.* And Jeremy has always known whose side she was on, and frozen her off when her sympathies drifted in his direction, because their father could sometimes be unspeakably cruel to her as well, and she would have welcomed a temporary respite from battle. They might have stood together then, if he'd allowed them to. She sees them, still children, holding hands while their father rages and their mother begs him to stop, more tired than angry, a vision she has only imagined.

And here are the letters, in various hands and tongues,

which show that he was loved and desired, desired above all, in the most lubricious ways, ways she would never have imagined possible. Language she's never seen written outside the walls of public lavatories. And yet they aren't dirty, not in the end. Love letters, she supposes she has to consider them – because if not, what else? – kept in a shirt box their mother must surely have discovered years before Rachel did, who had simply been looking for socks that could be used as bed socks. She would have opened it, as Rachel did, and read the contents. Had she been surprised, as Rachel was, and continues to be? Surprised and shocked to the point of disgust? Had she always known and been relieved to find her suspicions confirmed? Or had she simply come across some final letter, some letter that had sent her upstairs to pack her bags while her father ranted downstairs, she imagines, although she doesn't remember herself. All she remembers are the stories that have been told. And why hadn't she, Rachel, had that kind of courage? The courage to leave before she was left. I should be able to talk about these things with Jeremy, Rachel tells herself, sliding a folded sheet of notepaper back into its envelope, and is furious with him because she can't, and because this is his fault.

When she hears a noise, she snaps the box shut, afraid that Jeremy has surprised her, but it's only her father. He's woken and is banging his walking stick against the bed frame with the last of his strength. With a sigh, she gets up to see what he wants.

5

JEREMY

The sitter arrives when Jeremy is still in his pyjamas, standing alone and silent in the kitchen, wishing he had brought from Paris a quarter-kilo packet of his favourite coffee. He hears the front door open and walks into the hall to find a small dark woman, Asian, hair tied behind her neck, searching for something in a shopping bag. She's about to walk straight past him when he raises his arm to greet her or block her, he isn't sure. She looks across, sees him and stops.

'I'm Dhara,' she says, head to one side, hand still in the bag, suspicious. 'And you are?'

'Jeremy,' he says, buttoning his pyjama jacket. He jerks his head back and glances at the ceiling to indicate upstairs. 'His son.'

'Of course you are,' she says, 'the French one. Righty-ho,' and she smirks to herself, clearly recalling something not to his credit that she's been told, by Rachel, he supposes. She moves round him, face-to-face, their roles reversed until he finds himself stepping backwards onto the welcome mat, and the woman, pugnacious, her hair tugged back into a plait, is barring his way to the rest of the house. 'The baby of the family. I didn't recognise you at first, but I do now, my love.'

'That's what we always used to call him,' calls down Rachel from the landing. The French one? thinks Jeremy. His sister noisily descends, holding a plastic bucket slightly away from her body. 'He's not much of a baby any longer, mind you. Put on a bit of weight recently, haven't you, Jeremy?' Her tone is infuriatingly jolly, as though she were carrying a birthday cake into a room full of children.

'I have my own little brother too,' says Dhara, taking off her anorak and hanging it beside the door. Recognise me? he thinks. My love? Put on a bit of weight? Beneath the anorak, Dhara is swathed in a vast, elaborately knitted cardigan like something designed for the ski slopes thirty years ago. She grins. 'Vikram will always be my baby. Not that he's likely to put on weight.' She looks Jeremy up and down with unjustified affection as he edges his way back into the hall. Her bosom is large and low. 'Oh no, he plays rugby, you see. He's a full back.' She pulls an appreciative face at the idea, as though she can see the man before her, flexing his thighs in mud-smeared shorts. 'He's a lovely big clever boy, my little brother is,' she says, rolling the word *lovely* round her mouth like butterscotch. 'You'll be meeting him later.'

'Will I?'

'Vikram is Dad's doctor,' says Rachel, impatient for some reason. She pushes past them both to get to the kitchen. 'You don't need to worry about Dad now that Dhara's here.' Jeremy, who is still, despite all the activity surrounding him, barely awake, can smell shit. He looks into the bucket to see a bundled-up white object he realises must be a nappy. 'And you don't need to worry about this either,' she says. Before he can speak, she's swept through the kitchen, picking up a large carrier on the way, and left the house by the kitchen door. Dhara is halfway up the stairs, shopping bag still in her hand. It's like a farce about human consumption, he thinks. Shopping and shit, entrances and exits. And here I am in my pyjamas, the unwitting house guest to whom all happens and by whom nothing is understood. How does she recognise me? Does that mean I should have recognised her? When Dhara reaches the half-landing she pauses, throwing her head back to call out his father's name. 'Reggie,' she hoots, and he's shocked. Not even his mother called Dad Reggie. 'I'm on my way up, Reggie.' Her voice is high-pitched and grating, with an irritated lilt to it, as though she's contradicting someone.

Jeremy, after searching for coffee that isn't instant and failing to find any, makes himself a cup of tea with a bag, prodding until the glue floats off to form a silky scum on the surface, adding milk but no sugar. He carries the cup into the glassed-in room his sister calls the conservatory, which always makes him think of music, and never of what he sees now: dusty geraniums and growbags piled against one another to form a barricade against the wilderness of the garden. His mother loved the garden, spent hours every day in it, working as hard as a man might, pushing wheelbarrows, wielding hoes, using implements Jeremy remembers from his childhood but can't name. There was a gardener he remembers, when he was no more than five or six, but something must have happened because one day he was no longer there, and no one would tell him why. His father's neglect of the garden since she left has always seemed to Jeremy the final straw of his contempt for her. He puts down the cup to rub a leaf between his fingers and is at once rewarded with the scent of lemon. My father is dying upstairs, he thinks, and all I have is anger and the scent of lemon from a leaf that has nothing to do with lemon, a leaf I only rubbed to clean it of its film of dust. How full of tricks nature is. Although, looking through the window, he sees that someone seems to have taken the garden in hand since his last visit. Perhaps there is a new gardener, he thinks.

'So you're Jeremy. Reggie's little boy. How you've changed.' Dhara is standing at the door.

'Reggie wants you.'

'Me?' said Jeremy. 'He wants me? My father wants me?'

'You are Jeremy, aren't you?'

'Dad remembered my name?'

Dhara sighs, exasperated. 'I wouldn't be here telling you to go upstairs, now would I, my love, if he hadn't told me to tell you? Dearie me. He said to tell Jeremy to come here. I need to talk to him about something. And then he said something else I didn't catch because he doesn't want his bottom set in today, for some reason, and he's hopeless without both sets of his teeth.'

'But Rachel said . . .' Jeremy is playing for time.

'Oh, *Rachel* said . . .' snaps Dhara, her hands on her hips. She's tiny, despite her bosom. He could pick her up and move her the way you would a child to clear his path, and run into the hall and out of the house. Why didn't he think of this at once? He'd be at the station long before Rachel could catch him, safely on the first Eurostar back to Paris by noon, back home before people have finished their post-lunch coffee. Coffee. He'll nip into town for a decent coffee just as soon as he gets the chance, he decides. There must be a café somewhere in Whitstable that knows how to make a drinkable espresso. 'You don't have to listen to everything Rachel says,' Dhara is telling him. He stands up, part of him about to flee the house for good, and realises with a shock that he's still in his pyjamas, unshaven, his teeth unbrushed, his bowels still

45

waiting patiently to be moved. He sees, as if in a vision, the malodorous bucket in his sister's hand.

'Anyway, you'd better get a move on,' Dhara says. *Because his father is going to die at any minute* is what she doesn't say. And if my father does die, thinks Jeremy, how will I feel as I run down the drive in my jim-jams to know he'd called for me, that his final wish had been to speak to me? Perhaps he has some closing need to apologise, to justify himself. That would make sense. And so Jeremy is carried upstairs on a wave of baffled, grudging curiosity, measuring his capacity for forgiveness against what his father might say and finding it, as always, wanting. Measuring himself.

His father has been propped up with pillows and is sitting almost upright, his gaze fixed on the door, although Jeremy can see, as he approaches, the filmy albumen of what must be cataracts and beneath them a blue he doesn't remember. Has his father always had blue eyes, he wonders. Is it possible he has never noticed this before? He is shrunken, half the size Jeremy remembers. He's about to walk over to the bed when some movement outside the window, a bird perhaps, attracts his attention. He crosses the room to look out. Directly beneath the window is the garden, and then, as he raises his head a little, the red-brick wall, almost hidden by fruit trees, and then, in the distance the grey-white sea, the colour of the sky. Even the scuds of cloud, moving from right to left like words on a screen, are sea-like, wave-like. The only flaw in the harmony of sea and sky is a wind farm he has no memory of, the giant white vanes rotating slowly as the same wind turns them. He thinks of that dreadful poem by Spender about pylons. 'Like nude giant girls', he called them. As though pylons bore any resemblance to naked girls. Not that he's any more of an expert on girls than Spender was. And what do these resemble, he wonders, other than themselves. He hates the word 'like', he thinks suddenly, as though everything has to be coupled up, closed off. As though *this* always had to be *that*.

'You there?' says a voice from the bed.

'Hello, Dad,' he says, turning round. His father's head jerks in the direction of the voice.

'Get me my teeth,' he says. He raises an arm and points at his soft, half-open mouth in a jabbing, exasperated way, as though accusing some foreign body. 'My other teeth, for God's sake.'

'Dhara told me you didn't want them,' says Jeremy conversationally, his heart sinking as he glances around the room in search of a set of bottom teeth. He hadn't planned on nursing.

'Who's Dhara when she's at home?' his father says, or this, at least, is what Jeremy hears. The old man's voice is muffled; he sounds as though something soft and loose is alive and moving in his mouth, pressing down against the tongue. Perhaps it is the tongue itself, no longer manageable. 'And who are you?'

When I'm at home, thinks Jeremy, completing the question. And who am I when I'm at home?

'I'm Jeremy. You told Dhara you wanted me.'

'Just fuck off, will you?'

The first time he heard his father swear he was seven years old and his father was at the top of a ladder. He was fixing boards, tongue and groove, to replace the old ceiling in Jeremy's bedroom with a new Scandinavian pine look when he hit his thumb with the hammer. 'Fuck!' he said and Jeremy, holding the base of the steps and staring up at his father's arse, was struck to the core to hear a word he'd thought only older boys, far from the hearing of adults, would ever use. He waited

47

until his father could be left alone then ran downstairs to tell his mother what he'd heard. She was mincing horseradish she'd rooted up in the garden, but he didn't realise at first and he thought she was crying because she too had heard the awful word his father had uttered. He stood at the door and watched her howl, her shoulders bent over the table. When she moved to one side, to wipe her eyes on a towel, he saw the dull gleam of the mincer.

Jeremy tries again. 'Dhara said you said you wanted me.'

'Not you,' the old man says. 'The other one.'

'Rachel? She isn't here. She'll be back soon.'

'Rachel?' The old man stares at him blankly.

'Your daughter.' A short pause, during which his father fixes him with a furious expression on his face. 'My sister.'

'No, no. Hell's bells. Not her.' He struggles to free the arm beneath the sheet.

'Not her,' says Jeremy. 'Not me. Who do you want?'

'I told you who I want. The other one.'

'Which other one?' Jeremy's voice rises, exasperated.

'The other *him*.'

'The other him? There is no other him. There's me and there's Rachel.'

The old man shakes his head, furious. 'Not you. Not her. The other *him*,' he says again. 'Oh my God,' he mutters. He seems to be on the brink of tears. 'Take me,' he says.

'You shouldn't worry too much,' says Dhara, who has appeared in the room and is standing behind him. 'Half the time he doesn't know what he's saying.'

His father's fists, lying on the top of the duvet, bunch up. The duvet cover is floral, the colours of an English garden, and the old man's hands are hard and livid against the woven pastels, green and pink and lemon, hard and tight with blood, smaller than Jeremy would ever have imagined, more like the tortured claws of some old bird than human hands. He reaches out to take one, expecting his father to pull it away, but he lets it rest, and Jeremy is surprised to see how smooth and dry it is, as soft to touch as it is hard to see. He holds the hand in his, convinced that his father will retract it, but the old man's eyes are closed now and the hand relaxes, the fingers, tapering and paper-like, opening out. He holds the hand in his until his father seems to be asleep then lets it go, placing it with all the delicacy he can summon onto the pale-green intricacy of a large, improbable leaf, a glistening tropical leaf that has somehow found its way into this Egyptian cotton bower of roses and rhododendron.

'I'll just sit here if that's all right with you,' says Dhara. Jeremy turns round to see the woman settling into an armchair by the window, her bag at her side where a cushion ought to be. She is reaching down beside the chair to pick up a book. He's about to ask her when they first met when he sees the cover.

'What are you reading?' he asks her, but there is no need. He already knows. He recognised the book immediately.

'It's just some nonsense I found here,' says Dhara. 'It's by someone called . . .' – she flicks the book over to see the front cover, the flame-haired woman, bosoms heaving, collapsing on the ancestral lawn – 'Nathalie Cray. You wouldn't believe it but it's practically all I could find to read that isn't about business and the Second World War. Your dad's a funny sort. He's got a whole bookcase-full in his study. I didn't think I'd like them – romance isn't my thing, really, I like something that hasn't just been made up by someone, you know, some-thing *real* – but they do get to you in the end somehow.' She giggles. 'Some of them are pretty racy too, I don't mind telling you. Perhaps that's why he bought them, the old goat.'

'You don't know what he meant, do you?' *Old goat?* he thinks.

'I'm sorry, my dear?' She looks up from the book.

'This other him he's talking about?'

'Oh well,' she says. 'He does that sometimes. He thinks there's someone else who should be here.' She puts a finger on the page to mark her place. 'You don't have another brother hidden away now, do you? Some twin over there in Paris? In gay Paree?'

Jeremy shakes his head, determined not to show irritation. Does she even know what she's said, he wonders, and if she does, does it matter? Who on earth is she? His gay, gay Paris, so far away from the stifling malodorous air of his father's bedroom, and here he is, after less than a day, as though he has never been anywhere else. 'Not to my knowledge.'

'Oh well,' she says again, 'he talks a lot of nonsense, to be honest. He's a sweet old thing, but the top storey's not what it was.'

Jeremy, startled, feels the need to defend his father from this attack, but Dhara has returned to her book. Her lips are moving. It strikes him that he might be able to lip-read sufficiently well to identify the passage, but his father's hand moves in his and Jeremy turns to see his eyes glaring up at him with a blind intensity.

'Is there something I can get you?'

His father smiles at him for the first time.

'This is another nice mess you've got me into,' he says, in his normal voice. And Jeremy is sitting in the living room of another house, the house before this one or the one before that, watching television with his father. The fire is lit and the room is overheated, his bare thighs are hot and scratched by the crimson moquette of the armchair, which is too big for him; he feels like a half-fledged chick inside the egg. His father is laughing and he is laughing along with him as two men try to push a sofa through a first-floor window. One of the men is fat and the other is thin and everything the thin one does is wrong; is always wrong. The fat one sits on the safe half of the sofa as it swings, half in half out, and fiddles with his tie and, although the sofa might fall and the thin man be crushed beneath it as he runs out of the house and into the street, his father continues to laugh, and so does he, Jeremy, one eye on his father, one eye on the screen. At this moment, as the fat man plays with his tie and the thin man brushes the dust from his hat, the sofa forgotten above his head, he loves his father with all his heart. And then the sofa begins to slide towards the street.

6

JEREMY

Armand Grenier's Paris apartment was in a building over-looking the leafless trees and asphalted paths of Parc Monceau. Jeremy had left the completed manuscript there the week before, with the concierge, who'd weighed the manila folder in her grasp as if considering whether her duties obliged her to take it from him or if she had some contractual right to refuse it. Now, as he stood outside the door beneath the columned porch, his hand reaching up to press the inset bell beside Grenier's name, he saw through the diamond-shaped pane of coloured glass in the door the same small woman walking towards him, adjusting her apron.

His mother had given him a portable typewriter when he went to Exeter, an Olivetti Lettera 22, a brand-new sky-blue jewel, perfect as a scarab in its zipped-up case. 'Now you can write me nice long letters every day,' she'd said and, for a moment, with her standing in front of him, her hands on his arms, he'd imagined he really would. He would sit there at his desk and tap out his letters home, and for posterity. He would have so much to tell her, he thought, which turned out to be half true. So much would happen and yet so little of it be tellable, to his mother at least.

He'd barely used the typewriter during his time at university, and had left it with friends when he first came to France, to reduce the weight of his luggage, preferring to fill a series of small black notebooks with his various moods and thoughts, *pensées* he would soon be too ashamed to reread but unable to throw away. The manuscript he had left for Grenier was the largest thing he'd produced on it so far: 248 foolscap sheets, double spaced, filling the beige folder, with the words *Knife in the Heart* on the front in what passed for italic script; he'd laboured over this in pencil and then with a special pen he'd found in a shop in the Latin Quarter and Indian ink from a small black bottle, molasses dark, like medicinal tincture. Each day, after writing longhand and then typing it up, he'd done a precise count of the words, calculating how many more would be needed, how much he'd already earned. Grenier had talked about a lump sum at the outset, but some half-remembered advice from a friend at university made Jeremy think he'd make more if he was paid by the word, and so he'd insisted on that. It's what we do in London, he'd said, and Grenier, to Jeremy's surprise, had believed him. At once, he regretted it. He should have known that anything Grenier might agree to would be to the older man's advantage. Still, he had the bill in his pocket, folded twice and slipped into a luxuriously thick cream envelope from the same stationer's. He would find a way to give it to Grenier. He had no choice; he was down to his last few hundred francs. He would have rent to pay before the end of the week, and food to buy. He was tired of bread and cheese and more bread. And wine.

The concierge watched him close the double doors of the lift and press the button, only returning to her cubbyhole as the wrought-iron box began to rise and he was out of harm's way. When it clattered to a halt and he opened the inner door,

Grenier was already there, holding the outer door open, his smile as wolfish as ever.

'My author,' he said. '*Mon auteur.*'

'*Bonjour,*' said Jeremy, awkwardly stepping out of the lift, his way partially blocked. 'Er, hello.' There was a moment it seemed possible Grenier would take him in his arms, kiss his cheeks, hug him in some inappropriate way, and Jeremy sensed himself brace, but unnecessarily; Grenier stepped sharply back and waved his hand towards an open door to Jeremy's right.

'In here, my dear boy,' he said. So they would be speaking English, thought Jeremy, with relief.

The room into which he was ushered looked less like the study of a publisher than the bedroom of a courtesan. It reminded Jeremy of a television production he'd seen of Zola's *Nana – fin de siècle*, overheated, a room that felt like an orchid magically transformed, corrupted, into living space. Between the two high, deeply curtained windows overlooking the park was a purple chaise longue, on which Grenier clearly expected him to sit. He would remain standing apparently, in the full morning light as it flowed in from outside, although for a moment Jeremy, with a flutter of unease, imagined the older man sidling down beside him, a snake-like movement so insinuating it would barely be noticed, Jeremy's sense of disquiet including a brief interrogation of Grenier's desirability. It wasn't the first time he'd considered this, and not only with Grenier. He'd walked whole afternoons around certain *quartiers* of Paris, imagining himself the kept boy of suited businessmen he saw leaping from taxis and letting themselves into the subtle darkness of foyers. He saw himself, petulant and available, his bare arms raised from the scented Egyptian cotton sheets, more often naked than not, a plaything without an unselfish care in the world. Men older than he was, although not old, in their mid to late thirties, with lives outside the real life they would share with him – shallow, perfunctory affairs of wives and children, lives they would leave by the door with their dark-blue cashmere overcoats and briefcases, their tailored jackets, as finely cut and stitched as the one Grenier wore that morning. He favoured the English lord look, Jeremy had noticed, which put him off a little.

'And now,' said Grenier, walking towards an ormolu-encrusted console table against the opposite wall and picking up the folder Jeremy had left with the concierge, 'to business.'

'Actually, I've found one or two things I'd rather like to change,' Jeremy said before Grenier could continue.

'I thought so,' said the man, with a smile, holding the folder between his hands in much the way the concierge had, as though its value depended on its weight. 'A perfectionist.'

On the contrary, Jeremy, assuming the worst, had intended to protect himself from Grenier's criticism by anticipating it. But Grenier was opening the folder and extracting the sheaf of typewritten pages with the satisfied air of someone who could have asked for no more suitable gift than this. He let the sheets fan slightly out, then waved them as though their ability to flutter in the over-warm air of the room were an integral part of their charm.

'I think this may be the start of a long and fruitful collaboration,' he said. 'You have captured the – how shall I say it? – the lascivious but essentially spiritual tone I was seeking. The episode of the entombment, for example . . .' He riffled through the manuscript, pursing his lips and smiling, pursing and smiling, while Jeremy fidgeted against the velvet cushions of the chaise longue, wishing he were somewhere else, wondering if he would be paid in cash, and today, or would have to wait. When the sheets of paper cascaded from Grenier's hands, accompanied by an oath, in French, he leapt to his feet. He and Grenier stooped simultaneously to gather the manuscript up. With a thud that echoed, or seemed to echo, around the boudoir-like room, their foreheads met. Grenier staggered back, clutching his temple, then fell. Jeremy found himself kneeling, his hands stretched out imploringly as his patron moaned and rolled in a curtailed arc, his legs bent awkwardly beneath him. At this point a telephone began to ring from the hall. Jeremy, suddenly aware of a throbbing pain in his head, was about to answer it, but Grenier caught his sleeve.

'No,' he said, his voice unexpectedly commanding. He struggled to his feet and left the room.

By the time he came back, Jeremy had sorted the sheets of paper out and was standing beside a small bureau inlaid with mother of pearl, its upper surface covered with framed photographs. The photograph he had in his hand showed a young woman, as young as Jeremy was now. She was sitting on the neatly trimmed grass of what looked like a park or formal garden of some sort. She was wearing a summer dress with a floral print and light shoes. Her head was thrown back in laughter as she stared towards the camera.

'This is my mother, isn't it?'

Grenier took the photograph. 'Vanessa. Yes,' he said.

'I didn't realise you'd known her this long.'

'Your mother and I are old friends.'

'I thought she was a friend of your wife.'

Grenier returned the photograph to its place.

'She is. She is how I met my wife.'

'So you knew my mother first?'

'What is that expression you English use? We go back a long way? Or perhaps that is more American?'

Jeremy looked at the other photographs. They were all black and white, tightly arrayed as fish-scales, each gleaming in its polished silver frame. It was a miracle he'd spotted her. Everyone looked the same in old photographs, as though their purpose was to remind those who looked at them of an age that had passed, of how they would all become part of their period and nothing more. There was a photograph of a little girl, grimacing at the camera, he would have sworn was Rachel. He might not have noticed his mother if he hadn't recognised the dress. It was one she'd kept in her wardrobe, pushed to one side on its hotel hanger, hopelessly dated, too small to wear as she'd gradually put on weight, and then no longer fashionable when she'd lost it. He'd wondered why she hadn't given it to a jumble sale, or made it into something else – a dress for Rachel, perhaps, a peg bag. It had roses splashed over it, red and orange, against a white background. He'd like to see her, he realised, right this minute and talk about his life with her in a way he never had, the way two adults might. And now, as he thought about it, he remembered the name on the hanger: Hotel Martinez, Cannes.

'Do you have any more of her?'

Grenier shrugged. Gingerly, he touched the side of his head, where a lump had begun to form. Jeremy echoed the gesture, wincing when his own fingers touched his own bump. Grenier grinned, then sighed.

'I don't know. Perhaps.' He walked back to the table in the centre of the room, where Jeremy had replaced the manuscript in its folder. 'There is one small thing I'd like to discuss with you.' He picked the folder up. 'Now, let me see.'

It had taken him no time to think of the story. Conquistador meets Aztec princess. Conquistador falls in love. Princess Zuma resists, in spite of herself, filled with the pride of her race as it battles with her heart, irresistibly drawn to the foreign soldier. She is captured and humiliated. Released into bondage, a jewel in Don Ramon's crown, she fights without success against the love she feels for her new master. She is in his chamber, chained loosely to the wall, when her people attack the invader's palace and overwhelm her captor. He is about to be sacrificed in a brutal Aztec ritual when Zuma intervenes. He is mine, she announces. He is mine to do with as I will.

He'd always been good at making up stories, even, or especially, as a child – stories in which he was brave, resourceful, above all exonerated. He'd tell them to Rachel and, when he had to, his parents, although his father never really listened, even when Jeremy addressed his every word to him. His father had a way of sitting, his feet planted firmly on the carpet, his hands on his knees, that made Jeremy uncomfortable, as though he were flimsy and might get blown away, or swept from his father's path by the merest gesture. Rachel was easier; Rachel would listen, her big face close to his, her eyes wide open, like saucers their mother once said, and that was how he always saw them after that. Like two great empty saucers, waiting to be filled with something – milk perhaps for the cat, or a dribble of scalding tea for it to cool enough to drink. He'd tell her stories that scared her, and was always surprised to see how easy that was, as though she could be scared by practically anything. He'd wondered, now and again, as he sat at his Olivetti and typed, what she'd make of *Knife in the Heart*; whether she'd be as excited as he was by certain passages; whether, at times, she'd feel the same kind of shame. But that shame was reserved for the maker, surely, he thought.

And now, as Grenier seemed to be about to read an excerpt from the manuscript, he found himself blushing. He had an impulse to protect his mother's photograph from what was being said, to pluck it from the rest and press it against his chest, her face against his shirt, so that nothing of what he had written could be heard. But Grenier put the folder down again and took Jeremy's hands in his.

'Tell me, Jeremy, who are you?'

'I'm sorry.'

'What I wish to say is' – he paused – 'with whom in this book do you identify? Which heart is yours? Which knife?'

Jeremy eased himself from Grenier's grasp.

'Vengeance shall be mine,' he said.

7

JEREMY

The café is in the main street, near the supermarket, charity shops on either side. It has a small table chained to the window frame outside, with two fold-out slatted wooden chairs, also chained, beside it. There is a *Free Wi-Fi* sticker beside the price list Sellotaped to the inside of the glass. Jeremy orders a double espresso, sits down, and opens his laptop. By the time the coffee arrives, he's deleted a dozen or so emails and is reading one from Armand Grenier, his publisher, telling him that there are interesting developments and that he needs to complete the book he's supposed to be working on. There's a link to something called *Thérèse Philosophe* by a certain Marquis d'Argens, downloadable from the Bibliothèque Nationale, apparently, and an implicitly barbed comment that it might provide him with inspiration. Should he have heard of him, wonders Jeremy. Some aristocratic filth merchant from the days of the Revolution, no doubt, a minor de Sade. Grenier does this, taunts him with literary porn of one sort or another, as though he should be raising his game.

Still, interesting developments. This ought to be welcome news, a spur to action, a distraction to Jeremy, who hasn't thought about his novel since the day he received Rachel's call about his father. How long ago was that? Can it really be less than a week? Just before leaving Paris, as the train filled up around him, he'd sent Grenier a short text to tell him he had to go away on family business, which must have made him wonder; Jeremy doesn't really have family business since his mother died. But so far there's been no reply. Now, from the tone of the email, Grenier doesn't seem to know where Jeremy is, and Jeremy would like to maintain this ambiguity for as long as he can. It's not that he isn't writing his tot of words a day; he's barely thought about writing at all. It's the simple fact of Grenier not knowing he's in England that makes his physical presence in Whitstable, sitting outside a café at half past ten on a Thursday morning, somehow less real, as though an essential part of him will remain in the studio flat in Batignolles for just as long as Grenier thinks he's there. As though Grenier represents whatever there is in his life that makes it real. Which is absurd.

He doesn't answer. He will, but first he needs to think about what to say. What kind of interesting developments could there be, in any case? His brand of soft-core romantic porn is hardly the sort of thing to appear on shortlists or be snaffled up by editors with a name-making reputation. Still, something must be on the cards for Grenier to sound so keen. Maybe he's about to be translated into Turkish, or transformed into a comic strip. Miss Cat-o'-nine-tails vs Whipping Boy. He hasn't done a superhero twist yet. That would be fun, he thinks. Maybe he can tap out a sentence or two before the urge to write abandons him. Cheered by the idea, he finishes his coffee, taps on the glass and points at the cup, nodding when the girl at the machine mouths, 'Another one?'

His mobile rings as she's putting the tray down on the table. It's the chorus of 'Tainted Love', Jean-Paul's idea of a joke; Jeremy's idea of a joke gone sour. They both jump, coffee slops over into the saucer, soaking his biscotti.

'I'll fill it up again for you, shall I?' the girl says. Her T-shirt has the words *Barista 100% Colombian* written across the tightly fitting front, although she's clearly Kent-born and bred. Still, the coffee's better than he expected.

'If you would,' says Jeremy. 'That's very kind.' But he doesn't look at her as she goes back into the café. He's staring at the screen on his phone. It's a Paris number, and his heart is beating. It's not in the memory, but that means nothing. It's a landline, perhaps an office or a restaurant, a payphone in a *café-tabac* if payphones still exist anywhere. People don't always use their own phones. It might be Grenier, and he isn't ready for Grenier, but he'd answer if he knew that it was him. He'd bluff and prevaricate; he's good at that. It's the thought that it might not be Grenier, but Jean-Paul, that blocks him. He can't speak to him like this, knowing how far away he is, and having to explain it, and not being able to clear up any misunderstanding they'd be bound to have by calling a taxi and finishing the conversation face-to-face. He stares at the phone until it stops ringing and the coffee has arrived, the same coffee, he suspects, but that's all right, at least his sodden biscotti have been replaced. He smiles up, grateful, then realises that the ringtone will have given him away. His hands rise to his head. Whoever has called will have heard that unfamiliar English *brrr-brrr* and will have understood at once that he is here. Irrationally, he glances up and down the road, as though expecting to be discovered. Would Jean-Paul track him down, from Batignolles to Whitstable High Street, even if that were possible, and how would it make him feel, he asks himself, after the shock of it had passed? Flattered? Unnerved? Perhaps a little frightened?

He drinks his coffee. All plans to write a paragraph or two have faded from his mind, replaced by Jean-Paul's last burst of rage. How many times had he insisted that Jean-Paul had no reason to be jealous, until the word had meant nothing to him either. Who else would want me, he'd said, and will always regret having said, and Jean-Paul had stormed into the bathroom and slammed the door behind him. He's going to kill himself, Jeremy had thought, and banged on the door and then the wall beside the door. Don't do it, he'd cried, but Jean-Paul didn't answer. When he came out, he'd packed his washing stuff into a bag. The mattress was already half upended by that point. Jeremy had watched him go before glancing at the window opposite. For the first time, the young man who lived in the room behind it, whose presence had been the unknowing occasion for all this, was looking directly at him, across the courtyard with its fine-leaved tree and its zinc-plated roofs. He was standing, his hands on the low wrought-iron balustrade, his eyes on Jeremy, shaking his beautiful head from side to side. And Jeremy, abashed, had stepped back into the darkness of his room and wished he were dead.

And if the call really was from Jean-Paul? He stares at the number a second time, trying to work out to which part of Paris it might belong. If the call really was from Jean-Paul and he wanted to make peace? He scribbles the number on a scrap of paper he finds in his jacket pocket, a Monoprix receipt for a smoked half-chicken and a bag of salad that triggers an anguished moment of homesickness, taps in the first two, then three, digits to see if any other number he might have in his phone memory shares them. And if Jean-Paul really wanted to make peace and here Jeremy is, hundreds of miles away, with the French coast tantalisingly almost visible across the Channel? The Marais. A number in the Marais. And what the fuck is

Jean-Paul doing in the Marais mid-morning? Who does he know who lives in the Marais? Why isn't he at work? Is he waking up in some man's bed and waiting for coffee to be brought to him, the way he does? Playing with the curl of hair beneath his navel in that half-distracted, half-teasing way he has? I'll just call Jeremy, he'll have decided, see how things are, tell him where I am, see how he feels about that. I'll hurt him, that's what I'll do. Why not? It's Wednesday morning and I don't have a care in the world . . .

At this point, Jeremy's negative reverie comes to a halt. Why do I punish myself, he thinks, when all I have to do is redial the number and find out who it was, most likely some call centre touting for trade, a reminder of a bill he hasn't paid. Not Jean-Paul at all. He's about to do this, thumb hovering over the icon, when he hears someone call his name. He turns to see Dhara perched on a man's bike, her feet barely reaching the ground as she struggles to a stop. She's wearing her anorak, which does at least cover the cardigan beneath. The basket at the front of the bike contains a carton of milk and a cake box, tied with raffia.

'Reggie felt like an éclair,' she says. 'So I got us all one.' Jeremy stands up to hold the handlebars, tilting the bike towards him, one hand on the contents of the basket, so that Dhara can dismount.

'It's Reggie's bike,' she explains, unnecessarily. 'You can push it if you like. Then we can walk along together.'

Sensing he has little choice, Jeremy settles the tab and thanks his waitress before setting off alongside Dhara, his father's bike trundling awkwardly between them.

'We mustn't keep him waiting too long or he'll have forgotten he wants one and then we'll have to eat it.' Jeremy feels her eyes on his belly and sucks it in.

'Should he be eating cake?'

Dhara laughs. 'Oh, I don't think it matters what he eats now, do you? He probably won't eat it anyway. He'll take half a bite and then put it down and ask for something else.' She looks up from Jeremy's stomach to his face, her expression mischievous. 'We won't tell his doctor about , though, will we? Just in case.'

'Your brother,' he says. 'The rugby player.'

She nods. 'That's the one.'

'He must be a lot younger than you are.'

'Well, that's not a very gentlemanly thing to say, is it? And how old do you think I am?'

'I'm hopeless with ages,' he says, 'I never guess them right.' Which is true, but not enough for Dhara. She prods him. There's an air of familiarity about her, of family even, a presumption of intimacy, on what grounds he doesn't know, that's starting to grate. She's gurning up at him, like a child possessed. Who is this woman?

'How long have you called Dad Reggie?' he says, before she can jab her finger into his ribs a second time. There'll be a bruise where she poked him first, he's sure of it.

'Oh, I don't know,' she says. She pats the cake box. 'As long as I've known him, almost.'

'And how long is that?'

She shrugs. 'That depends on how old I am, doesn't it?'

'I suppose it does,' he says. He's being teased, which irritates him.

'So, then, Paris,' she says. 'I've never been. I've never trav-elled at all, really. It must be very romantic. Do they still have all those cancan dancers?'

He looks ahead. To his relief, the garden wall is within sight.

'Paris,' he says, pauses. The grips of the handlebars are slick beneath his hands. He's sweating in the unexpected warmth of the late morning. The cream in the chocolate éclairs will be off by now, he thinks, which will serve her right for not taking them home immediately. Who is this woman, he wonders again, and what does she want from them all? Money?

He hasn't thought about money before this moment.

'Rachel's missed you, you know,' Dhara says, apparently not interested to see if he will continue. 'She'll say she hasn't, I know. I know what she's like, she's the last to complain about anything. But I see things. She's so glad you're home again.'

Once again, this unwarranted cosiness. 'I think that's my business, don't you?' He corrects himself. '*Our* business.' Of course, he's thinking. The money. It won't be long before Denny turns up at the door, upturned riding hat in hand, to see what can be shaken down from the family's money-tree. And then he thinks, *home*? Is that where he's supposed to be?

She's silent until they're in the garden and Jeremy is leaning the bicycle against the wall beside the kitchen door. Then, lifting the cake box and carton of milk from the basket, she says, 'Family is the important thing, you know.' She shakes her head reprovingly. 'You've hurt your father a great deal all these years. I think you ought to know that, and Rachel won't tell you. He deserves a better son than you have been to him.'

Before Jeremy, shocked, has a chance to answer, she has disappeared inside the house.

Rachel comes halfway down the stairs. The light from the landing window behind her reduces her to a silhouette. He's about to ask her who the hell Dhara thinks she is, in a loud enough voice for Dhara to hear, but Rachel starts in first.

'Well, thank God for that,' she says. 'I thought you were never getting back. You're supposed to be here to help me, Jeremy. You can't just wander off into town whenever the mood takes you.'

'We've brought some cakes back for Dad,' he says. He'll talk about the other business later. 'He told Dhara he wanted a chocolate éclair. She's putting them on a plate and making some tea for us all.'

'Daddy can't eat cake,' snaps Rachel. She sighs. 'I knew this would happen, that you'd get back here and disrupt everything.'

Jeremy sighs. 'So what would you like me to do, Rachel?'

'Oh, I don't know,' she says, exasperated. 'Go and see if the tea's ready. Tell Dhara to bring it upstairs. Even better, bring it yourself. It's about time you sat with Daddy for an hour or two.'

She turns on her heels and goes back upstairs. He can hear her speak, and then their father's voice, his tone as querulous and aggrieved as hers, but their words escape him. He climbs the stairs slowly. He still has his bag on his shoulder, with his laptop in it. He will introduce an Indian maid, he decides, into the dungeon scene he has planned for a later part of the book, when the tables are turned and Lady Mirabelle receives her comeuppance. A small, inquisitive Indian maid who will pay dearly for her impudence. And so the balance of the world will be restored.

8

JEREMY

Rachel is standing above him when he wakes. He isn't sure
where he is at first, and starts with fright at the bright-edged,
looming figure of his sister. But then she steps back and
straight away he sees her differently, as someone small, manageable even, her round pink face creased with exasperation. He
has been here before, he thinks, half supine beneath her,
struggling to wake, but he can't remember when, or where.
He stirs, still half asleep, his buttocks dead against the hard
outer rim of the armchair. He must have slid down as he
slept, his arse caught in the trough between upholstery and
frame. He clenches while smiling up, squeezing it back into
life. 'Hello,' he says.

'You're not much use, are you,' says Rachel. It isn't a question.

'Aren't I?'

'He's wet the bed.'

Jeremy wonders what she's talking about until his eyes
follow hers across the room towards their father's bed. It's
more elevated than a normal bed, with a frame along one
side, like a child's cot, even in the details: the gadget that
picks up noise and sends it to the monitor downstairs, a sort

of teddy bear with an aerial sticking out of its head. The nappy draped over it, ready to be used. The nappy that Jeremy, presumably, should have put on his father. And now he remembers Dhara saying something about taking the soiled one downstairs as she went, and would he, could he? And yes, of course, he'd said, yes, of course I will. Just leave it to me. And he would have done it too — although God knows how — if some thought hadn't distracted him, some thought about his flat in Paris he couldn't quite bring back to mind, perhaps about Jean-Paul, and his father's reposeful, regular breathing, his lips slightly parted, his hands folded peaceably on the sheet above his chest, so that it seemed unkind to wake him. The nappy could wait, he'd decided. Let sleeping dogs lie.

And then Dhara had gone and he was alone in the house, apart from his father, which scared him in an unexpected, disconcerting way. His father, in bed, asleep, seemed dangerous and unpredictable, capable of anything, of death even. His bare hands on the top of the sheet like crumpled paper gloves, emptied of everything but the occasional twitch of air.

And now Rachel is shaking their father awake in her efficient, uncaring way. 'Come on, Daddy,' she's saying, 'buck up, we need to put your whatsit on now. Jeremy's not been doing his job. It's what they always say, isn't it?' — jiggling the old man's shoulder and rolling him onto one side — 'If you want something done properly, you're better off doing it yourself.' But then she turns to Jeremy and hisses to him to get over to the bed to help her, she can't shift him on her own. Jeremy starts up, the blood rushing back into his legs. He's no idea how long he's been asleep, no idea what time it might be. His laptop is open on the floor beside him, but the screen is dead. Rachel is flapping around, his father lying limp beneath her hands, staring up at the ceiling in a lost, hopeless way, his mouth hanging open, a look that Jeremy has never seen before, and is shocked by, and filled with pity, which also shocks him. 'Help me lift him up,' she says, hooking the leg of the nearby chair with her foot and dragging it towards her. His father is wearing a sort of nightshirt, rucked up above his waist, as Dhara must have left it, for ease; his legs are chalk-white, hairless, thin as bone and yet soft-looking, like putty. Jeremy turns his head away, as though not wanting to be seen. When Rachel heaves the old man up and shifts him, Jeremy moves the chair until it is under his buttocks, hollow and wrinkled as emptied seedpods. 'Get me some clean sheets,' Rachel says, settling the old man onto the cushioned seat, lifting his legs away from a tangle of dirty sheet, tugging his nightshirt vainly down to cover his lap. His penis is larger than Jeremy might have expected, plump in the general scrawniness of the surrounding body, bare of hair, the testes dark and loose in their crinkled sac. 'They're in the airing cupboard, bottom shelf,' she says. 'In the spare room.'

And Jeremy wanders off to find them, shaken by what he has seen, the startling vividness of it, and yet how ordinary, how utterly predictable. He is shaken by a tenderness he finds in himself, as though he has seen his father for the first time, in some essential, hitherto hidden way, and yet also been exposed to the eyes of others, some part of what he is stripped bare, defenceless. What am I doing here? he asks himself. He pauses on the landing, casting his eye from door to door, suddenly as lost as if he had never set foot in this house before today. 'The spare room,' calls Rachel, behind him. 'For God's sake, Jeremy.' The spare room? he says to no one. The spare fucking room? And which fucking room would that be?

He can barely remember which room in the house is his.

'You can't be trusted with him, that's the problem,' she says when they are both in the kitchen. She is sitting at the table, playing with a teaspoon, Jeremy is making tea. Dhara is upstairs again, with her knitting. She showed Jeremy what she was doing as she passed through the kitchen, a scrap of pink wool the size of an airport paperback, destined to become the back of a cardigan for a great-niece, due next month. 'Do you have children?' she asked him, and he felt as though he'd already answered this question, but wasn't certain. Her words to him on the walk back from town that morning still rankled. 'No,' he said, shaking his head in what he hoped would be understood as mock disappointment; the mockery was important to him. But Dhara rapped his hand with the tips of her long white needles. 'There's still time for that,' she said. 'You're lucky, you see. You're a man. Men can go on fathering right up to the end.' She giggled at this, rolled her eyes and left the room. Leaning against the sink, Rachel watched Dhara go before saying, in a voice that was loud enough for her to hear, 'She's taken a shine to you.' Dhara chortled from halfway up the stairs. 'I'm perfectly happy as I am,' she called back. God help me, thought Jeremy. How much longer can I take this? Less than twenty-four hours had passed and already he was losing all sense of himself in the dreadful wash of home.

'Really?' he says now, squeezing the tea bag against the side of the cup. 'How strong do you like it?'

'I just need to know that I can leave you,' she says. 'Alone with him, I mean. Without having to worry myself sick.'

71

He throws the tea bag towards the bin. It falls six inches to the side, on the clean tiled floor. He stares at it, willing it to rise, to dispose of itself in some magical way. Rachel doesn't seem to have seen. He'll leave it there and see what happens, he thinks, as he turns to his own tea bag, his own over-brewed mug of English Breakfast. Someone will pick it up sooner or later. It's a small act of defiance – infantile, uncivil – and he's perfectly aware of this, but doesn't seem to have the strength to behave otherwise; he's becoming a child again, with the limited resources of a child for naughtiness. 'There's always Dhara,' the same mood makes him say. He recognises, and immediately regrets, the hint of sulking in his voice, but it's too late to call it back.

'That's true enough. I don't know what I'd have done without her these past few months,' she says, taking the mug and peering into it doubtfully. 'Well, years, if I'm being honest. Milk?'

Jeremy stares round the kitchen, orientating himself, then crosses to the fridge. 'I've been meaning to ask you.' He's seeking safer ground. 'How much does she cost?' He puts down the plastic bottle of milk more forcefully then he intends.

'Cost?' Rachel pours milk into her mug, then pushes the bottle towards Jeremy, who ignores it. 'What do you mean?'

'Dad needn't worry about money, surely? It's just that, well, I wouldn't want you to have to foot any bills that need paying.' This is the last thing he planned on saying. He sips his tea, sans milk, sans lemon, praying she hasn't heard.

'You've no idea who Dhara actually is, have you?'

'Why should I have? I'd never seen her in my life before yesterday. I just can't help wondering if there might not be something in it for her. I don't know. How much influence does she have with Dad? I mean, really,' he says, and pulls a face. '*Reggie?*'

Rachel laughs, without humour, as though some long and bitterly held theory about Jeremy has finally been proved right. 'She's been with Daddy on and off for decades now. You must have seen her before yesterday, dozens of times. You probably didn't notice.'

'Well, she didn't know *me*,' says Jeremy hotly, although this isn't what he wants to say. It isn't even true. Of course she recognised him. The Paris one, she'd said, or something like it, as though each European capital has provided a home and identity to a son of Reggie. What he wants to say is *with*? What do you mean by *with*?

'I thought everyone knew about Dhara and Daddy.' Rachel sips her tea slowly, staring across the rim at Jeremy as if over those half-glasses librarian spinsters wear in films. She's gloating; there's a look to her face that recalls his father's – judgemental, amused, contemptuous at root; a look his father can no longer manage, which ought to bring comfort to Jeremy, but doesn't.

'Are you telling me she's one of my father's fleet of other women?'

Rachel puts down her mug, nods. 'Yes, I suppose I am. At least that. Head of the fleet, probably. I thought you knew. I thought everyone knew, to be honest,' she says again, shaking her head in wonder at Jeremy's ignorance. 'She was here before Mummy even moved out. You *must* remember her.'

He slumps down at the table, all the wind knocked out of him.

'It's like one of your books,' she says.

'Is it?'

'Yes. Unlikely, unsuitable. Embarrassing, finally, I suppose, although everyone's used to it by now. Which just goes to show you can get used to anything.'

'Thank you.'

'I've got nothing against her,' continues Rachel as if she hasn't heard. 'It's Daddy I'm angry with. The selfish way he's behaved all round. As though nobody ever matters except himself.'

'Really?'

She stands up, rinses out her mug under the tap. 'No, not really. Not even Daddy.' She bends down to pick up the tea bag from the floor. 'I wonder how that got there,' she mutters, dropping it in the bin with a groan. 'Not any longer.'

'I thought you were never angry with Dad. I thought he could do no wrong in your eyes.'

'I don't know why you thought that. You were never here to see, in any case. You buggered off just as soon as you could. You and Mummy. Both of you as though no one here needed you.' He's startled by this, the idea that he might have been needed. She turns and looks at him, the same look as before, superior, unforgiving, but overlaid by a new touch of tetchiness, like that fifth flavour the Japanese are so keen on – his mother would have known the word for it. 'You don't think life just stopped because you weren't here to watch it, do you?'

'I don't believe it,' he says. But he does. He can see his father bending to hold the Asian woman, younger, more delicate than she is now, her hands bunched in front of her to push him away, his mouth on hers like a weight on freshly pressed cheese. And there is his mother, silent as he is silent, watching the scene unfold like something from one of his novels, which Dhara must surely know he wrote, sitting there in her shapeless Tyrolean hand-knitted cardigan, revelling in the sexiness and the cruelty of it all as though it were something exotic to be sampled in measured doses. There they both are, mother and son, thwarted, excluded, watching the show from the door. Reginald and his oriental concubine.

'It was all over years ago,' Rachel says. 'But she still kept coming round. Daddy didn't mind, I don't think. He never said anything to me, anyway. I think he liked it, to be honest. She's been running the house for years.' She pauses. 'You really didn't know, did you?' A second pause. 'I'm sorry, Jem. I thought you were having me on. It never occurred to me you might not know. I'm just so used to it, you see. And now there's Vikram too, of course.'

She hasn't called him Jem for years. Little Jem, she used to call him, and he only discovered this was also the name of a type of lettuce when he came back to the UK one summer and had to shop for himself. There he was, crisp and small under cellophane, ideal for sandwiches. Maybe this is why he's not ready to accept her apology. He's consumed by unexpected anger, as though she's been hiding something from him, this complicity, on purpose all these years. More than anything, he wants to escape from this place where no one is who they seem. The family home, he thinks, with its self-serving webs of intrigue and deceit.

'Vikram?'

'Dad's doctor.'

'And Dhara's brother, you said.'

'Did I? Is that what I said?' She pulls a face. 'Well, yes, that's right.'

'You said he'd be coming today?' he says as Rachel moves towards the door.

'He generally pops in at the end of his rounds.'

Jeremy considers her back for a moment before speaking. 'What does he have to say?'

'About?'

'What do you mean, about? About Dad.'

'What about him?'

'You know,' he pauses, unexpectedly reticent. 'About how he is.'

She stops and turns round to glare at Jeremy, eyes narrowed into slits, her head slowly nodding, her top lip curling. 'Oh, now I get it. Now I see what you mean. About how long he expects him to live?'

Jeremy shrugs. 'Well, yes.'

'Because that's all that matters, isn't it?' Her tone is openly hostile now. It is as though they had never spoken about Dhara, never shared anything in their lives but rancour and unspoken resentment; had never shared either of their parents. She is bristling like a challenged dog. 'To you.'

'It's what matters most to him, I should think.'

'And what matters to him, of course, is what matters to you. Well, naturally. You've always been the thoughtful one in this family, haven't you? You've always been the first to put yourself out.'

'Oh, for God's sake, Rachel, you surely can't want this to be dragged on for ever,' he snaps. 'We're not at some bloody debating society.'

'This, as you put it, is our father's life.'

Jeremy shakes his head. Is she right to be angry? What does he know? He wishes he had some idea what to say, or do. He can't take her hostility, which has somehow transformed him into his father's willing executioner.

'I don't know why you came home,' she says. 'I don't know what you expect from us.'

'Because you called me, Rachel. And this isn't home, not to me anyway. It hasn't been for decades. It might be home to you.'

'I called to tell you he was on his deathbed. I didn't call to fetch you home.' She pulls a contemptuous face. 'I'm sorry. Wrong word. *Here*.'

'So you'd like him just to go on like this, would you? Lying there like a helpless child.'

'He's perfectly comfortable,' she says. 'I make sure of that.' For the first time she sounds defensive. Despite this not being a debating society, Jeremy feels that he's scored a point.

'So long as comfortable means he's got a dry nappy on and someone's put his teeth in the right way up, I suppose,' he says, pressing on.

'Which won't be you,' says Rachel. She walks across to the table. For a moment he thinks she's going to slap him. It won't be the first time. She was always a heavy-handed child. Once, he'll never forget it, she dropped an empty coal scuttle on his head to stop him playing with her shoelace. When he told his mother, in tears, a trace of his own fresh blood on his fingers, she told him that boys should be able to defend themselves without running to their mummies and he can still see Rachel, smirking, through the kitchen door.

But she doesn't hit him this time, whatever her intention might have been. She rocks on her sensible heels, then slumps back down into the chair and cradles her head in her hands, her elbows on the table. She almost knocks the milk bottle over, but Jeremy doesn't move to steady it. He realises he's trembling with rage. He'd leave the kitchen if it didn't feel like a kind of capitulation, of *rapprochement*. 'Do you know,' she says, her voice muffled, 'I wish you'd just fuck off. You just waltz in here like the prodigal son, expecting everyone to love you, and now you want to kill Daddy off. I hate you sometimes.'

He sits where he is, silent. He's never felt so angry, yet so resourceless. Of all the thousand tones he might take, not one seems to fit. He'd like to tell her that prodigal doesn't mean what she thinks it means, and that he has been prodigal, in ways she will never know, or understand. To tell her how his whole life has been a waste, an expense of spirit. But this isn't the moment. More than a tremble, his whole body is shaking; he daren't raise a hand to see how much in case she looks up and catches him, reduced to this. How can one other person make this happen with so little effort, with so few words, as though some dreadful primitive force had caught him with the edge of its cloak as it swept past. He feels like the whimpering, burdened child at the feet of the giant Cruelty from an illustrated book he read almost fifty years ago, about just deserts and redemption, although none of that made much sense to him then and maybe still doesn't. He doesn't do redemption, he thinks. He'd like to hit her back, but she hasn't given him that chance. She never did. He has always had to defend himself in other ways.

'Hello!' hoots Dhara from the top of the stairs. 'Anyone there?'

'I'll go,' he says, before Rachel has a chance to stir.

His father is staring at the window, waving an arm while Dhara moves the curtain a little this way, a little that, her face a picture of weary concern. 'He says the sun's in his eyes. He doesn't know what he wants, that's the trouble,' she says, but before Jeremy can respond his father bellows, 'I bloody

78

do!' with a force that astonishes them both. He's raised himself up from the pile of pillows behind him, his shoulders jagged as fledgling wings beneath the cotton of the nightshirt. 'I bloody do,' he says again, more weakly, his face lifted to the ceiling as if appealing to some higher authority. Does Dad believe in God, wonders Jeremy, stepping forward, finding his way barred by Dhara, who is hurrying across to straighten the pillows, which have slumped forward, before the old man collapses back against them. 'We can't have you getting pressure sores, can we?' she says. Is this what bed sores are called now, thinks Jeremy; is the word bed too brutal a reminder? So many tricks to learn, so many terms and trials, and then he dies and none of it will be needed until Jeremy himself is lying in some other bed, and listening to those around him talking across his shroud-tight sheet. But who will there be for him, in the place of this dying man's children? And is God there for his father, or is there some other thing, some presence that resembles God, some unsuspected, otherwise undemanding, deity, to provide what comfort is needed? Because what other use could God, or his understudy, have? 'What can you see, Dad?' he says, his voice low, embarrassed, as if what he really wants is to speak to himself. His father is shaking his head, or trying to, against the plumped-up boundaries of the pillows, a bony shell against the enveloping softness. He no longer seems to have the energy to speak. But Jeremy's wrong again.

'You never came,' he says.

Jeremy looks at Dhara, who shrugs.

'I'm here now,' he says.

His father looks at him, his half-blind eyes filming over. 'You never came,' he says. 'I sent for you. I had it all written down, and the money ready for you. Everything.'

'I don't know what you mean.' Jeremy, helpless, glances at Dhara, who has settled herself into the armchair and taken up her knitting. She must be used to this sort of wandering, he thinks, after all these years, used to where his father's mind might go, but it doesn't feel like wandering to Jeremy so much as accusation, an accusation he can't defend himself against. He senses that whatever he might say to appease his father's anger will only incriminate him further. And he feels a rush of anger for this importuning old man, for his refusal to help him. 'What money?' he says.

His father is holding his hand out, pointing towards the bedside cabinet. 'In there,' he says. 'It's in there. My address. It's where you have to take me.' He starts to recite in an urgent sing-song way, like a child with a poem he has learned by heart for some reward, a string of words that may or may not have sense, that in this case make up an address, an address without end like the one Jeremy wrote in his first encyclo-paedia, in his baby writing, in scarlet crayon, an address that began with the name of his house and ended with the universe. Listening, startled and affected despite himself, Jeremy recog-nises fragments of that first address, of the house he grew up in as a child, of his grandparents' house, and other numbers, other streets, a mosaic of identifiable buildings and streets and towns, postcodes and counties, that, placed together, lead everywhere and nowhere, the meaningless scraps that make up a whole, identifiable life. 'Oh, Dad,' he says.

'Don't worry,' says Rachel's voice from behind him. He turns round to see her standing in the doorway, with a man he doesn't recognise staring over her shoulder. The man's taller than she is, and younger, dark-skinned, in a shirt and tie. Jeremy assumes he's the doctor, Dhara's brother, and is relieved, although he'd prefer it if Rachel weren't here.

'It isn't the first time he's done this,' continues Rachel, crossing to the bed. 'He thinks you're the taxi driver. He wants you to take him home.'

9

RACHEL

Rachel has arranged her father's letters as well as she can into groups, according to who wrote them. Sometimes there is a name, sometimes an initial. Sometimes, though the notion makes her cringe, there is a nickname or term of endearment. *Squeaky* is one and *Your cuddly-wuddly Bunny* another. Did he encourage this sort of thing, she wonders, responding in like fashion perhaps, his own nickname changing from one lover to the next; but she will never know unless she can trace the other half of these odd, sordid dialogues, and that would mean unearthing who each of these women was and, heaven forbid, approaching her. She couldn't bear to do that. What she has, and it is already more than she wants, in ragged piles on her dressing table, is the single strident voice of the person who appears to have loved her father, or the single voices rather, one after the next, although there appears to be some overlap at times, a cooling off here coinciding with a warming up there, a fading reproach and an advancing promise nestled together, each unaware, opportunely, of the other. There are almost always dates on the letters, and almost never addresses, which is reasonable, she supposes. Time in an affair is of the essence, while the beds in which the affair takes place are not in the home, but in hotels, temporary havens of one kind or another, illicit secretive spaces in which no one is at home.

She can't find the letters she wrote him anywhere.

What else is really missing, though, apart from the answering voice of her father, the words she can only imagine, is her mother. How curious, she thinks, that the only woman her father has ever been married to should have left no trace of herself, no written record. Perhaps they were always together when they were in love, when what they felt counted, as she and Denny were. There had been no need to write letters, not until he walked out and then it was too late; he'd never have read them even if she'd written. He made that plain enough, or his solicitor did.

Still, what a life her father's led. She can't help but admire him, against her better instincts, if that's what they are, and not something taught her by others, people she's trusted and been betrayed by. A dozen women and all this emotion, all this subterfuge and deception, all this passion, always passion, passion and reproach and more passion, all these words expended to make up for their being apart. He could have married again, more than once; he could have married Dhara, for heaven's sake, and she's wondered why he didn't, wondered was it Dhara's colour and dismissed that thought as unworthy, but not entirely, wondered how she would have felt if he had. If she would have felt jealous, as she would have had every right to, or – even worse – ashamed, rejected. The opportunities were there, certainly, and the craving doesn't seem to have weakened until the last few years, the final decline.

The most recent – and most explicit – letter, from someone who signs herself 'V', dates back to 1991, when her father was already more than seventy. She picks it up again, the last blunt nail in her father's romantic coffin. But romantic's not the word for what she reads, unfolding the letter for the umpteenth time, glancing at what it contains with a shudder as if to check that nothing has changed. She had no idea that people actually *licked* each other's bottoms for pleasure. The only bottom she's ever touched, apart from her own, for hygienic purposes, is her father's, it occurs to her now, although not, dear God, with her tongue. And to find out there's a word for it as well, at her age! What a dirty old bugger he must have been, she thinks, disgusted and – again, despite herself – amused, almost admiring, as though some glancing reflection might fall on her, illuminate her. What a life! And, as she thinks this, there is an unexpected, unnerving sense of a distance, hard and new and unwanted, opening up between them.

Still, she thinks, shaking the feeling off, these women were lucky to have known him in the end. That's what she gets from these letters, whatever else they might be saying: a sense of their good fortune, in spite of it all. A sense of grace, she'd say, if she were religious. Blessed by him, in their way. As she has been, she supposes. She has been blessed by his love for her, although she can hardly remember all that, and doesn't want to, not now they're so near the end.

She folds the letter up and slides it back into its envelope. Would she ever have written letters like this to Denny, assuming she had written? Sexy letters, like this? When they first met, and he'd taught her so much and then gone off to gymkhanas and left her alone at her father's house for days on end, weeks sometimes, without a word. Because she was mistaken, they hadn't always been together; there had been times when she might have written, as these women wrote to her father. A love letter, brimming with passion and desire, and the hint of reproof these letters required, because the other person was somewhere else, was beyond reach. As Denny had been so often at the start, before they were married. And then there'd been a phone call from some hotel lobby, just to put things right again, and she'd forgiven him. Time and time again.

She knows the kind of letters she'd have liked to write, if she had. Filled with passion, yes, but also recrimination, streaked with her tears. What a fool she'd been to trust him, to love him and let herself be hurt. She had the sense that her father had always let these women down gently. He was always kind, in the end – she knew that. She knew how kind he could be. He hadn't just walked out on them to sleep with some little whore he barely knew. He hadn't run off to Austria with her finest stallion and a stable girl.

People make so much fuss about love, she thinks, stacking the letters into a single pile. She plans to show Jeremy one of these days, to see what he thinks should be done with them. She'd do it now, but she's unaccountably shy, as though she'd written the letters herself, as though to show them to him would be a sort of confession. Sometimes she imagines her father's funeral and there, at the heart of it, is the farce of unknown women arriving and finding themselves all in one place for the first time, sidling into the pews like courtesans before their lord. In the old days, they'd have had their throats cut and been burnt, she thinks, and this idea provokes more pleasure than is comfortable. And then there's Dhara to be found a place for. And herself, of course.

Not that her mother was that much better, in the end. What was that horrible word Denny always used, smacking his lips over it? That's it. Goer. A bit of a goer. Their mother was a bit of a goer, in both senses of the word. Messing around with men, then up and off. She can't help wondering where all their sexy genes ended up. Look at her, early sixties, practically a virgin again after all these years. She's even found herself picking up one of Jeremy's dirty novels and flicking through it, just to remind herself what love must be like. But the very idea disgusts her, and what she saw of the sex in the book didn't help. Such filth, where on earth does it come from? From Little Jem? Just look at him. Hard to imagine Jeremy making love. Hard to imagine him *rimming* someone else, although she assumes that rimming will be part of his erotic repertoire. What she sees when she thinks of Jeremy and sex is that look of pathetic yearning she's caught in his eyes when he spots a man he likes the look of. His neglected puppy look. Like that man on the train. Like this afternoon, with Vikram. 'Hello,' he'd said, darting forward, hand outstretched, all smiles and wanting to be picked up and stroked. 'I'm Jeremy.' And Vikram had taken his hand and shaken it and said, 'I'm Vikram.' She'd felt quite sick. I could put a halt to that nonsense pretty sharp, she thought, but she kept her mouth shut. Now wasn't the time to talk about Vikram, especially not to Jeremy. Dhara's always tended to keep Vikram hidden, from her at least. She must have seen how uncomfortable he makes Rachel feel. She doesn't know where to *put* him, that's the problem. He's family, what with the business of Dhara and Dad, but it's not in a way she likes to contemplate. Sometimes he behaves as though he belonged here too, as he does, she supposes. As they all do, she and Jeremy as well. He's certainly worked wonders in the garden these past few months, though, she'll say that for him. It's almost as beautiful as it was when Mummy lived here. But who knows what goes on when she isn't in the house to keep an eye on things?

'Vikram's going to help us move Dad nearer the window,' she said.

Dhara was packing her knitting up into her bag. 'I thought you were coming later,' she said, complaining, but her tone was generous. 'I wanted to get him settled first.' She hurried across to the bed. 'He's been going on about the sun getting in his eyes today, I'm not even sure he wants to be moved any longer.' She stroked the old man's arm. He turned his head in her direction. He's practically blind, Rachel thought, with a wave of pity, his milky gaze like something in a dream. 'Do you, my love?' Rachel has never called her father *my love*, or anything like it.

Vikram put down his doctor's case near the door and rolled up his shirtsleeves. 'Come on, then. It won't take a moment. These beds have wheels, don't they? All we need to do is shift the armchair a little to the right and then we can push it over.'

'It's plugged in,' said Rachel. 'The mattress is plugged in. You can hear the pump.' Although she was so used to it by now that she had to make an effort to hear the low, constant hum of the box attached to the foot of the bed, regulating the air in the mattress, keeping her father's body free of pressure sores, making his last few weeks liveable. End of life pathway, that's what the nurses call it, which she finds reassuring, as though everything was happening exactly as it should, according to plan, the road marked out. What a godsend it is, she always thinks, and free, all of it free, how lucky we are to live in this country. How does Jeremy manage in France?

'It should be long enough to reach the window,' said Vikram. He'd walked round to the other side of the bed and was holding the flex up. His arm was bulky, smooth, a lovely caramel colour. You could see he played rugby from the size of him, a big deep chest, a solid neck. What a lovely man he is, she thought, how proud Dhara must be of him. She couldn't resist glancing across to see how Jeremy was coping and almost burst out laughing at the sight of him, mouth open, practically drooling, as Vikram put the flex down and positioned himself to push, and Dhara tugged at the armchair in a futile attempt to move it out of the way. He only moved when Vikram smiled across and suggested Jeremy take the other side of the bed; his mouth snapped shut. 'Righto,' he said.

Her father seemed oblivious to all this excitement, to the presence of Vikram beside his shoulder, lying there, staring up at the ceiling with his unseeing eyes, his hands on the sheet, his body so shrunken beneath it he might as well not have been there, the only bulkiness around the middle, where his nappy was bunched. Gone to nothing. All those women, thought Rachel, all that burgeoning. Loins, that's the word I was looking for. Biblical. Burgeoning loins and now there's barely enough to make a ripple in the sheet. 'There are brakes on it,' she said. 'We'll need to take them off.' She bent down to see where they were, her right ear pressed up against the humming pump. Somewhere behind her, Vikram had lifted the armchair clean from the ground while Dhara made anxious, admiring noises. Rachel straightened up, caught Jeremy's eye. He pulled a little face of appreciation, as though he knew what she'd been thinking, and didn't care – as though he saw her as an accessory. Perhaps he did. 'You have to move this,' she said, pointing to a metal lever with her foot.

Her father began to stir, moaning and rolling his head from side to side. 'Hang on,' she said, 'I'll see what he wants.' She pushed Jeremy away and bent over the bed until her face was inches from her father's. His breathing is getting worse, she thought, harsher and weaker at the same time. The last time Vikram had listened to his chest, he'd shaken his head, glancing across at her in a gloomy, unsurprised way, and she'd thought, oh well, we're almost there, and immediately been ashamed of herself. That's why she'd been so furious with Jeremy, she thought now, so fierce with him – because she'd felt uncovered. All that talk of his about death and wanting to hurry things up. She'd understood at once what he meant, because she'd wanted it herself and tried to pretend she hadn't. 'What is it, Daddy?' she said. 'What do you want?'

'Leave me alone,' he said. 'Let me die.'

'Don't be so foolish,' she said, her heart turning over in her chest. 'You don't want everyone hearing that sort of nonsense.'

'Let me die,' he said. 'What do I have to do to die?'

She straightened up.

'You take that side of the bed,' she said to Vikram. 'Jeremy and I will do this side.' She ignored Dhara, who was fussing with the curtains.

And now here she is, with the proof of his life stacked up beside her like outstanding bills to be paid. With a sweep of her hand, the letters scatter on the floor, at her feet, and she is bending down, immediately regretful, to gather them together again as though her life depends on it, gathering them into a rough, creased heap between her stockinged feet. She's darned the tip of one, she must be the last person left alive to darn a stocking – to wear a stocking, come to that – but the stitching has come undone and her big toe is peeking out, the nail too long, yellowing, curved, like something you'd find on an animal. She's letting herself go, her nails uncut, the stables abandoned to the care of Eric, who's all right in fine weather, so to speak, but come a hint of storm and he's blown off course, and now there's storm all the time, this constant talk of crisis, if she isn't careful she'll end up without a penny, the horses sold off or worse, and then what will happen? At least she'll have the money from the house, this house, she thinks, her share of it anyway, and before she knows it she's started to cry. First her mother, and now this. How dare he want to die, she says to herself. How dare he. After all she's done. Men are so selfish.

And she still hasn't found the letters she wrote to him.

10

JEREMY

Jeremy asked his mother about Grenier on her last visit to Paris before she died, when she'd stayed at l'Hôtel. She'd agreed that his most recent flat, a largish studio at the Père Lachaise end of Menilmontant that he shared with a Brazilian barman called Gilberto, wasn't quite the place for a woman in her early sixties.

'Oscar Wilde died here,' she said, as they waited for someone to carry her single case to her room, 'but I expect you knew that, didn't you?'

He nodded. 'It used to be called Hôtel d'Alsace,' he said, 'but I expect *you* knew that.'

She glanced at him sharply. 'That's quite enough cheek from you, young man,' she said, turning away to follow the porter and her case. 'Your old mother knows a lot more than you imagine.'

'I saw a photograph of you,' he said some moments later, as she opened the window to the room and looked down into the street, and he stood behind her, disregarded. 'A few months ago.'

She didn't answer, not at once. He thought she might not have heard, and was relieved in a way. He'd been foolish to bring it up.

'So tell me about this photograph,' she said that afternoon, when he'd forgotten all about it. 'Where exactly did you see it?' They were sitting outside a café, waiting for their drinks to arrive. She was playing with a copy of the novel he'd written, which he'd foolishly decided to give her to see if she'd be shocked – she wasn't – and to prove to himself that he wasn't ashamed of what he'd done, although he was. The act of presenting his mother with the vile, cheaply made and bound little book, albeit wrapped in the loveliest and most expensive paper he could find, and inscribed 'To my mother, my inspiration', which had struck him as witty at the time and now only confirmed his shame, had shown him to himself in a way he couldn't like or pardon. He'd rip it from her hand if he could, throw it into the nearest bin, grind it beneath his foot, reduce it to the unreadable pulp it really was. '*Knife in the Heart*,' she'd said, leaving a little space between each word for him to squirm in. She'd cast the handmade paper, torn, irretrievable, to one side and flicked through the book with a sideways smile, pausing now and then as though scanning for a passage to read to someone else, who wasn't there, who would judge him. Now, with a little laugh, she put it down.

'At Grenier's flat.'

'Really? The one in Paris? Well, yes, I suppose it would be.'

'Yes,' he said. 'Do you know it?'

She ignored the question. 'How is he?'

'He said he's known you for years.'

'Did he really?'

'Before he met his wife, he said.'

She nodded, then slipped the book into her bag. 'I'll read this later,' she said, 'when I'm alone. I suspect it's that sort of book.' She looked at him. 'I didn't know you had it in you.'

'I thought it was the other way round.'

'What was? I don't know what you mean,' she said. 'Oh, look at that, Jeremy! How sweet!' She gestured towards a *bouledogue* pup, no larger than a trussed chicken, attached to the wrist of an overweight, middle-aged man by a paste-encrusted collar and lead. The man was dragging the dog along behind him as it pissed, in fits and starts, on the ankles of passers-by; he had a straw-blond toupee, over-tight green trousers, a red carnation in his buttonhole. He glanced briefly at Jeremy as he skirted the café tables, then looked away with a moue of distaste. May God forgive us, thought Jeremy, for we know not what we do. Or, rather, we do know exactly what we do, because we are too self-absorbed not to, but we pretend we don't, which is even worse. We make ourselves ridiculous in order not to pass unnoticed, because invisibility is worse than ridicule. Doesn't Foucault – someone he's recently been reading, or trying to – say something about that? Armand, who recommended he read Foucault in the first place, will be bound to know. Still, he thought, surely there must be some other option? May I never grow old, or fat, or vain, he swore to himself. Or own a dog. Or need another person. Well, no, not that. May I need and find another person. He didn't count Gilberto. He never did. He knew he should, but Gilberto's love for him, the effusiveness of it, made him doubt his own capacity for love, and love Gilberto less.

'I thought that she introduced you to him,' he insisted.

She watched the man turn the corner before turning to him, with a little shake of her shoulders, and answering. 'Did you? I wonder why. In any case,' she continued, dismissive, 'What difference does it make?'

'None really, except that I don't know how you met him. I'm curious, that's all.'

For the first time since she'd arrived in Paris that morning, she seemed absorbed. Even the hotel room he'd found for her had failed to arouse more than a perfunctory attention. 'What did Armand have to say about it?'

'He didn't. I mean, I didn't ask him.'

'You thought you'd cross-examine your old mum instead, did you?'

He laughed, but he'd noticed that she remembered Grenier's first name. 'You just looked so happy, I wondered why.'

She scrutinised him. 'Is it that unusual for me to look happy? Isn't that what people usually do for photographs? Look happy? I expect he said *fromage* or something silly, and it made me laugh. Isn't that what people do?'

'Well, that's just it,' he said. 'It didn't look as though you were doing it for the camera. You were just sitting in this park somewhere and you had that dress on that you always liked so much, with flowers all over it, and you had your head thrown back and you were laughing at the person who was taking the photograph. Well, not at him, exactly, and not for him either. With him, I suppose. As though there were just the two of you in the world.'

She patted her bag. 'You seem to have found your vocation, Jeremy darling. Writing romantic fiction.'

'Did you love him?' he said, annoyed, at least a little wounded. The *darling* was new; he wondered where she'd picked that up. He'd never been called darling by anyone before that afternoon. He felt as if the word were holding him at bay.

'Dear me, Jeremy, all this for a photograph,' she said, but her voice was uncertain. I've rattled you, he thought, and was satisfied. People needed to be rattled, sometimes. It did them good. Why are you here, he wondered. To be rattled? Shall I rattle you, really? Rattle the bars of your cage, or mine?

'I really don't think my emotional life is any of your business,' she said, with a thoughtful, almost regretful smile that suggested the opposite. 'I am your mother, after all.'

After a few glasses of wine that evening, she was more forthcoming. 'He was my first Frenchman, darling. I don't know quite what I expected. Roses, perfume, champagne. But he wasn't that sort of Frenchman. He was just very, very sweet, and very affectionate and then, when he met Hilary and fell in love with her instead of me, which wasn't at all what I'd planned, very gentle and very cruel all at the same time. He said that all he thought about was me and, do you know, I think that might have been true. But I didn't think it then. It took me ages to forgive him.' She paused, then emptied her glass. 'I'm not sure I should be telling you this.' She paused again. 'I never forgave her.'

'I thought you were best friends?'

'Were,' she repeated, with emphasis, then sighed and looked away from him, as though he had hurt her somehow. 'Quite. Were.' Lighting a cigarette, she looked ill and tired suddenly. He was shocked. And then she smiled and was herself again. 'I thought I was here in Paris to have a little fun, dear, not disinter old bones.' She glanced round for a waiter. 'Shall we have coffee?' she asked him, then, opening her bag, added: 'This is on me.'

Which was a relief.

The next morning they both had hangovers, although Jeremy's seemed to be worse. This was unfair; he'd called a halt at the third brandy, while his mother had continued to order Calvados until well into the early hours. He'd found her a taxi and then walked home, swaying a little, discordantly humming one of the songs Gilberto sang as he cooked beans and sludgy grey-green dishes in their tiny kitchen, often in little more than an apron, like a burlesque parody of a maid. *Coraçon*, the song went, and then *coraçon* again, as far as he could remember, although surely there must be more to it than that. As he headed home to his shared one-bedroomed flat, he saw Gilberto's plumpish olive-hued bottom before his eyes, a shiver of smooth hot dew-damp skin, the wink of a puckered arsehole, a general sweaty squidginess, and wondered whether a rendezvous between Gilberto and his mother might not best be avoided, for all their sakes. How on earth did this happen, he asked himself out of the blue, the question a nasty surprise, and yet not entirely a surprise – a surprise he'd been avoiding. He meant this business with Gilberto. Gilberto Gil. And *that's* the name of the man who wrote the song I can't remember the words of, he thought, as he walked alone through central Paris, the city of love, his feet half breaking into a clumsy dance. *Gilberto*, he hummed, or said, or sang, *Gilberto*, followed, once more, by *coraçon*. A loop, he said, I'm in a loop of love, except that of course I'm not, I'm not in love at all. And then that other song entered his head, *I'm not in love*, he sang. Oh no. A song he hates. And then another song, one they'd played in the restaurant while his mother talked about Grenier, his brand-new book squirreled away in her bag, for some undefined, impossible to imagine, later. A song he recognised but couldn't remember, sung by – was it? – Dalida? In Italian? How potent cheap music is, he thought, unoriginally, although he couldn't recall off-hand who'd said this first. Especially in a language one understands not a word of. And now it was two o'clock in the morning and he was very tired.

He was just about to turn off Rue de la Roquette when a door opened some yards ahead and someone – a man – came out. The man was tall, so tall he had to stoop to pass under the lintel, so tall he needed sticks the height of a man – an ordinary man – to support his upper half. He was scrawny and dressed, despite the cool night air, in a T-shirt and trousers that reached to just below his knees. His calves and arms were bare, blue-white in the light of the street. Young, no older than twenty-five, albino pale, his hair cropped short and dyed in patches, brown and orange against the blond. Jeremy darted back into the semi-shadow offered by the nearest wall. The man paused for a moment, glanced once myopically in Jeremy's direction, and then began to move, halting, his sticks before him, towards and across the empty street. Jeremy, not breathing, watched from his almost darkness the long slope of the back, the four emaciated legs, two human, two artificial, the hair, the hair above all, the hair of a parodist, the knowingness of it, the wit. Giraffe, thought Jeremy. Giraffe made man. And how does one live with what one has? Hours later, he lay awake in bed, his hands behind his head, Gilberto snoring gently beside him, thinking of what he had seen. He hadn't spoken of it; he wouldn't have known how. His face was wet with tears. How does one live with what one is?

He didn't mention it to his mother either. She was waiting for him in the hotel foyer, with sunglasses holding back her fine grey hair and a large straw bag hanging from the crook of her elbow. 'Today,' she said, sliding her free arm through his, 'I want to do something exciting. An exhibition, perhaps. But not the Louvre. Something that will shake me up a little.'

'I need some breakfast first,' he said. 'I've got a splitting headache.'

'You need someone to look after you,' she said, lips pursed. They were outside the hotel. 'I'm surprised you don't have

97

someone already.' She pulled him to a halt and turned to face him. 'You don't, do you?'

He shrugged. 'Not really.'

In that case,' she said, 'I shall have to take you in hand myself.' She brushed his fringe from his forehead, which was hot and damp with last night's alcohol. 'Hair of the dog, my dear.' She paused. 'And then you can tell me what "not really" means.'

'But he was the one who picked *me* up,' said Jeremy, leaning forward, earnest, his elbow practically in the ashtray. He'd been smoking his mother's cigarettes all morning, but she hadn't seemed to mind. On the contrary, she'd pushed the packet in his direction more than once, with lighter, and then replaced it with a full packet when the first was empty. They were on their second coffees and third cognacs at this point, and Jeremy's barriers had been dismantled, glass by glass. 'He was really keen. I mean, you know what it's like, Mum, when someone sort of makes it so obvious, you just sort of, well, go along with it.'

'Yes, dear,' she said. 'It's called seduction.'

'I suppose it is,' said Jeremy, although he'd always thought seduction was about making the loved one feel valuable, unique even, not imposing oneself upon him to feed some pressing, selfish need. He hadn't told his mother that the seduction had taken place in a station latrine, at three o'clock in the morning. 'And I am fond of him,' he said, unforgivably relieved when his mother looked unconvinced. 'Honestly.'

'As long as you know what you want,' she said, and it wasn't clear to him quite what she meant, whether the corollary of what she had said was that knowing would be enough, whatever the situation he found himself in; or if knowing would be the trigger that initiated change. If she had continued, *you should go out and get it*, he would have been frightened and thrilled, and obeyed her. He would always obey her, if only she would tell him what to do. As it was, he suspected she had told him to cherish his kernel of self-knowledge, to hold it still and silent to his mouth, as though nothing else would be required to nourish him. Self-knowledge and Gilberto, in eternal dispiriting conflict.

'Well, I wish I did,' he said to clear matters up.

'And what about your sister, with that appalling Dennis,' his mother said, wilfully changing the subject, it seemed to Jeremy, who hadn't begun to exhaust the subject of himself. 'Do you understand her? Because I'm sure I don't. There's something so, well, unpleasant about him. I know we aren't supposed to say people are common any longer, but—'

'I thought he was a baronet or something?'

His mother laughed briefly. 'I hardly think so. That may be what he told Rachel, of course.' She lit a cigarette. 'I had lunch with her last Tuesday, in a place she likes near Victoria station. Not *my* cup of tea at all. She said she'd never been happier. I didn't believe a word of it. She's been borrowing money from your father and giving it to him, you know. She says they're going to open a stable or something. You can't imagine how often I rue the day your father bought her that filthy pony.'

'I suppose it is *their* money, not just hers,' said Jeremy. 'Now they're married, I mean.'

'And what about *your* money?' his mother said, abruptly angry. 'Who thinks about that? After all I've done.'

I do, thought Jeremy, all the time. I think about nothing but money. He shrugged. 'You know what Dad's like.'

'All too well.' She looked worried. 'Have you been in touch with him?'

He shook his head. 'You always tell me it would be a waste of time.'

She pursed her lips, stubbed out her cigarette. 'I wonder sometimes,' she said. Opening her bag, she took out an envelope and gave it to Jeremy. His book was still there, he noticed. 'Don't look just now,' she said. 'But don't worry. You won't be disappointed.'

'Thank you,' he said.

'I love you so much. You do know that, don't you? If only I could click my fingers and solve our lives. I would do, you know. But you know that. I know you know. You're my only son.'

He nodded. 'Of course I know.' And although he meant it, he let her wait a moment before adding, as he was meant to do: 'I love you too.'

He didn't see his mother again for almost five years.

11

JEREMY

Vikram gets to the house early with the book he promised Jeremy. It's written by someone Jeremy has never heard of and whose name he can barely pronounce, and is the kind of book he would not normally read for several reasons, but Vikram wouldn't countenance Jeremy's not borrowing it. 'You absolutely must,' he said as he left the house yesterday evening, after the long, half-whispered conversation they'd had in the hall while Dhara and Rachel settled his father in his new position by the window, 'it will enlarge and enrich your life.' His accent has a residual Indian tinge, unlike his sister's, which is pure Kent. On the cover of the book, an oddly sized paperback with a nastily glossy surface, is a painting of an enormous tropical bloom. It reminds Jeremy of the flower that emerges from its bud once every hundred years and stinks of rotting flesh, but he could easily be mistaken. Botany isn't his strong point. Not that the book, from the look of it, deals with anything as materialistic as botany. The tumescent bloom is surrounded by a host of floating ears, or what appear to be ears, hovering like cherubs against the vivid orange background as though waiting for words to issue from the fleshy technicolor petals at their heart. There's a pseudo-religiosity about it that Jeremy doesn't like at all; the book has the odour of self-help and, which is worse, self-publishing. Queasy, he takes it from Vikram's surprisingly small dry hand. 'Thank you,' he says, 'I look forward to reading it.'

'In this world, we spiritual seekers,' says Vikram with a dazzling smile, 'must help one another out.' And Jeremy is instantly lost in the bounty of this smile, as welcome as a lifebelt flung into a dark and hostile sea. Upstairs his sister is changing his father's nappy, as far as he knows, and he is waiting for the toast to pop up from the toaster, but none of this matters as Vikram takes the book from his hand and flicks through it, his features pursed into a look of such erotic concentration there is no air left outside it. All Jeremy can do is lean forward slightly, towards the source, and hope to breathe.

'Move him into the light,' says Vikram, closing the book in a conclusive manner and holding it out like a small bare tray. 'One of your many fine poets spoke of this, I believe.'

'Wilfred Owen,' says Jeremy. 'The sun.'

'Yes, I am also thinking of your father,' says Vikram. 'To be a son is a full-time job.'

'No,' says Jeremy. 'Wilfred Owen said to move him into the sun. The sun,' he says, glancing towards the window. He feels foolish now, pedantic. 'Not the light,' he continues, as if determined to make things worse.

'And now your father is in the blessed light of the sun,' says Vikram, 'and his son is down in the hall, standing here with someone who should be starting morning surgery in twenty minutes or he will be in hot water.' He lays a warm, comforting hand on Jeremy's arm. 'I shall be seeing you very soon.'

'I do hope so,' says Jeremy, his voice sounding absurd to him, dark and throaty, as though filtered through catarrh. He watches Vikram run to his car, which he has parked at the end of the drive. Jeremy takes a few steps out of the house, under the porch, his arm raised in a half-wave, before realising he is still in his pyjamas. They are black silk and cost more than anyone should ever spend on nightwear, but he is glad that Vikram has seen him in them. Is it racist, he wonders, to think that an Indian might be more likely to appreciate pyjamas? Perhaps the word itself is Indian, like tiffin, or bungalow. These particular pyjamas come from a shop in Paris, in the Marais, and he bought them to celebrate something, he can't remember what. Jean-Paul must have had something to do with it. He has the pyjamas still, the occasion for celebration they represented long forgotten. And now, despite himself, he is thinking about his father and the rest of Owen's poem, which he once knew by heart. It is a poem about death and resisting death, and acknowledging the impossibility of that resistance. The clays of a cold star. I should have been a poet, he thinks, if only I had had the talent. He has published one book of poetry in his life, thanks in part to Grenier's beneficence, and no one, to his knowledge, has bought it, which is proof of a sort that fate can be kind when it chooses, can spare the individual blush. But he still picks his copy up and reads the words out to himself, at night, after at least a bottle, when no one else is around to listen, and is moved by them, and wonders if perhaps he is a poet, after all. Perhaps, he thinks, Vikram would like to hear what I have written some evening, when the two of us are alone. One of your many fine poets, he said. What company I might keep.

'Was that my naughty Vikram bothering you?'

He looks up to see Dhara. 'I didn't know you were here,' he says.

She laughs, a guttural laugh he doesn't expect from her. 'He can be a bit of a pest when he wants to be,' she says. 'Don't you start encouraging him now, or we'll never get rid of him. Mind you, we don't want him neglecting Reggie either.'

'Well, he seems to be very nice,' says Jeremy, immediately wishing he'd said something worthy of the man, or nothing. *Reggie* again.

'Oh yes, he's *very* nice, he is,' says Dhara, laughing again. 'You want to hear what the senior doctor at his surgery has to say about him.' She looks at her watch. 'He should have been there half an hour ago.'

'Rachel's with Dad?' he says.

'Yes.' Dhara studies him for a moment. 'She's just so pleased you're here, you know. You're a godsend.'

'It's too much for her, I can see that.' Is that what Rachel said? That he was a godsend? She'd more or less told him to fuck off the day before.

'No, no, what on earth do you mean? Not the work here, that's not what I'm talking about.' Dhara's tone is dismissive, and also protective of his sister, as though he can't be expected to understand, but should, even so, be trying a little harder than he has done up to now. 'I can help her with all that. I just think she was missing you. You should be here, with her, with your dad. It's what families are for, isn't it? To help one another out.'

'That isn't the way our family works,' says Jeremy, irritated now at the thought that she and Rachel should have this intimacy. Who is this woman to tell him – or anyone – what's required by familial duty, or love? But of course, he's forgotten, she's more part of his family than he is.

'Yes, well,' says Dhara, pushing past him to reach the sink. She rinses a cloth out and he wonders what was on it. He hasn't seen his father yet this morning. He'll go up when he's had his breakfast, he decided earlier, before Vikram's arrival threw him off course. The toast has popped up from the toaster and is now lukewarm, which means the butter won't melt. He read once that cold toast took less butter and was therefore less bad for you, and made up his mind immediately that he would never eat cold toast. He despises the healthier option on principle, as though he will knowingly damn his own body before being told what to do with it by someone else. It is one of his small rebellions, like leaving the tea bag on the floor to be picked up by someone else, or refusing to straighten his mattress back at home, because why should he? It isn't his fault it's halfway up the wall, but Jean-Paul's. And Jean-Paul, one day, will come back to put it right, until which time it will remain his fault. But now, with Dhara's eyes on him as she rinses and wrings, and rinses and wrings who knows what bodily fluids into the sink, he takes the toast and puts it on a plate.

'The butter's in the fridge,' she says, as if talking to a child, 'unless you want that low-fat alternative that's friendly to the heart. That's next to the bread bin. And there's some marmalade on the shelf over there, next to the tea. It's homemade.'

'Thank you,' he says. 'Did you make it?'

'Don't be silly,' she says. 'I do have a life, you know.'

Rachel has asked Jeremy to take a look at all these letters and now here he is, sitting in the room he's always thought of as his mother's, which has now become Rachel's, just as the room he once considered his is now nothing more than the room in which he sleeps when he is here, a guest room, really, but

105

without the comforts a guest might expect. The making and the unmaking of the house – that long and, for him, unheeded process that has almost erased him, and his mother, it would seem, from its heart. Which is as it should be, he knows this, as they were the ones to walk out, so he can't complain, but there is that niggling resentment he can't entirely quell as he looks around, remembering. And he wonders now why it never struck him as odd that his mother should have her own room. Didn't parents sleep together?

Rachel had hustled him out of their father's room this morning and told him she had a favour to ask him. Before he could consider what this might involve, she'd shown him the piles of letters on their mother's dressing table, which is no longer their mother's but still has brushes he remembers – a hair brush and a clothes brush with a silver back, the shape of a pencil case, the kind of things no one owns now, he imagines, but that were once seen as essential. Does Rachel use them, he wonders, as he sits on the bed with the first pile of letters beside him, the earliest to have been written, feeling dirty, wishing he'd had the courage, or good sense, to refuse to read them. But he has never been much good at refusing Rachel. What he doesn't understand is why she should be so keen to poke her nose into their father's business, and to poke his nose into it as well, as though an unwarrantable curiosity shared were somehow lessened. Because what they're doing, what he's about to do, with their father dying no more than thirty feet away, is unforgivable. Can't this be left until later? He stares into his mother's mirror. Left until after he's dead? Isn't the Dhara business enough? But his reflected features, anxious, unshaven – he needs to buy new blades – are merely a distraction, offer no answers, no reassurance.

He picks up the first letter, still in the envelope, and opens it. From the date he works out that his father must have been in his mid-fifties, and Jeremy almost fifteen. The letter is long, six closely written sheets of pale-blue paper covered on both sides, with crossings-out and corrections on almost every line as though the thoughts of the person writing it were running slightly behind her pen. How odd to hold a letter in his hands again – it's years since Jeremy has received anything longer than a postcard; even his fans use emails – and to realise that the person who wrote it may still be alive, may still be feeling these same emotions, that his father may even now be thinking about this woman, whose name, he sees, is Lindsay, or something like that, it's hard to tell from the hurried scrawl on the final page, an old man lying in his cot-like bed with his eyes closed, the curtain protecting his face from the light of the late morning sun.

He starts to scan it but almost immediately gives up. Apart from the difficulty of reading through the web of rectification, and the nervous, over-emphatic loopiness of the script, there's a familiarity in the language itself, the insistence, the same few words – I miss you, darling; you know how much I love you; I can't bear the thought; your hands, your mouth, your heart – reiterated with such fervour, such candour. Imagine if he wrote like this, he thinks, how quickly his audience would disappear. But he doesn't put the letter down; after a moment, during which he turns once again to the mirror to interrogate himself, he reads on, skipping from one paragraph to the next as if he is looking for something specific. And it seems that the letter is aware of this, because Lindsay, if Lindsay is the name, begins to talk about a Hotel Metropole, and arrangements to meet in a pub called the King's Head, and what to wear, nothing too showy, apparently. There is someone at the office who mustn't know, though which office, hers or his, isn't clear. This is the kind of intrigue Jeremy enjoys. Dad must have been fucking a colleague, he thinks, and he wonders if his mother knew; they were still together then, after all. He looks at himself and sees her, his mother, looking out at him; the older he gets, the more he resembles her. He raises an eyebrow as she might have done, then smiles, sliding the letter back into its envelope and picking up another.

He's still there two hours later, when Rachel comes in with a sandwich and two cups of tea.

'It's bacon,' she says. 'Sell-by date yesterday. I thought we'd better use it up.'

'That Lindsay was rather intense,' he says. 'She wasn't very pleased when it all came to an end either.'

'Do you know, I don't think he kept the last letters,' says Rachel, sitting on the bed beside him. 'I always get the feeling the stories end too suddenly. I think he must have thrown them away. I suppose they were the upsetting ones.'

'I'm surprised he didn't just throw them all away.' He bites into the sandwich, melted butter running down his chin. God, he thinks, he's missed this. 'That would have been the safest option.' To protect himself from us, he thinks, but doesn't say. As though what we thought mattered.

'Yes,' she says. 'Denny always did. In the bin outside, in a large brown envelope. I think he bought them specially.'

'He didn't have them delivered to the house, surely?'

She shakes her head. 'Of course not. Neither did Dad. Did you notice on the envelope? He had a PO box in Canterbury.'

'So how did you know?'

'How does one ever know?' she says. She looks at him in

the mirror. 'You've got bacon fat all over you,' she says, with a smile, passing him a folded piece of kitchen paper from her pocket, not turning her face. 'You must have been betrayed at some point. How did you know?'

'Strangely enough, I never have.' Finishing the sandwich, he wipes his chin and then his hands with the tissue. 'I've never been worth the trouble of lying to, probably. When my partners find someone else they prefer they just move out.'

'Don't do yourself down,' she says sternly. 'No one will love you if you don't love yourself.'

They stare at each other's reflection for a moment, as though they have both been caught, engrossed, in front of the same film, before bursting into laughter.

'I can't believe I just said that. It's the influence of Dhara,' she says. 'It must be.'

'Or her brother, perhaps. Excellent sandwich, by the way.'

'Who? Oh, Vikram, you mean.' She pauses, sips her tea. 'You've taken a bit of a shine to him, haven't you?'

He'd normally deny this sort of thing, out of habit or to avoid the risk of seeming foolish, but Rachel's question startles him into truth. 'Yes,' he says. 'I think I have.'

'Well,' she says, taking the crumpled tissue from his hand and putting it on the empty plate. 'Good luck to you.' She stands up. She seems to be on the point of saying something. He tenses. But something changes her mind. Her smile is wry. 'He could do worse, whatever Dhara says. Not that I think he's of your persuasion.'

'You've talked about me with Dhara?'

'Of course not. It wasn't necessary. She saw you watching him go down the path. You were all gooey-eyed, she said. She didn't look that pleased.'

'I don't see why.'

'Well, she'll have her reasons,' said Rachel after a moment. 'She said what, exactly?'

'What I said. Gooey-eyed.' To his surprise, Rachel pauses at the door and turns to look at him, a smirk on her face. 'Horrible expression, isn't it? God knows where she picked it up.'

12

RACHEL

Rachel is looking at what appears to be Jeremy's Facebook page. She's never seen it before, and wouldn't be looking at it now if she hadn't found it open before her on the computer she uses for stables business. Normally she's faced by spreadsheets and pestering emails that always seem to need immediate replies in a way that real letters never did, and then there's the website she had made by a young IT person in Rochester, who expected free riding in return, which always needs updating or downloading or whatever the term is, and is more trouble than it's worth. She didn't realise what she was staring at to begin with, she's never ventured onto Facebook, or wanted to, her life's too busy for all this nonsense. But then it clicked. It doesn't have Jeremy's name, of course, but Nathalie Cray's. There's a photograph of a woman, airbrushed to such an extent that it may not even be a photograph, her hair an evanescent mass, her head titled alarmingly back as though avoiding an unexpected blow, her shoulders enveloped in something gauzy and apricot-coloured, a shade or two lighter than that of her face. She's smiling a taut, bright smile, and that's hardly surprising, thinks Rachel. How pleasant it must be to be the figment of someone else's imagination, the work of an artist, she supposes, though this is hardly her idea of art. Behind the woman's face is a sunset superimposed on something less savoury, which might be a dungeon. There's the shadow of a stone wall and what look like iron rings hanging off it.

She's not sure how much more of this she wants to see. She's always been mildly disgusted by Jeremy's work, as though it were one of those off-putting foreign cuisines based on raw fish or some robust form of insect life, deep-fried. She just can't fathom where it comes from. They grew up in the same house, after all, with the same parents. They ate the same food. Jeremy even wore her cast-off clothes for a while, until they were no longer suitable. She's heard all this talk about nature and nurture, but neither of them can explain to her just how *different* brother and sister can be, nor why this is. She'll never understand. Maybe it is their parents' fault, she thinks, or more probably the fault of one of them. And she knows which one to blame. She looks at Jeremy sometimes, when he's busy with something else, and all she can see is their mother the way she was towards the end, with slightly more weight and less hair; there isn't a shred of their father in him. Anyone would think Mummy had simply snapped off a piece of herself, like a succulent, and fed it until it grew. 'Now that's a nasty thought,' she says to the screen.

'What is?'

She almost jumps from her chair.

'What's what?' she says. She turns to see Jeremy slouching against the door frame.

'A nasty thought.' He is grinning, his top teeth biting into his bottom lip. Their mother's grin, she thinks, and suppresses a shudder. 'Now that's a nasty thought,' he repeats, in a voice that might resemble hers if it were lower-pitched and less hysterical. Is this how she sounds to him? Like a woman on the verge of madness? 'That's what you said. I wonder what it was. It can't have been anything you were looking at.'

If she didn't know him better she'd think he was teasing her. But Jeremy doesn't tease, or doesn't tease her; she has no idea what he might do with others. Or perhaps she just can't tell when he *is* teasing. Perhaps he does it all the time. Denny always said she had no sense of humour.

'I've no idea what I meant,' she says. 'You've interrupted my train of thought.'

'I didn't know you were on Facebook,' he says.

'I don't even know what Facebook is,' she says.

'You could like me, if you were.'

'That's very generous of you,' she says. 'I didn't know I needed your permission.'

'No,' he says, walking over and taking the mouse from her hand. 'Like this.' He moves the little arrow thing across the screen so quickly it takes her a moment to find it again, settled on a box that says Liked. 'I've liked myself already,' he says, and she wonders what on earth he's going on about. 'Well, Nathalie Cray, that is.'

'Who is she?' she says.

'My alter ego,' says Jeremy. 'I thought you knew all about her. There's a shelf full of her novels over there. They're amusing Dhara no end. She's working her way through them, one by one.'

'Don't be silly,' she says. 'Of course I know that. I mean, the actual woman in the picture. Who's the woman? Is she real?'

Jeremy smiles. 'She does look rather artificial, doesn't she? But no, she's real enough, in her way, although we have played around with her a bit. She's a friend of the man who publishes me. One of Mum's friends, well ex-friends, really. You've never met him. She used to be a dancer at the Moulin Rouge. She married an Oxford don and retired from the stage. You couldn't make it up.'

Rachel doesn't believe this for a moment. 'I never actually thought of you as having a publisher,' she says.

'What *did* you think? That the books emerged fully formed from my left thigh? Print on demand, Olympic style?'

He's in one of his clever-clever moods. She should be grateful, after the moodiness of yesterday and the closeness earlier today, which has left her shaken and uncertain where she stands with him, and regretful, anxious that she's opened herself up too much. But she's never known how to answer him when he's like this, whether to pretend she understands him and play along, or slap him down at the start.

'I suppose I just thought you'd paid for them to be published yourself,' she says, having decided on the latter.

'Ouch,' he says, still smiling, but she's pleased to see she's hurt him. 'Actually, the only things I've ever paid to have published are the things I'm most proud of.'

It's clear he's waiting for her to ask, but she won't give him the pleasure. 'Can you show me how to get back to my email?' she says. 'I don't know why this Facebook business popped up out of nowhere.'

'I sent Dad a copy,' he says, ignoring her, his little demonstration of power almost laughable. 'I don't suppose you know where it is?'

'Where what is? I'm trying to find my email.'

'My book of poems – well, translations of poems really. It had the picture of a soldier on the front of it, quite menacing for poetry. I thought he might have kept it with the Nathalie stuff, but it isn't there.'

'He never showed anything like that to me,' says Rachel. 'I don't know why you bothered. He's not really a poetry lover.'

'No, I know that.' He reaches across her, does something with the mouse, there's a click and the Facebook page is replaced by her email account, as if by magic. She'd ask him how he'd managed it if she wasn't so fraught with irritation. He's too close to her, his arm against her shoulder, almost embracing her, his breath near her ear, but she doesn't want to move away from him; she wants him not to be there, that's all. She wants her distance back, if she can find it.

'If he kept it, it'll probably be in here somewhere, with all these other books.'

She's set up her computer in her father's office. It's a small room, overlooking the drive; he must have chosen it so that he could keep an eye on whoever was coming and going. He hated not knowing where everyone was, still does. The desk is facing the window, with filing cabinets between the window and the door, and bookshelves covering the other walls. There aren't that many books on them: a set of great works of literature their grandfather had collected in parts from the *Daily Express* at the turn of the previous century and had bound in leather; some Reader's Digest condensed novels, unopened; paperbacks their mother must have left by women writers no one reads any longer; biographies of Victorian politicians; a flurry of business books her father had bought when business books started to appear in station bookshops; a German--English dictionary, heaven knows why; an atlas or two. Her father was never a big reader, and had no patience with fiction, let alone poetry. I've got no time for made-up stuff, he liked to say, I have more than enough on my plate dealing with the real world. The remaining shelves are stacked with trade papers of one kind or another, magazines, manila files. The last few years he worked from home, or pretended to, until the directors arranged for him to be bought out. The world of plastics will never be the same, he said, but Rachel hasn't noticed any significant changes. Plastic is plastic, indestructible. She'd see him staring out through the window as she drove up to the house, and pip her horn to greet him. The business plans she produced during those awful years when she was being groomed to take over will still be here somewhere, she imagines, filed inside boxes, as useless in their way as Jeremy's poems must have seemed to him. Perhaps they were catalogued side by side under Offspring: Disappointment.

'I can't imagine him working in here,' says Jeremy, his tone more amenable. 'He was never at home when we were children, do you remember? Mum used to send us to bed before he'd get back. We didn't see him for days on end – I didn't anyway. You may have done. He always found time for you. It's funny though, isn't it, how no one ever went on about male role models then, when most children practically never saw their fathers? It hadn't occurred to anyone that men might be needed as role models. Or women for that matter. People just grew up. And then we'd have those mad weekends, when we all had to pile into the car and get dragged round castles and eat picnics. And they'd row endlessly about where to stop. And we'd always end up fighting in the back of the car and getting slapped.'

Rachel doesn't remember it like that. What Rachel remembers are days of warmth and light, and the roughness of her father's sports jacket against her cheek as he hoists her up to be bristly-kissed and then, with a whoop, she is hurled round onto his shoulders and they are racing down the frightening, infinitely steep side of a hill and the whole world is falling away while her mother screams out their names behind them, the voice fading further and further as they fly towards the valley, her bare knees under his hands, holding her firm and safe. How sad it must be for Jeremy, she thinks with surprise, this new thought breaking through her anger, how sad it must be never to have known what she has known. Is that why he's alone, and has always seemed to be alone? He has never had anyone like Denny even, never mind their father. He has never been loved by their father, not really, not the way she has. No wonder he writes the things he does. No wonder he's so bitter about love.

'I've been thinking about that time you came to stay with me, in Paris,' he says. 'The last time you came, do you remember? After Denny walked out on you.'

'And you were sick in a bin.'

'Oh yes. I'd completely forgotten about that.' He smiles. 'No, I was thinking how unsympathetic I'd been. I should have been more thoughtful.' He shakes his head. 'I'm sorry.'

'My God, Jeremy, that must have been fifteen years ago.'

'You can still remember my throwing up in a bin. It wasn't so long ago.'

'I remember we had a perfectly disgusting Chinese meal.'

'Although that wasn't what made me sick.'

'It was that awful bar you took me to. To see what I'd do.'

'Yes,' he says, laughing. 'I blame the nuts. Which isn't something you often hear in bars like that, I don't suppose. Or perhaps it is.'

She can't help laughing herself, although she isn't quite sure she's got the joke, other than that it's probably vulgar. Sometimes Jeremy reminds her of Denny, in that at least.

'And the hotel wasn't much better. I'd so hoped I'd be staying with you,' she says, surprised to feel that hurt once again. 'How could you have stuck me in that awful place?'

'I'm sorry about that as well,' he says. 'I had no idea you'd mind. To be honest, I thought you'd prefer it to staying with me. I always had the feeling you thought I lived in a state of total disorder. As I do, I suppose. And my place is so small. There's barely enough room for me.'

She's about to ask him why on earth he imagined she would prefer a shabby room in a cheap hotel, shared bathroom on the landing, to her own brother's home, however small, when Dhara calls out her name from upstairs. Her voice is urgent.

'Coming,' she calls back, hurrying from the room, with Jeremy trailing behind her.

Her father is lying on the floor, with Dhara bent above him. 'He just rolled out,' she says, breathless, 'when I wasn't looking.' She grabs him, just above the shoulders, her fingers at each side of his neck, her thumbs in the deep hollow beneath his chin, and lifts him an inch or two from the floor. 'You silly old man,' she says and, before anyone can stop her, she has begun to shake him as hard as she can. His face is horrified. 'Help me,' he says across her shoulder, in a voice made jerky by Dhara's furious jiggling. 'She's trying to kill me.'

'For God's sake, pull her off,' says Rachel, but already, before Jeremy has a chance to move, she's on her knees beside the woman and her father and holding them both, folding them in towards her, as if to feed them at her breasts, thinks Jeremy, left outside this odd three-figured *pietà*, wondering what to do. And then, just as abruptly, Rachel has pulled Dhara off herself and is telling him to get Dad back into bed, but gently, *gently*, he might have broken something. Dad's mouth resembles more and more the toothless screaming mouth of Munch. As the women stumble away from him, locked together, with

Dhara still struggling to be free, his hands flutter up to his face; the resemblance is stronger than ever. Jeremy crouches down beside him.

'Are you all right?' he says.

'Of course I'm not all right,' says his father. 'These madwomen have almost squashed me to death. I've had enough of all this palaver. Hasn't my time come yet? Can't you get me out of this?' There are tears in his eyes. 'For pity's sake.'

'I wish I could,' says Jeremy, primarily to himself. Cautious, he slides his hands beneath his father's body. To his surprise, his father's arms shoot up like the mechanical arms of a toy and lock themselves around his neck, in a tightening vice. As he straightens his back to lift them both, the old man rises with him, almost weightless, his face as close to Jeremy's as it's ever been, so close he could practically kiss him, his warm breath smelling sweeter than he'd ever have imagined. He hugs the old man, his father, to him, their cheeks briefly touching, and places him gently onto the bed.

'There you are, then,' he says when his father is lying back and staring at the ceiling as though he has seen something move there and is trying to work out what it might be. 'There we are.'

'I told him not to try to get up without help,' cries Dhara behind him. 'He's a naughty, wicked old man.'

'Show some respect for him, can't you!' Jeremy starts to his feet and turns to face the two women, who huddle together, his one hand raised as if to strike. He can't believe he's doing this. He's feels as though he's hovering above the scene, entirely detached from his rage, enjoying it even, as though he's been spurring this hopeless, ineffectual person on to act for ever and is finally rewarded. 'Dear God! He doesn't deserve to be shouted at like that. Why don't you just fuck off?' He must be crying, because otherwise he would be able to see them clearly; as it is, they're smeared and crude, like figures in a crayon drawing of a child. Rachel steps back, shocked. His voice breaks. 'Just fuck off, will you? Both of you. Leave me alone with him for a while.'

13

JEREMY

Gilberto died just over a year before Jeremy's mother, in a hospital bed a thousand miles from hers. He and Jeremy hadn't been living together for three years by that time. Gilberto had moved in with another waiter, from El Salvador, who had come to Europe to change sex. This was just as well, said Gilberto later, when he was dying, what I need right now is a woman's touch and Miriam has given me that. Jeremy looked over at Miriam's bony, capable hands as they detached the full bag of urine from the catheter, truck driver's hands for all the scarlet nail varnish, and felt both wounded and relieved. Gilberto had called him after a four-month silence to say that he had Aids and did Jeremy know what that was, and Jeremy had said that he did – although he wasn't sure – and had heard nothing more of what Gilberto was saying at the other end of the line, wherever that might have been. Long after Gilberto's sobs and accusations and apologies had died away, he sat with the phone in his hand. He was living in what had once been a maid's room, at the top of a building, with the bathroom on the landing. It was his seventh or eighth or, maybe, ninth flat in Paris, depending on how he defined the word flat, and he shared it with no one, which was just as well, it occurred to him, when he finally replaced the receiver and stood up, almost falling over because his left leg, which had been curled beneath him, had gone dead. He stamped his foot, shocked by the brutal return of sense. He began to shake. The room was cold, and barely furnished. There was a shelf with plates and glasses over the sink. I have no one, he said. I'm twenty-eight years old and I have no one in the whole world. I have no one to call and commiserate with and condemn, as Gilberto has called and condemned me. Someone on the landing outside began to call down the stairwell a name he didn't know. The building is full of people and I have no one and Gilberto is about to die.

Jeremy wasn't condemned, or not in the way he'd supposed. He was condemned to relief, when his own tests showed him negative, and anxiety, because it might be too soon to tell and the tests would need to be repeated, and guilt, because he had heard some people were carriers and perhaps that was what he was, and anger, because maybe, just maybe, Gilberto had known and said nothing, and resentment, that this should be happening at all, to anyone. He was condemned to all this, but none of it mattered, or mattered quite so much, when he finally went to Gilberto's new flat and found him reduced to skin and bone, with an odd, tear-anointed stoicism he'd never have imagined or expected, so that, for the first time, he almost fell in love with him, this new bedridden man, as fine and brave as the earlier Gilberto had been plump and evasive. He was glad now that he hadn't been the one to end it, that Gilberto had left him – anything else would have been too hard. He sat beside the bed with the familiar smell of Gilberto in his nostrils, aftershave and something sweet he had never been able to place, some cream he used on his skin, overlaid by other smells, lotions and shit and dope, because Gilberto refused to give up dope, and sweat, however often he was bathed. Miriam was a treasure and a saint. What would my father make of me now, wondered Jeremy, sitting in this overdecorated, overheated room, with a skeletal ex-lover in the bed and a transsexual fussing over them both, singing a fado as she folded towels, and nappies.

Miriam had read his books, and loved them. The men in them are so cruel, she trilled. She insisted he sign her copies, dictating a dedication that made him blush to write for its effusiveness and vacuity. He'd published six by that time, with Grenier continuing to pay him by the word, plus a lump sum for translations in Portuguese, Spanish and French; a German edition of *Knife in the Heart* was about to come out that autumn. It felt as though the world were clamouring at his gate. Well, not at *his* gate; hardly anyone knew who he was. He'd used a series of pen names, suggested by Grenier, each more absurd than the last; he'd had to copy them from the cover, letter by letter, when he signed Miriam's well-thumbed copies.

Grenier sold them mail order, or through newsagents and specialised outlets. Jeremy knew the sort of place he meant: second-hand bookshops down side streets near provincial stations, the kind of shops he'd sought out as a teenager to buy nudist magazines like *Health and Efficiency*, cutting the best men out and gathering them together, like bucking, unbroken colts in a corral, to paste into a scrapbook secreted beneath his bed. The books had had what was known as word-of-mouth success, to his shamed delight. In order to make it into actual bookshops, albeit on a dedicated shelf beyond the reach of children, Grenier suggested Jeremy tone down the more extreme sexual practices, and Jeremy had done his best, removing a ladies' horsewhip here, a roughly studded lingam there, but his inspiration failed him when things became too domesticated. His sexual imaginings refused to be tamed. With the books and occasional translations, he made barely enough to live on, but his mother still sent him occasional cheques. He still thought of his mother, of what she must have made of the book he had given her to read, of how foolish he'd been to imagine she might be proud of him for having become a pornographer in the city of her heart.

Gilberto's death changed that, although not immediately. Jeremy was halfway through another book, with Grenier calling him on a daily basis for an updated word count, when he seemed to wake up to what he had done. He read through the sheets of manuscript he'd stored in a box beside the kitchen table, and despaired of finishing. Set in a loggers' community in Canada in the nineteenth century, the novel told the tale of a group of lumberjacks who had captured a Native American girl and were using her for their pleasure, until she was rescued by the braves of her tribe and returned to her home, along with the ringleader. The second half of the novel would have dealt with her revenge and final capitulation, as the man she loved was shattered and yet refused to be shattered – was reduced to a chattel by love. He'd written the same book half a dozen times already, changing the setting and the names, the instruments of torture to fit the epoch, the narrative following its familiar arc from brutality through escape and vengeance to eventual submission. This final part was the part that Miriam loved, the harsh man broken, and begging to be saved. Vengeance is mine, as Jeremy had said to Grenier, and Grenier had smiled, and nodded. Vengeance is always mine.

But the second half wouldn't come. It was true that men were cruel, and deserved what they got, but wasn't he a man as well? And Gilberto? Wasn't Gilberto a man? And not only Gilberto. Other friends were dead, or dying, and friends of friends. Didn't they all deserve a little hope? A little love that wasn't just revenge? He threw the manuscript away, fishing it out of the bin the following morning, rewriting it with Grenier breathing, literally at times, down his neck. The mood became more romantic. The native girl had an ally from the outset. Nathalie Cray was born.

When the book, entitled *Cabins of Passion, Tepees of Desire*, came out, he sent a copy to the last address he had for his mother, somewhere in mainland Greece. She'd mailed him a cheque with a postcard of a loosely woven sack containing live frogs, waiting to be skinned and eaten according to the legend on the back, and a second one, without a cheque, some months later, of a monastery perched on a column of friable red rock. He tried to read sense into this sequence of images, but was thwarted. The messages were upbeat. She said she was reliving her youth, or living it for the first time, and hoped that he was happy. When he told Grenier what he'd done, Grenier laughed.

'You already have your mother's approval,' he said. They were sitting on a patio at the back of Grenier's house outside Paris, drinking chilled white wine. Grenier's wife, Hilary, had been with them until a few moments earlier, but was now in the kitchen. Jeremy could hear her voice in the distance, talking to whoever was preparing lunch. He hadn't mentioned his mother in Hilary's presence. She'd asked him once about her old friend, her tone forlorn, regretful, and it was evident from the way she turned her head towards the window while he spoke that her duty had been done, and that she had no further interest in his mother. She treated him in a similar fashion, as though not quite sure what he was doing there in front of her, an unsuitable applicant for her attention. He wondered what she had planned for their lunch, something that showed him how unnecessary he was to her well-being without being overtly ostentatious. She was a tall woman, with hair arranged into a taut chignon, more French than the French. When the three of them were together, she insisted on using her second language, addressing Jeremy with '*vous*', looking askance at her husband when he failed to do so. As soon as she had disappeared inside the house, her low heels clicking on the parquet, the two men relaxed into English.

'I'm not sure that I do,' Jeremy said.

'Oh, your mother has always loved you, you know that,' said Grenier, dismissively. He leaned forward, his forearms between his knees, an oddly boyish posture. He was wearing cotton twill trousers and a loose white shirt; his hair was longer than usual. He had a look on his face that reminded Jeremy of someone else, he couldn't think who. Jeremy was overdressed, in a jacket he couldn't take off because his shirt was torn on the sleeve. He hadn't expected this sort of heat in May. It would be cooler in the house, but Grenier had insisted they sit where they could see the roses. He'd had them brought over from England – it was part of his Anglophilia, he said. There was a place in the Midlands that created hybrids. Some of them were scented; Jeremy could smell them from here, sweating in his frail white ironwork chair, already on his third glass of Pinot Noir.

'Where did you say she was?'

'Somewhere in Greece. They eat frogs there, apparently. I thought only we did that. The French, I mean.'

'Alone?'

'I shouldn't think so. She didn't say.'

'How does she manage, do you know?'

'For money, you mean? I suppose she has a pension. She's old enough now. And Dad gives her something, I'm sure.'

'I'm glad to hear that.'

'I can give you her address, if you like?'

Grenier shook his head. 'No, no. I don't think that would be a good idea at all. But I'm happy your father continues to provide for her.'

'Yes,' said Jeremy. 'So am I.'

'And your sister?' said Grenier after a moment.

'My sister?'

'Yes, what is her name again?' Grenier waved his hands in the air as if the name could be retrieved.

Again? thought Jeremy. 'Rachel. What about her?'

'Is she well? Happy?'

'As far as I know, yes,' said Jeremy. 'I don't really have much contact with her, to be honest.'

'She lives near your father?'

'Yes,' said Jeremy. 'They're very close.'

'And you're not?'

'Not at all,' said Jeremy, puzzled by this conversation. Grenier had never before shown such interest in his life outside Paris. 'We couldn't be more different.'

Grenier nodded slowly. 'You say she's married?'

'I didn't,' said Jeremy, 'but, yes, she is. To this dreadful man. Dennis. He's mad about horses. They both are.'

Grenier nodded again.

'Do you see him ever?'

'Dennis? Not if I can avoid it.'

'No, not Dennis. Your father.'

'Not really.'

'I don't suppose he's ever mentioned me,' said Grenier.

'Well, no,' said Jeremy, increasingly bewildered. 'He doesn't know you, does he?'

'No, of course not.'

'So?'

Grenier brushed this question to one side. 'Still, it isn't good, you know. A man needs a father.'

'What an odd thing to say.' Jeremy emptied, and refilled, his glass, as though the entire conversation hadn't been odd. More than odd. Inexplicable. 'I'd have thought it depended on the father.'

'When did you last see your father?'

At this point, Jeremy, with a sense of respite, began to laugh. Grenier, slighted, raised an eyebrow. 'I'm sorry,' said Jeremy, 'but there's a famous painting called that. You probably don't know it. A bunch of Roundheads are asking a boy where his Cavalier father is, or it might be the other way round. And the little boy won't talk, although how we're supposed to understand that from a painting, I don't know. It's all about filial loyalty, very touching stuff.'

'And what would you have done?'

'I'd have shopped him immediately.' He looked at Grenier. 'You're very interested in my father suddenly.'

'I'm curious,' he said. 'Curious about you.'

Jeremy felt uncomfortable. 'I don't see why. I'm an open book.'

It was Grenier's turn to laugh. 'You are a very closed book indeed, *mon petit*.' He stood up. 'I think we should see what Hilary has prepared for lunch,' he said. Jeremy followed the other man into the dark, cool interior.

'I wanted you to come today,' said Grenier, when his wife had left them alone after their meal, 'so that we can talk about the future.'

Jeremy was drunk. He nodded slowly.

'I think we can begin to market you more widely,' he said. 'I wasn't sure until I'd read the new book a second time and gathered some other reactions to it, from people in the business. All of them extremely good, I'm delighted to say. You've managed to channel your often rather perverse inspiration into a much more, what shall I say, *domestic* genre. If I were your father I'd be very proud of you.'

'You're obsessed with my father today,' said Jeremy, who had heard only the last part of what Grenier had been saying. He stood up, more sharply than he intended, knocking his chair over behind him.

Grenier held up his hands, in mock surrender. 'Calm down, my dear boy. You have almost broken my nose once,' he said. 'I see I must be careful when I discuss literature with you.'

'I'm sorry,' said Jeremy, reaching down to pick up the chair. 'I'm feeling a bit pissed, actually.'

'Good wine. The best. You'll be fine after a brief siesta. Let me show you to your room.'

'My room?'

'You'll be sleeping here tonight. You don't think I would allow you to return to Paris before we have finished our conversation? Another cognac before you take a little rest?'

Jeremy slept uninterruptedly for eleven hours, waking at three o'clock in the morning with a fierce thirst and no idea where he was. He was lying in a larger, more comfortable bed than he was used to, in total darkness, naked. He had been dreaming about a trial at which men asked him for information about a painting. He had sworn he could tell them nothing, but that was a lie. He knew it; they all knew it. He was being dragged from the room into a garden filled with roses, their thorns buried deep in his flesh, when he heard whatever the noise was that had woken him. He reached out to his right for a lamp, and found a flex hanging down beside the bed. His fingers walked its length until they stumbled on a switch, which he pressed. Instantly, the room was filled with golden light. He blinked and lifted his head from the pillow with a low, unearthly groan to see Grenier, cross-legged in pyjamas of crimson silk, perched like a guardian troll on a stool beside his bed.

14

JEREMY

Jeremy is standing beside the window of what used to be his father's office. He has moved his work in here after two weeks of trying to write, laptop on knees, in whichever corner of the house he can find a moment's peace from Rachel, from Dhara, from the various needs of the place, his father's included, although his father's needs are those that irritate him least. He still doesn't know why this is; it's as though his father has been replaced by some milder, more docile being, as though he'd been exorcised of a demon Jeremy had always assumed was not the diabolic occupant of his father, but his father himself. Even this room, which ought to repel him as the final dwelling place of the public face of his father, captain of industry, mogul in the world of plastics, seems to offer an unexpected, melancholic haven for what he knows he should be doing, his father's work ethic like a whispering presence beside his ear. Two mornings ago, after drinking his usual double espresso in the café he'd decided was *his* in town, he'd bought a memory stick, come home and transferred the interrupted adventures of Lady Mirabelle onto it from his laptop. He walked into the office, holding out the small black stick before him, like a divining rod, and found Rachel staring at a spreadsheet with a look of confused irritation. When he reached round her and slid it into an empty USB, she jerked hastily to one side, her attention shifting from screen to stick as though it were an exotic sexual object, a mini-lingam, a pocket-sized pleasurer. Silent, she stood up and left the room.

He has been working on his novel since then, or trying to. Rachel can't stop him, although she's made it clear she'd like to. She wanders in every hour or so, nonchalantly reads what he's written over his shoulder while he grits his teeth and resists the urge to flick back to XTube, or whatever he's been looking at, the sound turned off – her metal-tipped heels on the tiles of the hall alert him to her arrival. She's behind him, but he can *feel* her shrug, her moue of disgust, as she turns and sweeps out of the room. Moments later, she's calling for him, apologising that he's had to be distracted from his – pause for effect – creative work. Or maybe it isn't for effect. Maybe she's actually trying to be nice, despite decades of ill-feeling. Maybe she's noticed he's still on the same paragraph each time she looks at the screen, and has started to feel sorry for him. These days, as days turn into weeks, anything seems possible.

This is the kind of room I have always wanted to write in, he thinks when he's back at the desk, and yet now that he has it almost entirely to himself he continues to suffer from writer's block. It's the first time in his life this has happened. Whatever shortcomings he may have as a writer, he's never run dry before now. After decades of soft-focused industry, Nathalie Cray has failed him. He knows he should write through it, but there she is, stubbornly refusing to cooperate as the chastised gardener languishes in Lady Mirabelle's dangerously well-equipped cellar, and the Indian maid is waiting for her turn at the whipping post. Maybe that's the problem. He no longer has the urge to punish Dhara that impelled him to introduce her into the plot two weeks ago. Nathalie, in the meantime, has taken her yapping lapdog and her Ethiopian chauffeur, and is dividing her time between Paris and Los Angeles.

He's almost relieved when he opens his email account and finds the latest in a series of messages from Armand Grenier. Each one is terser and more insistent than the one preceding it, a bolero of entreaties and cajoling. There is an interest, stateside, apparently, and it's hard to imagine Armand adopting such a term if it weren't a cut-and-paste job, which gives the claim some authenticity. There is the usual stuff about new markets being opened, and audio books and e-books, and being prepared for the next wave from wherever it might come. Jeremy has been holding him off with optimistic promises and bulletins of his father's health, and, at the end of each reply, Armand has added a comment about this, with best wishes for his father, and Jeremy and Rachel, as though they were all one happy family and he were part of it. But despite this you must come back, Armand insists, if only for a day, we have so much to discuss, and it must be in person, although he won't say why. He loves being mysterious; Jeremy's known this for years, it's part of his being French. In this most recent email Armand promises to pay for his Eurostar ticket, a day return, and lunch anywhere he chooses if only he will pop back to Paris and *talk*. Jeremy's tempted to call and explain why this isn't possible, not now. The truth is that his father could die at any moment. But the real truth, because there is always more than one truth, and one that is more real than the others, is that he doesn't want to move from where he is. Paris can wait. Grenier can wait. Nathalie Cray can wait. Jean-Paul, may God forgive him, can wait. He is stuck in a slow-brewing viscous stew of his own making, a stew of sentiments – about his father, about himself – that he has never imagined he would feel, and that do him, he thinks, a credit he's not sure he deserves.

He closes his email, stands up and walks across to the window once again. In the garden, to the left of the drive where Rachel's car is parked, is Vikram. It's his day off from morning surgery and he's been working in the garden since soon after breakfast. Dhara made them both toast and coffee, but Vikram took his outside almost immediately, leaving Jeremy in the kitchen. Now Jeremy, half concealed behind a curtain, one hand at his throat, watches the man tie loose shoots of wisteria onto a trellis against the high red-brick wall at the far edge of the lawn, which he has already mown bowling-green short. The wisteria is in flower and Vikram is struggling beneath a tumbling curtain of purple blooms, rough twine in hand, secateurs gripped between his teeth. He appears and disappears, like some minor god in a mannerist fresco, from beneath the waves of colour. Jeremy is pretty sure he won't be seen as he pulls out his mobile phone from a trouser pocket and takes a swift photograph of Vikram, arms raised and united in Saint Sebastian fashion, white teeth bared round the gleaming secateurs in his mouth, haloed by imperial purple blossom.

'So here you are,' says Rachel. 'I was wondering.'

He barely has time to slip his mobile back into his pocket before she is standing next to him, in full view of the garden.

'Vikram could do with a hand,' she says. 'Unless you're busy writing?'

Her tone is increasingly unreadable. This remark, which a fortnight ago would have seemed at the very least sarcastic, is now infused with a gentle, even anxious quality, as though she really cares about his work, his writing. Yet what can she

134

know? He hasn't told her about his block; perhaps she has gathered it from his manner, the difficulty he has in concentrating, responding to simple questions, going about the daily business of shared living in the house that is slowly, it dawns on him, beginning to feel like his. She must have noticed by now that the words on the screen don't change.

The only other person he feels entirely aware of, absurdly, is his father. He has the impression that everything done in the house and garden is somehow instigated, or directed, by the bed-ridden semi-conscious man, who should have died ten days ago, if not before, whose continuing existence is a mystery to them all. He lies there, is rolled from side to side, his bags replaced and filled and emptied, his medicines administered. Vikram checks his heart and shakes his head, the district nurses wash and powder him and change his dressings, and sit in the armchair making copious notes in babyish script, so littered with abbreviations and jargon they make no sense to Jeremy at all when, after they have gone, he sneaks a look at the bulging file. One of the nurses, a woman barely out of her teens, said how wonderful he and Rachel were to look after their father, not all children would do the same for their parents, and Jeremy blushed and felt ashamed of himself, because he never really wanted to come. But he was also angry to have been so misrepresented. He felt false, he supposes now, but there's also a lingering sense – of what? Of Duty? Of simply *wishing* to be here? – that makes what the nurse said true; which is even harder to accept.

It will soon be a full moon, another, older nurse had said, closing the file and standing up, casting a significant glance at the bed and then the sky, still filled with light. Rachel told him later she'd heard that more people died at the full moon than at any other time of the month, and he had a sense of the naturalness of death's harvest, and was reconciled to the idea, and then felt both frustrated and relieved as the full moon waxed and waned, and his father continued – in his needfulness and his innocence – to run the house. Some days, he took his laptop up to his father's room and sat in the armchair with it balanced on his legs, untouched, the screen-saver telling him to *get back to work* in lilac italic script, watching his father's chest rise and fall beneath the sheet, a movement so slow, so subtle, he found himself holding his own breath with the tension of it. At these times, with the two of them, father and son, no more than six feet apart, surrounded by the bedroom's silence, the silence of the sea-reflecting sky and the distant slowly turning vanes of the wind farm – all that energy being made from nothing to be wasted on nothing – he tried to locate the anger he had felt for more than thirty years, the anger he had felt against his father. But it wasn't there any longer. He has been won over, and now he is bereft. Perhaps his block is simply this. He's no longer angry enough to write.

On one of these occasions, when Rachel had driven over to the stables and Dhara was cooking downstairs, he opened a new file on his laptop and began to write something else, not a memoir exactly, an apology perhaps, or a justification, as though he's been asked to plead his case. He tried to recover the first memory of his father, some primal recall that wasn't the facsimile of a snap from the tin box in the sideboard of the dining room, a box he'd been shown by Rachel some days before in a shy, yet challenging way, as though she expected him to refuse to look inside it; some genuine memory. He almost had pushed it away unopened, but photographs of the past, of one's own past, are like cherries, impossible to resist, and he'd dipped in. The first one he'd found that touched him was one of his father and this small, neatly formed child that was Jeremy then, his blond hair parted and brushed, his white knees emerging from wellington boots, the two of them drinking tea from large pottery mugs in a garden he remembers only through photographs of this kind. This isn't his first memory, surely; it isn't a memory in any case, but a sort of Rorschach test, a rectangle of deckle-edged cardboard telling him something he may not want to know about himself, but without intrinsic significance. Two people, fifty years ago, united by mugs of tea his mother must have made for them, and brought out to the garden where his father was working, itself a rare event, perhaps on a tray. And so he began to write about a tray he remembered, a black lacquered tray, inlaid with ivory. *My mother had a tray she would use for special occasions, but not only that. Or perhaps her idea of special included me.* He sat and wrote until Rachel arrived and asked him what he was doing. 'Nothing,' he said. 'Just editing. The boring stuff.'

She nodded, glancing across at the bed. 'Is everything all right?'

He nodded back. 'He's fast asleep.'

'That's good,' she said, and left.

And now, with Rachel standing beside him in the office and glancing across at the computer to see what he's written, he wonders if she remembers the tray, if perhaps it still exists in a cupboard, neglected, covered in dust. When he and his father were drinking their mugs of tea, she must have been somewhere in the house, he thinks. He doesn't remember her having friends. How odd to think of those years he had his mother to himself, though, with his father at work and Rachel at school, and Little Jem too young to know how perfect his life must have been. How often has that been true, he wonders now. How often has he let perfection slip past him, and seen only horror and tedium and opportunities for fear? Out of the blue, he sees the giraffe-man glancing up and down the street from the sheltering safety of the doorway before venturing onto the pavement, and is filled with an indiscriminate, all-encompassing sadness for which he has no name.

'Yes, you're right,' he says. 'I'll go and see what I can do in the garden.'

Vikram is halfway up a ladder, gathering the overhanging wisteria shoots and pinning them to a web of netting and wire. Jeremy, who knows nothing about gardening, can't help thinking this arrangement improbably flimsy. He takes hold of the ladder as if to steady it, his eyes at the level of Vikram's knees, and stares at the solid, linen-clad rump of the man, whose trousers have ridden up into the crack to form a tangled rose of material. Above the rump are the back and the muscles of the shoulders, moving beneath the taut white cotton of a T-shirt, on the front of which, as Jeremy already knows, there is an image of a cartoon hedgehog holding a rugby ball as he runs. There is a smudge of blood on the man's left forearm, just beneath the elbow, and a long, fine scratch, from a thorn perhaps, bright red on the burnished amber of the skin. There is an odour of onion, sweat and soap; Jeremy breathes it in with surreptitious rapture. When Vikram turns his head to look down, he steps back, self-conscious, and almost trips over the abandoned secateurs.

'Watch out,' says Vikram, his face in shadow. 'You're just in time.'

'I've come to help,' says Jeremy, unnecessarily.

'Well, you can pass me that drill over there,' says Vikram. 'I need to fix this wire or everything will collapse. That would be a fine state of affairs.'

Jeremy passes him the drill and watches from a few feet

away as Vikram concentrates on the task, his bottom lip caught beneath his teeth. He's slightly goofy, something Jeremy hasn't noticed before and is immediately thrilled by. He loves the old-fashioned quality of Vikram's English, as though he's learned it from the early days of television. When Vikram hands him down the drill he stares at it stupidly for a moment before reaching up to take it.

'You need to spend more time in the sun,' says Vikram. 'You're far too pale, you know. Vitamin D deficiency is very dangerous.' He comes down the ladder, sliding the last two rungs, and they are standing together, close enough to touch. He is taller than Jeremy but not by much, an inch or two. His hair is gleaming with natural oil or new sweat; it flops in a wave across his forehead, the brightest black, a raven's wing. Jeremy wants to ask him how old he is, but equally doesn't want to know the answer. Too young, a warning voice whispers. Old enough to be your father's doctor, a second, more insinuating voice replies. When Vikram lifts a hand to Jeremy's face it is all he can do not to start back. His heart is pounding.

'You have a wisteria petal,' says Vikram, plucking at Jeremy's hair, his fingers light. 'There, that's better.' He shows Jeremy a scrap of violet blossom in the palm of his hand. 'This is God's work,' he says.

'But you're here, aren't you? I mean, to give him a helping hand when required.' To Jeremy's relief, Vikram smiles.

'We must all toil together,' he says.

For a second, Jeremy expects him to continue *in the garden of the Lord*, which is not at all what he wants to hear. 'It's very good of you to come and help us in your free time,' he says quickly. 'I don't know what Dad would do without you.'

Vikram, bending down for the secateurs, ignores this. 'We both need to be more careful,' he says.

Jeremy, for whom nothing is simple, sees this as a warning. 'Careful?'

'You might have cut yourself on the secateurs, which I inadvertently left open when I put them down. There is a small catch here, you see,' he says, and Jeremy watches his fingers open and close a tongue of grass-stained steel. 'It holds them shut. You placed your foot on them earlier, when you were fetching the drill for me. You're lucky nothing happened. You might have cut yourself and I would have been to blame.'

'Oh, you mustn't blame yourself,' says Jeremy, shaking his head at the idea. 'I can be very clumsy sometimes.'

'Is that true?'

'Oh yes,' says Jeremy. 'Very.' He pauses. 'I need looking after.'

Vikram gathers his tools together, bending over once again. Jeremy's eyes flicker down to the sliver of bare skin between the T-shirt and the belt.

'And now I think we should make ourselves some tea and sit here in the sun,' says Vikram, straightening up in a determined manner. 'We have earned a break. And you need your vitamins.'

'I've done nothing at all,' protests Jeremy, delighted by this idea, relieved that his brief attempt to flirt appears to have passed unnoticed.

'You have been in Reginald's study for some hours. I could see you quite clearly by the window as I worked.' He smiles. 'I've had my eye on you, you see.'

'Oh,' says Jeremy.

'Did you know he calls Dad Reginald?'

'Who does?'

'Vikram.'

Rachel pours herself another glass of wine.

'Do you call him Reginald?' says Jeremy.

'Well, of course I don't. I'm his daughter.' Rachel sips her wine the way people sometimes count to ten, to avoid being hasty. 'I don't know why you're so upset,' she says eventually.

'I'm not upset.'

'You certainly seem upset.'

'I just don't understand.' Jeremy is drunk.

'What is there to understand?'

'Nothing in this house makes sense.'

'Now you're being silly.'

'You can't say I'm being silly. I'm not a child.'

'You *are* a child. When you behave like this.'

Childishly, Jeremy pokes at his salad. He's had more than enough to eat by this stage in the evening, intricate pockets of chicken breast with some ersatz, herby substance in the middle, five minutes in the microwave *et voilà*, with tubs of three-bean salad, all of it bought in from M&S or Waitrose by Rachel on her way back from the stables. He had no idea how reliant Rachel was on ready meals, not that there's anything wrong with them, but he'd always thought of himself as lazy in this regard and imagined his sister to be more competent. He's partly disappointed and partly vindicated. What he wants the food to do is counteract the wine, but he knows this won't happen as he forks the final beans into his mouth, and feels slightly sick.

'I'm not behaving like anything,' he says. 'I just am.'

At this, Rachel snorts with laughter and he realises that she has also had too much to drink. They have finished a second bottle and started a third, and now, as Jeremy stretches out a hand towards it, he sees that much of that has also been drunk. Indeed, by filling his glass, as he now does, he manages to finish the bottle. Chardonnay. Three empty bottles, and the flurry of noise upstairs has nothing to do with either of them, which means they have served their purpose, he thinks, as Rachel stands up all at once and flaps around, and he wonders what on earth can be happening. She leaves the room and he hears her talking to Dhara on the stairs, but their voices are both too low for him to follow the conversation.

Rachel comes back into the kitchen. 'He's taken a turn for the worse,' she says. 'We'd better call Vikram.'

15

JEREMY

Grenier told him to sit down. They were in the Parc Monceau flat. Jeremy's initial suspicion that this was a fuck pad, or whatever the elegant equivalent of that term might be, the befittingly *chic* term for it, had been confirmed by the departing presence of a woman, who offered him her hand as she left, then led Grenier into the hall with a murmured endearment, her arm in his. Jeremy heard a slap, an affronted squeak, a stifled moan. The front door opened, then closed. Back in the room, Grenier made no reference to the woman, which established his relationship with her, in Jeremy's eyes at least. She wasn't much older than Jeremy was, in her mid-thirties perhaps, and had been wearing a glove-leather jacket that looked as though it had cost more than Jeremy's entire wardrobe, which wouldn't have been that hard. He still stored most of his clothes in a broken suitcase pushed beneath his bed, along with stuff Gilberto had left and never had time to collect.

He watched her cross the park beneath him while Grenier shuffled papers on a desk. She looked round once, up at the window where Jeremy was standing, and raised the small bag she was holding in a half-wave before walking off. He was startled to feel a twinge of jealousy, as though he'd thought Grenier belonged to him and had only now discovered the truth. The half-wave she had given him, that little gesture of acknowledgement, complicity even, seemed to suggest they were both in the same business. We're both his chattels, he thought gloomily, paid to provide our humble, but necessary, services. Which was true enough. He was feeling out of sorts that morning. Two bills – water and gas – had arrived; he still didn't have enough money to install a phone in the flat. He was tired of being poor, of relying on handouts, of waking at four in the dark pit of the morning with a sense of anguish he couldn't pin down, and then pinning it down and lying there, awake and fretting, until early dawn.

'Sit down,' Grenier said again.

'I'm sorry if I've interrupted something,' said Jeremy. He sat down on the chaise longue between the two windows.

Grenier thought for a moment, then shook his head. 'Not at all.'

This was the first time Jeremy had seen Grenier after his visit to the house outside Paris. He'd woken that morning with a headache and the sense that what he had seen had been a dream, contradicted by an equally vivid sensation that it had not and that Grenier really had been watching him sleep. Certainly, he or someone had stripped Jeremy of his clothes and placed them on a chair, where Jeremy found them the following morning, his trousers folded neatly along the crease, his shirt on the chair back beneath his jacket, his underpants laid out flat on the folded trousers like a courtroom exhibit, his socks rolled loosely into balls and inserted one in each shoe. Jeremy had no memory of this uncomfortable familiarity. In what might or might not have been a dream, Grenier had smiled at the waking Jeremy and then, with an odd flowing movement, like water in a film reversed, he had risen to his feet and left the room, and Jeremy had continued to lie there, temples throbbing, before eventually falling asleep again, or dreaming he had. When he came downstairs after dressing, he found Grenier's wife in the hall, car keys in her hand. She drove him to the station in silence, only turning her head to look at him when he was about to leave the car. 'Do give your mother my love, when you see her,' she said, to Jeremy's astonishment. 'Of course I will,' he said.

He'd spoken to Grenier several times since then, on the telephone, but neither of them had mentioned the visit. Now, with the older man in front of him, it was hard to see him in pyjamas, hard to imagine him awake and silent in the unfamiliar room, legs crossed beneath him, his gaze fixed on the bed in which Jeremy was sleeping. Hard not to feel observed as Grenier turned his head towards Jeremy now, in the heart of Paris, in this overdecorated rococo fuck pad, and looked him up and down. He's seen me naked, thought Jeremy, he's touched my skin, held my still warm, worn underpants in his hands. At this image, of the older man easing his pants from beneath his arse and gently down the deadweight of his legs, an unsolicited erection overtook him. He squirmed on the purple velvet in an effort to subdue it, but Grenier seemed either not to have noticed or to be utterly indifferent.

'Sales are excellent,' he said, with satisfaction. 'Really excellent.' He walked across to the flimsy console table at the other side of the room to pick up a magazine. 'And look at this.' After flicking through the pages, he folded it open at a photograph of a woman Jeremy had never seen before. 'Meet Nathalie Cray.'

Jeremy stared at the face in the photograph. His erection softened.

'She doesn't look much like me,' he said.

Grenier laughed.

'I think that may be to our advantage,' he said. 'If you read the article you'll see that no mere man could compete with Nathalie.'

Grenier was right. The magazine was an in-flight magazine produced by a charter company Jeremy had never heard of. The article contained a potted biography, a sort of review and a short extract from *Cabins of Passion, Tepees of Desire*. It was disconcerting to see the words he'd produced with nothing in mind but the amount of money they would earn him, driven on by coffee and handfuls of cashew nuts, now surrounded by ads for offshore investment and timeshares in Madeira. He looked at the photograph more carefully. Nathalie Cray was a thirty-something-year-old woman with elaborately arranged blonde hair and too much costume jewellery, a pouting lower lip, heavy mascara and a single manicured hand at her neck, covering, as Jeremy told someone later with great hilarity and little regard for the truth, a multitude of chins. According to the article, she was born into an army family in the south-east of England, but had studied in Italy and France and now lived in Greece, on an unnamed island, with a fisherman artist. She had left a rich husband and various lovers in search of herself, the article said – her elusive essence, the quest for romantic fulfilment that had inspired her novel. It struck Jeremy that some of these details seemed to refer to his mother, distorted but still recognisable in a glass darkly sort of way, and he wondered if this was intended. If so, Grenier had been unwarrantedly cruel, because surely this was Grenier's work. The coyness of it all made him cringe. His mother would never forgive him the phrase *elusive essence*. She would sooner die.

The article gave a brief, somewhat guarded synopsis of

Cabins of Passion, Tepees of Desire, followed by a paragraph of effusive praise that only someone paid to do so could produce. This was followed by a half-page extract, a scene from the novel that Jeremy now had only the vaguest memory of, in which the logger comforts the kidnapped native girl after the first part of her ordeal. He read it through as rapidly as he could, squirming with humiliation at first and yet soon struck – even impressed – by its sheer facility, as though an infinitely shallow voice, the voice of a mean, cheap, indolent, morally evasive spirit, had channelled itself through his. It was literary possession, he told himself, drawn to the grimy horror of it like a dog to its vomit, the fingers of a twelve-year-old to a half-formed scab on his shin. He didn't feel shame so much as curiosity and, underlying that, an echoing, inexplicable absence of disgust. He was less the creator of this lurid stuff, than a radio, for whom all utterance was potential, tuned into a distant crackling station of bottomless vulgarity, a station to which all notion of indignity was foreign. He had been taken over by the paste and gimcrack spirit of Nathalie Cray, this painted, ageing blonde who might be his mother, or Grenier's latest whore, his face turned out, turned inside out, towards the world. She breathed through him, this woman, her tawdry notion of love and commitment acquired their power of speech through his. *He lifted her bleeding chin in his powerful work-scarred hand, the scent of pine sap still on it. Her tears were like ice against his skin. 'I will see that you come to no more harm,' he said. She looked up at him through misted eyes. 'I am yours,' she said. 'You may treat me as you will.'*

'I thought you'd be pleased,' said Grenier.

'Oh yes,' said Jeremy. 'I am. I'm delighted.' He thought for a moment. 'We'll need to talk about money, won't we, though?

If sales are so good. I mean, about how much I get, and so on. Maybe we can renegotiate a little?'

Grenier didn't reply to this. Jeremy put the magazine down. 'I want to talk to you about my mother,' he said.

He wrote to his mother that afternoon, still drunk from lunch, longhand. He repeated what Grenier had told him, in words as close to those he had heard as he could manage, his memory racked by doubt. It was hard to start the business of writing, but after the first few sentences had been dragged from his pen, the letter flowed. It was a love letter of sorts although he didn't know it, a muddle of recrimination and loss and desire that Jeremy would never have imagined he could write, to his mother least of all, a letter that forced itself out, like Nathalie Cray, from some unwelcomed and unacknowledged part of him, a place without censors or wisdom or self-respect. He signed it, folded the half-dozen scribbled sheets unequally into three without reading them through, pushed them into an envelope. It took him half an hour to find her latest address, someplace in Greece he'd never heard of, by which time he had a headache and might have changed his mind if he hadn't already put a stamp on the damn thing, and sealed it. That's what you are, he told himself, petit bourgeois, pathetic, a snivelling mummy's boy who can't bear the fact that your mummy told you a lie, and you have to punish her. So cheap you can't throw away a fucking stamp to save your life.

Cabins of Passion, Tepees of Desire was the first official Nathalie Cray novel. The rights were bought from Grenier by an American publisher that specialised in soft-core romantic fiction for women, on condition that Jeremy, or Nathalie, toned down a few of the scenes. It wasn't the violence that worried them, but its explicitness. The repeated use of the word bruise, in particular, was an issue. Jeremy was taken out to lunch by the woman who dealt with European rights at La Coupole, a choice so hackneyed and so right his every prejudice was confirmed. He ordered foie gras, *choucroute garnie* and champagne, and enjoyed watching her eyes shift over to the prices, her pale-pink mouth tighten but say nothing. She ordered salad, the kind with gizzards in it, and mineral water, which she sipped in the thoughtful, reluctant manner of someone doing something unpleasant but potentially life-saving. She was very thin. She was wearing an exquisitely cut white linen dress, and a long gold necklace she played with as she spoke; her nails were polished and the same pink as her lips. She reminded him a little of his mother – she had the same distracted air, as though waiting for someone else to arrive who might relieve her of the monotony of her present company, but lacked the smile that made it possible to forgive this. But maybe he could not forgive her simply because she was not his mother; his mother was countries away.

Pushing her salad around her plate, she asked him about Paris and what else he did there. He drank too much too quickly, and became confessional in his usual over-chummy, *faux*-uninhibited way, the way that led to regret and self-loathing. Indifferent to her growing ennui, then perversely invigorated by it, he told her about the horror of doing business translations for under-the-table payments and private lessons with sulking children in the kitchens of the rich, but all the time he was talking he was thinking about his mother, and imagining how different – by which he meant better – his life might have been if she had been, well, different – by which he meant better once again – or if he had, or if something had. It always came down to this, that something had needed adjustment, improvement, and he still had no idea what it was, nor when it should have happened, nor at whose hands. There existed drugs that produced this kind of alienation, he knew. Perhaps there were also drugs that could set things right. He wondered afterwards how much the woman had taken in. He had a vision of her nodding head, her vacant smile. I should have been Nathalie Cray, he thought.

At the end of the meal, after Jeremy's second coffee, the woman, whose name his distracted mind – to his horror – had completely mislaid, picked up the change from the bill and slipped every centime of it into her bag. She gave him a brilliant smile. 'I'm so glad we'll be working together,' she said, but her eyes were already on her perfectly tailored coat, in the hesitating hands of the waiter, and he had the sense of her slipping away from him, as slick and unctuous as the pâté that now sat so heavily on his stomach. Half an hour later, he was sick in the toilet of a bar.

His mother had always encouraged him to eat. She had a theory about appetite, as she did about most things, that indifference to food was a sign of indifference to life, than which no crime was worse. She tested recipes on him from glamorous parts of the world, dishes the older Rachel pushed away with determination, and that he was teased and cajoled into tasting. He understood later that she was bored, so deeply bored that a squirt of cochineal into the soft white mess of a rice pudding was, at the very least, a passing distraction, a burst of blood-red at the heart of the awful blandness she was being forced to undergo.

How much she must have hated staying at home, he thought, when he thought about the past, in the house in Whitstable, and before that, when all he can remember is an echoing kitchen and a bedroom wall. All those hours spent fiddling in the garden, the orchard, the conservatory. All that bottling of fruit. How much she must have wanted to leave. So why hadn't she? They could have lived together, the two of them, and eaten the products of her questing imagination three times a day. He still resented her for that, for those meals *manqués*, the hues and tangs of them, the textures, sheer as silk or rough as pelt on the tongue, that fifth taste he could never recall the name of, that made some foods more adult than others. They could have worked their way through Escoffier, adapting his dicta to their own special needs. His father and Rachel could have eaten their paps and puddings and mashed potatoes together for the rest of their long, dull, tasteless lives.

16

RACHEL

Rachel is holding a fortified vitamin drink to her father's mouth but the plastic straw, concertinaed in the middle, is no more than lodged against his slightly parted lips. He's breathing badly, a guttural rasp, but at least it's regular now. The night has been long and anxious, sleepless for them all. Vikram went and came, went and came. He told them not to worry, but you might as well tell a dog not to bark. 'Try to drink some,' she says, and she can see the effort he's making from his eyes, which are now so pale and watery it's a wonder he can make her out. Perhaps he can't. She's had the impression more than once recently that his eyesight is so poor he's waiting for her to speak before he commits himself. She might be anyone, some dark shape looming over him as he squints up. Jeremy, Dhara, Vikram. Anyone at all. Weeks ago, before Jeremy arrived, the poor darling said one of the district nurses was a good son, apparently, calling her Jeremy and then another name she said she couldn't catch but that Rachel suspected was Vikram. The nurse didn't mind; they're trained to deal with that sort of thing. But Rachel minded. Who knows what else he might say. She can't bear to watch him decline like this, the barriers falling all round him.

Sometimes she looks at the tablets in his scratched little plastic cup, the morphine and the water retention pill and the stuff he's taking for his heart and the little pink one she can't remember the purpose of, and wonders if twice the dose would be enough, or whether she should hold something back, let nature take its course. No one would know, she thinks, and then, It's what he wants, he's said so a hundred times. But part of her is scared, and part of her is shocked, and part of her – perhaps the largest part – can't bear the thought of life without her father, so that to bring it to an end, however *right* that may feel, is too awful to contemplate. What would she do without him? Her eyes fill with tears; these days, they're hardly ever dry. 'Just a drop, Daddy, try a little harder, you've got to eat something,' she says, and, uncomfortably like those of a baby, the thin, dry lips grip the straw and start to suck and his gaze at her, blurred and myopic and washed-out as it is, gives every sign of having seen her, and of trusting her. Which is what love comes down to in the end, she thinks. To be seen, to be trusted.

That was always Denny's problem, that he couldn't see her, not really, however hard he looked. Because he had looked at her, she knows that, she can't believe otherwise. Not just the way he'd looked at other women either, as though deciding whether to put a tenner each way on them, that hateful appraising manner he had, and not just with women, with everyone. With her, she's still convinced of this, he had made an effort. The evening they'd met, at one of those fake barn dances people used to organise then, he'd been wearing jeans and a checked shirt and cowboy boots, and he'd been so slim and sexy, and adult somehow, and they'd both had the same knotted handkerchief round their neck, which was how they'd started chatting, or that's how she remembers it. He'd made her feel adult as well, not just a child to be coddled and then rewarded. They'd had sex that first time, proper sex, something she'd never done before, although it was clear to her even then that he had, and she'd found some straw caught in her bra strap the next day. She still has it somewhere, with other scraps of the past she can't bring herself to throw away.

She sees him suddenly, years after that, they must have been sitting in a pub somewhere, when people were still allowed to smoke, and his eyes were screwed up, and there was a Johnny Cash song on the jukebox, 'Train of Love', the song they'd first danced to at the barn dance or she would never have remembered. She'd thought it was the song that was making him cry, and sat there and listened to the lyrics for the first time. Then, when the song ended and his expression didn't change, she decided it was the smoke in the room and suggested they took their drinks outside to finish. But it wasn't that either. He'd snapped at her to leave him alone, and then walked across the bar and made a call from the public phone near the gents. It was their local pub, she remembers now, the place was filled with people they knew, people they dealt with, some of them even friends, people they had dinner with. One of those horsey pubs they always went to, because you never knew who you might meet, there was always someone who might turn out to be useful. Rachel had felt people's eyes on her as she watched his shoulders hunch up, the tension in his neck, the skin of it changing colour. She watched him fiddle in his pocket for loose change to feed the phone, his knees bent, and noticed for the first time how much weight he'd lost these past few months. He'd been eating out a lot, work dinners mostly, but there he was, as thin as when they'd first met, his trousers hanging off him. He needed to buy some new clothes, she thought. He needed looking after. But she knew, or with hindsight she thought she'd known, that she wouldn't be required for that.

She was right. A few weeks later, he came home in a new tailored suit, with his hair cut into a sort of fringe; he hadn't had a fringe in twenty years. He looked ridiculous, and she told him so, but that didn't stop him. That was the first time he'd had an affair, she worked out later, when she had time on her hands. The fringe was the giveaway. The second give-away, a year or two later, was when he began to change his underwear every day. What a pig he was. How could she not have seen that earlier? Why had he never changed his under-wear for her? Why do women bother? She wonders how long it took with the new one before he reverted to sleeping in his pants.

'How is he?'

She turns to see Jeremy at the door. She'd forgotten he was even in the house. She shrugs. 'He won't eat,' she says.

'Hello, Dad,' he says, not answering her directly, just walking across to the bed and placing a hand on their father's bony shoulder. She feels ignored, but brushes aside what she feels, or tries to, for everyone's sake. Still, when the old man moves his head towards Jeremy with what sounds like a murmur of greeting, and the straw is dislodged, she can't resist a reproving tut. Why? she thinks. Why him? She lifts the bottle away. 'Well, see what *you* can do,' she says, handing it to Jeremy, hating herself and the anger in her voice which is, she recog-nises immediately, nothing but envy and resentment, and the feeling that she will never finally have what she deserves. She's being excluded once again, shoehorned out of her father's life after all these years, decades even, in which Jeremy has been less than nothing and she has been everything. And now look at him. He's wormed his way back into the house like some disease that springs to life after years of lying dormant, more virulent than ever. Like syphilis, she thinks.

But Dad's pushing the bottle away with a feeble, shaking hand and a grimace of distaste, as though they're trying to poison him, and Jeremy is looking to her for guidance, so baffled and hopeless by what he sees that she is sick with guilt. 'It's no use,' she says, her voice breaking as the fatigue of the night hits her – she hasn't slept a wink for over thirty hours. 'He's just not interested.'

'He'll die if he carries on like this,' says Jeremy in a voice so low, so unobtrusive she barely hears him, and she wonders if she was meant to hear or if he was talking to himself. How lost he looks, she thinks, her little brother – Little Jem – her anger wiped away by a wave of unwanted tenderness. How easily he's worn down by trouble. It occurs to her to say, We all will, Little Jem, we'll all die. But that won't do either of them any good. It isn't even true, if you think about it. As long as you're alive you're alive and after that there's nothing, so what sense does it make? She's got no truck with all that religious nonsense. You leave no one, everyone leaves you. They've never had that comfort in her family. Mummy, maybe, towards the end, with that Greek man in tow. And just look at how Jeremy's changed his tune about Daddy's dying. A couple of weeks ago he was champing at the bit; now he's on the brink of tears. It's all part of this great new friendship between them, she thinks.

'What time is Vikram coming?' he says. So that's it, she thinks. He's waiting for Vikram. And the anger washes back.

'I've no idea,' she says. She pauses. 'I'm surprised you don't know.'

'Know what?'

'Know whether he's coming or not. After all your little chats together. All your little conflabs in the corridor.'

He doesn't answer.

'It's a bit embarrassing, actually,' she continues, her voice quite calm, 'the way you pester him. I'm surprised he hasn't told you to back off. You won't get anywhere with him, you know, if that's what you're thinking.'

'I wonder if anyone else in the entire world still uses the word conflab,' he says after a moment, as though he is leaving her time to regret what she has said. She might have done if he'd said something else, something kinder and less stuck-up.

'Oh, I'm probably wrong about that as well,' she says, bridling. 'I'm sure they don't use it in Paris, that's one thing.'

'Well, no,' he says, with one of his irritating smiles. 'They tend to speak French in Paris.'

'Because you are rather pressing him, you know,' she says. 'I couldn't help seeing you both in the garden yesterday. You didn't give him room to breathe.'

'That seems to be all anyone does in this house,' he says after a pause. He's backed away from the bed and is picking up things from the dressing table by the door. It's odd that Daddy should never have got rid of it, she thinks, as Jeremy picks up a clothes brush, long and thin, with a decorated back, that must have belonged to their mother when they still slept in the one room. That long ago. It can't have been sentiment, surely. Perhaps he used it on his suits. Perhaps other women have found it useful.

'Watch other people,' continues Jeremy, putting the brush back where it was, adjusting the position of a tray filled with cufflinks, looking at her face through the dressing-table mirror. 'Dhara told me she'd been watching you.'

'She'd been what?'

'She'd been watching you in the kitchen. She said you were

157

opening and closing the fridge door as if you couldn't remember what you were supposed to be doing.'

'I don't believe you.'

'After breakfast this morning, it was. She was standing by the door, she said, and she watched you for a good five minutes before you even realised she was there.'

Rachel can't believe Dhara would go behind her back to Jeremy and say such things about her, such cruel nonsense, as though she were going senile. I don't remember seeing Dhara at all this morning, she thinks now, not before I bumped into her in the hall and told her how Daddy had been during the night, and she'd known already, of course, because Vikram had called her. She'd been on her way in, surely? She still had that awful old yellow anorak on; Rachel distinctly recalls wanting to suggest she buy a new one, or, even better, a proper coat of some kind. She isn't surprised, though, that Jeremy should repeat it, and revel in repeating it. It's just what she'd expect from him. Except that he isn't repeating anything. He's making it up. It's the old Jeremy showing through all this love for Daddy, all this lovey-dovey family nonsense; it's the little liar showing his true colours all over again. He's spent his whole life telling stories, and now he's paid to do it, so there's no way of stopping him. It's like an itch.

She glances at the time on the DVD player Dhara uses to watch her Catherine Cooksons on. It's just before lunch. Which means that she was downstairs opening and closing doors like some loony old woman less than four hours ago. So what was she looking for? She sees herself in the kitchen, holding the handle and staring at the shelves, at the cheese and boiled ham and pack of low-fat citrus yogurts and the empty butter dish and the family-sized tub of cholesterol-reducing margarine. Is that what she wanted, the margarine?

And then she forgot what she wanted? Because she knows in her heart that what Jeremy says is true. She's been seen at her weakest by Dhara. Because Jeremy is right about that as well. That all we do in this house is watch one another, waiting for flaws to reveal themselves, waiting for glimpses of bare flesh into which we can twist the knife. That's how it has always been, since long before Mummy left, although nobody has ever said so, and ever since then as well. Only Daddy's immune to it, above it somehow, like the heart of the hive. He's sleeping now, his lips slightly parted, a drop of the vitamin drink on his chin, but his breathing sounds rested in a way it hasn't for days, as though he has settled on just the amount of air he needs to stay alive and no more. I love you, she says to herself. I don't know what I'll do without you. I love you and I forgive you everything. And she feels her heart ease at the thought of these words.

When music blasts from downstairs, Rachel and Jeremy look at each other.

'That's Debussy,' says Jeremy.

'It certainly doesn't sound like Dhara's kind of thing,' says Rachel. 'She's more of a Shirley Bassey fan.'

'It could be Vikram,' says Jeremy.

'Calm down, dear,' she says. She's about to tell him why Vikram, whatever either of them might feel for each other, or Jeremy might feel for Vikram, is out of bounds for Jeremy, because surely the same rules apply, even between men. But Jeremy is already bounding down the stairs like an excited child. She stands up and crosses the room to hear what comes next. Dhara is saying something about there being a friend of Jeremy's here, and Jeremy is saying, Oh, I thought it might be Vikram. No, no, says Dhara. She hears them cross the hall together, with Dhara talking thirteen to the dozen, but she can't make out a word, the woman's voice has dropped to a whisper. The sitting room door opens. Dhara finally stops talking.

Then Daddy sits up and stretches his arms out towards her – she can see this through the mirror, his mouth half open and gasping for breath, a sort of noise coming out of his throat, or his chest, or from somewhere that isn't him, that can't be him – and she's turning back towards the bed, all at once anxious and scared; oh God, please no, not now, she is saying to herself, with all this happening, and Rachel is quite alone as the silence downstairs is broken and Jeremy speaks, his voice raised. But he's speaking in French and then he laughs and she can't understand a word of what he says.

PART TWO

(1985)

17

JEREMY

The call comes when Jeremy least expects it. He's had the phone in his flat for just over two weeks now; it never seemed worth it before. He had other people's numbers and the payphone in the *café-tabac* below the flat was close enough for him to call them when he needed to. But now here the thing is, ringing out from beneath the sofa, where he thrust it a couple of days ago, in a moment of agonised pique, after someone called him by mistake and insisted his number wasn't his, but belonged to someone else, someone French, whose line he has apparently stolen.

He was waiting for a call, it was true. If he forces himself to think about it, the reason for having a phone is that he hopes Jean-Paul will call. He left his number scribbled on the back of a postcard of the Eiffel Tower, which was intended to make Jean-Paul laugh, a private joke he might not even remember having shared, and given it to his concierge, who put it in her apron pocket. No doubt it's still there, buried in greying fluff, creased and grease-stained and forgotten. Still, nothing risked, nothing gained, as the saying goes, unless, as he suspects, he's remembered it incorrectly.

He's never understood the process that condemns his

English to slowly crumble into awkward shards and husks of language without a corresponding improvement in his French. Even now, after more than five years, he can find himself tongue-tied or, even worse, blabbering and incontinent. Arranging for the phone to be installed was the sort of nightmare that initiation rites must be for youths in tribes in Central Africa. His latest novel is set in the Belgian Congo, more or less, and initiation rites are uppermost in his mind. He played with the idea of circumcision, both male and female, but decided his readers weren't ready for impromptu genital surgery. He opted in the end for something milder, a prolonged spanking over a sort of primitive gymnasium horse with totemic potency, endured by the Belgian officer at the hands of a local chieftain's daughter and her brutish underlings.

He's about to turn on the television when the phone rings. Jean-Paul, he whispers to himself. *Enfin* Jean-Paul.

The party was in an apartment that overlooked Les Halles. Worried he might be late, Jeremy had arrived too soon, just before nine, and knew no one. He'd been invited by a middle-aged, overweight art critic he'd translated an article for and then rebuffed when the critic had stroked his leg under a table. Jeremy had been under the impression that the critic was the host, but there was no trace of him in any of the large bare rooms, although the flat had the air of someone in the *beaux arts* business, the off-white walls interrupted by modishly unframed canvases that reminded Jeremy of more famous canvases, by artists whose names he knew. There was a lot of sub-Twombly graffiti, and shapes in smears of blood-toned acrylic that resembled human organs against washes of beige hemp. Young men in crisply ironed shirts and faded 501s turned away from each other to examine him as he drifted, half-empty glass in hand, from window to window, observing the horror of the new Les Halles from above for the first time. Not that he shared the fashionable disgust for the place. He adored FNAC, and the black boys from the *banlieues* who hung around the place on Saturday afternoons, some of whom would be spotted later in bars a few blocks to the west – or if not them, boys much like them. He'd taken one home once and they'd talked about Genet, or he had, and the boy, well, more than a boy, a youngish man, had listened, or appeared to listen, his softening mulatto dick in Jeremy's gentle, stroking grasp. How different they were from these preening, acid-faced, pencil-thin culture queens, coupled off against the iciness of their own making, curdled by dissatisfaction. Where was his only friend, the critic? He hated them with all his heart.

Yet who am I, he asked himself, to censure? From what lonely and precarious pulpit do I deign to judge? Where, with the lights of the artificial gardens beneath me, and the dark, all-devouring commercial hole at their heart, do I belong? He stared at the immaculate skin of the window instead of through it, and he saw the party behind him reflected, bright and cold, as though he were peering in from outside, hovering above the desecrated square on angelic wings. I could be like them, he said to the glass, these men in their candid shirts and *faux*-workmen's jeans, who come and go and talk of Michelangelo, if that's what I want, if only I tried harder, thought less about myself and what people think of me. Too much thought, he thought, and not enough instinct. He felt as though embarrassment were his natural state, as though he'd been born to blush and skulk, and see the world reflected, and dream of revenge.

'Hello,' said someone behind him. He turned round.

'Hello,' he said.

'You're English,' the man said. He was Jeremy's height, and weight, perhaps a little stockier, and, at a rough guess, in his late twenties or early thirties, as Jeremy was. He was wearing jeans, like everyone else in the room, and a pale-green polo shirt. He had dark hair and brown skin and white, evenly spaced teeth, with slightly long canines. He was impossibly good-looking.

'Is it that obvious?'

'No, you blend in well,' the man said, with a soft French-American accent. 'But people talk.'

So I have been noticed, he thought. Some spiteful queen in this freezer compartment of a room has deigned to acknowledge my presence.

The man offered him a cigarette. Jeremy had given up smoking two years earlier, but the fear that the man might walk away if he refused was too strong.

'Thank you,' he said. He watched the man's hand cup the flame of the lighter against an imagined breeze, then bent his head towards it. He could smell the scent of the man, and beneath that scent, the man himself, his skin, his sweat. His arm was covered with fine hair turned blond by the sun. He looked up to see the man's eyes on him, amused.

Jean-Paul sold clothes in a Daniel Hechter store in the eighth arrondissement. Jeremy dropped in to surprise him the day after the party. He had a hangover and a sore throat; he'd barely slept and had only the faintest recollection of walking home. Jean-Paul had left the party early, but he'd spoken to no one else there, and kissed Jeremy goodbye before he left with a kiss that barely grazed his lips. He'd placed his hands on Jeremy's hips while he kissed him and then, as he moved away, let them slide up to his waist and startlingly clench the flesh, a teasing, testing clench, as though Jeremy were being measured up, or even softened up, for later. *Au revoir*, he'd said, the first time he'd spoken French all evening, and Jeremy, his breath failing, the skin at his waist still hot from the pinch of Jean-Paul's fingers, had answered him in the same, newly exotic tongue.

He hated this kind of shop. Only the terrifying thought that he might otherwise never see Jean-Paul persuaded him to walk through the swinging glass doors into the over-chilled, overpriced, cathedral-hush-like air, the lustre of a world that seemed to have no place for him, that barely deigned to notice him, that, when it did, despised him with all its brittle diamante heart. In his jeans front pocket was an almost full soft pack of Winston, the brand Jean-Paul had coaxed him with the evening before. He'd smoked two on the way to the shop, in the hope they would ease the soreness of his throat by some mysterious homoeopathy, but the pain was even rawer than before.

He sidled across the off-white carpet towards a rack of jackets as flimsy as shirts and began to slide them along the rail until he had gathered the strength he needed to glance around. When someone walked over and asked him if he needed assistance, he shook his head. 'I'm here to see Jean-Paul,' he said, his voice harsh and broken, faintly high-pitched. 'Jean-Paul? Jean-Paul isn't in this morning,' the man said, and Jeremy's glance caught the smirk. He coughed to clear his throat. 'He isn't ill, I hope?' he said. The man shrugged. 'Was he expecting you?' 'Not exactly,' said Jeremy. He turned to go. 'Who shall I say was looking for him?' the man said, following Jeremy as he walked towards the safety of the street, past pullovers stacked like grounded, humbled rainbows.

Jeremy saw the man, one pace behind him, through a mirror. His feet were oddly long for his body. He had a waist that Jeremy could have circled with his hands; perhaps Jean-Paul's hands had already measured it. 'It doesn't matter,' he said. 'I'll call him at home.' 'You have his number, then?' said the man, blatantly incredulous, standing at the threshold as Jeremy half walked, half ran down the street.

That was the first disappointment. The second came a few days later when the number Jean-Paul had written on the foil of an empty Winston pack was answered after the umpteenth ring. 'Jean-Paul?' said Jeremy, cringing at the keenness in his voice. He'd been standing in the bar for almost an hour, dithering about whether to call. 'No,' said the voice at the other end, the brusque voice of a man he didn't know. Jeremy's nerve failed him. He hung up. His hands were damp with sweat. If Gilberto were still alive, he thought, he would have called and asked him what to do. Gilberto would have known, would have instilled in him the fortitude he lacked. But there was no more Gilberto, Gilberto had been dead for over a year, and Jean-Paul had given him this number for a purpose, surely, and told him where he worked, and people shared apartments all the time, not only with lovers. He would call again, he decided. But first, he would have another cognac.

When Jean-Paul answered the phone, Jeremy was already drunk enough to ask him out to dinner. Jean-Paul agreed. 'Come round to my flat first,' he said, 'for an aperitif.' Hand shaking, Jeremy scribbled the address on a paper napkin. He lay in bed, the scrap of paper in his hand, unable to sleep, a foolish grin on his face, wanked out.

This was the way he always behaved, drained of sperm, love-struck, too dazzled to actually see the loved one – the would-be, never-had, potential loved one – already on the edge of feeling as woe-struck as if the affair was ended and he had been abandoned, cast aside on an unmade bed to weep himself dry, *déjà aimé*. The only songs he could bear at times like these were sung by Julie London, Billie Holiday, or at a pinch Marc Almond. He was twenty-seven and he had never been in love, not properly, unless he had been in love with his darling dead Gilberto, which he doubted. But he had also *been in love* a thousand times, a solitary, ingrowing sort of love that left him weak and tearful and goon-like, furious with himself and the larger, disinterested cruelty of the world, furious that, once again, the subject of his affections had ignored him, or rebuffed him or, worst of all, been sweet to him before moving on. This was the sort of *being in love* Jeremy knew best, and Gilberto must have felt this for him, because all the signs had been there: the pettiness, the jealousy, the unvoiced and unreasonable demands. It was as though love's only purpose were to frustrate him or, if he was lucky, condemn the other party to the same frustration.

So he wasn't surprised when he found himself outside the building Jean-Paul lived in, waiting in vain for the doorbell to be answered. He stepped back, stared up, the windows narrowing as they rose towards the roof. He had no surname to cling to, but the number suggested a flat near the top of the building, one of those ex-servants' places with a shared bathroom on the landing. Maybe he shared a telephone line as well; it wouldn't be the only duplex in Paris. Perhaps he was on the landing at this exact moment, waiting for the gruff-voiced man who'd answered the first time to flush and vacate the lavatory before returning to his own room, opposite Jean-Paul's, closing the door behind him as Jean-Paul flipped the lock and sat on the still-warm seat to evacuate his bowels. Encouraged by this image, Jean-Paul with his jeans around his ankles, Jean-Paul reaching round to wipe his arse, Jean-Paul, the most beautiful man he had ever been about to dine with and then fuck, standing to hike up his jeans, Jeremy tried again. His finger still on the button, he pressed his face against the glass of the door, saw a passage, beyond it a court-yard, a tree, the light fading from everywhere.

That was when some movement reflected made him turn. The road was narrow, a side street off Rue Saint-Jacques, small shops, a bar, the doors to the flats above with metal grates and glass, and there he was, the giraffe-man, after – what must it be now? – five years, stooping to leave a shop that sold art materials, his sticks painted orange and white to match his hair, pausing for a moment as if to remind himself where he was and then heading left, towards the river. Jeremy thought of Gilberto, of how he had kept the man a secret from Gilberto, the fact of having seen him, as though to have seen him had rendered him complicit in – what? His disgrace? His weirdness? His remarkable failure to conform? His courage? His sense of humour? As though what Jeremy felt had been bound by shame, bound and twisted like some tortured bonsai into a shape that could only parody its true nature, whatever that was. He thought of how this unshared secret had been the end of his shared life with Gilberto, and how this had seemed coincidence at the time, and possibly was. Who knows? Who knows what might have happened if Jeremy had never seen the giraffe-man? He was fifty yards ahead of him now as they headed north towards the Sorbonne, his passage as halting and spectacular as some royal progress while the street lights flickered on and the bookshops closed, Jeremy trailing behind like some anxious, hopeful stray in search of a home and a little understanding, all thoughts of Jean-Paul briefly driven from his head.

*

He pulls the phone out from under the bed by the cord, dislodging the mouthpiece from the stand. It's no more than halfway to his ear when his sister's voice rings out. 'And about time too. For God's sake, Jeremy, where have you been? I've been calling all day. What's the point of letting me have your phone number if you never answer? Hello? Hello?'

'Out,' he says. 'I've been out.'

'I've just heard from Mum's new boyfriend,' she says. 'You'd better get a bag packed pronto. Apparently, she needs us.'

18

RACHEL

Denny is shaking his head in his usual way, as though she's a complete fool. He's buttering his toast with the bread knife, but she can't say anything; he's in a filthy enough mood already. Mornings like this she wonders how he puts up with her. Before the call came he'd been holding the newspaper as if something foul had been wrapped in it, at arm's length, his face mercifully hidden from her, although she knows his customary expression so well – hard, pinched, contorted with disgust – it hardly needs to be seen. She can't imagine why he still bothers to buy his daily paper, or any paper, or listen to the radio for that matter, since all the news ever does is reduce him to near apoplexy. What is it this time, she was about to ask him – unions, immigrants, the price of petrol – when the phone rang and she had to go out to the hall. 'It'll be for you,' she said, not expecting him to move, 'at this time of the morning.'

But it wasn't. It was for her, although she didn't realise this at first. What she heard to start with was a foreign man in a state of some excitement. 'I'm sorry,' she said, 'you have the wrong number.' 'No, no,' the man's voice insisted, 'you are Rachel, yes? The daughter of Vanessa Eldritch?' And there it was, like a stab of heartburn, her initial thought. She's still using Daddy's surname. How dare she do that after what she's put him through? 'Yes,' she said, but her resentment distracted her and it wasn't until she heard the word *hospital* that she began to listen again. 'I'm sorry?' she said. 'Can you repeat that?' It serves her right, she thought, as the man babbled on.

'Why in God's name didn't he ring your bloody brother?' Denny is grumbling now, his mouth full of half-masticated toast. 'Mummy's boy.'

'They don't have his number,' she says. 'He's only just got a phone.'

'Oh yes,' says Denny, food churning, a shred of peel on one of his front teeth, 'I forgot. They don't have mod cons like telephones in Parisian garrets.'

'I'll have to call him myself.'

'*La* bloody *Bohème*.' He takes another bite of toast, swills it all down with tea. She watches him sometimes, and wonders if he's aware of what he looks like when he eats, the way he hunches over his plate, if he's bothered to fetch himself one, as though he's scared it might be whipped away from him before he's finished. Is this what he was like when they first met and she fell in love? Is this how he was brought up, as though every morsel were threatened? What a monster his mother must have been. 'It's a fucking miracle he hasn't got TB, or that new thing they're all dying of.' He flicks his fingers in his usual impatient way. 'You know. Gay cancer.'

'It's not called that any longer,' she says. 'There's a new name for it.'

'Same difference. Same filthy behaviour.'

She's looking through the mail on the worktop to see if she can find the letter Jeremy sent her, with the number in it. Denny's right, of course, as ever. Absolute madness not to have a phone these days, especially if you choose to live abroad. She wonders what keeps Jeremy there, in Paris. She's barely seen him these past few years, and all they've done is argue. She couldn't believe it when he confessed he was homosexual, without a trace of shame as far as she could see, that awful evening in the pub near Victoria station, before he caught the train to the ferry. She hadn't wanted to meet him, but he'd insisted. I've got something to tell you, he'd said. Something important. And she'd thought, well finally, he's getting married. We can only hope she isn't French. Please let him come home. And then he'd said it. I'm gay. Gay what? she'd said. She hadn't understood at first. Gay totally, he'd said, gay one hundred percent, and made a silly laugh. He was drunk by that point and she supposes, when she recollects the scene, that he thought she'd also be drunk. You aren't going to tell Daddy, she'd said, and he'd laughed again. Oh I don't think it would come as much of a surprise to Dad. But you haven't actually done it, I hope, she'd said, and he'd said, Told Dad? and she'd said, No, you know, *it*, and this time he'd laughed in her face. Of course I have, he'd said. It's not just theory, you know. There's practice too. And then, with another stupid giggle, he'd said, And I've had lots of practice. She'd walked out on him at that point. He could have spared her that stupid dirty comment, she thought, and still thinks. At least he could have spared her that.

He'd left the pub a few moments later and found her wiping her eyes on her sleeve, standing there on the pavement, and she's never forgiven him for that. Just don't tell Daddy, she'd said through her tears. And, to his credit, he never has, as far as she knows at least. She can only hope he doesn't pick up his new phone one day and call home. That's just the sort of cowardly way he would do it, she thinks, as she finds his letter between a circular from the Show Jumping Association and a gas bill she thought Denny had already paid. Hardly a letter, a torn scrap of exercise book paper in an envelope, with a number and *Call me! Jeremy x* scribbled on it. He was such a good-looking boy as well, though never in the same league as Denny. Surely he could have found a woman who could have helped him. She still feels this – how many years is it now since he told her? Eight? Ten? Twelve? She's still convinced he's never really tried. And now there is this awful business in New York, with all the homosexuals dying like flies. Not much gaiety there.

'So what's wrong with the old lady, then?' Denny stands up and brushes the crumbs from his shirt onto the floor.

'I'm not sure,' she says. 'I couldn't understand him.'

'I don't understand why all your family has to hook up with foreigners.'

'That's not fair,' she says.

'Even your father, with that bloody Paki.'

'She's Indian.'

He laughs. 'That makes all the difference, does it?'

'I don't know why you're being so horrible, Denny. My father's never done anything to you.'

He picks up the paper, throws it down again. 'This country's going to the dogs. No wonder everyone's leaving. We've got bloody pop stars raising money for Ethiopia now.'

Is that so dreadful, wonders Rachel, but she knows what the problem is. Money. It's all so much harder these days, and Daddy's refusing to give them a hand with some of the bills hasn't helped. She told Denny he'd say no this time, but nothing would put him off. And now Daddy's being funny with her as well. She feels like telling him she's all he's got, but she wonders if that's true. Denny's right about that as well, in his way. She never goes over to see her father without finding Dhara there. At least the boy has been sent off to her own family in India. Seeing him there with her father would be too much to bear.

'I suppose we'll have to send some money to her, is that it?'

'Well, no,' says Rachel. 'I don't think that's the problem. I think he just felt we should know she's in hospital.'

'In hospital, you say?'

'I told you, Denny.'

'You never said anything about her being in hospital. In Greece? I don't much fancy her chances.'

'I suppose someone ought to go and find out what's happening to her,' says Rachel. She wasn't going to say this, but Denny's tone has irritated her. Of course she told him. If he'd been listening to her, he'd have heard.

He lights a cigarette. 'You aren't thinking of going, are you? Don't be stupid.'

'I'm not being stupid. I think she needs me. She is my mother.'

'Why don't you let mummy's boy go? You've got his damned number, haven't you? You could have given it to Zorba, or whatever his name is, and saved yourself the bother.'

She knows it's worry that's talking. This isn't the Denny she fell in love with, and married. He's sick with worry, that's all it is. Seeing him there in front of her – his hair uncombed, his cheeks unshaven, a stain on the front of his shirt, which he should have left out to be washed, crumpled because he wore it yesterday, hanging out over his trousers, his socked feet cold on the kitchen tiles – it's all she can do not to run across and hug him to her, hug him back into shape and youth and happiness, make him love her as much as she loves him. If only they had more money, she thinks. And then she thinks, astonished that the thought hasn't come to her before today, that Mummy might be able to help. She's always had enough, and more than enough, and not only what Daddy gives her, Rachel is sure of it, although she's never asked herself the source of it, nor quite wanted to know. She's never quite trusted her mother. Denny saw through her at once, the first time they met. You're nothing like her, he said as they sat in the back of his car, his hand beneath her blouse, she thinks she's so special, he said, his mouth on her neck, his breath in her ear, the other hand forcing its way between her thighs, she thinks she's so fucking special.

'Oh, Denny,' she says. 'She is my mother.'

She calls the number her mother's friend gave her, the number in Greece, several times but there's no answer. He must be with Mummy in the hospital; she hopes so, anyway. Between these attempts, she goes upstairs and stands at the guest bedroom window and watches to see what Denny is doing at the stables. It's a long way off but she has her binoculars, hidden behind the curtain. Not that there's any need to hide them; Denny never comes in here. If anyone sleeps in here, it's her, after one of their rows, when she knows he doesn't want her near him. The first few times she's frustrated – there's no sign of him. He's in the office, she imagines, trying to make some sense of it all. It's a miserable day, overcast, the occasional drizzle of rain. The fourth time she looks, though, he's walking across the yard. He's smartened up, thank goodness, changed his shirt, shaved; he must have sneaked back into the house without her knowing. He'd still be the man she fell in love with if he only lost a little weight. His longish hair just suits him, though it often doesn't suit men his age. She'll trim it for him if he'll let her. She always does a good job, even Denny admits it, and the hairdresser he goes to in town has become so expensive recently. She hasn't been to a hairdresser herself for months, not since they had to settle that extortionate tax bill and she went through a list of their spending and crossed out whatever wasn't absolutely necessary. If only he'd give up smoking, she thinks, as she watches him light a cigarette and then stand there, staring up at the sky. When he turns towards the house, without quite realising what she's doing, or why, she steps back from the window, lowering the binoculars. Her cheeks are hot. She waits for a moment and then leans forward a little to see if he's still looking this way, but he's walking towards the stable door, throwing the half-smoked cigarette to the ground and grinding it with his foot. Maeve is coming out of the stable. She stops and says something, pushing her fringe back from her forehead, tucking her blouse into her jodhpurs. Raising the binoculars, Rachel fiddles with the focus to get them both into the picture, Denny and Maeve, but before she's had time to do this, Denny has stepped so close to Maeve she can no longer see the girl. All she can see is Denny's back as they go together into the stable.

And that's another expense, she thinks. A stable girl. A girl who does what she would do for nothing, and better, if what she's seen of the girl's work so far is anything to go by. But Denny insisted. Don't worry, he'd said. You needn't do anything. You're busy enough with the house, the cleaning, the cooking, although he knows how much she hates cooking. All those times her mother made her beat egg whites until they were stiff and butter cake tins, all that fiddling with food, as though it made it any better for you. She'd sooner muck the stables out than cook. But he wouldn't take no for an answer. He'd organised everything himself, put the ad in the local paper, interviewed the candidates. She'd have thought a man would be more use, but Denny said people liked to deal with girls, by which he meant men did. She isn't stupid. She knows he's got an eye for a pretty face, and all the rest of it as well. At least he flirts with them in front of her, she tells herself. Not like those men who sneak off and do it behind their wives' backs. She watches him sometimes, in pubs usually, but not necessarily; anywhere will do, a point-to-point, a restaurant, a supermarket queue. He stands up straight, chest out and tummy in, puts on that silly grin, his eyes all over the shop. It used to break her heart, she told him so too, you demean me, she said, but it didn't make a scrap of difference. I'm only being pleasant, he'd say, you wouldn't want me to behave unpleasantly, would you? You ignore me, she said, I might as well not exist. But I'm doing it for you, he said. To show you how much I trust you.

And then, suddenly, she didn't care anymore. She watched him as if he were someone on television, on *Candid Camera*, and didn't feel anything very much. These days, seeing him flirt, what comes over her is a sort of love and pity, as though they both know how hopeless he is. Nobody wants him, she thinks, except me, and this is a comfort to her, a comfort she never imagined she'd feel, or need to feel. She wants to save him from the poor opinion of other women by loving him all the more. Maeve appears at the stable door, glances round, looks over towards the house and then goes back in. Rachel puts the binoculars back behind the curtain and walks downstairs to the hall.

This time, a man answers and she recognises the voice at once. 'I'm calling about my mother,' she says.

'You are Rachel,' the man says. He sounds on the brink of tears.

'I've been calling all day.' She wonders if he'll understand. But he's bound to understand. Mummy doesn't speak Greek, or didn't the last time they saw each other. She and her boyfriend must be able to communicate somehow. The thought of the word boyfriend makes her shiver. She tries to imagine him as he talks, and what she sees is a waiter from a local kebab shop Denny sometimes stops at as they drive back from a night out, a thin man with spider monkey arms and too-long hair. She wishes she knew his name. He told her, but she didn't catch it.

'All day I have been with your mother.'

'Is she very ill?' Rachel asks, although she doesn't want to know, would rather imagine the worst than have it confirmed. Her imagination has never been up to much, has never prepared her for the truth.

'She is dying, I think.'

'Oh no,' says Rachel, 'you must be mistaken. That can't be true. She isn't nearly old enough to die.' How stupid I am, she thinks. What made me say that? Of course she's old enough. Everyone is old enough to die. She rests her free hand momentarily on her stomach. Even children die.

'She needs you, Rachel. You must come. You and your brother. You will speak to him, yes? You promise me you will come. You and he.'

'Yes,' she says, her tone almost as urgent as his. 'I promise.'

'Soon.'

'As soon as I can.'

'I will tell her.'

180

'No,' she says, quickly. 'Don't do that. Let it be a surprise.' Because you never know what might happen. Her mother will be lying there waiting and no one will come. And that will be the worst thing of all.

19

JEREMY

They meet in Athens, at the airport. Jeremy lands first and stands in the damp heat of arrivals, his shirt and trousers sticking to his unsunned flesh, dithering about how many francs to change to drachmas, chain-smoking and blaming Jean-Paul for the carton of Winston he bought at Charles de Gaulle. He's flown in on an overpriced charter from Paris; it's the first part of a package that includes not only connecting flights to a hotel he won't be needing on Hydra but also, and more usefully, a return flight, scheduled exactly one week from today, though God knows whether he'll be on it. He's physically sick with worry; he voided his stomach on the plane, although not in the paper bag provided, something he has always half wanted to do, but never quite found the courage for. He returned to his seat, the taste of vomit on his breath, the regurgitated vestiges of a limply industrial *croque monsieur* he'd wolfed down before leaving Paris. There was turbulence. Somewhere beneath him, apparently, was the Adriatic. The weather in Athens, the pilot informed them, was hot and humid. He sat there, head thrown back, an unread, unopened *Libération* on his lap, fretting whether the woman in the next seat could actually smell him, and whether he should apologise, and in which language. She didn't look French, or English; she crouched beside him, her face pressed to the porthole, her bony back like the carcass of a chicken. She was wearing a crocheted lime-green waistcoat she might have made herself and loose beige slacks. In the end, he closed his eyes and tried to sleep, but all he could see in the semi-darkness, apart from the veins in his lids, was his mother in some primitive hospital bed, strapped in and punctured by tubes of various colours and thicknesses, like a chart in a biology textbook.

He could kill Rachel. 'I'll tell you what I know when I see you,' she'd insisted three days ago, as though telephone etiquette forbade the exchange of anything more informative, or emotionally taxing, than deferment. Perhaps she thought he'd break down. Well, isn't that what he's done, without interruption, since she told him what time she'd be arriving in Greece and put the phone down on him? Isn't that what made him sink to his knees in the impossibly constrained space of the airplane lavatory and heave up his ersatz breakfast? He still feels queasy. She was due to land over an hour ago, but her plane's delayed. It can't be her fault this time, but that doesn't encourage him to forgive her. Nothing does, ever.

He looks at his watch and then at the board, which still gives no arrival time. He stares around the airport, glances at soldiers wandering or dawdling in pairs with machine guns poised against who knows what potential danger. He's too hot and sweaty, too exhausted and anxious to pay them his usual discreet attention, to give them points and tick them off his checklist. All he can think of is his mother. His mother in hospital, in a Greek ward, his mother alone and abandoned somewhere in an iron-framed bed, waiting for him to get there. His mother already dead, or so near death she won't know who he is. Not that, he thinks. Not that. He hasn't seen her since Paris, how many years ago now? Three? Four? And whose fault is that, he thinks, if not hers?

He walks out of the arrivals hall into the greater heat outside and lights a cigarette, watching the flame of the match burn straight in an air so still it feels like some other element. There is a newsagent's kiosk across from where he's standing, by a bar with a half-dozen tables beside it. He left his unopened paper on the plane and can't be bothered to dig out the book he's supposed to be reading from his rucksack. He wouldn't in any case be able to concentrate on it. Perhaps there will be an English newspaper, he tells himself. A crossword would do it, distract him sufficiently. He drifts across.

The side of the kiosk is covered with newspapers but they're all in Greek. A man's face appears, over and over again, on the daily papers and the magazines, an old man, gaunt, with thinning grey hair and a moustache. He could be a politician, except that he's wearing a check shirt open at the neck, or a writer, perhaps, but no writer in the world warrants so many front pages, not even in death. The man has a skewed, ironic smile on his lips, as though he's told a joke that no one else has understood. Other photographs show him without the smile, but with the same shirt, looking tired and ill. Jeremy stubs out his cigarette and returns to the arrivals hall. The board says Rachel's plane is due in half an hour.

She's flustered, irritated with the service on the plane, the insolence of the man who checked her passport. She can't see the point of leaving Athens until he tells her just how far from anywhere their mother is. 'Even if we go this afternoon,' he says, 'we may not make it tomorrow. I've spent hours trying to work out timetables, but nothing seems to be very clear.'

She looks at him, her expression saying, What else would you expect? We're abroad.

20

JEREMY

'I don't know about you,' says Rachel, shaking his shoulder roughly, 'but I haven't slept a wink all night.' She is bending over the bed, blocking the light from the window. Jeremy doesn't know where he is for a moment. Then, with a wave of misery, he remembers. The search, in vain, for a taxi. The overcrowded, under-ventilated, five-hour coach journey in stifling heat. Their arrival at a neon-lit hotel that was worse than even he could have imagined, its floors glossy with filth. The grimy receptionist who had mutely confiscated both their passports before resolutely handing over just one room key. Rachel, sitting on the bed, crying: 'This is no place to die.'

He struggles into a sitting position, the mattress giving beneath his elbows. The last thing he recalls from the previous night is deciding not to take off his shoes because of the state of the floor, and Rachel saying something about the sheets not having been changed and covering her pillow with a scarf. A glance at his feet confirms that he still has his shoes on, along with his trousers and shirt, buttoned tightly shut at the wrists and neck. He has slept on the top of the bed, as Rachel no doubt has done, or lain there at least, unblinking. Like him, she is fully dressed.

'I haven't even washed my face,' she says, with a shiver. 'I've never seen such a filthy bathroom. There are cockroaches behind the basin.'

'I'm surprised we have one at all,' he says.

'I suppose the water's drinkable.'

'I shouldn't think so for a minute. You haven't, have you?'

She shakes her head, but he's not convinced. Oh God, he thinks, she has. I know she has. 'There's a bin beside the loo,' she says, 'with loo paper in it.' She shudders. 'Used, by the looks of it. It was just the same at the airport. You don't think it's like this everywhere, do you? This level of filth? I'll never know what possessed Mummy to choose to live here.'

He swings his legs round. 'You can hardly judge a country from one hotel room.' But the same thought has crossed his mind, more than once. He can't remember now if his mother had met Andreas before she came to Greece or after; perhaps he has never known. They've been in touch so little these past years, after that letter of his and her reply. Had she come on holiday, and fallen in love? Some pick-up in a bar, on a beach, that turns into a life together? Isn't that what he's always imagined for himself? How typical of his mother that she should have got there first. He stands up. 'Let's get out of here,' he says, brushing away whatever traces of the linty pillowcase, the greying cotton bedspread, might have attached themselves to him. 'I'm hungry, and I need some coffee.'

An hour later they are sitting on the wooden seats of a train as it pulls out of the station. Rachel has grumbled her way through an English breakfast in a harbourside bar, and a journey in a taxi that ended in a brief squabble with the driver about money, a squabble he managed to settle while she was bent over behind the taxi to fiddle with her suitcase, the fabric of her dress drawn taut across her bottom. They'll need to talk about money soon, thinks Jeremy. She's got loads more than I have. So far he has paid for everything: the bus from the airport, the bus from Athens, the lukewarm moussaka of the night before, the hotel, the English breakfast, most of which he left, and now this final outrage, a fare that surely must have been twice what it ought to be and the man insisting that he also be given a tip. He was mentally converting drachmas into francs when Rachel straightened up, pulled at his arm, and pointed across the station at the only train. 'That must be ours,' she said. 'You'd better get the tickets. I'll look after the cases.'

Forty minutes later he is pushing a ragged curtain aside, leaning out of the window as the train gathers speed. 'I don't believe it,' he says. 'It's steam.' He closes the window abruptly to keep the smoke out. He might get a smut in his eye, he thinks, like that E.M. Forster heroine, and then fall hopelessly in love with a local. The day is already hot and promises to get hotter; his arse-crack is sweaty and itching after thirty-six hours in the same pair of pants.

'I believe it.' Rachel has taken a *Daily Telegraph* quick crossword book from her bag. 'How long is this going to take?'

'As far as I can tell, four hours.'

She harrumphs. 'You can't be serious.'

'And then we have to try to get a bus to where Mum is. It's the next town on, but the train doesn't go there.'

Rachel sighs. 'I can't understand what possessed her. Didn't she think of how much trouble it would cause everyone if anything happened to her in this awful place?'

'People don't think that way,' says Jeremy.

'I do,' she tells him and, yes, he says to himself, you do.

That is exactly the way you think. What was that expression people used to use? I'm a martyr to myself. It's a refined sort of egotism, the denying kind medieval would-be saints indulged in. He can see her, wolfing down her own cold vomit in some freezing cell, convinced she's pleasing God and bene-fiting her immortal soul. Rachel falls in love on a Greek beach and her first thought is to fend the man off, gorgeous though he is, the man she's sought her entire life, and to leave this earthly paradise of sand and sun and calamari, to return to the utter greyness and loneliness of her own dull home, not for her own sake, but for the convenience of others. What an appalling, smug, self-centred woman she is, he thinks. He glances across at her, sitting opposite him on the wooden seat, her biro poised above the puzzle. What in God's name shall we do together for the next few days? If only I could have come alone. I know that's what Mum would have wanted. Her only son and her lover at her bedside. And his mind swings back to the man he saw in the hotel room last night, the second man, whose door stood open, whose dark eyes followed Jeremy as he lingered momentarily in the corridor before walking on to his shared bedroom and his irate elder sister, perched on the edge of the bed like some malignant bird. Who knows what might have happened if he'd been alone? He might have fallen in love, as his mother has done, and grown old and ill, years later, and been cared for by Andreas, or whatever the man's name might be, some Greek name, oh I don't know, Patroclus, yes, that would be nice, something classical, like one of those men from Mary Renault, one of those hot heroic men, he thinks, who loved and died together, his eyelids slowly closing.

He's shaken from his dream when the train comes to a jerking halt in open country. There are fields of what looks like corn on either side, endless bright yellow fields. It looks more like rural France than Greece. He wonders for a moment where he is, until Rachel leans over and prods him with her biro and he remembers. He's on a train between Volos and some town whose name he doesn't recall, but that doesn't matter because the train stops there, and there is nowhere else for them to go until they leave it.

'Here,' she says, 'read this.' She gives him a magazine, a copy of *Newsweek*. 'I got it at the airport. I thought you might like to see what's going on in the rest of the world.' As opposed to France, he assumes, taking it from her and thumbing through it. He's about to put it down when a face catches his eye. It's the face of the sick old man he saw all over the news-stand at the airport. He starts to read the article, then puts the magazine down, shocked.

'Did you know about this?' he says.

'About what?'

'Rock Hudson. He's dying of Aids.'

She shakes her head. 'Surely not? I mean, he isn't . . .' she pauses. 'Is he?'

'Well, yes,' says Jeremy, 'he is, actually.'

'Oh dear,' she says. 'I didn't know.'

'That was the point,' he says. 'That people didn't, I mean.' He looks at the photograph again. 'If they hadn't printed his name beside the picture, no one would know even now.' He sighs. 'A friend of mine at Exeter had sex with him once.'

'Oh no,' says Rachel.

He nods. 'Oh yes. In a hotel bathroom in Florida.' He thinks back. 'Fifteen years ago it must have been. Before he started university. His father was a lawyer in Los Angeles, or knew one. He fixed him up with a job, I don't remember exactly what. To get some experience of life, that was the idea

190

anyway. It worked. He spent most of the year having sex with film stars, or he said he did.' Shall he tell her about the morning this friend, whose name was Jake, pulled down his jeans and pants in the middle of Jeremy's room in college and sprinkled delousing powder over his genitals, like castor sugar on apple pie? Better not, he thinks. But the memory of this, and of Jake's blond bush, which surely he ought to have shaved off, and short plump penis, stays with him as he picks up the magazine again and starts to read about Rock Hudson.

'You don't know anyone, do you?' says Rachel.

'What do you mean?' He puts down the magazine. He knows full well what she means.

'With, you know, Aids.'

'No,' he says. 'Not now.'

'But you did?'

'Yes,' he says. 'I lived with someone. He's dead now. He died a year ago, in Paris. We'd already split up. It happened quite fast. It doesn't always. With some people it can drag on, apparently.'

'I'm sorry,' says Rachel, awkward. Is that why she kept her clothes on, he wonders. To protect herself from me.

'We aren't the only ones to get it, you know,' he says, enjoying her wince at the 'we'. 'Other people do as well. Homosexuals. Haitians. Heroin addicts. It helps if what you are begins with an aitch. Horse-lover, for example. I'd watch out if I were you.'

'I don't know how you can joke about it.'

You would if you'd watched Gilberto die, he thinks. 'You don't need to worry about me, though. If you were worried, that is. I've been tested.'

She shakes her head. 'I'm so relieved,' she says and, for a moment, he believes her, believes that she cares about him.

He is moved. He leans over to put the magazine beside her and is about to touch her knee, the lightest possible gesture of affection, when she continues. 'It would kill Daddy if you died like that.'

Half an hour later, with a shudder that shakes the entire carriage, the train comes to a halt. They have stopped in what might be a station; beside the railway line is a platform of cracked concrete and a small yellow building the size of a garden shed. Rachel has spent the past twenty minutes wandering up and down the train in search of a lavatory that works. Thwarted, she has returned to her seat. 'Are you all right?' Jeremy asked her the first time she walked past. She shook her head, but didn't stop. She was walking rapidly, her buttocks clenched beneath her dress. When she came back some time later, he didn't look up. Now, as the other half-dozen passengers in their carriage open their windows and stare out across the empty fields, she sighs so deeply he's anxious about her for the first time.

'Are you all right?' he asks again.

She shakes her head once more, but this time she speaks. 'My stomach's upset.'

'Did you find anywhere to go on the train?'

'No,' she says. She stares round, as if afraid she might be overheard. 'But I absolutely have to go.'

Other passengers have left the train and are standing in clusters along the crumbling platform. 'Maybe there's a loo in the station.'

'What station?'

'We seem to have stopped at a station,' he says.

'How can it possibly be a station?' She starts to her feet, winces. 'It must have been that vile moussaka last night,' she says.

Or the tap water you drank this morning in the hotel bathroom, he thinks, but doesn't say. 'Well, it won't hurt to look.' He stands up. 'Come on.' He holds out his hand to help her, and to show his sympathy, but lets it fall as she leaps to her feet and pushes past him to get to the door. Jeremy follows. By the time he leaves the train, she's running along the platform to the yellow shed, hitching her dress up as she goes. Her thighs are large and white. Nobody else seems to have noticed. His shirt is sticking to him as he walks towards the shed. The air is heavy with the scent of something growing. Chickens have appeared and are pecking for food between the wheels of the train. In the silence, interrupted only by the distant conversations of his fellow travellers, he has a sense of peace so foreign to him he wonders if this is what it must be like to die. He feels as though something has broken in him, something that has held him back and stopped him breathing. He wonders if he is having a heart attack, but surely that would involve some sort of pain and what he feels at this moment is so far from pain he can no longer imagine what pain might be like. He places his hands together on his chest. A slight wind lifts from the fields to his right and the whole rough sheet of yellow grain, or whatever it is, ripples and heaves. And then he catches the scent, and he is back in a hospital room in Paris, holding a basin, Gilberto too weak to move, a male nurse bustling into the room and pushing him to one side, slipping on latex gloves before rolling the dying man onto his flank. He walks round to the back of the shed.

Rachel is slumped against the wall in a crooked, ungainly half-crouch, her dress hitched up above her waist. Her knickers, stretched taut between her parted knees, are smeared with diarrhoea. There is more on the ground and up the wall, on both her sandals, and, as he sees when she reaches out to him, on the side of her hand; she must have brushed against it while struggling to stand up. As she wriggles to maintain her balance, her face alive with the vileness of it all, her pubic tuft flashes dark against the blue-white of her shit-streaked thighs. He's never seen it before.

'Get these off me,' she says, plucking feebly at the crotch of her knickers, at an unsoiled scrap of cotton, falling back with a squeak of horrified disgust. 'For God's sake, Jeremy, get these filthy things off me.' She bursts into tears. 'I feel so *dirty*.'

By the time they have tidied her up, her shoes and knickers rinsed off in water from an adjacent tap, her hands and arse wiped clean with a packet of paper tissues Jeremy finds in his pocket, their train has gone.

21

RACHEL

They get to Kalambaka late evening. Rachel has been sitting in her own filth for hours now, how many hours she neither knows nor cares. She can smell herself on her hands, her clothes, in the air around her. People on the train they finally catch, about to sit in seats near hers, have looked her over in a puzzled way as though they can't match what they see with what their noses tell them, and then moved on, affronted, to other parts of the train. Jeremy is sitting opposite her. Occasionally, he leans forward to pat her leg, to comfort her, she supposes, or remind her that he's there, but she's still too angry with him to touch him back, or speak. She has been humiliated in front of him, and it will take time for her to forgive him. She only has to look at him and be met by that look of embarrassed concern to feel the same anger rise in her, and the same shame. It is not his fault, she knows that, but she will still make him pay for it.

Their cases are waiting on the station platform, beside a man who hurries towards them as soon as they leave the train. He's older than they are, tall, with overlong greying hair and a beard, dressed in what look like white pyjamas. He raises his hands in their direction and the sleeves fall away from thin dark forearms. He has sandals on his feet and skinny ankles, with the trouser legs flapping around them as he approaches. He's got a biblical air about him that Rachel doesn't like at all. She hates ostentation. She can't imagine why the railway people should employ someone dressed like this to take care of their luggage, although thank goodness someone has. Please God don't let him get too close, she thinks. But he's on them before she has a chance to move away. She flinches when he tries to take her shoulders in his hands. She's watching his face, his nose, for disgust, but Jeremy has already pulled him off her and is shaking his hand. Of course, she thinks, how stupid I am. This must be Mummy's boyfriend.

'I am so happy to see you. I don't understand why your cases are here and you are not. They are your cases, yes?'

'Yes,' says Jeremy. 'We had a little accident.'

Oh please God, no, she thinks, he's going to tell him what happened. She sticks out her hand to distract them both, immediately wishing she hadn't. She isn't sure how clean it is. The second train also had no working lavatory; you can only do so much with tissues and a cold water tap. 'I'm Rachel,' she says urgently, 'and I'd be very grateful if you could take us to a decent hotel.' Her stomach is beginning to work again. She can actually hear it, like some small creature gurgling in mud. She can't work out why no one else seems to be aware of it.

'But we can drive to my home,' he says. 'It is only two hours from here.'

I'm going to cry, she thinks. I know I am.

'We've had a dreadful journey,' says Jeremy, to her relief. 'Do you think we could spend the night here and then go tomorrow? Is your house near to the hospital?'

'Yes, the hospital is in Ioannina. I live not far from where it is. We can leave early tomorrow perhaps, and be there by ten, when we can visit. They will not allow us to enter the hospital before that.' He flashes an unexpected smile. 'The doctors must do their work first. First science, then love.' Andreas glances at his watch. 'Now, anyway, it is too late. She will be asleep and the hospital is closed.'

They are sitting in his car, an orange Citroën 2CV, Jeremy in front and Rachel behind with the cases, when Andreas points to the nearby hills. 'If we have time I will take you to see our famous monasteries,' he says. 'They are very special. There are no other monasteries in the world like them.'

'That will be lovely,' says Rachel, because any conversation is better than sitting there waiting for him to ask about the smell in the back. 'Maybe before we leave?'

'How's Mum?' says Jeremy suddenly. 'Were you with her today?'

'I am with her every day.'

'Is she comfortable?'

'Comfortable?'

'I mean, are they treating her properly? Is she getting the medical care she needs?'

'Oh yes,' says Andreas. He is hunched over, too large for his car, like one of those insects that eat their partners. That's it, she remembers, a mantis. A praying mantis, sandals and all. She looks at the mountains. Why on earth would a monk want to live in a place like that? She's never seen what there is to admire in these people who cut themselves off from the world to pray, as though there weren't so many more useful things they could be doing. The good of the soul is all very well, she supposes, but someone's got to put food on their plates, even if they do live on beans and cheese or whatever it is they eat. Jeremy was telling her on the bus from the airport about monks who won't eat eggs because they come from female hens, or some such nonsense. The thought of food makes her gorge rise. Please God, let her make it to the hotel before she has another accident.

The car is making an awful racket, as though a wheel's about to fall off, and the top half of her window is flapping about like a broken wing. What an odd car for a grown man to have, she thinks, and she wonders what he does for a living, dressed the way he is. She'd expected someone a bit like Daddy, someone that age at least, but she couldn't have been more wrong. Now that she's seen him close up she realises he can't be that much older than she is, no more than a year or two, which makes it even worse than she'd thought. Jeremy is asking him for details of Mummy's treatment and she's trying to listen, but her stomach is in revolt and she's afraid she might have to ask him to stop where they are, in this rundown suburban street, where everyone will be able to see her.

Oh God, she asks herself, why did I come? I don't even love her, not really. And she is so shocked by this realisation that she slumps back into the car seat, as hard and stiff as a metal garden chair. What hell is this? she thinks. I don't deserve it. If only Denny were here, and they had a proper car. If only Mummy were well and didn't need her.

An hour later they are sitting in a restaurant eating spit-roast chicken and village salad, as Andreas calls it. Rachel is picking at hers, but at least she has had a shower and changed her clothes. Jeremy and Andreas are talking about the monasteries near the town, but she's hardly listening. She's wondering how her mother is now, whether she's still

198

awake and waiting for them to come. How awful that would be, she thinks, to be lying there in a strange bed, surrounded by foreigners. Walking towards the restaurant, she asked Andreas if he'd phoned the hospital and he nodded, but said nothing, and Rachel didn't want to insist. She doesn't want that kind of intimacy with him, she supposes, as though it were only through him that she could be close to her mother. Not that she is. The last time they were in the same room was the day she married Denny. She'd turned up with a friend from London, a playwright, she said. Rachel can't remember his name, but she remembers the way he looked Denny over as though he were a stud horse before shaking his hand; she remembers as if it were yesterday how long it took him to let the hand go. Denny didn't notice, but he was oblivious to that sort of thing in those days. Everyone was. When she mentioned it later, as they were leaving the hotel for the airport, he looked puzzled and then said something like, Oh yes, your old ma's nancy boy.

She hadn't known about Jeremy then, thank God, or she might have given the game away. Denny knew, though, she found out later. I've always thought your brother was a bit of a shirtlifter, he announced once, in front of other people at a dinner dance, and she thought she'd die with shame. Looking at Jeremy now as he leans forward, his bare arm on the table almost touching her mother's boyfriend, she wonders if he fancies his chances with him. Isn't that what they're like? Ready to make love or whatever with anything in trousers? No wonder they're dying of this awful business.

And all at once, in this small, over-bright restaurant, the face of Rock Hudson appears before her eyes. Surely he can't have been like that, she thinks. Rock Hudson. A man who had everything. Doris Day. She'd always thought they were lovers. And now here he is, dying of promiscuity like some vile beast. And Doris, where is Doris? Is she by his bedside, in Paris? And who will get all his money? People used to say that Denny looked like Rock Hudson, and it was true. He did.

'Do you live in Mummy's house?' she says.

'I'm sorry?' Andreas is startled. Jeremy looks shifty, as though he's been caught out, and then offended, as though she's spoken out of turn. If she has, it's also on his behalf. He should be grateful.

'Someone has to ask these questions sooner or later,' she tells him, not looking at Andreas. 'We have to be prepared.'

'We live together,' says Andreas. 'I don't understand your question.'

'Do you work, Andreas?' She wishes she had a surname for him, so that she could call him that and whatever the Greek word is for mister. She hates this cosiness with a man she's never met before, some Mediterranean gold-digger. She wonders how much he's responsible for her mother's state of health. Perhaps he's been poisoning her slowly, so slowly that no one has thought to check. If I could get her back to England, it occurs to her, perhaps she'd live. And then, as the repercussions of this dawn on her, she asks herself what good that would do. While she was sitting on the train all she could think of, apart from the smell, was Denny, his head in his hands, and that spike with all the bills on it, that spike she's wanted to take away from the office just in case. He's been so desperately worried recently she can see him doing something foolish. She walked into the office once and found him actually crying, her Denny, crying his eyes out like a child, and that Maeve girl standing there next to him, hands in her hair, not knowing what to do, without the sense even to call his wife. It's awful what money can do to people, she thinks, how low it can make them sink when they haven't got it. And now this man is talking about some sort of holy workshop he's set up – no, sorry, holistic workshop, whatever holistic means when it's at home, and Jeremy is nodding beside him like one of those toy dogs people used to have in cars, gullible as ever, always agreeing and agreeable. Little Jem, that was her name for him when they were young. Little Jem, everyone's favourite, except Daddy's. And hers.

'And my mother, what does she do?' she asks.

'She is with me in everything I do,' Andreas says stiffly. 'She is my partner, and my love,' he says, and his voice breaks on the final word. Jeremy's hand snakes out to stroke his arm.

'Oh, leave him alone, Jeremy,' says Rachel. 'Why are you always having to touch people? They aren't bloody pets. They don't need stroking.' She's had enough of this. She's barely touched her food, such as it is. She's scared to eat or drink in case the diarrhoea starts again. She can't hear a word of their conversation without wanting to scream. She stands up. 'I'm off to bed.' She stares at Andreas as if daring him to contradict her. 'We have an early start tomorrow morning if we're going to see my mother.'

'Six o'clock,' he says.

'Six o'clock is fine by me.' She leaves the restaurant without saying good night to either of them. Glancing back through the window, she sees their two heads close together, as though they are sharing secrets.

They have separate rooms tonight. She insisted. Not that Jeremy put up much of a fight. He's trying to take control of the situation, she's noticed, by paying for everything, and she's happy to let him. He must be making more money from his dirty little books than she thought. She takes off her blouse and skirt, then goes into the bathroom to see if her dress is drying. She hasn't brought nearly enough cool clothes with her. She expected good weather, but not this relentless heat. The skin on her face and arms is uncomfortably red from the time she spent at that dreadful place, hardly a station, where they waited for the next train, with Jeremy bleating on about the nature of time and how it was the journey that mattered, not the arrival. She wonders sometimes what he did at university, and what she might have done if Daddy hadn't realised how much use she'd be working with him at the factory.

She looks around the room for a telephone, to see if she can get hold of Denny, but there doesn't appear to be one. She isn't surprised. The place is clean, she made sure of that before taking it, but basic. A single bed with a picture of the famous monasteries above it, a wardrobe, a table and chair, a bathroom with the same plastic basket beside the loo for paper, and a sign above it reminding her to use it in four different languages although not, she notices, Greek. It's how they'll have been brought up, she supposes, but still, how strange. She's heard that in some countries people use their hands directly. Jenny, the girl at the hairdresser's, told her once about a holiday she'd had in some Arab country, heaven knows why, where there hadn't been any paper at all, or lavatory come to that, just a hole in the ground and a tap. It doesn't bear thinking about.

All at once she wonders what she must have looked like when Jeremy came round the corner of that shed and found her with her knickers round her knees and, for the first time, she sees the funny side of it. She swore to herself she'd never tell a soul, but maybe a slightly doctored version of it will amuse Denny. She takes off the rest of her clothes and stands directly beneath the ceiling fan in the middle of the room, stark naked, thinking of Denny, finally cool and clean.

22

JEREMY

She is in the last ward off a long, bare, airless corridor. Jeremy follows Andreas past a series of half-open doors into a room with white-painted beds along both sides and a window on the far wall. It's another hot day and the window faces south-east so that, entering the room, Jeremy is momentarily blinded by mid-morning sunlight. Rachel must be behind him, but he doesn't turn round to check; he's given up on Rachel after last night. He's never understood her inflexibility, her odd little moods, her rudeness with people she doesn't recognise as part of her tribe, as one of us. For all the good she'll do their mother she might as well have stayed in the car or, even better, at home, with her horses and husband.

On the way to the hospital, she didn't speak a word to Andreas, other than to mutter complaints whenever he overtook anyone or drove in a way that wouldn't suit a vicar's wife in rural Sussex, while Andreas glanced over his shoulder to see what her problem was, his face concerned, his driving more erratic than ever. Jeremy asked her how she was feeling as they left the hotel, *for which he paid*, and she told him to worry about himself not her, which neither answered his question nor, given her tone, expressed concern for him or for how he might be feeling.

The truth, although he doesn't share it, is that he has a headache and shooting pains in his neck because he drank too much retsina last night, and is feeling nauseous, only partly because of the wine. He's inclined to blame the sun, which is too strong for him this morning. He blinks and turns his head from the bare hard light of the window towards the beds. Andreas, out of tact, he imagines, is hanging back by the door. Jeremy looks at the old women, ranged along both sides of the room, four beds to each white wall, as the women, or some of them, look back at him, while others stare up at the ceiling, and others have their eyes closed. But he can't see his mother.

He's about to ask Andreas if he's sure this is the right ward when Rachel lets out a little gasp, and pushes past him.

'Oh, Mummy,' she says. 'Oh my God, Mummy.'

Later, when he is back in Paris, alone or with Jean-Paul, he will think about this moment over and over again and find no peace. He will run his mind's eye round the ward, from bed to bed, as if along a series of photographs scattered on a desk or along an identity parade of similar, almost familiar, but finally unknown faces, and still he will fail to see her among the other old women in their metal-framed hospital cots, white sheets pulled up to the chin, or pushed back because of the heat, pushed away by bare arms burnt brown with the sun or blue-white with the lack of it because they have been in hospital so long, their faces turned towards him, some curious, some not, or staring elsewhere and seeing nothing. He will hold each face against the mental image he has of his mother's, except that mental isn't the word, he has never had an image of his mother that wasn't in his blood, his heart, that didn't touch him beneath thought. And yet he didn't see her, he will insist in a sort of self-flagellation, so hard on himself it hurts, but never quite enough. He didn't see her. He would like it to hurt more.

It was Rachel who found her out, his big sister Rachel who ran in her clumsy, stumbling way down the centre of the ward to the last but one bed on the left, her arms already stretched out ahead of her, already moaning. It was Rachel who enveloped the frail, bald, *unknown* woman in her grasp, and lifted her bodily from the bed and hugged her, and rocked her backwards and forwards like a frightened child, and started to wail in a way he had never imagined her capable of.

It was Rachel who reached his mother first, while Jeremy stood at the door beside Andreas, who put his hand on Jeremy's shoulder, and squeezed it gently, and whispered words he didn't catch, or want to hear. Jeremy stood there and was afraid to move. That was the truth of it.

And now Andreas urges him forward. 'I told you,' he says. 'She is very ill. But you are in time, and your sister also, and that is good. Yesterday, I didn't say this to you, but I was worried we might not arrive before the end. But now we are here together, we three. This is what she wants, I know this, what she has wanted all the time, after we knew, when they told her there was no hope. I thought to telephone you many weeks ago, but no, she said, no. They will try to take me away and I want to be here, to die here. I want to die where I have lived with you.'

His voice is low and quiet, hypnotic almost, as though he has prepared this speech and no longer needs to think about what he says. It says itself. And Jeremy listens to this with half an ear as he walks towards the bed, and he can see his mother now, because Rachel has moved to the far side – fat, sweaty, ungainly Rachel in her flowery frock – and she is looking at him with an expression he can't fathom, of contempt for him, of fear, and for the first time in his life it strikes him that he has no idea who she is or what she's thinking, and that this might be his loss. And his mother has raised a hand to welcome him, so thin and veined it is more like a fragment of muddied glass.

'Hello, my darling,' she says and her voice is so hers, so much stronger than he expects, that for a moment he thinks she will live, she will be all right. All this, these undeniable markers of death – her baldness, her fragility, the bones at her collar like blades sticking up through the skin and draining it of its colour, an odour he can't quite place, medicinal and sour – all this is a passing thing.

'Hello, Mum,' he says, his own voice weak and breaking, strange to himself.

'Hello, darling. Aren't you going to give your mother a kiss?'

'Of course I am,' he says. Leaning forward, his hand on the sheet beside her shoulder, he sees her wince, briefly, before his lips touch her cheek. He steps back, acutely aware of the weight of his body, of its health. 'Oh, Mum,' he says. 'I'm so glad I'm here.'

They spend the first day taking it in turns to sit beside her bed for as much time as they're allowed. The hospital is lax about visiting restrictions, leaving whole families clustered round beds in the ward for hours on end, playing cards and peeling fruit and interrogating staff, and there are times Jeremy wishes someone would ask them to leave more often than they do. A nurse they grow to know and like, a sturdy woman with long grey hair in a bun and a few words of English, has hugged them both briefly a number of times and offered them glasses of water, which Jeremy accepted and Rachel refused. There is one hard chair and they take it in turns to use it, while the other one perches on the bed. Sometimes Andreas is with them. At other times, during the morning, they see him talking to doctors in the corridor before they are all hustled out to wait in the car park, where Jeremy smokes one cigarette after the next. And then the doctors go and they are let back into the ward, like dogs into a house.

At first their mother asked them both to stay with her, hanging on to their arms, their wrists, with an unexpectedly strong grip, pulling herself towards them. But that didn't last. The first one to be sent away, not long after their arrival, was Jeremy. They had been sitting in painful silence for long minutes, neither of them wanting to talk to her in front of the other, or that was how it felt to Jeremy, who cradled his mother's hand in his while Rachel fussed with the sheet corners at the bottom of the bed. Neither of them had the courage to ask her how she feels, nor what she knows, although Andreas had told them already what she knows. She knows everything.

At the most it's a matter of days, he explains to them this first afternoon, as they stand together in the hospital car park. They have left her sleeping, eaten *tiropita* bought in a local bakery, drunk soda water from small glass bottles. Jeremy would like a cup of decent coffee but all that's available in the bar near the hospital is instant, with long-life milk. Andreas has refused the cigarette Jeremy offered, with Rachel tut-tutting to herself about how on earth he can smoke when Mummy is dying of cancer, and is talking, in his thoughtful, almost guarded way, about how he met their mother. He calls her Essie. No one has ever called her Essie before. When he started, Jeremy thought he was talking about someone else. It wasn't until he said *your mother* that Jeremy began to listen.

He is telling them about the day she came to see him at his farm. 'It isn't really a farm,' he is saying, 'it's only a small piece of land, but I prefer to grow the plants I need. I call it my farm, in any case, and Essie likes that. The man at her hotel had told her about me, that I have my workshop here, my holistic workshop, and she wanted to know if I could help her. Essie had headaches, did you know that? No? She never said? Bad headaches. That first morning she asked if she could help me by working in my garden and I said yes. Not because I needed help, you understand, but because she did.' He looks at Rachel. 'I think you also have headaches,' he says.

Jeremy sees her shrug, shake her head. 'You used to,' he says quickly, before Andreas can continue. 'I remember. When you had your period.'

She blushes. 'I don't remember that.'

'You'd benefit from some holistic treatment,' Jeremy insists, determined to make her suffer. 'Especially if you knew what it was.'

Andreas touches his arm, and he is instantly ashamed. 'I only meant . . .' he began.

'You think your headaches are psychosomatic?' Andreas says, looking at Rachel, purposely avoiding Jeremy's eyes.

She turns away, and then back with an air of defiance. 'I don't believe in that sort of rubbish.'

'Good,' says Andreas, to Jeremy's surprise. 'Because, you know, there is no difference between *psyche* and *soma*, between the mind and the body. They are one. So how can one influence the other? You know this, don't you?'

'I know Mummy's dying,' she says, glaring at Jeremy.

'And there is nothing we can do about this,' he says. 'Essie

209

knows this, but I think you don't know it, not yet. Not entirely.' He takes her hand and holds it for a moment, gradually twisting it round until the palm is up, then uses his other hand to fold the fingers shut as though around something only he can see. 'It is time to go back,' he says. 'She will be waking soon and I don't wish for her to feel abandoned.' He leads Rachel back towards the hospital. Jeremy follows, a few paces behind.

Later that first day, when Rachel has been driven by Andreas to his house to change into something cooler, Jeremy is finally alone with his mother. Her eyes are closed and he doesn't want to wake her. He sits beside the bed on the single chair and looks down at his mother's face in a way that's normally not permitted, the way a man might look at his lover's face or a mother at her child's, concentrated, unfiltered, unwavering, himself invisible to the other. He sees the frailness of the skin around and over her eyes, larger than they should be now that the rest of her face has shrunk back to its essence. Before these strange hot days, he's never seen her without lipstick, she'd never leave her bedroom without it. Often, it was all the make-up she used and she'd replace it as it wore off, or transferred itself to cups and glasses. She'd pass the scarlet tip over her lips, rubbing them together in a way he'd imitate later in his own room with a wet red Smartie, then reach in her bag for a tissue to blot the excess colour off. Now thin and drawn in an odd closed smile against her teeth and gums, her lips are as colourless as the rest of her. She's been out of the sun too long. He stares at her, at the texture of her skin, at the fluffy patches of off-white hair, at the honeycomb of pores and film of sweat. No, not sweat. Horses sweat. Women glow, she's always said, and there is a sort of glow about her, some light from somewhere inside, unless he's imagining it, or wanting it so hard it's true. Her nose is red, the tip of it, as though she has a cold, and there are tiny broken veins in it, and in her cheeks. He'll never have this chance again to see her properly, he thinks, and he's scared it will end, so scared that, perversely, he doesn't want her to wake. He bends further in to see more closely, but the closer he is the less he sees. When he can feel her breath on his lips, he pulls away.

'Aren't you going to kiss me?' she says, her eyes still closed.

'Of course I am,' he says, and does, a light kiss on her cheek.

'That was nice.' She smiles. 'You have a very gentle touch.'

'Thank you,' he says.

'You always have had. When you were a little boy you used to kiss me every morning on my cheek, just like that. Do you remember?'

He shakes his head. 'I was a little boy,' he says.

'You were my little boy.' She turns her head towards him. 'I'm so glad you're here,' she says.

'So am I.'

'You won't leave me, will you?'

'Of course not,' he says.

'Because Andreas will need you too.'

'He's taken Rachel back to his house. With our cases.'

'Our house,' she corrects him, ironic, proud. 'We built it together.'

'You built a house?' he says

'Yes. It was something Andreas had always wanted to do and I thought, well, why not? We spend too much time in other people's houses, old houses, don't you think? It's like wearing other people's unwashed clothes. We get so fetishistic about the past. Sometimes you just want to pull it all down and start again from scratch. So that's what we did. You can see the island from it. Do you know about the island?'

How strange this is, he is thinking, as they talk about his mother's house and the town she has chosen to live in, which he first saw this morning from the window of a stranger's car, as though nothing had happened, as though he were here on holiday and his mother were about to show him the local sights. She is telling him about the hilltop monasteries they saw, from a distance, the day before, but his mind is elsewhere, wondering how much longer she will live. He takes her fingers in his hand and strokes them while she talks about a restaurant Andreas will take them to. There is a part of him that is listening to her words and a part of him, more deeply centred it seems, that is listening to its vehicle, her voice – the cool, appraising, slightly distrustful tone it has always had, as though she's more likely to be amused than not, amused but not convinced, but will nonetheless reserve her judgement. She's started to tell him about her spoken Greek, and how dreadful her accent is, when he hears a woman shouting in the corridor. Heart sinking, he realises at once that it is Rachel. He can't make out what she's saying, but he'd know her high-pitched anger anywhere. His mother seems not to have heard but, when Rachel bursts into the ward, she turns her head towards the door, anxiety clouding her face for the first time. 'Oh dear,' she says.

'I've told them,' says Rachel, stomping, an unleashed fury, towards the bed. 'I've had enough of all this nonsense. You're coming home with me.'

23

RACHEL

Rachel identifies her first, with Jeremy still gawping at the window as though he's never seen the sun before and the hippie boyfriend hovering somewhere behind them both, refusing to be shaken off. Her mother's lying on her back, but she's turned her head towards the door, lifted it slightly from the pillow, then let it fall back. After the first shock of seeing her reduced to this, to skin and bone, all Rachel can do is run towards her through the ward. She hears her own voice echo round the room as if from a distance, and the voices of the other women from their beds, but she takes no notice of them. Everything is lost to her but her mother's eyes, so glaring and demanding, demanding as a child's, as they scan her face and then glance off her face and stare behind her, behind Rachel, disappointed almost, anxious, looking to see who else there is.

'Oh, Mummy,' says Rachel, her heart a mixture of pity and pain, and rage, and jealousy, because what her mother is searching for is Jeremy, it's just so obvious, so bloody obvious. You could have pretended just this once, she says to herself. Just this once you could have pretended that you were pleased to see me.

She hugs her mother to her, forcing the woman's head away from Jeremy and into her breasts, her neck, forcing the woman not to see her son. She is blinded by tears, choked by a hacking, angry crying that rises in her throat and nose. She can feel her mother resisting for a moment and then, through lack of strength, give in and let herself be held, but with her head still stirring, unsettled, against her daughter's body. Rachel feels so big beside her, enormous, out of place.

'Oh, Mummy,' she moans again, her voice thick with snot. She's closed her eyes, to stop the tears and to block out the sight of Jeremy, but she can feel him there still, on the far side of the bed, like a starved dog waiting for a scrap of food from the table. And Mummy is holding out her hand and speaking for the first time, her voice much stronger than anyone would expect, asking him for a kiss as though Rachel weren't even there.

But after half an hour, or maybe more, of awkward, barely interrupted silence, their mother sends Jeremy away, and off he trots, with Andreas, who's been hanging around the ward, a step or two behind him. 'Come and sit here next to me,' her mother says when Jeremy and Andreas have left the ward, and Rachel does as she's told, moving up from the bottom of the bed where she has been smoothing out the sheet and making herself useful, anything rather than sit there and wait for someone else to speak, each word of hers a sort of unwarranted affront apparently, taking the chair that Jeremy has occupied as though he had a right to it, finally relaxing. Her mother's face has become familiar to her again, as though she has always been this taut and pale, as though there were nothing more to worry about. 'Now tell me how you are,' her mother says. She rests her head back on the pillow, her eyes closed, her lips drawn tight in what might be a smile. Rachel feels foolish talking to a woman who could be asleep, or laughing at her.

'I'm fine,' she says. Despite herself, she wishes Jeremy were here.

'You're looking tired,' her mother says, opening her eyes again. 'I worry about you.'

Rachel doesn't believe this for a moment. 'There's no need to worry about me,' she says quickly, more piqued than she would have wanted. 'I'm fine, honestly.'

'And your husband?' She pauses.

My husband? She can't remember his name, thinks Rachel. 'Denny? Denny's fine as well.' She reaches for a tissue from a box by the bed and wipes a film of sweat from her mother's forehead. 'Is there anything I can get you? Are you thirsty?'

Her mother moves her head slowly from left to right against the pillow. It's a ridiculously small pillow, or stack of pillows rather. Rachel is reminded of the princess and the pea, and the memory is so appropriate to her mother that she wonders if she's had this thought before, of her mother sprawled in the lap of luxury, complaining. Daddy always said how impossible she was to satisfy, how endlessly demanding. 'Nothing was ever right for Vanessa,' he's said a thousand times, whenever her name comes up, as if to forestall any discussion, head off any other, more trenchant, criticism. Even when Rachel called him to say she was leaving for Greece, and why, he said, 'She was spoiled, and I'm afraid that I was the one who spoiled her.' He made it sound as though Mummy's illness were a final self-indulgence, an act of spite directed specifically at him, to shame him in some way. She was shocked. She hasn't told anyone this, and Jeremy hasn't mentioned their father once.

'How's Reginald?'

'Daddy? He's fine too.'

Her mother smiles at this and then, to Rachel's surprise, actually begins to laugh. 'What a wonderful life you all seem to be leading,' she says. 'All of you fine. It's like a film by Frank Capra.' She opens one eye to see Rachel's face. She looks as though she's winking. 'I don't suppose you know who Frank Capra is, do you?'

'I never have time to go to the cinema these days.' Rachel's determined not to be annoyed, or not to show it. Determined not to be hurt. Her mother has always made her feel stupid and now, with the woman dying before her eyes in this awful foreign place, she feels unprotected, unarmed. Her spite will die with her, she thinks. She is immediately ashamed.

'And England?' her mother says. She's making small talk, it occurs to Rachel. It's like some sherry thing at Denny's club.

'Oh, England's fine,' she says.

Later, standing in the car park outside the hospital with greasy feta pies in their hands, Andreas tells them she'll be dead by the weekend, if not before, and Rachel's first, appalling, thought is that she would have bought a return ticket if she'd known, and saved some money. Her second thought is less a thought than a sense of emptiness and fright she can't explain, an airlessness, as though she herself were about to die. Later, he begins to pester her about her headaches, though how he knows about them she can't imagine, unless she has foolishly mentioned them to Jeremy and he has blabbed. This dotty Greek, who could so easily have told her just how ill Mummy was before they arrived, is spouting some nonsense about herbs, because that's how they first met, she supposes. She thinks of her mother, in some patch of foreign land where he

216

grows his herbs. Essie, he calls her. No one has ever called her Essie, to Rachel's knowledge. She wonders what her mother thinks of it. She'd always insisted on Vanessa with everyone; she'd even tried to get them both to use her name, as though she felt ashamed to be their mother, but that hadn't worked, with her at least. Jeremy was different in that as well. He'd have called her Lady Bountiful if she'd asked him to, and she's surprised he doesn't; she's always been generous to a fault with him. Oh Mummy, she thinks, with an unexpected twitch of pain, why have you always held me that little distance away from you, at arm's length, as though you still haven't made up your mind about me, about whether I'll do or not? As if I was something to be ashamed about, or explained away? I wish to God I was at home with Denny, she thinks, while Andreas gathers the scraps of greasy paper from their hands and carries them across to a nearby bin. 'She may have woken up,' he says, walking back to them with his innocent smile, and then, in his odd, affected English, 'I don't wish for her to feel abandoned.' And it's all she can do not to tell him to just bugger off and leave them be, tell him that it's no concern of his. Except that it is. He calls her Essie. Essie, she says to herself as they walk back into the ward, feeling the word in her mouth as something foreign, and not entirely welcome.

'This is the house we built together, Essie and I,' Andreas tells her later, as they get out of the car. It's a long, low place, made of lime-washed concrete, with a flat roof, all of it blinding white in the sun, and bare earth between the car and the building. It reminds her of the stables back at home, apart from the smell. Here, instead of horse manure, is the scent of some herb she can't place. Thyme, perhaps. The windows are small, square, shuttered, evenly spaced in a row along the otherwise unadorned wall. It's a stand-offish sort of place, she thinks, as she closes the car door behind her and smooths the creases from the back of her skirt. She's sweating in the heat. All those times she's imagined her mother in Greece she's had this picture in her head of vine-covered porticoes and geraniums in pots, of red tiles on the roof and that blue you see in the advertisements. But the shutters are painted dark green and there isn't a plant to be seen. Andreas hurries ahead, carrying her case before she has a chance to take it from him, and opens the door. 'Come in,' he says, standing back to let her pass. She steps across the threshold. What she expected were terracotta floors and beams and woven rugs. What she finds is a room that seems to occupy the whole house, and opposite the door what looks like an entire wall of glass, with a lake beyond it and, at the centre of the lake, an island. 'Oh,' she says, despite herself. 'How lovely.'

'It's our lake,' he says.

'Yours?'

He laughs. 'Well, not only ours. We share it with everyone else.'

The sun is above the lake, its reflection visible in the water. Rachel is startled by the beauty of it, and then resentful. 'So this is where Mummy has been living,' she says.

'Yes.' He takes her case through a door to the left. 'This is your room,' he calls back, over his shoulder. 'There is also a small bathroom, but you will have to share it with your brother. I am sorry.'

'Thank you,' she says. 'That's fine.'

'Can I give you something? Some water?'

'No,' she says, then realises how churlish this sounds and changes her mind. 'I mean, yes, I'm sorry. A glass of water, please.' But when it comes, on a small silver tray hanging beneath an ornate handle, like an empty birdcage, she no longer wants it. Even water would make her sick. The anger she's been feeling since she arrived in Greece, anger with Jeremy and with her mother, anger with her body, which has let her down and dirtied her, and with this tall attentive man who is standing beside her, a look of concern on his face as she puts the full glass back on the delicate ornate tray, anger with all this beauty she hasn't expected and doesn't want, and with the money this house must have cost for all its apparent modesty, because she isn't entirely stupid, all this anger is about to come to the surface and it is all she can do not to hurl the glass to the floor.

'Let me show you our wonderful house,' he says. Before she can stop him, he has put down the tray on a long wooden table and taken her by the elbow. 'You were surprised when you came in, I saw that,' he says, leading her across to the wall of glass. 'You expected something small and dark. This is the effect we wanted, to move from the darkness promised by a closed wall into the light of the world beyond. Like an aperture,' he pauses, as if uncertain of the word. 'An embrace, perhaps, but out, not in. I'm not explaining this to you very well,' he says. 'I'm sorry. Essie, your mother, is the person who should explain.' He pushes a panel of glass to one side and the heat floods in. 'That is our lake,' he says, pointing with his free hand, the fingers of the other hand clenched, unrelenting, on her elbow – she'll have marks there when he lets go. 'The lake of Ioannina. There are boats from the town that carry people across to the island. There are restaurants there. Perhaps we shall go before you leave.'

She shifts a little to release her arm. But when he walks away from her, towards the opposite side of the house from the room she has been given, she follows him, unexpectedly lost. He opens a door and they are in a second room, not much smaller than the first, set at right angles to it, with most of the walls concealed by bookshelves. Mats, of the kind people use for exercise, are arranged in two rows on the floor. 'This is our healing room,' he says. 'The morning sun is strongest in here. Later, it moves round to other parts of the house.' He crosses to the nearest window, beckons her across with a smile. 'You can see your bedroom, look, over there.' Again, he points. She's keeping her distance, she doesn't want to be touched by him again; she can still feel the pressure of his hand on her arm. For a moment, she wonders why she should trust him. A woman, alone, in a house she doesn't know, with a man she doesn't trust. But now she's being silly. She follows the line of his finger and sees not only the window he's expecting her to see, which is also shuttered, but the space between, paved, with a small pool at the centre, and low stone benches around it. The window of the main room is to the left of this, but she hasn't noticed the pool before now. She wonders how she could have missed it. The house is playing tricks on her, she thinks. 'There are four bedrooms over there,' he says. 'Come with me and I will show you.'

They're back in the main room when she stops. 'I suppose Mummy paid for all this,' she says.

He seems surprised, although surely he must have expected to be asked sooner or later. Who wouldn't have expected it? Jeremy, perhaps, but Jeremy has never had any sense of money. He's done nothing but throw it away since they arrived. So much waste, she thinks. He has always been a wastrel.

'Not all of this, no,' he says, after a moment. His face has an expression of distaste, as though he's been given something bad to eat. He picks up the tray and carries it across to a kitchen area at the far side of the room. It's open space, she thinks, in an unconnected way, I've always wondered what people saw in it. Her mother must have spent hours here, cooking her outlandish meals for them both. 'What's a healing room?' she says.

'You know the word *healing*?' he says. His tone is sarcastic; it's the first time he hasn't sounded like some brain-addled Eastern guru. She's annoyed him finally, which gives her considerable satisfaction.

'Of course I do,' she says, her tone matching his, or trying to. 'It's just that I've always assumed you needed to do a bit more than sprawl around on the floor. To be *healed*, I mean.'

'Sometimes that can be more than enough,' he says. 'If people really want to be healed.'

'Like Mummy, you mean?' she says. 'Or doesn't she want to be healed? Is that what you're saying? Why don't you heal Mummy in your healing room?'

He stares into her eyes until she has to turn away. 'There is so much anger in you,' he says. 'I ask myself where it comes from. Essie has spoken to me about your father. About what he did. That must be hard for you to accept.'

'How dare you bring up my father,' snaps Rachel. She still can't bring herself to look at him. She'd hit him if she dared.

'Essie's anger was damaging to her. Even now, she cannot speak of your father without anger. It is part of what is killing her, this anger.'

'You're not saying Daddy's responsible?' Rachel seethes. She sees herself from a distance, the child she is. She could cry with rage. 'That's it,' she says. 'I've had enough of this. You're the one who's killing Mummy with all your healing nonsense. How dare you accuse my father!'

The blood leaves Andreas's face. How odd, she thinks, to see someone so tanned look drained like this, as though he's been stripped clean of everything but shock. 'I will show you the bathroom,' he says stiffly.

'I don't want the bathroom,' she says. 'I want you to take me back to the hospital this minute.'

24

JEREMY

Jeremy hurries Rachel out of the ward before she can say another word. 'For God's sake, calm down,' he hisses, marching her past the row of gawping old women in their beds. To his surprise she lets herself be led, all the way down the corridor and out of the hospital. She is shaking. The second he lets her go, she turns on him. Her face is flushed and damp with sweat; there's a tiny pool of it glistening in the hollow of her upper lip. Behind them both, at the edge of Jeremy's gaze, two nurses are sharing a cigarette. They stop talking to watch, detached but curious, as Rachel starts to rant. She's spluttering with rage.

'He's stolen all our money to build himself a house,' she says, as Jeremy steps back. 'And now he's killing her, you can see what he's been doing up at that awful place. He's had her lying on *mats*, Jeremy. No wonder she's nearly dead. We've got to get her away from him before it's too late.'

She's gone mad, he thinks. 'It's already too late,' he says. 'Can't you see that?'

'You're not a doctor,' she cries. 'What do you know?'

'I've seen people die before,' he says.

She looks at him, puzzled, and then with contempt. 'Well, of course you have. I'd forgotten. All your nancy-boy friends.'

'She can't be moved from here, even if it were the right thing to do,' he says, ignoring this for now. 'Which it isn't.' He'll get his revenge when she least expects it. 'Even if it's what she wanted herself, which it *obviously* isn't.' He reaches in his pocket for a cigarette, lights it while Rachel twitches in front of him. 'I mean, have you even listened to her? She loves this place. She loves him. Have you the slightest idea what she's thinking, or feeling?' He takes a drag, exhales the smoke as slowly as he can. 'You know what it is, don't you? You've gone completely bloody bonkers.'

'We've left him alone in there with her,' says Rachel, glancing from side to side in a jerky, anguished fashion, as though she's heard nothing of what he's said, or couldn't care less. 'He'll talk her round again, you'll see.' She sucks in her breath as though her life depends on it; the puddle of sweat drips down onto her heaving chest. 'Of course, I know *you* don't care. You don't give a damn about money, do you? You're not desperate. You've been throwing the stuff around as though it grew on trees ever since we got here. I suppose you imagine it makes me feel inadequate. You do, don't you? That it makes me feel like a failure compared to you. As though I wanted your bloody money. You think you're a writer, don't you? An artist.' Her tone signals new heights of disgust. 'Well, let me tell you something, Jeremy, in case you don't already know. You're nothing but a bloody pornographer.' Unexpectedly she lurches towards him, burns herself on the cigarette. 'Oh shit, shit, shit.'

'I've had enough of you,' he says, with as much composure as he can find in himself. He can't believe what he's heard. Not the insults; he's known what she thinks about him for years, and this knowledge has consoled him in his darker moments. It's the astonishing news that she's under the impression he's rich, just as he was, of her, until this moment, that's thrown him utterly off balance. And yet, all at once, everything makes sense. She's here for the money. She's here to take whatever money their mother might leave and run off with it to her loathsome Dennis.

He has nothing more to say to her. He's about to go back into the ward when she lunges again, this time at his shirt, plucking it from his back. He resists, there is a rip. It is his favourite one, a white linen shirt he bought with the first money from *Cabins of Passion*, the shirt he was wearing when he met Jean-Paul. 'Oh my fucking Christ,' he says, spinning on her and thrusting her away.

'You're filthy!' she screams.

'And you're mad!' he screams back. She stumbles, falls sideways. Before he quite grasps what is happening, she is down on one knee in front of him, awkwardly, both hands on the gravel, and he is pushing her again, harder this time, with a surge of glee. She lands on her shoulder, twists round like a floored beast, bare legs thrashing in the air as she struggles to regain her balance. She is gasping for breath, flushed. He steps back, excited by what he's done, thrilled by the sight of her lying on the ground in front of him, her skirt ridden up to her thighs, her knickers showing as she rolls back onto her side, pulling her knees up towards her chest. She's on all fours when he shoves her a third time, with the flat of his shoe. He's never felt stronger, or more alive. He's about to kick her when someone grabs his arm. Turning to see who it is, he's tugged away from his sister by one of the nurses he noticed before. The other one is helping Rachel to her feet. Both of them are talking, but in Greek; he's not even sure what their tone is. Rachel is being held now, and he recognises the nurse as one he's seen in his

225

mother's ward. She's stroking the back of Rachel's head. Rachel is reaching round towards him and saying it's his fault, and there is blood on her hand, where she has broken the skin on the gravel of the car park, the palm is black with blood and dirt from the ground. She'll need to get that dressed, he thinks, and then, mildly hysterical, it occurs to him that it couldn't have happened in a better place. It's a hospital. He wants to reassure her, to say there's bound to be a doctor somewhere. I almost kicked her, he remembers, and wonders at himself. Mum would have told him not to be such a bully. If she could have seen him though, and known how he felt, he wonders what she'd have thought. She's only yards away, as the crow flies. He can feel her presence.

'If you breathe a word of this to anyone,' his sister says, 'I'll never speak to you again.'

When he enters the ward there's no sign of Andreas. His mother is lying back, her eyes closed, her hands crossed on her breast. For a moment, heart stopped, he thinks she's dead. He glances around the place as he hurries to the bed, but no one seems to have noticed or, if they have, to care. When he takes the chair beside her, his back to the door, she opens one eye and smiles a little before closing it, against the sunlight perhaps. 'I'm just going to have a little sleep,' she says. He nods and thinks of taking one of her hands in his, to hold it and feel the life in it, but decides in the end to leave her as she is. The smile is still on her lips. He wonders what she's thinking, if anything, or dreaming. He's tempted to close his own eyes. It occurs to him that what he really wants to do is talk to her about Jean-Paul, tell her what he remembers about him, how they met, every detail of it. He wants to tell her about his wrists with the fine dark hair, his sleepy, bedroom

226

eyes, which is how he recalls them now, slightly hooded, in league with the half-smile, the bedroom mouth if such a thing exists, half-smile, half-pout, his legs crossed on the sofa, not crossed exactly, an ankle resting on a knee, held there by the hand, the strong-looking capable hand, the crotch of his jeans looking full but not too full, not *frighteningly* full, the polo shirt unbuttoned, the hint of darkness against the pale green of the cotton, the kind of chest he loves, the soft abrasiveness of hair on his lips. He wants to tell her that this time he has found the man for him, the man of his dreams, all those pretty things. He wants to practise on her, practise the language of love for when he's back in Paris. He's got a hard-on and he's on the point of waking her when someone touches his shoulder. Andreas.

'Rachel?' he says. His mother opens her eyes.

'She's gone for a walk,' says Jeremy. 'She's upset.'

His mother looks at Andreas. 'Go and see if you can find her,' she says. 'See what you can do. Calm her down, darling.'

Jeremy would tell them both how unlikely it is that Andreas could calm her down, although surely Andreas must already know this, but he wants to be alone with his mother. As she wants, he suspects, to be alone with him.

'He won't be much use, of course,' she says, confirming this, the minute Andreas is out of earshot. 'He's just been telling me about how she behaved in our house.' She reaches across for Jeremy's hand, strokes it. 'He says she was like a rabbit caught in the headlights. They say that here as well, you know. I expect it's universal, wherever there are rabbits and headlights.' She pauses, her hand, her voice, all of it stilled. 'What is the matter with her, do you think? She's seemed so unhappy for so long now.'

'I didn't know you'd seen her that much,' he says.

'Oh, I've been back once or twice,' she says. 'I haven't told you all my recent movements, you know.'

She's flirting with him again, the way she has always done, if only he'd known. He'd thought for years that this was how mothers normally behaved, with this lightness of touch. He hadn't appreciated how extraordinary she was.

'Andreas has taken a liking to you,' she says. 'You will be good to him, won't you? Treat him well. It will be so hard for him when I die. He's come to depend on me more than he should have done.'

'Don't talk like that,' says Jeremy.

'Like what? Like someone who's going to die? I've told you enough lies in the past, my darling. It's time to be honest.'

She's right, thinks Jeremy. He has a sense of time being whipped away from him, from beneath his feet, and of falling, and of having no mother. He can't imagine how that will feel. She's right. It's time to be honest. 'That letter I wrote,' he says.

'Ah yes,' she says. 'That letter.'

A woman on the other side of the ward begins to shout. Jeremy turns his head to look. She is waving her arms in the air and staring at the window as though trying to attract the attention of someone outside.

'Poor thing,' his mother says. 'She thinks she can see her husband.'

'Where is he?'

'Dead, darling. He was killed during the war. The Germans.' She taps the side of her head. 'It was a terrible time.'

'I thought you always said you had a good war.'

She looks mischievous. 'That's also true,' she says. 'But I didn't lose anyone I loved.'

'Not until you left Paris,' he says.

'That's what Armand told you?'

'You know it is. I told you everything he said.'

'That I'd left the love of my life and gone back to England to marry your father because I'd . . . how did you put it? That's it, because I'd lost my nerve.'

'Yes,' he says, reluctantly. He wishes he hadn't mentioned the letter, not now. He wishes he hadn't written the letter in the first place. None of this will matter, he thinks – the past, the things we may or may not have done. We can start afresh every day. Now there's a thought.

'And you believed him?'

'Yes,' he says. Perhaps he has understood nothing, ever.

'Because that's what you do, isn't it, darling?' She rests her head back on the pillow. She can't bring herself to look at him, or perhaps she is simply too tired. 'You believe what people tell you.'

'Not always. Is that what you think I do?' She's hurt him now, made him feel small and gullible, as if trusting someone is a sort of infirmity, and he wonders if that's her aim, to wound and belittle him. What does it mean to hurt, and be hurt, when you're about to die? Is it more important, or less?

'I did love your father, you know,' she says. 'To start with. I loved him very much. And I didn't love Armand quite as deeply as you seem to think.'

'He thinks you did.'

'Still?' She looks at him now. 'Does he know you're here?'

'No,' he says, 'I didn't tell him.'

'I'm glad.' She sighs. 'I wouldn't want him to see me, or think of me, like this. He always attached so much importance to the way people look. I imagine he still does. But you'd know more about that than I do.' As if she has just thought of something, she smiles. 'He told me he thought you were charming, did you know that?'

229

'No,' he says, surprised. And then he remembers that night, when he woke and saw Armand at the foot of his bed.

'Oh yes,' she says. She's staring at him with extraordinary concentration now, but her voice is fading in and out like the voice on a car radio. He takes her hand and holds it as firmly as he dares. 'He was so pleased when I sent you to him.'

'You sent me?'

'Well, you couldn't stay in England, could you, darling? It was killing you. Besides, I had a debt to pay.'

She's said this so often to him in the past, how he'd die if he didn't get out, live somewhere else, both then and later, when he was already out and it was a matter of congratulation and shared triumph, his own precious life so heroically secured against the ogre of his father and his father's world, except that he's no longer sure if any of it was ever really true. He hasn't thought about it for years. He lives where he lives. What did she save him from in the end? Himself?

'I suppose not,' he says. Only now does he hear what she said about a debt. He wonders what she means.

'Besides,' she says, but her voice has almost gone. Her eyelids are heavy, she sounds as though she's half asleep, or worse.

'Besides?'

She lifts her hands, then lets them fall back onto the sheet. The burn scar on her arm is longer, more livid, than he's ever seen it, but, of course, it's the arm itself that has shrunk. Her breathing is weaker by the second. She's about to speak, but something, some pain he can only imagine, intervenes, and she shudders, then winces, and he's not sure if she's wincing at the pain or at what she's saying. 'Armand would have made such a terrible father.' She pauses, draws in air. 'I couldn't let him be her father.'

'Her father?'

'But he was there for you, wasn't he, darling?' She struggles to open her eyes. 'Fair exchange is no robbery, isn't that what they say?' She smiles. 'It's not the sort of thing I normally believe, but maybe they're right after all.' She moves her nearest hand towards him. He reaches out to take it. He wants to ask her what she meant about a debt. He can hardly hear her; he has to bend forward, his ear beside her mouth, to catch her words. Her breath is sour, he wishes it weren't, or that he hadn't noticed. His mother has always smelled so sweet, of face powder and flowers. 'Call me the nurse, will you, darling? I think I need some drugs.'

Standing up, he waves at a nurse by the door just as Rachel comes back into the ward, Andreas behind her. 'Tell her Mum needs some help,' he says, but Rachel runs across.

'Oh, Mummy,' she says, pushing him away with brute force, as though he has no right to be near them. 'I'm here now.' But a moment later the nurse is also there, holding his mother's wrist, and Andreas is coaxing them gently from the bed, despite Rachel's tearful clinging, and Jeremy's rage, which he cannot express. He's unexpectedly aware, as he hasn't been for over an hour, of the rip in his shirt, and at once he's reminded of Jean-Paul. I haven't had a chance to tell her about him, he thinks, and maybe I never will. But of course I will, I'm such a fool. And he imagines how her face will look as he talks to her about love and how this time he has found the right person, as she has done in Andreas, and how this time everything will work out right for him, although it never has before.

And then he thinks about her strange last words, although he doesn't know this, he has no idea that she will never speak again, as the nurse calls for a second nurse, who runs down

231

the centre of the ward, and Andreas holds her face in his hands, his mother's face, bare and gaunt, and he wonders what she means about Armand making such a terrible father, a terrible father to *her*, and how it couldn't be what he thought it was, because that would make no sense at all. Perhaps she meant *him*. Is that possible? He must have misheard, or she's confused, muddled by pain. And then she utters a sort of moan from deep within, a noise he has never heard before and prays he will never hear again, as his mother's life leaves her, and as she leaves them.

25

JEREMY

They say goodbye to Rachel at the airport. It's a small airport and they watch her while she fumbles with her bag at security, dropping her passport and boarding card, her cardigan slipping off her shoulders as she bends to pick them up. She's been crying on and off all morning, and now she starts again. Jeremy sees her fumble for a scrap of paper tissue in her pocket and blow her nose. When her passport has been checked, and she's about to disappear from view behind a partition, Jeremy raises his hand in a final salute, but in vain; she doesn't turn. Andreas touches his shoulder lightly, to comfort him. 'Don't worry about me,' says Jeremy. 'I'm glad she's gone.'

Rachel has spent the last few days since their mother died in a hotel in the centre of the town, refusing to return to the house. She imagined there would be time to fly home and back, reinforced by the presence of Denny for the funeral, but to her, and to Jeremy's, surprise, this has already taken place, two days after the death, in a small brick-built Byzantine-style church just outside town that Andreas said they had chosen together for their marriage. This news, that Andreas and their mother were married, was the only thing that brought brother and sister together, although briefly. They hadn't known. For the rest, all Jeremy has received from Rachel is an aura of hostility so impenetrable he's made only the faintest attempt to break it down. A smile ignored, the briefest touch shrugged off. When he said she was being foolish not to come back with them to the house, she said, her voice charged with loathing, *That murderer's house? I'd sooner die.*

The only time she said more than a few words to him was to ask for his help in returning to Athens, and it was obvious from her tone how much this brief, apparently conciliatory, moment had cost her. That was when they discovered that Ioannina had its own small airport, with direct flights to Athens. I'll never forgive you for making me stay in that filthy hotel, she said, and that's one more item on the list, he thought then, of crimes for which he'll need to seek absolution in some way that's still not clear to him. I'll think about it later, he decided, when I get back home. Now, leaving the airport, sweating in the heat, he sees the ravaged and unrecognisable face of Rock Hudson stare out at him, repeated a dozen times, from the glass-panelled side of a newspaper kiosk. It's the same magazine cover he saw when he arrived, or looks like it, which means he has been here for less than a week. Is that possible? You've outlived Mum, he murmurs to himself, and to Rock. We all have.

They're at the car when Jeremy says, 'I didn't know Mum believed.'

'Believed?'

'In God.'

'She became a member of the church here before we were married.'

'Is that why she did it? So that she could marry you?'

Andreas shakes his head. 'It was her idea. I had no need to marry her in a church. I am born Greek Orthodox, but it has no great importance for me.' He smiles. 'She took theology lessons, and adopted a Greek name. Eleni. She was baptised in the lake, in a white dress she had someone make for her. Very beautiful. She told me she felt born again. Our neighbours brought her gifts of bread. She was very moved.'

'Like a born-again Christian,' says Jeremy. He can't believe this version of his mother.

'No, I don't think like that. I think she simply felt new. Clean, perhaps. Like a new person.'

'You saw a side of her I never did,' says Jeremy, wondering if Andreas will hear the resentment in his voice.

'I saw all of her, I hope. I saw her whole, entire. I think perhaps no other person did.' For the first time, Andreas sounds distressed, and Jeremy regrets his bitter tone. Andreas turns his face away. 'I'm sorry,' he says. 'This is not a competition to see who knew Essie best.'

'But you called her Essie,' says Jeremy. 'Not Eleni.'

'I called her Essie,' Andreas says. He starts the car and pulls out of the airport car park. 'And now I will take you to the island.'

The boat carries them across the lake to the island, the minaret of a mosque emerging from a wooded shore and then disappearing as the boat pulls in to moor at a jetty. The shoreline on either side of the dock is hemmed by beds of dried rushes, but Andreas leads Jeremy away from the water towards what looks to be the island's only village, a cluster of two-storeyed stone houses along narrow lanes, a couple of restaurants. One of these has a loosely woven sack hanging beside the door. When the sack moves, Jeremy looks more closely and sees that it's stuffed with live frogs, glistening in the sunlight as they clamber across each other, webbed feet pressing onto open eyes and ears, to reach the outside of the sack. He remembers the postcard his mother sent to him. He looks at Andreas, who nods. 'Frogs' legs are a speciality of the island,' he says.

A little further on, the wall of a house is covered with bells of various sizes, the kind that hang around the necks of cattle and goats. Ten minutes more and they are standing outside the mosque he saw from the boat. Another ten and they are standing outside a monastery. So many different faiths, so many closed doors and walls, within spitting distance of one another. You could walk round the entire island in not much more than half an hour and Jeremy wonders again how his mother lived here, surrounded by all these cloistered men and flower-filled stifling alleys and shifting reed beds, surrounded by frogs in sacks and clanging bells, so far from the world she loved, of style and laughter and wit, the world she'd left his father in order to find elsewhere. But maybe he'd understood nothing. Maybe she'd been looking for something else entirely, and discovered it here.

'It's time to eat,' says Andreas. They stop outside one of the restaurants they'd passed earlier, then go inside. There is a woman at the far end of the room, beyond the tables, beside a door that leads out to a garden. She has a sack of frogs beside her and is reaching in as one reaches into a carton of popcorn, her wet hand coming out of the sack with a frog in it that she flings onto a wooden chopping board, hard enough to stun the creature, then chops in half. She throws the top half, head and forelegs, into a bucket beneath the table and skins the still twitching lower half with a single gesture, as cleanly and indifferently as if she were peeling off a glove, throwing the back legs into a bowl already half full of half-frogs, almost translucent, alive with them as they kick and struggle, as though still not fully aware of what they've been reduced to, still filled with the last trace of fight.

'I don't think I can eat those,' Jeremy says. 'I feel a bit queasy.'

'It is not the only dish,' Andreas says. 'Come into the garden. There are some tables with shade over there, beneath those trees.'

'Essie read all your books,' says Andreas, pouring the last few drops of wine into Jeremy's glass. 'Not only the ones you sent to her.'

'I didn't think she liked them,' says Jeremy. It doesn't strike him at once that he has no memory of ever having sent his books to his mother, apart from *Cabins of Passion, Tepees of Desire*. She must have ordered them herself, he thinks later, and been ashamed to say so. Perhaps she hadn't wanted to tell him what she thought of them, talk about her disappointment.

'No, that wasn't it. You mean, because she didn't write to you?'

'Well, yes, I suppose so. Apart from a postcard.'

'She found them difficult to read in some ways. But she was also amused.'

'Amused?' Jeremy isn't sure how to take this.

'She said that when she read them she could hear you as a child, playing with your sister. You fought a lot, she told me. You were always fighting over small things: toys, privileges, jealousies. And now that I have seen you together, I can understand what she meant. She said you were happier apart. I thought it was strange that this didn't seem to worry her or to make her sad. Most mothers want their children to protect each other. But now I understand that too. Essie wasn't really born to be a mother.'

'My books reminded her of me as a child?'

'Yes.'

'Have you read them?

'Yes, I have.'

'Do you think they're like children, I mean, like stories about children fighting? Is that what she meant, do you think? Because they aren't supposed to be. They aren't supposed to be about children.' But how would she have known about them, he wonders, unless someone kept her informed? She wouldn't have seen them reviewed, that was certain. Armand?

'I didn't at first. I thought they were written with great skill – you have a way with words – but I didn't like them. They made me feel . . . what is the word . . . grumpy?'

'Grubby?' Jeremy suggests, snippily.

'Thank you, yes. Grubby. But now I think I do.'

'Like them?'

'No. Not that. But I see that, yes, they might be like stories of children. I remember once Essie talking to me about a phrase you have. My English is all her work, you see, she wanted me to have a good command of your language so that she would never be misunderstood. She said that when people want revenge they say they are getting their own back. It is as though something that once belonged to them has been taken and they must have it again to be peaceful. And we talked many hours about what this something might be. Pride, we thought, or face, or what the Italians call *bella figura*. But we could find nothing that justified revenge, nothing of any real importance. And I think your books are about that, about getting your own back from someone. But you don't know what it is that you want to get back either, nor who from. And so you become obsessive and cruel.' He pauses. 'I'm sorry,' he says, in his slow, measured way, as if that might make his words easier to bear. 'I am too blunt.'

'No,' says Jeremy, although he *is* too blunt, and Jeremy is deeply hurt. 'I've never imagined anyone would take them seriously, not really. They're wank books, you see, that's all. That's what they're for,' and he mimes the act of masturbation in case his mother has neglected to teach her foreign husband the word 'wank'.

'Someone has hurt you,' says Andreas.

Jeremy laughs. 'Oh, people have formed queues to do *that*,' he says.

Andreas nods. 'And yes, there is also self-pity in your work.'

'I hadn't realised I was revealing myself so entirely,' says Jeremy, now irritated. 'I thought everyone assumed I was Nathalie Cray, for a start.'

'You have a soft heart,' says Andreas, after a moment's thought. 'You flew here to be with your mother. You cannot bear to see a dead frog skinned. And yet people are tortured to death in your books and you pretend this has something to do with love.'

'That isn't true,' says Jeremy hotly. 'That's not what they're for at all. I told you.' And he repeats the gesture of wanking until he notices a man at a nearby table nudging his girlfriend and pointing towards Jeremy with a grin. He wants to say that he's changed, that his books have changed since Gilberto died, but doesn't know how.

Andreas smiles. 'It is fiction, of course. I'm sorry.'

'In any case, I only write them because I'm asked to,' says Jeremy. 'I do it for the money. My mother was never supposed to read them.' So why had he given her a signed copy of *Knife in the Heart* five years ago in Paris? And what had he written in it? Some nonsense he can't bear to remember, and can't forget. Why had he sent her *Cabins of Passion* if not to receive her praise?

'I see,' says Andreas. He calls the waiter over, gives him some money.

'Please,' says Jeremy, 'I'll get this.'

'No, no,' says Andreas, standing up, brushing crumbs from his clothes. 'It gives me pleasure to offer you lunch.'

They spend the afternoon in the room overlooking the lake, drinking more wine, talking about Jeremy's mother. Jeremy cries more than once as Andreas turns the pages of photograph albums he has never seen before, had no idea existed. He sees his mother as a girl, as a young woman, in the dress she was wearing in the photo in Grenier's apartment, with his father, with Rachel as a child, with him, less often with them both. More recent albums show her as she travels – in Istanbul and San Francisco and somewhere in India – after the divorce. She is cooking, or standing beside a bridge, or shopping. He had no idea what she was doing in those years, his first years in Paris. She was always so vague about her plans. She'd change her mind at the last minute, meet someone new, develop some new enthusiasm. He saw her life as enviable and mysterious, and as something that excluded him always, as though his life were the dark side of a minor moon that orbited hers – her life, her world. He's never understood this before, not fully, this anger at how little she has given him. He has always thought of himself as privileged to have been her son. And now he sees her in the company of people whose names he will never know, laughing, her head thrown back, or with that look of passionate concentration he always hoped to provoke in her, and so rarely did, it seems. With him she was always distracted, always looking out of a window or leafing through a glossy magazine, always on the point of leaving.

Andreas must see how upset he is. When Jeremy gets up from the couch and walks across to stare, or pretend to stare, at the lake, Andreas also stands up and puts his arm round Jeremy's shoulder. 'She will always be with you,' he says, and this is so far from the truth, as Jeremy sees it, that it is all he can do not to laugh. 'She will always be with us both,' says Andreas, and Jeremy nods, and looks at the island as hard as he can until his vision clears.

Later that afternoon, when Andreas is busy somewhere and has left him alone in the house, Jeremy picks up the phone, trying to control his shaking hand, and dials the number he has been carrying around with him since he left Paris, a number that never seems to end, so many numbers to remember, because he has remembered, even the prefix for France, as if he'd known he'd be calling from somewhere else. The scrap of paper he has had in his wallet has no other purpose than to act as a talisman, a reminder that Jean-Paul exists beyond the febrile walls of Jeremy's sexual imagination. He finishes the number and waits as two countries get their act together, a noisy, buzzing, clicking procedure during which so much might go wrong. He's about to give up, redial, or not redial, when the call tone starts and then, before he has had a chance to consider putting down the receiver, because what is the point of this call other than to compound his misery and sense of loss, a voice answers and it is the voice of Jean-Paul, a voice he has expected never to hear again.

'Hello,' he says, in English. 'It's me.'

'Hello, me.'

Is this a joke, thinks Jeremy, or does he really have no idea who I am? How many me's can there be in the world of Jean-Paul? 'Jeremy,' he says quickly, as if he'd been interrupted.

'I know that. I was wondering where you'd got to,' says Jean-Paul.

Jeremy feels sick with joy.

'Were you?'

'I've been calling you but you're never in.'

'I'm in Greece,' he says, 'I'm calling from Greece.'

'You're on holiday in Greece and you didn't tell me,' says Jean-Paul. 'Now I'm really upset.'

'No, don't be,' says Jeremy. Please God, not that, not now. 'It's family stuff, I'll tell you all about it when I get back.' He pauses. The line is awful, crackling with static. For a moment, he wonders if the charming, amenable man at the other end is Jean-Paul at all, or someone else.

'I'm sorry about that evening,' the voice says. 'I had to go out. I've been calling to explain.'

'Don't worry,' says Jeremy, but the line has gone dead and all he can hear is his own voice echoing back at him, saying the word *worry*.

Andreas goes to bed before Jeremy. Jeremy finishes the final bottle of wine, then wanders into the healing room to see if he can find the copy of *Knife in the Heart* he gave his mother, but there are too many books and none of them are his. He finds an illustrated volume of Greek sculpture and lies on one of the mats, his shirt unbuttoned, the book propped on his chest, the black-and-white plates scraping his nipples as he turns them, his penis stiffening as the perfect nudes parade before him. Finally, he puts the volume to one side and unzips his trousers, jacking off until he comes with a long, silent shudder. He lies on the mat, exhausted, then uses his shirt to wipe the sperm from his stomach. Trembling a little, he stands up, replaces the book on the shelf, then takes off his shirt and steps out of his trousers. He looks around the room as if he has no idea where he is nor how he has arrived there. Leaving his clothes on the mat, he walks to the far end of the room and opens the door.

This is the part of the house his mother slept in, with Andreas, always with Andreas. There is a short corridor, a brightly coloured woven carpet on the floor, windows along one wall leading to their room. He follows the corridor to its end, then opens the door and walks across to the bed, as silent as the lake outside. The blinds have been left undrawn and the room is barely illuminated by the cool light of the moon. He lifts the single sheet protecting Andreas. Slowly, he slides himself in behind the other man, who is also naked. He slips an arm around his waist and waits. Andreas shifts a little beneath Jeremy's arm and then takes his hand and holds it, their fingers entwined into something that is both a cage and an embrace.

They lie together until both of them are asleep.

26

RACHEL

Rachel is sitting in Heathrow arrivals lounge, her suitcase beside her. She left a message with Maeve last night that she'd be there at five-fifteen, but now the plane's landed over an hour after the scheduled time she's worried that Denny might have had some other engagement and not been able to wait. She was lucky to have found Maeve at the stables so late, but if only Denny had called her back, as she'd asked, they could have sorted out a plan B. There's never a plan B these days, it seems to Rachel, whose head is splitting from the landing and all that ear-popping business, which she's always hated. She might have burst eardrums, the woman in the seat next to her said; that would explain it. She'll talk to Dr Slocomb about it as soon as she gets home. Which, this minute, is all she wants from the world: for Denny to walk through the revolving door and pick up her suitcase and drive her home. At least she's lost weight these past few days, after that dreadful episode on the train, and all the filthy foreign food she's been expected to eat. Now that she's safe and sound in her own country, with all the familiar shops around her, it's hard to believe what's happened. Hard to believe that Mummy's dead and buried, or cremated, perhaps. She isn't even sure of that.

She couldn't bear to watch at the end of it, that awful funeral. She doesn't know what she'll say to Denny about it all. And now there is that nasty gurgling sensation again. If she wasn't looking out for him she'd nip across to Boots and see what they have for upset stomachs.

Here he is finally, pushing through the crowds of people as though he owns the place. He's lost weight too since she left, she notices, and at once she feels a twinge of guilt. He'd starve to death without her there to look after him. 'Here you are,' he says, and when she stands up to be kissed he moves her roughly to one side to pick up her suitcase. 'You might have let me know which terminal. I've been driving round like a bloody fool for over half an hour.'

'I'm sorry,' she says. 'I didn't know either. I thought you'd be able to find out when you got here.'

'Oh you did, did you? By shouting from the car, I suppose.' He takes her arm with his free hand, traps it beneath his own. 'Fucking airports. It's all done for the Saudis these days, the whole of London's running rings round itself to keep them happy. Petrodollars, that's what it is.'

Rachel tries to keep herself from crying, slows down, stops, gripping his forearm with her elbow so that he can't get away.

'So the old girl's snuffed it, then,' he says, after a moment. He does care, she thinks. She blames the traffic; he hates driving in traffic. 'Must have been a bit of a shock.'

'Well, yes,' she says.

'You seem a bit peaky yourself,' he says, looking at her for the first time, his blue eyes finally turned to hers. 'I hope you haven't caught anything.'

'Oh, Denny,' she says, 'it's been awful.'

'Has it, love?' he says, concern in his voice for the first time. 'Well, yes, I suppose it must have been. I don't suppose your pansy brother was much use either.' He pauses, looks round the concourse of shops, fast-food outlets, and all at once she knows what for. And she's right.

'I know what you need,' he says. 'A snifter.'

It's the first time they've made love in ages. He starts off as usual, with the lights dimmed on that switch he's had installed, his hands working up beneath her nightie until they reach her breasts, pushing the cloth up as he goes so that she's lying with rucked-up rolls of fabric beneath her back. She turns her head to one side to avoid the whisky on his breath, but the bristles of his chin are already scratching at her neck and she takes his head between her hands to lift it away from her for a moment until he jerks away and nuzzles back down between her breasts, his beard scraping at the skin where she caught the sun in Greece, nudging and grunting a little, like a puppy after milk. Her hands fall away as he forces her legs apart with his knee, levering it until her thighs fall open and then his fingers are inside her, parting her roughly. Not yet, she whispers, not yet, Denny darling, but he doesn't hear, he's too busy. He's playing with her breasts and she lies there, hoping he won't be too rough, the way he can be. Sometimes he hurts her so much it's all she can do not to cry out, but she doesn't want to interrupt the flow of his passion for her, his nails like pincers on her nipples, the graze of his teeth, not tonight; it's been so long. She'll let him do what he wants. He thrusts his penis into her; instinctively, she tenses. Yes, he mumbles against her flesh, that's it, like that, she can feel his hot wet breath rasping at her like a file. And then, before she's had time to respond, he's spent and lying on top of her, with one long exhalation, all the dead weight of him pinning her down. She tries to move him a little to one side, to breathe herself, but he settles his body more firmly on hers with an irritated wriggle. Minutes later, he's asleep and snoring. She lies still until she's sure he won't wake, then edges out from beneath him. All the exhaustion accumulated over the past two weeks has disappeared and all she can think of is Mummy in hospital, as though everything else she has ever known about her mother has been wiped out, to leave her with an image as flat and unforgiving as a final demand, and as difficult to ignore.

Next morning, in the kitchen, his dressing gown hanging open, Denny makes tea directly in the cup while Rachel glances through the newspaper, reading nothing, her eyes flitting from headline to headline, resting briefly on the by-now-familiar face of the dying actor. When she glances up with a sigh, she sees Denny's penis, sore-looking, shrunken into its nest of hair. I must get over this aversion, she thinks. 'Have you told Daddy?' she says.

He sips his tea. 'About what?'

'About what happened in Greece,' she says. She can't bring herself to say the words Mummy and death. She can't believe he needs to ask.

'Didn't feel it was my place, my dear,' he says. To her surprise, he walks across and strokes her hair with his free hand. She leans a little into the stroke. It's as though she has only now come home.

'You're right,' she says. 'I'll do it this morning.'

'You just relax,' he says.

'How have things been here?' she asks him.

He shrugs. 'More bloody bills. The Fletchers have pulled out.'

'But I thought they'd promised?'

'Horse thieves and liars,' he says. 'It's in their blood.' He strokes her hair again, more firmly this time. 'I don't suppose the old girl thought about you, did she?'

'Thought about me?'

'You know, financially.'

Oh, she thinks.

'She must have had a fair bit of, well, you know—'

'Money?'

He steps back. 'There's no need to say it like that,' he says.

'Like what?' She genuinely wants to know what tone he's heard. For herself, she has no idea. She wishes she did.

'As though I were some money-grubbing, I don't know—'

'No,' says Rachel. She'll let him stew in the greed of his own juices for a little. She wants to force him to ask her what she means. When he doesn't, when he furls his dressing gown around his nakedness, as if to protect himself, and moves even further away from her to lean on the rail of the Aga, holding his cold tea in both hands, she stands up. 'I'm going to call Daddy.'

'*No* what?'

She smiles to herself. This time, at least, she's won. 'No, she didn't think about me. Financially. At least, I don't think so. I told you about the set-up in the car last night. You don't remember, do you? How she was living with this dreadful Greek who's spent all her money on some hare-brained clinic? You weren't listening, were you? I didn't think you were.'

He spreads his arms, mutely pleading. When the dressing gown falls open again, she sees his penis twitch. 'I heard every word,' he says. 'Every word.' He steps across and pulls her to him and they stand in the middle of the kitchen, his penis stiffening against her nightie. Is this what she wants, she wonders, and then, when he kisses her, she slides her own arms around him, still not sure, and lets herself be kissed.

Half an hour later, they have showered and eaten breakfast together. Not another word has been said about money. So Rachel is surprised when Denny tells her they'll be having a lodger.

'I thought we could make a little bit of cash from the room at the end,' he says. 'Every penny helps.'

'The nursery?'

'That's the one. Maeve's been thrown out of her bedsit in town, you see, and sleeping here means she can get off to a good start in the morning instead of turning up late one morning in two. She'll save on transport, she'll pay us rent. We can't lose.'

'I'm not sure about the nursery,' says Rachel.

'But it isn't, though, is it? It isn't a nursery.'

His tone is so reasonable she can't argue against it. But how can she be reasonable?

'It's time we moved on, love,' he says. And the 'we' is a sort of comfort to her. She thought he'd moved on ages ago, and left her, frozen into stillness.

'I suppose so,' she says.

Ten days later, the phone rings. Denny leaves them both at the table and goes into the hall to answer it, coming back a moment later.

'It's Madame Pompadour,' he says.

Maeve giggles. Rachel puts down her glass and leaves the room.

'I see Denny's glittering wit remains undimmed,' says Jeremy.

'You know what he's like,' says Rachel. 'He means no harm.'

'So you got home safely?'

'Yes. Are you calling from Paris?'

'Yes. Back last night.'

'You stayed until last night? I thought you had a flight booked a few days ago?'

There's a pause. It's a poor line. Perhaps he hasn't heard. She's about to repeat herself when he answers.

'No, I had some stuff to sort out.'

'Oh.' Another pause.

'Look, Rachel, I've got some money for you.'

'Can you say that again?'

'Money, Rachel. Andreas sorted out the money. That's what I stayed for. He gave me a banker's order, well, two actually. One each.'

'How very generous of him,' she says, although what she wants to say is *How much?* She cranes round until she can see into the kitchen, to let Denny know in some way, but he's sitting with his back to her. He's talking to Maeve and doesn't notice. Maeve does, although she pretends not to.

'It *is* actually, Rachel. She left us nothing. What he's done is give us the money they had in their joint account. Most of it, anyway. I wouldn't let him give it all away.'

'It wasn't his to give,' she says, but inside she's exultant. With money arriving, they can move Maeve out.

'He's a good man,' says Jeremy. 'Our mother was lucky to have known him. You should have stayed, Rachel, honestly.'

'Oh, I don't know, Jeremy,' she says. 'I don't know what to think.'

Again, no answer.

'Are you still there, Jeremy?'

'Yes.'

'How are you?'

'I'm fine.'

'No, I mean, really.'

'Really? I can't believe Mum's dead. None of it makes sense, does it?'

'Is there anyone there with you?'

'No. I wish there was.'

'Is there anyone at all? In your life, I mean?'

'I don't know. I thought there might be. Now I'm not so sure.'

'I'm sorry, Jeremy.'

'Don't be,' he says and she wonders what he's thinking. That he'd rather be alone than be with someone like Denny.

'Denny's a good man too,' she says. 'You don't know him.' She glances into the kitchen and catches Denny's hand as it touches Maeve's hair, and the look on Maeve's face as she stares through the open door at Rachel, of bare-faced cheek and triumph. When Jeremy doesn't answer her, she says, 'No, I won't be sorry.'

It isn't until she puts the phone down and is about to return to the kitchen that she realises she never asked Jeremy how much money she was getting. Denny will be furious. And that, she decides, will serve him right.

PART THREE

(1977)

27

JEREMY

Jeremy is asleep. He is lying in a single bed in a large house on the outskirts of Whitstable, but he is also walking along a corridor filled with statues of naked athletes who turn towards him and smile as one, beckoning him with their marble hands. Before he can respond, the corridor comes to a halt and he is saved from what would otherwise be a fall to certain death by a wind that shifts him, leaf-like, onto a ledge. He is high above a wooded valley, high in the mountains, the same wind whistling about his ears. And then the wind carries him again and he is swimming in the warm soft air above an endless sea until one of the athletes from the corridor, the one with the discus, appears before him and kisses him, the marble tongue unexpectedly warm and wet in his mouth.

He wakes up, blankets on the floor, cold in the pre-dawn air from the window. It is four-fifteen. He knows this without needing to look at the clock beside his bed. It is always four-fifteen when he wakes up with the warmth and moistness of someone else's dream tongue still in his mouth and the dull throb of the hangover he will have the next morning already knocking gently at his temples. It is four-fifteen and it will be four-fifteen until he goes back to sleep, whenever that will be. It will always be four-fifteen.

'What time did you get in last night?' His mother is sitting at the kitchen table. She is listening to Radio Three, a cigarette in her mouth, a paperback splayed open in her hand. She treats books badly, snaps their spines to get to the matter they contain. Jeremy can't bear what she does to books.

'What are you reading?'

'Sybille Bedford,' his mother says round the cigarette. 'I adore her.' She shows Jeremy the cover, a baroque angel behind horizontal stripes of colour, red and green, in white italic script the title: *A Favourite of the Gods*.

'Lucky Sybille Bedford,' says Jeremy. He takes a bottle of milk from the fridge, drinks from it, then holds the bottle against his forehead.

'Well, yes and no,' she says. 'We do have glasses, Jeremy. And not only for wine.'

'I don't suppose there's any post for me?'

She shakes her head, stubs out her cigarette. Jeremy picks up her packet from the table, offers it open to his mother, who shakes her head, then lights a cigarette himself.

'I'm going to make some coffee,' he says.

'Lovely,' she says. 'I'll join you.' She watches him spoon coffee into the paper cone of the filter. He can feel her eyes on him, questioning. 'Are you expecting something?'

For a second he's tempted to tell her about the poems he sent off to the *London Magazine*, the ones sent back by *Agenda* and *Stand* and *Poetry Wales*, the ones he wrote during his year out in Montpellier in a series of small black numbered note-books, for posterity, and then typed up on his Olivetti in the dreary weeks he's spent at home since he got his degree. But telling her would mean showing her the poems, because of course she would ask to see them, and he isn't prepared for that. They're poems about love, about heartbeats and skin against skin, about dried flowers and the scent of freshly made coffee and suffering, and he doesn't want to talk about love or its intimate hinterlands to his mother. More than anything, he doesn't want to be forced to admit to her that the poems are works of the purest, and impurest, imagination. Publishing is one thing: showing his mother is something else. She said to him yesterday afternoon, in one of their endless conversations about his father, that it wasn't the business of men to talk about love, that there was something unattractive about it, and he held his tongue, as always on this topic, because to contradict her would be tantamount to confession.

'No,' he says. Pouring out the coffee into two cups, his back to her, he mouths, *It's white hot and our secretive bands of white / call out to each other across the grass* and immediately his dick gets hard inside his jeans. Surely someone out there must see how wonderful these poems are, how effectively they work on the body. Maybe there will be an answer tomorrow.

'So what time did you get in?' she asks again.

'Oh, I don't know,' he says. 'Late.'

'And you were with?'

'No one you know.'

'Try me.'

'Honestly, Mum, I didn't see anyone really. I just wandered round a bit.' If only all this weren't true, he thinks. If only he had something to conceal.

'He wanted to know what your plans were,' she says. 'Again.'

'Really? And what did you say?'

'That you were still deciding what to do. What else could I say? That you wanted to join the family business?'

'I suppose she just sat there next to him, pulling that face of hers.'

'You mustn't talk about Rachel like that,' she says, lighting another cigarette, not offering him the packet. Her little, formal punishment. But he knows how much she enjoys this kind of comment.

'This was at breakfast, was it?'

'Yes.'

'That little shared moment I never seem to manage to share.'

'I'll take you out for lunch to make up for it,' his mother says, 'if you can bring yourself to shave. And a slightly less obscene T-shirt wouldn't be a bad idea.'

Jeremy stubs out his cigarette and looks down to see which T-shirt he's slept in. *If it ain't STIFF it ain't worth a fuck.* 'Lunch already! Doesn't time fly.'

'And then,' his mother continues, as if he hasn't uttered a word, 'we can have a little chat about what we're going to do with you.'

'I'll wear a nice clean shirt, shall I? Then you can take me somewhere expensive.'

The oysters have come and gone, Jeremy has drunk a pint of Guinness and is halfway down a second, and his mother still hasn't settled into the purpose of the lunch, which is to make him suffer. He's drunk enough now, with residual alcohol still in his blood from last night, not to care overmuch what she says. He already knows what he wants to do with his life. He wants to avoid gainful employment. He wants to fall in love and have someone else take care of him, just as his father has done so unquestioningly with his mother. He wants to be kept, not necessarily in luxury, although he wouldn't refuse luxury, which he sees as his natural element. He likes the idea of being under someone's thumb, wriggling a bit but ultimately acquiescent. The way he justifies this when he's sober is that he wants to have 'time to write'; when he's drunk he doesn't need to seek justification. When he's drunk, he doesn't think about writing. When he's drunk, he doesn't think at all.

'So what are your friends up to these days?' she's asking him now, the menu in her hand, her eyes on what it offers.

'Oh, I don't know. Different things.'

'For example?'

'Teaching. Business. The City.' Getting married, he thinks. Falling in love. Finding homes together to furnish with significant objects, nourished by shared memories, clothed by the knobbly fabric of arguing and making peace. Making love. Some of them are having children, as though the world will go on for ever and as if that mattered.

'And these options don't appeal?'

'Come on, Mum. Really?' He shakes himself, mentally. 'Can you see me in a classroom? That awful year out in that vile *lycée* in Montpellier, I was dreadful. I hated it. They hated me. All those snide little Gallic faces sniffing at my French. It's a miracle I'd still be prepared to go back to the country. But I certainly wouldn't teach there.' He shudders. 'And business? A boardroom? I mean, Dad would have a fit if I went off to work in someone else's company.'

'And Rachel would have a fit if you worked in his,' she says. They laugh together. Mum's always ready to laugh at Rachel, given encouragement.

'Still,' she says, after a moment, 'there must be something you'd like to do. Use your languages, perhaps?'

'My language, you mean?' He wonders sometimes what she thinks he did at university.

'Well, yes, dear, your French. You *did* spend a whole year there, even if you didn't much enjoy it.'

'It isn't that good, to be honest.'

'I'm sure it's good enough to do *something* with.'

'But what *do* people do with French, other than teach? I just told you how much I hated that. I suppose I could write. Isn't that what people do in France? I could pretend I was Hemingway.'

'I suppose you could.' She sounds exasperated now, and slightly bored. 'I'm having monkfish,' she says, putting the menu down. 'And a glass of nice dry chilled Vouvray.'

'You could get a bottle?' he says, optimistic.

'You're drinking too much, Jeremy. I don't like it.'

'I'm just going through a bit of a bad patch, Mum,' he says. 'I'll be all right.'

'There's something I've been meaning to tell you,' she says.

'Really? Good news?'

'In one way, yes.' She lights a cigarette. He reaches across to take one for himself. 'I'm thinking of getting a flat.'

'Who for?' His heart leaps.

'For me, dear.'

He isn't sure he's understood. 'But what do you need a flat for?'

'What do women of my age generally need flats for? To escape from their wicked, brutal husbands, of course. I intend to escape from my wicked, brutal husband.'

He doesn't know what to say. He thinks she might be teasing him.

'Can I come with you?'

'I don't think it'll be big enough for two,' she says.

It strikes him that she's serious. 'But you can't just walk out and leave us,' he says, anxiously.

'How old are you now, Jeremy? Remind me.'

'It isn't about how old I am,' he says. 'I'm thinking about you.'

'Twenty-three,' she says after counting on her fingers. 'Twenty-four this year.' She shakes her head. 'And, no, you aren't thinking about me, Jeremy, so don't pretend you are. You're thinking about yourself. You're wondering what it will be like to have to deal with your father without anyone to look after you. I can't see Rachel defending your right to stay in bed all morning.'

He can't believe what he's hearing. 'But you've put up with him all these years. Why now?' He isn't that bad, he wants to add. But what does he know? He's been away for years and his mother has been here, in a town she doesn't like, in a house she has never shown any affection for, with Rachel and Dad going on about plastics all the time, and no sign that Rachel might leave and make a life of her own. No sign of any man, which doesn't surprise him. I might be the only thing Mum has, he thinks, finishing his second pint of stout. No wonder she's desperate. When she doesn't answer, just twiddles the stem of her empty glass, he calls the waiter over and orders monkfish for two and a bottle of Vouvray. As soon as the bottle comes, he takes it from the waiter and fills both their glasses himself. 'I can't stand waiters fussing about,' he says when his mother raises an eyebrow.

He butters a piece of bread roll, then another, suddenly ravenous. His headache has entirely gone. He feels alive, energised. A distant raucous rattle from somewhere beyond the terrace of the restaurant, an uninterrupted clacking and rustling that has troubled the edge of his consciousness since they arrived, now moves to its centre and lodges there. 'What is that noise?' he says.

'I can't imagine,' she says, distracted. She pauses to listen, her head tilted. You're still a beautiful woman, thinks Jeremy. No one should treat you badly, ever. He remembers seeing her – what? – no more than a week or two ago, rubbing cream into a fresh bruise on her arm. Was that Dad's work, he wonders now. 'Oh yes,' she says. 'It's that seafood shelling machine. You know, that thing sticking out at the side of the restaurant.'

He has no idea what she's talking about. He'll check later, he decides, when they leave, investigate this mysterious machine. They sit together at the table, the enigmatic noise between them, the half-empty bottle of wine, the memory of a bruise she didn't want to talk about. They are waiting for their fish to arrive and there seems, to Jeremy at least, to be nothing to say.

'I can't leave you alone with him, Jeremy,' she blurts out: the words he should have said to her. 'That's the problem now. You didn't have to come home, you know.'

'I'm sorry,' he says. 'I thought that's what homes were for. To come home to. The clue's in the word, I thought.'

'Oh no,' she says, easing the white striated flesh from the dappled skin of the monkfish. 'Homes are what you have to leave. I thought Exeter would have taught you that. Isn't that what university is for, to prise you out?'

'Well, I don't want to stay any longer than I have to.'

'I know that.' She puts down her knife and fork, wipes her mouth on her napkin. How useful food is, it strikes him, and all the business of food, to not say what it is we think but don't want to say, to be circumspect. And then all at once the tools are laid down and all that circumspection is pushed to one side. 'Your father can help you. That's why I'm still with him, for you. Don't you realise that? That you have nothing without him? Neither of us does.' She lights a cigarette. 'And now you're treating me as if I didn't matter at all.'

'No, I'm not,' he says, uneasy now. What does she mean when she talks about his having nothing? He doesn't intend to live off his father any longer than is absolutely necessary.

'Rachel will be all right. Now that she's practically taken on the image of her father. It's you I'm worried about. Rachel has her special arrangement with him,' she says, her tone acidic, 'but you've done everything you can for years to make him dislike you. If you weren't his son, he'd have thrown you out of the house years ago.'

'If I weren't his son, I wouldn't have been there,' he says, 'and anyway, I left the house years ago of my own accord. I didn't need to be thrown out. This is just a pause for reflection. Between one phase and the next. I'll be gone soon enough.' He hopes this is true. Perhaps he and his mother can live together, he thinks now. If she gives him a chance, he'll try to change her mind.

'But you're back now.' She stubs the cigarette out, exasperated. 'Your father's a dangerous man, degenerate. You don't see it, I know. You think he loves you. Maybe he does. But you have to trust me. He'll destroy you if he gets the chance, if only to spite me. You do know he has lovers, has had for years?'

Jeremy didn't, but he isn't surprised. He's always assumed, hoped even, that his mother has also had lovers. He pours what's left of the wine into his empty glass. What on earth did she mean by 'special arrangement'? By saying it in that way? He watches Rachel and their father sometimes, and there is a complicity he must have envied at some time, though he can't imagine why, nor remember when. But isn't that just the normal family dynamic, he thinks: aren't jealousy and confusion and eventual indifference also, in their way, arrangements?

'Is that what makes him dangerous?' he says, because his mother is waiting for him to answer. Yes, he thinks, we can live together, you and I. But who will pay, if not Dad?

'Don't be silly,' she says. 'That's what makes him manageable.' She picks up her bag and takes out her wallet, while Jeremy empties his final glass. 'Take this,' she says, giving him a wodge of notes. 'Go and pay the bill. I need some fresh air.'

The seafood husking machine is cantilevered out from the side of the building, rising like the arms of a praying mantis from the cladding of matt-black wood. They stand beside the surrounding fence, the sea behind them. They watch the wet conveyor belt rise from the wall and climb until its glistening load of shells, milk-white, blue-black, the living fruit removed, are dumped onto the ever-growing pile beneath.

28

RACHEL

Rachel wishes Daddy would trust her more. She hates the work, and perhaps he knows she does, however hard she's tried to hide it from him. He's always seen through her, made her feel defenceless, as though she weren't allowed to have secrets. Not even here. But that doesn't mean she isn't capable of doing the job. She made a special effort to gen up for this meeting with Smithson's this morning and now he's swanned into the office, her office for what it's worth, and picked up the file that wasn't meant to be read by anyone other than her and that has taken her days to prepare, and opened it. He's half leaning, half sitting on her desk, his ankles crossed, a growing smirk on his face as he glances down her notes, her meeting plan, her scribbled amendments, her figures. All her hard work and effort. Until the smirk disappears.

'Dearie me,' he says, shaking his head. 'This won't do at all. You might as well give the stuff away.'

'What's wrong with it?' She bites back *Daddy*; she's sworn to herself she won't use the word in the office. Besides, she wants him to think she's putting up a fight. 'I've been over the whole proposal half a dozen times.'

'Letters of credit? Are you sure? For such a small amount?'

She's never quite grasped the way letters of credit are supposed to work, and she knows he knows this.

'If you're prepared to do the paperwork, of course,' he says. 'Although if you pay yourself for the hours that entails, you're probably working at a loss. Fortunately, you won't be paying yourself. That'll be a job for muggins here.' He looks at his watch. 'What time do they get here?'

'Half past eleven.'

'Why don't you go and make us both a nice cup of coffee while I try to sort this mess out,' he says, and it isn't a question, or, if it is, it requires no answer, because he's already left her office, file in hand, and headed down the corridor towards his own. The word *mess* continues to smart as she follows him, turning off into the room with the photocopier and the kettle.

Rachel carries both coffees past Elaine, her father's secretary, whose job this ought to be. Elaine's eyes are fixed firmly on her hands as she types so as not to see the disdain on Rachel's face. Crossing into her father's office, she heads towards the desk. His right shoulder is angled against her, with one large hand holding a telephone receiver and the other scribbling on a sheet of paper that moves a little as he writes. He turns and, without looking at her, nods briefly towards the spot on the desk where Rachel is to put down the mugs. She does as she's told, her face set. Her only whole thought throughout this entire process, other than contempt for Elaine, has been one of flight.

He waits until they have driven a mile or two from the factory before reaching over to squeeze her knee. She doesn't move. She closes her eyes and listens to the noise of the car, the soft purr of the engine, the squeak of the leather as her father shifts his weight for easier purchase. She smells her father's aftershave, her father's sweat, the car upholstery.

'Sorry about this morning, love. School of hard knocks, I'm afraid, but we can't have you running the show just yet, can we? What would be left for your old Daddy to do?'

'That's all right,' she says. 'I understand. I don't expect special treatment even if I am your daughter and I'm supposed to be taking over the place at some point.'

'That's my girl,' he says. His fingers ease up her skirt an inch or two and stroke the inside of her thigh before he withdraws his hand. 'Fancy popping into the pub for a quick one? On me, naturally.'

'If you want,' she says. She hasn't forgiven him and he won't wheedle her round this easily. But she won't say no to a drink either, after wasting a whole day in useless anger. It's like fighting the weather, or politics – she ought to know that by now; as far as Daddy is concerned, she might as well just give in and let it happen, get on with it, move on. She'll drink her drink and smile and behave, the way she always does, and then she'll forgive and be forgiven. And one day soon she will find a man who will love her and take her away from this, from the factory and from her father. She sees them both at home, Mummy and Jeremy, conspiring together, and she knows what they're up to: any fool can see they're scheming to leave. Well, let them, she thinks, let them go. They're neither of them any use to her or Daddy. 'I could do with a gin and tonic,' she says, slipping her hand into his trouser pocket the way he likes it, to keep it safe.

Rachel's feeling a bit tipsy when they arrive back at the house. There's no sign of Jeremy. Mummy is in the sitting room but she doesn't stop to speak to her, just hurries up the stairs to her own bathroom. After letting the pee flow with a deep sigh of relief, the side of her head against the soothing coolness of the tiles, she washes her hands once thoroughly, and then again more slowly, sniffing the palms to make sure they're clean. Not quite, she thinks.

By the time she comes down, in her favourite flannelette pyjamas, her father is on the sofa with a half-eaten cheese sandwich in his hand, watching some news programme. Her hair is dripping from the shower; she's draped a towel across her shoulders to keep the pyjama jacket dry. Her father looks up at her as she stands there, then opens his legs.

'Come and sit here,' he says. 'I'll dry your hair for you.' He puts the remaining crust of sandwich onto a plate beside him and beckons her down.

'We do have a hairdryer, darling,' says Mummy, glancing at the plate on the cushion, but Rachel is already sitting on the floor, her flannelette-covered bottom on the carpet, her elbows at rest on her father's knees, like a child again, feeling his fingers work at her scalp through the roughness of the towel, relaxing back into him as he hums a tune she has heard a hundred, a thousand times before, a tune she can't remember not knowing, her father's insistent, demanding, all-encompassing lullaby that has rocked her so many times before into acquiescence. Her life's song, in the mouth of her father, wordless and without respite.

Next day is Saturday. Rachel has received an invitation through her pony club contacts to a barn dance this evening and has no idea what to wear. She considered asking her mother for help, but then decided not to tell her where she's going. She's worried one of her mother's friends might also be invited and be told she'll be there. She knows she's mad but she has this idea that her mother is ashamed of her and has organised a network of informers to have her shame confirmed. Some evenings, Rachel has been in a pub with her girlfriends, who are still the girls she knew at school, or from the pony club, many of them married now or living with someone, but only too happy to leave their husbands and boyfriends at home and spend an evening with Rachel, and she's seen older women she recognises, or thinks she does, and noticed the way they look at her, as if they're making notes. Well, let them, she's thought, and had another drink, or taken a cigarette from a friend and pretended to smoke it. Which really is mad, because her mother has always drunk too much, and smoked, and would probably be delighted to hear that Rachel was following in her footsteps. Maybe that's it. She wants proof that Rachel is her daughter too, and not just Daddy's little girl, as she likes to say, with that sarcastic twist to her mouth as though to be loved by her father were something she ought to be ashamed of. She'll drive over to Canterbury this afternoon, she decides, and buy herself a dress to wear that no will have seen her in before, a dress that will make her feel new, and some shoes to go with it, with heels. She hasn't spent any money on herself for ages.

She's leaving the house soon after lunch when Jeremy lurches down the stairs.

'Going out?' he says.

'What does it look like?'

Before she has time to hide them, he sees the car keys ready in her hand. 'You're not taking the car, are you, by any chance?'

'What if I am?'

'Good God, Rachel, I only want a lift somewhere. I'm not asking for a pint of blood.'

'Where do you want to go?' she says.

He grins at her as though she's said something hilarious. He's wearing a black T-shirt that's too small for him, with the name of some pop group on it, and jeans ripped at the knees, and he hasn't had a shave. His hair looks as though he's cut it himself with a pair of nail scissors. 'Wherever you're going suits me fine,' he says.

'I'm going to Canterbury, if you must know,' she says. 'You can come if you want, but I can't promise to bring you back.'

'That's fine,' he says. 'I'll find my own way home.'

As soon as they are in the car, he lights a cigarette.

'I wish you wouldn't,' she says. In response, he sighs and winds the window down. Which is better than nothing, she supposes, although she wonders why he always has to seem so belligerent, as though she'd committed some unforgivable offence against him. It's been like this for as long as she can remember, his sulking and off-handedness the only reaction she ever gets to her attempts to be pleasant to him. Because she does try. She does care. A couple of days ago she'd opened his bedroom door on her way down to breakfast with some clean underwear Ramona had left on the landing and he'd been lying with the blankets and sheet slipped off, in his pants and the T-shirt he'd had on the day before, his face pushed up against the pillow, his bottom raised up a little the way children sometimes sleep, as though they'd been folded and then dropped, and she was stabbed by such affection for him she almost cried out in pain. Affection for what, she didn't know, and still doesn't. The baby he once was, who'd followed her round and demanded her time, or the baby he still is, sulky and cynical and almost constantly in a mood, cheerful and wheedling when he needs a favour done or a loan to tide him over, as he usually does these days, although over to what he doesn't say. Or the baby she wants herself, perhaps, the baby she longs for and can't imagine except as a warm blur at her breast. But that's not a thought she's prepared to entertain, not today. Still, this evening, she thinks. Who knows?

'I'm going to buy myself a dress,' she says. She'll give him one more chance, she decides, to behave like a decent person, like a brother, or not: to behave the way he usually does, like a spoiled little shit. He's silent, and it strikes her that he's also considering which line to take. He throws the half-smoked cigarette from the window, the way Mummy does, as though he's abruptly bored. He's looking for some way not to commit himself to anything, to *her*. She can feel this as clearly as if he'd just come out with it and been honest with her, and said so. She wonders how this has happened, this lack of trust between them, as though attack were the only natural way to deal with situations, when they have grown up together, more or less, and know each other so well, or she likes to think they do. Because if they don't, who does? Maybe she's the one who's wrong, not him. Maybe she's never known him at all, just been Big Sister to his Little Jem. But he still hasn't spoken. With the vision still in her head of baby Jeremy, bottom up, creased cheek squished against the pillow, she's about to say something else, something calm and measured, mollifying even, although she's not sure what.

But she doesn't get a chance.

'Any idea what kind?' he says. He's turned towards her and is smiling. As far as she can tell, the smile is sincere.

'Oh, Jeremy,' she says, and her relief is palpable. 'I wish I knew.'

'I could give you a hand if you like,' he says. 'I don't know how much use I'd be.'

'That would be lovely,' she says. She's wondering already if

271

she's made an awful mistake. She doesn't even know which shop to start in. What possible help could Jeremy be?

'Is it for anything special?'

'Not really,' she says, evasively. But then, when the smile fades from his face, she changes her mind. 'Actually, yes, it is. There's a barn dance tonight. It's just one of those silly pony club things, near Rochester,' she adds hastily, in case he imagines he'd like to come. Anything but that. 'And I thought it might be nice to wear something new.'

'To go with your bit of straw.'

'My what?'

'You'll need a bit of straw to chew on, won't you?' he says. 'Isn't that what people do at barn dances? Swing their partners round and round, and chew on straw?'

'I suppose it is,' she says. He's teasing her, she knows that, but it's a gentle sort of teasing. The nearest she's been to a barn dance is seeing *Seven Brides for Seven Brothers* when she was a little girl, sitting on her father's knee one Sunday afternoon and becoming increasingly energised by the sight of all that being thrown around until her father abruptly put her down.

'You'll need to get one of those big skirts,' he says. She glances across to see if he's taking this seriously after all. 'You should have asked Mum. She's probably got one you could have borrowed.'

'Oh, you know what Mummy's like,' she says. 'It always ends up with her telling you what to do. She'd have wanted to do my hair and make me up. I'd have hated it.'

'You could do with a new hairstyle though,' he says. 'Or you could get one of those, what are they called? Wendy bands? One of those plastic things you stick in your hair? They're fairly cowgirlish.'

She starts to laugh. 'I can't see myself with a Wendy band,' she says. 'I'd just look stupid.' She's had the same haircut for as long as she can remember, shoulder length, side parting, an elastic band to hold it off her face when she gets hot or needs to stuff it up into her hat for riding. She gets a woman down the road to do it. She's never thought about having a hair*style*.

'No, honestly,' he says, surprising her again with his enthusiasm. 'I'll come with you if you like. We can look through one of those books they always have in hairdressers, you know, like sample catalogues.' He reaches across and touches a lock of hair. 'It's a lovely colour, your hair. I've always thought so. I wish mine was that colour.'

She fights back the urge to pull away and then, surprised and slightly unnerved, she feels the prickling of tears. 'Is it?' she says.

'What do you think of my new cut?' he says. 'I did it myself.' He pushes his fingers through the ragged mess of his hair.

'It suits you,' she says.

May God forgive her.

29

JEREMY

It's half past seven and Jeremy is standing outside a pub near the cathedral, a half-empty pint glass in his hand. He'd borrowed ten pounds from Rachel before she drove home some hours ago, her new dress thrown onto the back seat, her hair still stiff with lacquer. They parted on good terms, for the first time in weeks. He can't recall the last occasion they shopped together, maybe they never have, but it seemed the most natural thing in the world to be pushing size fourteen dresses along the racks of Dorothy Perkins, Miss Selfridge, Marks and Spencer's, with Rachel dithering beside him, shaking her head, behaving as though he were about to be arrested.

It turned out that he knew more about shopping for women's clothes than she did, something that surprised him as much as it failed to surprise her. Either that, or she hid it as well as he. He needn't have done, he thinks now, finishing his pint and going back into the pub to replace it. It might have provided an opportunity for the conversation he's been putting off for a decade by now, the conversation in which he tells her he likes fucking men, the conversation he has also managed not to have with his mother, for that matter,

274

who surely deserves to know first or, at least, before Rachel. It's odd, he thinks, that wandering around the streets of Exeter with his pink triangle on his lapel and telling pretty much everyone he met that he was gay within minutes of their meeting should have been so exhilarating, while telling his family is turning out to be so hard. Or maybe not odd at all. Maybe it's the least odd thing about him, this reluctance to open his heart to the only people in the world who might care what he is. Because it is all hot air, in the end; whether he's telling everyone or telling no one, it makes not one scrap of difference to the truth, to the dark corrosive secret at the core of him, which isn't his sexuality at all. He wishes it was.

At the acid heart of his shame, wearing him away as it trickles insidiously through his veins, is the fact that he's barely had sex with anyone, not since he was fifteen and his best and only friend changed school and didn't reply to his letters. After that came the twilight years of furtive ogling, and backing away from the threat of being noticed, such as it was, and cursing the meanness of his father, who could so easily have sent him to boarding school where boy-on-boy sex was rife, and who had chosen not to out of some ill-considered notion of egalitarianism, or so he claimed. And then came university and the sorry, single-figure clique of gay liberationists, with their sagging loons and weeping jags when one of them left another.

Well, fuck them all, thinks Jeremy now, watching the barman's hand as it takes his glass and fills it, watching the muscles in the stringy forearm fidget and twitch as the beer is pumped into the glass, his dick half stiff, his head already slightly heavy. It's cool in the pub, cooler inside than out. Outside the air is still mild, one of those long summer days they've been having these past few years, edging into autumn. He eases the shoulder of his T-shirt from his skin. Rachel will be dressed up by now and ready to go. He wonders what Mum will have thought of it all, assuming she knows. Will Rachel have modelled her new look, the way Jeremy used to as a boy, strutting up and down beside his mother's bed? Or simply slipped out of the house before she could be seen, and criticised?

They'd found a gingham shirtwaist dress in the end, despite all the odds, in a shop for older women than Rachel, and some white shoes to go with it. It wasn't until they had both had steak and ale pie and chips, and a couple of gin and tonics for lunch that he'd persuaded her to go to a hairdresser's. He'd sat there reading magazines, occasionally glancing across to see her anxious face in the mirror, perfectly happy with his lot, as though his life could offer him nothing more, nor better. You look like Doris Day, he'd said when she came out from under the dryer and the whole coiffure – no other word for it – had been brushed out in its sun-kissed splendour. Do I? she'd said, and then she'd giggled in a way that threw him. Maybe I'll meet my very own Rock Hudson this evening. Maybe you will, he'd said. He'd been tempted to tell her then, about Rock Hudson, about his friend at Exeter who claimed to have had sex with him. About himself. But he'd bitten his tongue, less to protect himself, in the end, than Rachel. Her innocence, her fragility, standing there in her oddly cut trousers and her oddly cut hair, with her hands clasped in front of her as though holding a phantom handbag with her bare-skinned heart in it.

He pays the barman and is about to take his beer outside again, because the public pavement, is, he feels, less emotionally hostile to solitary drinkers, when the barman points to his T-shirt.

'Going to the gig, then?'

'What?'

'Generation X. They're at the Art College tonight. Come on, mate. You telling me you didn't know?'

Jeremy's heart leaps. 'You going, then?' he says in his own uneasy stab at the vernacular.

The man looks up and down the bar, then shakes his head. 'Doubt it.' He grins. 'Still, you never know. I might just walk out. Fuck the bosses, right?'

The barman has a dotted line tattooed round his neck, with the words *cut here* an inch below the Adam's apple. It's an old tattoo, faded, although he can't be much older than Jeremy. Jeremy laughs, but it strikes him that this is exactly what the man *might* do, that he is dangerous, and unpredictable, and not necessarily friendly. He's not sure how he feels about this, but his erection knows. The barman's face is thin, his hair shaved almost to the scalp, but badly, almost as badly shaved as Jeremy's is cut. White lines run through the stubble like those meaningless markings in the South American desert.

'I might see you there, then,' he says.

The barman grins. 'You're on.'

Jeremy has enough money to get in and that's it, which doesn't worry him at first; he's had enough to drink. He stands at the back of the hall, beside a row of empty coat hooks. It's not a trusting environment. There's a support band he doesn't know the name of, but he recognises the singer as someone he's seen in the pubs in Whitstable and wondered if they were at school together, wonders if he's fancied him before this evening or if it's just context, and alcohol, and if that matters. He edges towards the stage, shouldering a way through the pogoing crowd, pogoing himself in a cautious fashion, all at once aware of how much he's drunk, stumbling and banging against indifferent others, until he's close enough to reach out across the string of lights and touch the ripped Green Flashes of the singer, identical to his own worn pair. For a moment, but he catches his hand in time, he almost does – he almost does establish contact. He's carried forward, oblivious to those around him, in the usual wave of envy and aspiration that strikes him when he sees a stage and someone on it who could conceivably, in a fairer and more caring world, be him. He hears someone shout out *Gary* and he shouts it out too, and lets a sudden surge towards the stage crush his chest against its edge. *Gary*, he shouts out, and the singer gobs at him, the singer's name is *Gary*, and it lands hot and wet at the centre of his forehead like a mark of caste. *Gary*, he shouts again, his voice pitched high, and then, rasping his throat for all the phlegm it's worth, he gobs back at the bare pale ankles no more than three feet from his face, the young man's ankles with a trace of black hair and a line of blue vein over the bone. His voice can barely be heard above the others, so he shouts louder, his sore throat dry with effort, and when a skinhead to his left throws beer at the stage he holds out his hands like some parched child for water, then licks them clean.

At the end of the set he wanders away from the stage, ears ringing. He feels in his pockets, checking to make sure there isn't some cash left in some deep corner, a handful of coins, a folded note that slipped through his fingers. It's happened before that he's mislaid money and then found it when it most serves, in the lining of a jacket, beneath a discarded pair of underpants. But this time he's disappointed. He has no money at all and his throat is on fire. He wanders across to an empty table at the back of the hall and sits down, scanning the crowd to see if there is someone he knows, someone from school, someone from the band, Gary, a semi-familiar face that offers some chance of a loan. But he's alone, as alone as he has ever been. He's sitting at an empty table in a hall full of people he's never seen before and will never see again and it strikes him, as he stretches his legs, and eases his sweat-damp jeans from his crotch, and then bends down to tie a shoelace that has worked loose during his manic dancing, his fan-worship, with his eyes at the level of unknown knees as they pass, invisible as a child in a world of adults, invisible as a dog in a pound, or a bubble of spit in a glass of beer, it strikes him that, because he is known to no one and need never return to this vile, inhospitable place in which he has no money or friends or visible means of sustenance, in which no one so much as deigns to notice him as he struggles back onto the orange moulded plastic chair, identical to the dozens of other plastic chairs stacked along the wall behind him, chairs that could easily collapse if they were pushed, chairs that might have been mould-injected and expelled in his father's factory, it strikes him that he can behave in a way that is consequent of this, congruent with this, with this invisibility. He can do, in other words, whatever the fuck he wants.

He stands up and begins to walk around the hall. He's staggering a little, but no one seems to notice, or care. He stumbles into a girl, who steps away, lifting her shoulders as if to shrug on a fugitive scarf, but doesn't turn to look at him, perhaps because he isn't worth it, which gives him a spark of courage as he heads towards the stage. Three guys are moving stuff round, carrying off the drum kit that was used for the first set, replacing it with a large one, with Generation X written on it. They've got long hair and faded purple loons, like throwbacks to an earlier era; they look like he looked when he was still at school, but horribly, magically, aged. He feels a wave of nausea and leans for a moment against the stage, his hands on the rough scrubbed wood. The main lights are on and he can see the stains of beer and gob, some of them his, made by his own body in his adoration of Gary. He wonders where Gary is and if he'd appreciate a zipless blowjob. There must be a dressing room or a corridor some-where backstage. He'll go and look, he decides. He might find the singer of Generation X, a tattooed bottle-blond he saw in a photo in *NME* and almost cut out to keep; he would have done if his mother hadn't been sitting in the room with him. Who knows, the man might be draped above the urinal, one hand on the wall, the other shaking the last few drops of piss from his dick, just waiting for Jeremy to come in and find him. Why not? Why not indeed.

He eases his way along the front of the stage, guided by the splintering wood and its patina of bodily fluids and spilled alcohol, to where a short flight of steps leads up into the sacred space beyond the curtain, the sanctum sanctorum, where sweat-damp T-shirts are thrown into corners and young men scratch their naked arses with bitten-down tobacco-ambered fingernails. He's about to tread on the first step when an uncontrollable thirst pulls him up, sharp as a halter. His throat feels like sand; or worse, like sandpapered flesh. He has to drink, he has to quench the fire inside him. I'm burning up, he says, to no one. He's checked his pockets for money, he knows this, but he checks them again. Still nothing. He glances up the steps and along the stage with an eye-narrowed furtive expression, like a cartoon cat burglar. What he wants to do is pussyfoot, lifting his legs one after the other, placing his toes on the ground, the pseudo-jazzy music playing behind him, like something out of *The Pink Panther*. But what he actually does is edge up towards the curtain, taking care to look nowhere and at no one, because to see is to be seen, and then, with his back to the wall, reach forward and shift the clammy, smoke-scented crimson velvet a little, pushing a double fold of the fabric to one side.

And there it is, rare and perfect as an orchid in the wild. He deep-sighs with satisfaction. He stretches out and takes the glass in his hand and lifts it, unhurriedly now, to his mouth. It is warm, but not intolerably so. It is flat, but that's to be expected. He places the lip of the glass against his own soft bottom lip and tips until the warm, flat beer flows into his mouth, across his tongue, and down his throat, like rain on desert sand, and his whole world is there, in the wonder of it. He drinks and only stops drinking when someone taps him on the shoulder.

'What the fuck do you think you're doing?'

Jeremy turns round slowly. He is no longer alone.

'I said what the fuck do you think you're doing?'

'Me?' This is a genuine question.

'Who the fuck else?' the man says. Jeremy's world has shuddered to a stop and he's not sure what this man might want from him, this man who seems familiar, his shaved head and dark eyes, his polo shirt with the yellow bands on the collar, on the black. The air around his head blows hot and cold. His cheeks are burning somehow, skewed into a sort of smile. The moment hesitates, as if waiting for the next thing to happen, and Jeremy doesn't know what this is. Or maybe he does. The man pushes Jeremy with his big hard hands towards the hands of another man, which twist him round and push a second time. Jeremy is standing at the heart of a circle of skinheads, three or four, maybe five, he isn't sure, there are men behind these men, men beyond those perhaps, petal upon petal, love me, love me not. The glass is taken from his hand and what's left of its contents tipped over his head. Some of the men surrounding him laugh at this, one man leans forward and rubs his wet T-shirt hard against his nipple, pinching it as he's spun, and turned, and twisted, all of this to general laughter. But the one in front of him now, as he comes full circle, the one who has poured the beer on his head, isn't laughing. His lips are drawn from his teeth in a cartoon-like snarl. He has long canines, sharp, off-white. He has freckles and a mole beside his nostril. Jeremy tries to pull his head back, to make some space, the man's sour breath in his mouth, but the face comes with it, as if attached to his, maintains its hold, the eyes on his, the breath in his breath. This face is new to him, blue-white in the glow from the stage as the lights in the rest of the hall dim and then die. There's a pent silence of expectation, the sort of silence that precedes the falling of an immense wave, and then the band comes raggedly on and Jeremy sees this, sees the musicians take their positions on the stage as he is spun again, giddy, nauseous by now, each revolution a gathering of speed. But then, as he ceases to resist, as he lets his body loosen, he thinks, yes, this is something new. The hub of their little game, he finds himself relaxing, supported, his fear of falling itself fallen away.

Until they move away from him, open up the circle and he's no longer supported, their arms outstretched now, their bodies withdrawn, and he's thrown around a space that no longer holds him up, he's stumbling and almost falling to his knees. But the man with the snarl doesn't want this, he has other ideas for him, and Jeremy is picked up by the armpits, lifted a little from the ground, held dangling like a child being lifted from the bath to be wrapped in a warm soft towel, rubbed down, taken to bed, tucked in and kissed goodnight. He knows the man now, or if not this man then one of the others – he was standing beside him and gobbing at Gary. They have this in common. They are one beneath the skin. How can he say this, he wonders, how can he make this known to them as they half drag, half carry him out of the hall, this brotherhood they have shared? How can he save himself from what they will do to him?

They take him to a space between two cars and drop him, and he flops down, eyes darting briefly until he closes them against what they will do. The side of his face scrapes roughly on the gravel as one of them puts a boot on the back of his neck and rubs it into the ground, as if stubbing out a cigarette, grinding it until the filter breaks and the last half inch of tobacco is reduced to shreds. The gravel goes into his mouth, scrapes against a tooth. Then he's kicked in the stomach, twice, and kicked in the lower back, and then a boot stamps on his thigh and that's the hardest pain to bear, which surprises him, and he hears his own voice, but high-pitched, screaming a little in a half-hearted, anxious way, as though he doesn't want to be heard. If he's heard, it will make this real. And then he's in some space where this isn't happening, some very small space, uncomfortable, airless, but if he can stay there long enough, and be quiet enough, he might survive. And so he curls up as tight as he can get. And then they step back and he's alone, unmoving, curled tiny as a foetus on a marble slab. He's cold; he's never felt this cold in his life before. Until something warm splashes on his neck and cheek and, that's nice, he thinks, until he realises what it is, and now the laughter has returned all round him and his hair is drenched by it, yellow and acrid and rank, with the faintest trace of beer so that, for a moment, unthinking, he lifts his thirsty head to drink.

30

RACHEL

Rachel's creeping downstairs, her new shoes dangling from her hand, when the sitting room door opens and her mother appears. She's holding a cocktail glass, with nothing in it but a bright red cherry on a stick. Rachel can see she's drunk from the way she slumps against the door frame, the glass tilted. Oh God, Rachel thinks. Here we go.

'You're going out?'

'Yes, Mummy.' Start with deference, she thinks.

'Where? No, let me guess.' Her mother takes a tentative step towards the stairs, thinks better of it. 'Sainsbury's.'

'Don't be silly, Mummy.' Damn her, she thinks. 'It'll be closed by now.'

'I'm aware of that,' her mother says. 'Still, I'm glad to see you're going out. It's about time someone had some fun round here.'

'Yes,' says Rachel, wretched, alert to danger.

'You've had your hair done, finally, I see.'

Rachel nods, but doesn't answer.

'What on earth are you wearing?'

'It's a dress,' says Rachel. Say nothing beyond what is necessary, admit nothing, reveal nothing that cannot already be seen. She feels like a foreign spy captured and strapped to a chair beneath a swinging light. She has only herself to protect, which somehow makes it harder. When her mother doesn't answer, she adds, hopelessly, 'It's new.'

'I thought I'd never seen it before,' says her mother, the faintest slur perceptible, her tone affronted. 'And where are you wearing your new *dress* to?'

'A dance,' says Rachel.

'A dance?'

'A barn dance.'

'A *barn* dance,' her mother says. She has that little dismissive smirk on her face that Rachel knows so well.

'Yes. It's a pony club thing.'

'A *pony* club thing.'

'Yes. A pony club thing.' She's had enough of this. She walks down the last few steps, then holds the final rail of the banister to slip on her shoes, grateful for the extra height the small heels give her. She is taller than her mother at all times, but she doesn't always feel it.

'And you choose to wear that funny little dress because it's a *pony* club thing?'

'For God's sake, Mummy, if you want to say something horrible, just say it.' Although she already has.

'But why on earth should I want to say something horrible?' her mother says, dragging out the last word in her nasty, sarcastic way, as if she'd never stooped to this before, as if the misunderstanding was Rachel's fault.

Rachel picks up the car keys and slips them into her bag. It's a clutch bag she's never used before, one that her mother gave her when she was still at school. Her mother had said she didn't want it any longer and Rachel had thought it was glamorous. It has glittery jet beads sewn on the outside and all at once feels too bright, too loud, too precious. She wishes she'd chosen something else, less noticeable, more her style. She prays her mother doesn't notice it.

'If you think it's suitable, I mean,' her mother says. 'For a barn dance. It's certainly very . . . well, rustic.'

'That's it,' snaps Rachel, at the end of her tether suddenly. 'If you must know, your precious son helped me choose it. We went shopping together, in Canterbury, this afternoon. So don't blame me if it isn't *suitable*. Blame him.'

'Ah yes,' her mother sighs, turning unsteadily, going back into the sitting room. The cocktail cherry slides from the downturned glass. Rachel resists the urge to pick it up and throw it away in the kitchen. 'That would explain it.'

'What do you mean? Explain what?' Rachel says, already regretting it. She knows already how little she wants to know.

'I suppose he said you looked pretty in it.' Her mother comes to a halt, but doesn't turn, just raises her voice. Rachel stares at her back, wishing the clutch bag were a knife.

'No.' He did say this though, more or less. He said it in the shop, when she came out of the changing room, in bare feet. You look gorgeous, he said, which is better than pretty, surely – more lavish, more extravagant. She'd loved him for that. No one has ever called her gorgeous before. She'd been sure he meant it.

Her mother continues to wend her uncertain way back into the sitting room, weaving across to the sideboard to tip what's left in the cocktail shaker into her empty glass. The television is on, the sound turned off. Despite the heat, there's a two-bar electric fire a little too close to the sofa. Rachel, drawn in her wake by hurt and anger and frustration, because there is something in her mother's spite she still doesn't understand, sees the fire. I'd better move that before I go, she thinks. She'll burn the place down, the hateful old drunk.

'He didn't?' her mother says, now curled on the sofa, her half-full glass precariously askew. 'So you bought it despite his advice to the contrary? That was brave of you. I'd never have dared in your place. He's such a tyrant in matters of taste.'

'No, he . . .' Rachel stops. Why do I bother? she thinks.

'*He?*'

'He chose it for me.'

Her mother purses her lips. 'Well, I think he's behaved very badly.'

'What do you mean?' Her mother sips at the cocktail. Answer me, you bitch.

'Well, you surely don't think he chose it because it suits you?'

Rachel feels cold. 'What do you mean?'

'How can I put this?' She ponders the issue for a moment. 'He's trying to make you look ridiculous.'

Rachel shakes her head.

'He's a very naughty boy, and I shall tell him so when he gets home.'

'I don't know what you mean,' says Rachel.

'It makes you look like a badly wrapped parcel, darling,' her mother says. 'The thing is, you really need a waist for a dress like that.' She struggles to her feet, slopping the remains of the drink onto the floor. Please God let it splash onto the fire, thinks Rachel, please let her die in a blaze of alcoholic flame, the drunken whore. I hate you, she thinks, but it isn't hate she feels so much as loss, and hurt, and a need to be comforted. She doesn't believe her, of course, Jeremy would surely never be so cruel; or she wouldn't have believed her if she hadn't had the same thought herself, ten minutes earlier, standing in front of the full-length mirror in her bedroom, her hands clasped in front of her waist, such as it is. She isn't fat; it's just the way she's made. She's built like a man, that's the trouble. She can't help being taller than everyone else in the family, taller than her mother and Jeremy, taller than her father. Sometimes she wonders where she's come from, if she wasn't just left on the step. She wishes she was a man. She wishes her father were here to help her. He always makes her feel loved, even when she doesn't deserve it. Where is he when he's needed? Why isn't he here at home to keep his wife in check? She feels like an animal trapped in a cage and harried, tormented, and she can't decide who by, her mother or her brother, she can't decide which way to turn, in which direction to hurl her pain and rage, whose hand to bite. Her mother in the meantime has stumbled across the room towards her and is trying to embrace her, fingers tacky with drink grasping her bare arm, the other hand snaking round her thick contested waist as though she wants to dance. With a deep shudder Rachel pushes her away.

'Do let me help, darling,' her mother says. 'I'm sure I've got something that would fit you.' How guilty she sounds now, how eager to make amends. The cruelty then was hers, thinks Rachel, but how can she be sure her mother isn't right? How can she be sure it wasn't Jeremy's intention to make a fool of her? Would he do that to her? Would he be that calculating? He was so sweet, the way he held the dresses up in front of himself, shaking the skirts out to show how they hung.

There is a grunt from below, followed by a tug. Her mother has slid to the floor and is struggling to get up. Rachel hears fabric rip.

'I don't need your help,' she says, not looking at her mother as she rolls about on the floor like a helpless child, giggling at the absurdity of it all. Fuck them both, she thinks. Fuck everyone. I shall enjoy myself this evening, whatever the cost.

The minute she walks into the barn she's happy. She's not sure why. She cried for the first ten minutes of the journey; she could hardly see the road through her tears. Then she stopped in a pub for a hurried G and T, and it seems to have done the trick. She's flushed, but that's the heat in the barn, which really is a barn, bales stacked along the walls and the centre of the floor swept clean for dancing. At the far end is a low stage, with a band on it playing something slow that sounds familiar – that's it, Roy Orbison – and three or four couples are dancing, no one she knows. There are fewer people than she expected, which is a relief, because crowds can be so intimidating. She's looking round to see if there is anyone she recognises when a girl from the pony club walks over and gives her a clumsy hug.

'Hello, Rachel. Love the hair.'

'Sally,' she says. She's forgotten about her hair. She touches it with her free hand; still stiff from the lacquer so that's all right. 'I don't suppose there's a glass of wine anywhere, is there? Just to get me in the mood.'

'No, but there's some absolutely lethal punch in a sort of tin bucket over there. Very authentic.' Sally giggles. 'I'm certainly in the mood. I think I may have had a drop too much already.' She looks Rachel up and down. Rachel tenses. 'So glad you could come,' Sally says. 'I wasn't sure you'd make it. You work too hard, you really do. Your father's such a slave driver.'

Rachel smiles, relaxes, returns the appraising look. Sally is wearing a dress not unlike her own: a small pink check, a full skirt, cinched-in waist. Jeremy may have been on her side, after all. 'I wouldn't have missed it for the world.' She slips an arm through Sally's. 'Come on, show me where this punch is hiding.'

Half an hour later, she is dancing with someone she's seen at dos like this in the past, and always thought out of her league. Tall, dark wavy hair a little longer than she'd normally like, strong chin. He's been introduced to her by Sally's sister, a girl she barely knows. This is Rachel *Eldritch*, she said, *you know*, and Rachel wasn't particularly happy about this, although he didn't seem to mind. She doesn't want to be her father's daughter this evening, or anyone else's. She didn't catch his surname, but his first name is Danny, or Denny, short for Dennis perhaps, and he has large firm hands, which he has just placed on her hips to pull her in. He reminds her of someone, but it's only when she remembers what Jeremy had said about her looking like Doris Day that it comes to her. Rock Hudson. He has bright blue eyes, though, which makes him even nicer. She can feel him against her, his chest against her breasts and further down, although she isn't sure of this, and isn't sure she wants to be, a hard something that might be his penis, or the buckle of his belt. Her heart is beating more rapidly than she'd like and she wonders if he can feel it too through the cotton of her dress and his shirt, a red and white check shirt open at the neck, as tight fitting as her dress, the pearly buttons pressing into her, unless she's imagining this, and if what she is feeling is actually her own heart, or his. He's sucked a mint before dancing with her, she can smell it as he bends his head down and brushes her cheek with his lips, a sharp peppermint tang, warm, with a touch of sweetness. He leaves his head close to hers, he's humming the words to the song in her ear, some song she doesn't know about trains and babies coming home. This isn't normally her sort of music. Country music, she supposes; Jeremy would hate it. Her arms tighten round Denny, or Danny, she must find out before things go much further, her hands slide slowly down from his shoulders to his waist, then stop, afraid. It *is* his penis, she's sure of it now, it's poking at her tummy, with a life of its own. She'd like to look into his eyes, but all she can see is his neck and the collar of his shirt. She's starting to wonder if they shouldn't both sit down somewhere and get their breath, and how she can make this happen, when he reaches behind himself to detach her hand from his back and leads her across to a vacant bale. He tells her to wait a moment while he fetches them both something to drink. He doesn't ask her what she wants, nor even whether she wants something to drink, but that's all right. She does. She's used to having her needs anticipated, in any case. Her father does it all the time.

She watches him stride off, bits of straw poking through her dress into her legs, scratching the palms of her hand as she leans back and pushes out her breasts, extends her neck, tucks in her tummy as far as she can; trying to be as gorgeous as he might want. She watches his bum flex in the tight blue jeans he's wearing, his shoulders swinging as he passes among the dancers, a properly cowboy sort of walk; she's excited, anxious, a little scared. When he waves to someone across the barn she checks immediately that it isn't another woman, then catches herself, catches the relief she feels when she sees it's a man, a man she knows from work, Graham from the accounts department, the keeper of Daddy's little secrets. She didn't know he was the horsey sort. Rachel, she tells herself sternly, you're just being stupid. She's had boyfriends before, but not like this man, and not recently, and she's never known her heart beat so fast over anyone. She can still sense his penis against her, like a shock, the aftermath of a shock, as if she's been slapped and can feel the skin burn where the hand has been. She can still feel his grip on her waist and then her hips, the way his fingers tightened into her as they danced. There's going to be embracing, said the song.

When he comes back with two plastic glasses filled to the brim with punch and a cheeky, eager smile on his face it's all she can do not to clap with delight. He gives her the glass and then he does that thing she's only ever seen in films, where they lace their arms together and drink, and she ends up spluttering her punch all over his shoulder. 'I'll have to take my shirt off,' he says, and starts to unbutton it right there on the bale, beside her. She shakes her head, snorting with laughter. 'I need a cigarette,' he says. 'Let's go outside. We can't smoke in here or we'll set the whole bloody place alight.' She tells him she doesn't smoke, it makes her cough, and he pulls the lugubrious face of a clown. 'You'll send me out there into the cold alone,' he says, 'without so much as a shirt to my back,' and he takes his shirt half off. His chest is hairy, but not too hairy, and muscled. She wants to kiss it. 'I'll come with you,' she says. 'To keep you company.'

The skin of his back is smooth and warm, it's like stroking silk, she thinks, her hands sliding inside his shirt. I can't believe I'm doing this. She's drunk, but that isn't it. She sees her mother suddenly, also drunk, slumped on the sofa beside the two-bar electric fire, but still cold, cold as a witch's tit, and thinks how much she'd like to be here with a gorgeous man, because there is no other word for him, his mouth on her neck, then nibbling at the top edge of her ear. How much she'd like not to be old any longer and to be loved, desired. What a cow Mummy is, her daughter thinks. When Danny's

(Denny's?) hand slips up her skirt, she tenses, relaxes, her legs falling apart with a sigh of nylon, how wonderful these full skirts are, how much room there is beneath them. Oh God, she thinks. Oh Daddy.

He stands up and leads her towards the cars and she thinks, with a flicker of panic, my clutch bag, my keys, I don't know where they are. But he's opened the back door of a car that's larger, and more comfortable, and more powerful than hers, and she lets herself be laid down on the seat, her knees raised and his head is down there between her legs and he's doing something she's imagined but never known, his tongue against her knickers, his strong tongue flicking against the cotton of her large white schoolgirl knickers, and there's a general wetness there she's not sure she can take, but her hands are reaching down around his head, pressing it into her, sharp and vivid as flame, and she's saying yes, oh yes. *Oh* yes. Oh *yes*. Fuck you, Mummy, she thinks. Fuck you.

When it's over they go back into the barn to look for her clutch bag, but can't find it.

'You'll have to drive me home, Danny,' she says.

He grins. 'It's Denny,' he says. 'You'd better start getting used to it. I think we'll be seeing a lot of each other.'

31

VANESSA

Vanessa wakes up with a jerk, one side of her body burning. She struggles into a sitting position, squealing with pain when her bare arm brushes the side of the electric fire. She has no idea where she is. She has been dreaming about a row of offices that open onto a terrace, and a panther trapped in a glass tank, like an aquarium. And then she knows exactly where she is, lying on the floor of her sitting room. She is feeling guilty about something, or someone, but can't remember why. She has had too much to drink, although it isn't that. It's something she has said, or done. When she hears a car pull into the drive, she struggles to her knees, nursing her burnt arm, and ends up with her face buried in the cushions of the sofa, a sudden fit of laughter half stifled by crimson velvet. She's like this, kneeling, arse in the air, shaking with hilarity despite her head, which hurts, and arm, which also and more immediately hurts, and her sense of guilt, which is growing, its source still unidentified; she's in this deeply humiliating position when she hears the front door open and – after what she will subsequently refer to, ironically, as a pregnant pause when she recollects this moment – her husband's voice.

'I see you've been enjoying yourself in my absence.'

This sets her off again. She hears him stride towards her and, for a moment, she thinks he's going to drag her to her feet, hit her perhaps: it wouldn't be the first time. But all he does is turn off the electric fire, muttering about waste, and then – she checks this with a sideways glance – walk over to the television, which appears to be on, in order to turn that off too. He picks up an empty glass with an exasperated sigh, puts it back on the sideboard, which, from the position in which she is lying, looks dangerously vertical. He really is the perfect housewife, she thinks to herself. She couldn't have trained him better. If only that were true. She's surprisingly comfortable. She could stay like this all night, and may do.

But now Reginald really does hoist her up, with a grunt, his rough hands lifting and twisting her upper body until she finds herself sitting where her cheek was only a moment before, and staring up. He's angry, she can see that at once, and she wonders why he's bothered to come back to the house if all he wants to do is make trouble. He could have stayed in one of his usual places, with one of his floozies. There's no need for you here, she wants to say. I don't need you. Jeremy doesn't need you. Not even Rachel needs you, poor girl, however much she might think she does.

And now she remembers why she was feeling guilty. I am a swine, she thinks. An absolute swine. Why did I do that? My poor dear girl. You must have caught me on the hop. I was jealous, is that it? Jealous of Rachel? Young and gauche, untried. Well, not entirely untried. His hands are still on her. 'Will you just let me go,' she says.

'I need to speak to you,' he says in his office voice, as though she's some underling on the payroll. 'I don't expect a sensible answer, you're obviously too drunk for that, but I'm afraid this can't wait.' He's wearing a suit and tie, as he always does. She wonders where he's been, and who with. She imagines him in some hotel room, the perfect master of commerce from the waist up, his trousers and underpants round his ankles, his socks held up by suspenders, some tart attending to his needs. He steps back from her, fiddles around in his jacket pocket, pulls out an airmail envelope.

'This arrived today,' he says. She stares up at him, as blankly as she can manage, fighting back this terrible urge to giggle at the image she has conjured up. He seems to expect her to answer, but there is nothing she needs to say. She's mildly curious, certainly, but knows she only has to wait.

'It's from someone called . . .' he says, extracting a letter from the envelope and shaking it open, 'Armand Grenier.'

'Armand Grenier,' she repeats, but not for him to hear, she doesn't care one jot about him. It's simply to have said the words, to have heard them said in a decent accent. From that to this, she thinks. How far I have fallen.

'It's in French,' her husband says, his tone contemptuous.

This does surprise her. Armand's English is almost as impeccable as his pride in it. He has always written to her in English, and not only to show off; to be close to her. And then it strikes her that Armand has written a letter to Reginald. How odd, she thinks. Why on earth would he do that? He's never met the man.

'I expect he imagines I don't read French,' he says. 'He was hoping to humiliate me by forcing me to ask you to translate it. Or Jeremy, I suppose. Or perhaps he thought I'd seek out some local Frog and pay to get it put into English.'

'Humiliate you?' she says. What a limited repertoire we have in this family, she thinks. Shame, and then humiliation, and then guilt. I'll make it up to Rachel somehow. How awful

I've been. Of course, I might also have been right. It's just the sort of behaviour I'd expect from Jeremy.

'You do know what this is about, don't you?' He's waving the sheets of paper around his head now, enraged, blood rushing to his face. She watches his anger mount, like milk in a hot pan.

'I've no idea,' she says. For now, this is true.

'I don't believe that for a minute. I don't believe a word you say.' He's incensed almost beyond speech. There is a growing tremor in his voice, the hand that holds the letter is shaking. He takes a half-step towards her, his raised hand curling into a fist around the letter. She feels a moment's fear, but that soon passes. He rocks back on his heels, like one of those bottom-heavy toys that won't be pushed over. The truth is that he's scared of her. He's scared of what he would do to her, if he could.

'You know damn well what this is about,' he says, spluttering.

'Do I? Actually, I don't.' Although she does know now, or suspects she does. She has been waiting twenty years or more for this. 'Why don't you tell me?'

'You whore,' he says. 'You filthy whore.'

'Well, you ought to know about whores, darling. You must be quite an expert by now, the time you spend with them. Filthy and otherwise.'

He throws the letter in her face, but even screwed into a ball the paper is airmail weight, flimsy, too insubstantial for such petty acts of violence. It falls to the floor between them, the pages fluttering apart. She's tempted to pick them up and read them, flatten out the crumpled sheets, recompose the letter as it was this morning. She'd never imagined Armand would have the nerve, or the reason. That must be why he wrote it in French, so that the letter could be written and yet not read. He must have hoped, at some unconscious level, that it would never be read; he was protecting himself from himself, from his need to confess. How droll, she thinks. Grown men can be such children. Of course, we both know – Armand and I – that the letter was meant for me in the end. Reginald is just a sort of prop, as he always has been. But how dare Armand drag him into this.

'You make me sick,' he says. 'I suppose you thought I'd never find out.'

'To be perfectly frank, Reginald, I haven't cared one way or the other for twenty years. Longer, probably. How old is Rachel now, exactly?'

'So it's true.'

Vanessa shrugs.

'And Rachel doesn't know?'

'Of course not.' She's tempted to say that all this has nothing to do with Rachel, but she's reasonable enough to see that isn't true. And yet Rachel is the least of her worries. In one way, she reminds herself, and is deeply tempted to remind him, it's an advantage that Reginald isn't her father.

'I suppose you think I should tell her she's the daughter of some French puff you had sex with when you couldn't keep your knickers on?'

'If that's what you feel is appropriate,' she says. She wonders how long it took him to get that line the way he wanted it. She can see him, sitting in the car, rehearsing, balancing one word against another, a proper little poet. How pleased he must have been by *French puff*. You witless oaf, she thinks. How vulgar you are.

'And then fobbed off on me.'

'I'm sure she'd love to know that's how you feel about her,' she says. 'That she's something someone neither of you has ever met has fobbed off on you.'

'It's got nothing to do with how I feel about Rachel.'

She stares at him, fixes his eyes with hers until he turns his head away. He knows what she's thinking, what she sees when she scrutinises him like this. He won't be hitting her now, she's sure of that, and that weight is lifted from her. I'm leaving, she thinks. I've had enough. It's a kind of illumination. She has been waiting for this to happen for as long as she can remember and now it has, and she is released. He has never seemed smaller to her, nor more absurd. She will go to Paris and she will ask Armand what the hell he thinks he's playing at, but she won't find it in her heart to be cross with him, not deeply, although she has every right to be cross. She will thank him, and then say goodbye to him for ever, and that will be his punishment. And then she will seek the life she has constantly been denied. The burn on her forearm is increasingly sore. She wonders if it will leave a scar. She will wear it as a badge.

'You know nothing about my feelings for Rachel,' he says.

She stands up, finally, with a sense that everything has been sorted out. 'You should be grateful Rachel isn't your daughter,' she says. 'It makes your behaviour with her slightly less inexcusable.'

'I don't know what you mean,' he says and she sees now that she was wrong. He would have hit her if she hadn't said this, or something like this: if she hadn't reminded him just how vulnerable he was. She sees at once that he would have struck her, on her face or wherever it would hurt the most, his need to hurt her taking the upper hand. I'm leaving, she repeats to herself. I'm leaving, and this knowledge is like an amulet against him, I'm leaving and I shall take them with me, both of them, my children, the children of my womb. One way or another. And you will have to live with it. And I shall expect you to keep me until my dying day, because that is what will hurt you most. Because all you have ever cared about is money. Money and sex.

'You know perfectly well what I mean,' she says.

'You've stolen my daughter from me,' he says, and then, to her horror, he begins to cry.

She is walking past him when the phone rings in the hall. She picks it up. She is asked if she will pay for a reversed charge local call. Of course, she says.

'Mum?'

'Jeremy? Is that you?'

'Of course it is. I'm in a bit of a mess.'

'Where are you? Are you in trouble?'

'No, not like that. I mean. I mean my clothes are dirty. And I've got no money. I tried to get a taxi but no one will take me. I got a lift, I thought they were going all the way, but they've left me in the middle of nowhere.'

'Dirty?'

'Look, Mum, can you come and get me? I'm on the Canterbury road, near the Royal Oak. You know it? Honey Hill, I think. Or maybe you can send Rachel?'

'Of course I can come,' she says. 'I'm on my way.' He didn't ask for his father, she notices, with satisfaction.

Dirty? she thinks.

She's about to pull out of the drive when a car she doesn't recognise, a BMW, pulls in. She swerves to avoid it, realising as her foot slips off the clutch that she's in no fit state to drive. Her head is spinning slightly, the burn on her arm has begun to throb in a way that frightens her. She's worried she may

300

have done herself some serious damage. She will pick Jeremy up, in whatever state he is, and then drive on to the hospital to have it treated. She hates and is scared of hospitals; it will be good to have company.

She sits, both hands on the wheel, as the BMW comes to a halt. There is a man she has never seen before in the driver's seat, a young man, and beside him, Rachel. The light has been turned on inside the car and she sees Rachel stroke the man's arm and say something, leaning towards him, before looking across at her. The young man winds down his window. Belatedly, distracted by pain, Vanessa does the same.

'Where on earth are you going, Mummy? It's past midnight.'

This is interesting, she thinks. She had no idea what time it might be. 'I'm going to get Jeremy. He's outside some pub on the Canterbury road.'

Rachel mutters to the young man, who nods. 'You look as though you need to rest,' she shouts across. 'Let Denny take you. He doesn't mind.' The young man smiles. He is very good-looking indeed, thinks Vanessa.

'It's all right,' she says. 'I can manage.' But Denny is already out of his car and has opened her door. He reaches into the car to help her out, inadvertently touching the burn on her arm. She yelps. Immediately, Rachel is beside him.

'You've burnt yourself. It was that stupid electric fire, wasn't it? I knew I should have turned it off before I left.'

Rachel has always done this, Vanessa thinks, blaming inanimate objects for the foolish things we do to ourselves. She's pleased to find herself having a cogent thought and is on the point of sharing it when Rachel takes her other arm and the two of them heave her gently to her feet.

'You don't need to go,' says Rachel. 'Just tell us where he is.'

'No,' says Vanessa, 'I must go. I promised.'

This is how she is with him, mouths Rachel to the young man, silently, but it's clear what she's saying; she must think I'm a total fool. *I told you what she's like.* Rachel shrugs, and so does he, with a grin that makes him more attractive than ever. My, my, thinks Vanessa, how intimate you two have become in so short a time, assuming you met this evening. Even the shoulders you provide to lean on are synchronised. She lets them lead her round to the passenger seat, dangling like a doll between two awkward girls. She's not sure how drunk she really is. She felt perfectly sober fifteen minutes ago, in the house, or thinks she did. Some of her apparently fragile state, she concludes, must be pretence, for someone's benefit, possibly hers. The truth is that, as ever, she's charmed by herself, by her thought processes, her emotions; it's always been her problem. Rachel's new young man, she thinks. This will take some getting used to, and not only for her. She wonders what Reginald will have to say about it. Poaching on mined territory. Perhaps she ought to warn the young man, or would that be too cruel? She's been cruel enough to Rachel already this evening, she remembers. Still, she'll have a chance to talk to him in the car. When she's safely seated and strapped in, she turns her head to see the two of them, Rachel and whatever his name is, kissing each other as if he were about to be sent off to the front. Well, she thinks, that was fast. Unless she knows nothing at all about her daughter, unless none of them does, which might also be the case.

As Rachel's boyfriend drives onto the road, Vanessa sees Rachel walk over to the house, the front door open, her father waiting on the steps, his arms stretched out to greet her. And the hunter home from the hill, she thinks, except that Rachel isn't the hunter. Reginald is. She turns her head to the right.

'We haven't been introduced,' she says.

'Denny,' he says. He twists towards her, offers her his hand. 'I think you may know my mother.'

'Really?'

'Do you hunt?'

'Foxes?'

'Well, yes,' he says.

She laughs. 'No. I don't.'

'In that case you probably don't. She lives for it. My father used to be hunt master. He's dead now, left us without a penny, but you wouldn't think so from the way she tries to run things.'

'Ah.'

'Where do I need to go?'

She tells him, then leans back into the soft upholstered welcome of the leather. The car is warm, over-warm, and she's tempted to simply close her eyes and sleep. He's driving fast, the way she likes to be driven, and the noise of the engine is a distant purr. Not exactly without a penny then, she thinks, but his interest in her daughter is certainly more understandable than it was before. Has he been as transparent with her, she wonders, as he has with me? He might as well have asked me what kind of dowry we're prepared to furnish him with. Still, she's in no position to criticise someone for thinking ahead, living as she has done off Reginald the cuckold's substantial income all these years. And now, with the image of the crumpled letter rising before her eyes, now that her gaff has been blown, she thinks, and yet not blown, because she still has the upper hand and Reginald knows it, why not share the spoils? Why not be generous?

She turns her head again to take a better look at the new acquisition. He is rather lovely, although he doesn't strike her as particularly bright. Not that brightness need matter; Armand wasn't that bright either, although he thought he was. She watches him turn on the radio, his thick, hairy wrist sticking out of the rolled-back cuff of his cowboy shirt. 'You don't mind, do you?' he says, when he notices she's looking. 'Not at all,' she says. He settles on a station playing jazz, which surprises her. People are so unknowable, finally. How pleasant, she thinks, to be here in this lovely fast car with this delectable young man, with nothing to distract her but the constant throbbing of her burn and Bill Evans, if she's not mistaken. Yes, Bill Evans.

And then she sees her only son at the side of the road, she'd know him anywhere, sitting on the kerb with his head between his knees. He looks up as the car approaches, his face bloodied, utterly forlorn.

'That's him,' she says. 'That's Jeremy.'

32

JEREMY

He doesn't recognise the car. Who the hell *is* this, he thinks, when it pulls to a halt and a woman leaps out of it, stumbles drunkenly on the grass verge, regains her balance and runs towards him, wailing, arms reaching out. He's already tensed to flinch from her grasp when he realises who she is. He starts to struggle to his feet and is half standing when she gets to him, his body one long dull ache with points of acuteness here and there: his chest, both legs, an ankle. Behind her is a man he's never seen: tall, thick dark hair, good-looking in a square-jawed way, a few years older than he is, in a cowboy shirt and jeans, sexy the way a *Playgirl* centrefold is sexy. Mum's brand-new bit of rough? I must be dreaming, thinks Jeremy, while his mother, still keening in an inchoate fashion, runs her hands up and down his aching sides as though searching for drugs. He wonders what he looks like. Dreadful, he imagines, or she wouldn't be behaving like this. He pulls away when she touches what might be a broken rib, falls back down to his knees. 'Ouch,' he says. 'Fucking ouch.'

'What in God's name has happened to you?' she says.

'I got into a bit of a fight.'

'A fight? Good God, Jeremy. You, in a fight? Whatever for?'

This idea, that fights might have some purpose, makes him giggle. But giggling makes him gasp with pain. Centrefold man moves closer, arms out to help him, then recoils, his face appalled. I stink of other men's urine, thinks Jeremy, and he wonders why his mother hasn't noticed or, if she has, why she's said nothing. She stinks of gin, which might explain it.

'He's pissed himself,' the man says, shocked. 'I'm not sure I want him in the car. I only had it cleaned yesterday.' Craning forward from the same safe distance, wrinkling his nose in disgust, he examines Jeremy more closely, as though he were roadkill, steamrollered flat and requiring identification. 'He might do it again.'

'You must have a horse blanket or something,' his mother snaps. 'You don't think I'm going to leave him here by the side of the road, do you?'

'I'm not incontinent,' says Jeremy, helpfully.

'Well?' says his mother, ignoring this. 'Chop-chop. You do want to see my daughter again, I imagine?'

'Oh,' says Jeremy. His mother raises an eyebrow.

'Hush,' she says. 'I'll tell you later.'

The man shrugs, opens the boot and pulls out something that actually is a horse blanket. He shakes it out and lays it on the back seat, holding the door open in a kow-towing parody of the willing servant. Jeremy struggles to his feet and starts to walk, wincing with each step, his legs trembling beneath him, towards the car. He feels unexpectedly queasy. Dear me, he thinks, I'd better not throw up in sexy hunk's clean car.

'Oh, darling,' his mother says. 'I think we should get you to a hospital straight away. What have they done to you?'

'No, no,' says Jeremy hurriedly, fighting the nausea down. 'I just want a hot bath.'

'You certainly need one,' says the man, beneath his breath.

'This is Denny,' his mother says, with a disdainful sniff. 'Rachel's new friend. He offered to drive me,' she adds, unnecessarily. Jeremy watches him put out a hand, pause in mid-air, think better of it, withdraw. Teasing, despite the pain involved in raising an arm, he offers his own hand, smiling as Denny, reluctant, takes it, squeezes with unnecessary vigour, then wipes his palm on the arse of his jeans.

'Hello, Denny,' he says, with a smile he intends to be winning.

'You wanted to go to casualty?' Denny says, to his mother.

'No, that's all right,' she says.

'That's a nasty burn on your arm,' he says. 'You should get it seen to.'

'That doesn't matter now.' She closes the door, glances out to the verge where Jeremy had been sitting as though she expected to see him sitting there still. He wonders what she's thinking about, if she's thinking about him and the fight he's supposed to have had. She knows he'd rather run than fight. What does she imagine has happened to him? She's calmed down so completely it's hard to believe she lost it so completely only five minutes ago, if that. He has no idea of time. Not since his first lift pushed him out of the car, when opening all four windows didn't suffice to attenuate the smell of him. His watch must have stopped before that happened. He remembers looking to see what time it was before finding a phone box and calling home. He remembers shaking it to no effect, and holding it to his ear. Waterproof doesn't mean piss-proof, apparently. How long has she been drinking? he thinks. All evening? All day?

All week? What a fucking miserable life she has. It's time she left. It's time they both did.

Denny turns the car round while she fiddles with the clasp on her seat belt, using her left hand. He's about to try to help when the tongue slides into place. She seems smaller than usual, diminished. She sighs, adjusts her skirt, then turns round to look at Jeremy. He's started to shiver, although he isn't cold. He is sitting on the cusp between the two back seats, in the middle of the horse blanket, which smells worse than he does and is covered with short, bristle-like hairs already working themselves through his clothes towards his skin. As the car heads back towards the house at a speed that must surely be over the limit, his T-shirt begins to steam in the heat of the car, a heady piss-scented steam, until Denny opens his window with a grunt and lights a cigarette. He's shivering again within seconds. 'What burn?' he says.

'It's nothing,' she says. 'I don't suppose I could have a cigarette?'

Denny gives her the packet and the lighter. She takes one for herself and one for Jeremy, lights them both, passes one back. When he takes the first draw he realises, in the general miasma of soreness, that he has also hurt his lip. His mother is turning on the radio. 'You don't mind?' she says. Denny shakes his head. His shoulders are set. He's far too good-looking for Rachel, thinks Jeremy. I'd fuck him. Jazz, which could be worse. His crotch is damp, he lifts himself from the blanket to pull the cloth away from his balls, then sniffs his hand. It's as though it never happened. He sees himself angelically hovering above, his body prone and curled on the floor, surrounded by skinheads with their dicks pulled out, pissing on him, his hair, his face, his crotch, his back, and his own dick stiffens in response: like calls to like. His ribs are aching, with each drag on his cigarette he's stabbed by pain, his lip stings, the skin of his cheek has been opened on the bone, when he grimaces he can feel the crust of dried blood on his face ease and crack and flake, he has bruises on both his thighs and an ankle, he knows without looking. Taking his clothes off will be torture. He'll be black and blue tomorrow. He's a fucking disaster. He grins to himself. *Poète maudit*, he thinks, then: *nostalgie de la boue*. So much French, so many men, so little time. Denny, the sulky dreamboat, is driving him home. His mother is humming to Ella Fitzgerald.

He's had a fabulous evening and it isn't over yet.

The house is quiet when they arrive. Denny waits in the car, the engine turning over, until they are standing at the front door, then drives away, gravel skittering beneath the wheels. Inside the house, the lights are off. His mother sighs with relief. 'We've had rather a difficult day,' she says, taking off her shoes. 'All round.'

'I'm going to have a bath,' Jeremy says.

'And tomorrow morning you will tell me exactly what happened to you this evening.' Her voice is stern. 'Every single detail. Do you understand?'

'Yes,' he says, his voice as faint and humble as he can manage. He has no intention of telling her anything. Already he's thinking of versions of the truth that might be more palatable, for his mother, for the world. And then he will write a poem, exploiting the rich gay argot he has never had the chance to use in conversation. The ghost of Hart Crane will envy him. He will turn his half-hour of humiliation, if that is what it was, into the timelessness of myth. His mother crosses the hall in the darkness. He limps behind her. His ankle can barely take his weight. Perhaps there is something broken, some small, essential bone. He reaches for the banister, to guide him upstairs.

When she pauses on the landing halfway up, he pauses behind her, grateful. 'That's odd,' she says.

'What is?'

'Look,' his mother says, pointing at the light in Rachel's room. Her door is wide open. Is that so odd? he thinks.

'She never leaves her door open,' his mother says, as if she has heard his thought. She hurries up the last few steps, Jeremy a dragging pace behind her, then stops at the door. Jeremy looks over her shoulder to see Rachel sitting up in bed and their father half standing, half sitting beside her, as though he's been interrupted mid-act. He's fully dressed from the waist up, shirt, tie, waistcoat, but he's wearing his pyjama buttons and slippers: half of him ready for the office, as always, and the other half ready for bed. Rachel is in a nightdress, as far as he can see. She is staring at Jeremy and his mother in what appears to be a state of shock, like someone who has just been woken from coma. We have no right to be here, he thinks. We've broken something up. Whatever is happening, it's none of our business. His mother is shaking. 'You filthy brute,' she says. His father slumps down on the bed and turns his head from Rachel to look at her. He doesn't see me, thinks Jeremy, although I must be visible, even to him. As far as my father is concerned, I might as well not be here. He's tempted to wave, if only every movement didn't hurt so much. It's been like this for as long as he can remember.

'How dare you talk to Daddy like that,' says Rachel, coming round from her trance-like state, staring furiously at their mother, 'after what you've done to him.'

310

'Leave it, Rachel,' his father says, still staring at their mother, cowed by something, harried into some dark fetid corner, which might make him more dangerous, held there by something he can see in his wife's face, hear in her voice. 'This is none of your business.' Whatever the business is, thinks Jeremy, it's between the two of them. Rachel doesn't matter either, although she imagines she does. She's tugging down the sleeves of her nightdress, as though ashamed of where her hands have been.

'After what I've done to *him*,' says his mother, incredulous. 'Do you have any idea?'

'I know that Daddy loves me,' says Rachel. What the fuck is all this about? thinks Jeremy. I've missed a bit somehow. I should never have left this house of horrors, because that's how he sees it. The garden, the kitchen, his mother's sweet-scented realm, and then, surrounding that, a sort of deadness in which his father and sister have lived, like polyps in rock, waiting to strike.

'Oh yes,' says his mother, 'he loves you all right. He *loves* you.'

'Leave us alone,' his father says in a low voice, as though he might not want to be heard. He sinks back onto the bed, deflated. Jeremy has never seen his father like this, subdued, unsure of what to do or say. You poor old man, he thinks. For the first time in his life he sees his father as ageing, his powers declining, in the shadow of death.

Rachel pushes her father's back. 'Get up,' she says sharply. 'You're too heavy. I can't move my legs.' And Jeremy watches their father rise to his feet and stand beside the bed. The dress he and Rachel bought together that morning has been thrown onto a chair. Rachel's hair is high and stiff with lacquer on one side, flattened on the other. Jeremy wonders for a second if she's had sex with the man in the car, whose name he's forgotten, and what it must have been like, and what exactly they did. It's hard to imagine, but he's trying. His father hasn't moved.

'Just get out, all of you,' says Rachel. Their father turns to look at her, but Jeremy can't see his expression. What he sees is the old man's shoulders sag and Rachel's face suddenly soften. 'Yes, Daddy,' she says. 'You too.'

'I'm going to have a bath,' says Jeremy.

When he wakes up next day, the pillowcase is stuck to his face with blood from the reopened cut on his cheek. Gingerly, he peels himself off the cotton, then tries to sit up, but the jab of pain at both sides of his chest is too acute and he falls back. Fuck, he says under his breath, and then, louder, hoping someone will hear him, fuck fuck fuck. He rests against the bloodied pillow, wishing he had a little bell to ring, some way of attracting attention to his needs. He groans. He groans again. On the third groan, his bedroom door opens.

'Hello,' says Rachel. 'You look dreadful.'

'I feel worse.'

'I'd stay in bed if I were you.'

'I intend to.'

'It's miserable downstairs.'

'Just for a change.'

She shrugs. 'It's usually about you.'

'What is?'

'When they argue.'

He's gratified to hear this. 'Are they arguing?' he says.

'No, actually, they aren't. Not now anyway.' She sighs. She's standing with one shoulder against the door frame, half in, half out of the room, her weight on one leg. She shows no sign of moving. 'They're behaving as though there was no one else in the house. They aren't even talking to me, let alone each other. They're sort of circling each other.'

'Like vultures.'

'Well, one of them ought to be the dead body, in that case, don't you think?' She gives him a rueful smile. 'I shouldn't be joking about it. Daddy was so upset last night.'

'I could see that. Any idea why?'

'Oh, I think he's just sick of her getting drunk and then disappearing. He didn't even know she'd gone to pick you up until I told him. And then I think he was disappointed.'

'Ah.' By me, he wonders, or by someone else. Did I ask for him? I don't remember. I suppose I just assumed that he wouldn't come and that Mum would. That's how it always has been, after all. Rachel is still by the door, as though wanting to be invited in.

'That dress,' she says. 'The one we bought yesterday in Canterbury.'

He waits. When she doesn't continue, he says, 'Yes?'

'You did like it, didn't you?'

'I thought it was perfect,' he says. 'And it worked, didn't it? What's his name?'

'Denny.' She looks awkward. 'I don't know.'

'What don't you know?'

She hesitates, her face red. 'He's taking me out for a drink tonight. He is nice, isn't he?'

'Well, he certainly looked nice,' says Jeremy, careful not to sound too enthusiastic. He doesn't want to scare her off. Why can't she always be like this, he asks himself. Chatty, confessional, needing him. Why can't I?

'So what happened to you?' she says. 'You look dreadful. You've got blood all over the pillow.'

'Oh, I just got into a fight,' he says.

'And lost, apparently.'

It is his turn to smile. He shakes his head.

'You ought to see the state they're in,' he says.

He stays in bed the rest of that day, and the next, reading desultorily, touching his cheek. His mother and Rachel bring him food on a series of trays, most of which he leaves, and mugs of tea. His father looks in once, but Jeremy has recognised his tread on the stairs and pretends to be asleep. On the third day, Tuesday, he gets up painfully, lies in a full bath until the water is almost cold, his hand on his cock, playing with it in a mildly scientific way until it stiffens. This brings to mind a joke from school that started, *You know when you wank in the bath and the spunk sticks to you?* And whoever said *Yes* became the joke. He wraps himself in a towel, then removes it in front of a full-length mirror in his mother's dressing room, astonished to see the lurid patchwork his body has become. He pulls on his loosest jeans and a baggy T-shirt and gingerly walks downstairs. His mother sees him from her vantage point in the sitting room. Her chair is surrounded by newspapers, books, empty cups, as though she hasn't moved in days. 'At last,' she says. 'I've been sorting things out. We're leaving.'

'Really?'

'Yes. You're going to Paris. It's all arranged.'

'And you?'

'Don't you worry about me. I'll be fine. We'll all be fine.'

He's going to ask about Rachel, and about money, but decides these questions can wait. He shrugs, then goes into the kitchen to see if anyone has made coffee recently. Sitting at the table is a young Indian woman, his age or perhaps a little older, gleaming black hair tied back behind her head, a bright pink T-shirt, enormous eyes. She is shelling peas. She is pregnant. She looks up and smiles at him. 'Hello,' she says.

PART FOUR

(2012)

33

JEREMY

Armand Grenier is in the armchair his father always used, directly in front of the TV. He's sitting with his knees apart and his trolley case between them, as if waiting for a flight to be called, his head cocked slightly, listening to the music that Vikram must have put on to keep him amused. When Jeremy walks in, Vikram makes an odd little gesture towards the armchair, as though he's performed a conjuring trick of some kind, while Armand springs up, his arms outstretched. He looks lankier, more scarecrow-like, than ever. Jeremy hasn't seen him for three or four months, but he seems to have aged years in that time. From his face he's brought bad news. This is all I need, thinks Jeremy, after all the exciting developments he's been emailing me about these past two weeks. Sooner or later, I shall have to tell him about my writer's block. And that will be that, he thinks, the sad demise of Nathalie Cray.

But unexpectedly Armand smiles and takes Jeremy by the shoulders. He kisses him on both cheeks. He starts to speak in French and Jeremy is thrown for a moment; he hasn't heard French since he got back to England. Armand is saying how good it is to see him, and why hasn't he been in touch properly, they have all been so concerned for him, and Jeremy is answering that he's fine, and he's been reading his emails and answering them surely? It hasn't been easy but he hasn't disappeared off the face of the earth, he says, his eyes rolling stairwards, immediately relaxed and at home. And who are *they*, he wonders, his heart leaping for a moment. How much he's been missing this, his second language, he thinks, and laughs out loud without realising it, his father momentarily forgotten. When Armand says, again, 'How good to see you,' this time in English, he wants to shut him up, he wants to maintain the illusion that he's back at home, in his own small flat, with Jean-Paul maybe, because if not Jean-Paul, who else? Madame Grenier? But do Jean-Paul and Armand even know each other? Of course they do. He introduced them once, at Charles de Gaulle, and Armand was snippy with them both, and called Jean-Paul a shop assistant, fortunately behind his back. All this is going through his head as, impulsively, he hugs Armand to his chest, holds him close. How good to have you here, he thinks, forgiving him everything, and fully breathes out for what feels like the first time that day, a sigh of relief so deep it shakes him. By the window, beside the stereo, as *L'après-midi d'un faune* moves smoothly, atmospherically, towards its climax, Vikram is beaming at them both. Jeremy looks at him, puzzled and then surprised, as though remembering, then closes his eyes. There will be time for Vikram later.

He's about to ask Armand how long he can stay, and what on earth has made him come, when he hears Rachel's voice call from upstairs. 'For God's sake, someone come up here now,' she's shouting, and Dhara is already halfway up the stairs by the time Jeremy has turned round to follow her. 'I'm coming,' he calls up, Dhara's body blocking the light from the landing window. Behind him hurries Armand, and it's too late to stop him, although this isn't his place, this isn't where he should be. Abruptly, Jeremy wishes he weren't here after all. Rachel is calling out for them to hurry, to hurry for God's sake, and Dhara has begun to wail, a low hiccupping wail of words he can't make out. He thinks it's Indian at first, some Indian language he doesn't know, but what she's saying is Reggie, over and over again, oh Reggie, she's saying, oh my darling Reggie. And then, pushing past them all, there is Vikram.

'This is the right way to do it,' Vikram is saying. Jeremy has been sitting beside his father for over an hour, holding his hand, feeling the warmth leave it. It's so much more gradual than he thought, as though there were no clear line between life and death, just the slow, soft, uninterruptable ebb of heat. He can't believe it, not really. He's watching his father's face, the eyes closed, the lips parted, the skin on his jutting cheekbones relaxed and slightly waxy, for any sign of movement. Perhaps what made his father his father is leaving his body as slowly as the heat of it, he thinks. Perhaps there is still some trace of him there, some residue of the man. Once, he was sure he saw a flutter in the throat and almost called Vikram: we've made a mistake. But he was wrong. His father is dead.

It wasn't like this with his mother. They'd been hustled out of the ward, been ordered to wait in the corridor while they prepared her. That was the word Andreas had used. Prepared. As though one can be prepared for death, he'd thought then, and thinks now. At least, this time, no one is here to hustle him out, no nurses, no frightened faces in adjacent beds, no foreign language. He wondered at first why Rachel wasn't here with him, or instead of him, because surely she has more right to this than he does, but she's locked herself in her room, Dhara says, she's breaking her heart. Dhara has loosened her hair and is sitting at the end of the bed, her hands in her lap, rocking gently backwards and forwards. Vikram has called the people who need to be called, he's known what to do. Armand has made tea and might be in the garden, or the conservatory. Jeremy doesn't know. He's here because he can't bear to think of his father not having someone with him, and, although he knows there is Dhara, and he knows what Dhara was, and is, it's not enough. It's up to him, in the end, and to Rachel. He looks at his father, both there and not there, the mystery of it, banal and implacable. You old cunt, he thinks, and it isn't with shame, he has felt no shame for weeks, but with affection. *Vieux con.* His father had understood, he knows that, understood the word, and understood what lay beneath the word. Better than Jeremy had done, he sees that now. He sees so much he couldn't see before.

He stretches his legs, which are stiff, and his shoulders, which ache. He has been in the same position too long. The tea Armand made for him is cold; a dirty orange scum has formed across the top of it. He glances at the foot of the bed, at Dhara, watching her rock back and forth, quite lost to him, in her own private place of grief. How long has she been waiting for this moment, he wonders. And now he remembers her, sitting, shelling peas, only days before he left the house for Paris. And pregnant, surely she was pregnant? Or is that a false memory? How untrustworthy memory can be. But he remembers her smiling across at him as he crossed the hall, so vividly it might have been this morning. She has been in his father's life as long as he has been out of it. To his astonishment, this thought brings tears to his eyes.

'I need to walk around a bit,' he says. 'Why don't you come

and hold his hand?' You have more right to it, he thinks, but doesn't say.

She looks up, nods.

'I'll do that,' she says. 'Yes.' She stands up as he does, and there's a clumsy ballet as they pass each other, between the bed and the window, Jeremy catching his foot behind the leg of the commode. He finds himself suddenly with Dhara in his arms and the two of them clinging to each other for dear life. Dear life, he thinks, the phrase flashing into his head, as Dhara holds him more tightly and he puts his arms around her, presses her head to his chest. She is crying finally, he can feel her breasts shaking against him, but his moment of tearfulness has passed and left him with a feeling of pity for Dhara, and for Rachel. He eases her away as gently as he can. 'I want to see how Rachel is,' he says.

Dhara's wrong, Rachel isn't in her bedroom. He wanders round the house, upstairs and downstairs, looking into every room with a sense of increasing urgency, until he comes to their father's office. The door is closed. She doesn't answer when he calls, in a low voice, 'Rachel.' He knocks, waits, knocks again. No answer. He's not sure what to do. He stands there. If she's in the room and wants him, she'll say so, he thinks. If she isn't, or doesn't, he's lost. He needs her as much as she must, surely, need him. He's about to walk off when he hears his name.

'Hello?' he says.

'Oh, for God's sake, Jeremy,' she says. 'Don't just hover. Come in.'

She's sitting in a corner of the room, in a small Victorian chair that used to be in the living room when he lived here, an armchair his mother used for sewing in because it had no arms. His father must have moved it in here; later he'll wonder why. He'd forgotten about it, hadn't noticed it, the fabric's been changed; seeing it now brings his mother back to him. Rachel's too big for the chair; it barely holds her.

'I knew it had to happen,' she says. She hasn't raised her head to look at him. She's staring into her hands as though she is holding something valuable, or dangerous, and doesn't know what to do with it.

'Yes.'

'But you're never ready, are you?' she says, lifting her head now and glaring at him with red, sore eyes.

'No.'

'It's easier for you,' she says, and he wants to answer her back, deny this. But maybe she's right, after all. Maybe his fate is always to suffer less than she does.

'I'm sorry,' he says, foolishly.

'What for?' She looks back to her empty hands. 'You didn't kill him, did you?'

'I'm sorry I wasn't with you when he died.'

'With me? With him, don't you mean?'

And this is true, she's right. He's sorry he wasn't with his father. But that isn't what he meant.

'You were with Mummy,' she says. He can't tell if she's offering this as consolation or as further accusation, as though, wherever he is, he is bound to be in the wrong place.

'We both were.'

'Yes, but she spoke to you. She never spoke to me.' She stands up to tug a handkerchief out of her skirt pocket, blows her nose into it, folds it and puts it back. A moment later, she takes it out a second time and sits down again, with the handkerchief in her lap. 'I always felt there was something she wanted to say to me, but never did. I never once felt that with Daddy.' She pauses, examines her handkerchief. 'Did you?'

'Not really, no.' He's still by the door. His answer is not an answer at all, but that doesn't matter. He'd sit beside her if he wasn't so afraid he'd be rebuffed. Rachel is so erratic. Afraid not for himself but for her, it strikes him; he wouldn't mind for himself. He's afraid she'll feel utterly alone. As perhaps she is. Only minutes ago he was holding a woman he barely knows and now he is looking at his only sister across the infinite few feet that divide them. 'Dad always said what he meant,' he says.

'He did, didn't he?' she says, then looks up again, more gently. 'Do you really think so?'

'Yes.' His eyes prickle with tears. 'Why don't you go and sit with him? While you can. They'll be here soon.'

'What do you mean?'

'The undertakers. Vikram told them to come this afternoon. He wanted to give us as long as he could.'

'They're going to take Daddy away?' she says, as if this fact has only just occurred to her.

He nods.

'I can't bear this,' she says, her voice flat, matter of fact. 'I can't believe it's happening.' She breathes in deeply, starts to cry, slowly at first, and then, after the first few gulps, with a frenzy that scares him, half suffocated by some force inside her, like one possessed. Her hands are scratching at each other, two animals trapped in the same small cage. She seems capable of anything, of flinging herself to the ground, of hurting herself, or him. He crosses to the chair, lowers himself slowly beside her until he's kneeling on the carpet, a supplicant, waiting for her to give him some sign that he might be tolerated. Her whole body shakes with the pain of it. Cautious, afraid still, he reaches his arms around her, knots his fingers together behind her far elbow in a sort of cat's cradle, some game their mother taught them, here is the church and here is the steeple, open the doors and here are the people, struggling to contain what won't be held.

Jeremy's in the garden when they arrive. Armand has sat beside him, in respectful silence, although Jeremy would have liked to talk, to be distracted. He'd have spoken himself if it hadn't seemed inappropriate. He tried at one point, telling the other man how the garden had been when his mother lived here, the roses, the clematis, a host of flowers he has no name for. Vikram has been pruning the wisteria, he said. Armand had nodded, said something about Vanessa always loving flowers, and Jeremy had said, I miss her, Armand, I miss her so much, with a lurch in his heart of surprise, as though he had never quite realised this before. So do I, said Armand. And then they had both stopped talking.

When Jeremy hears the doorbell ring and Vikram's steps in the hall, his eyes are closed; he could be asleep. Armand touches his shoulder. 'They have come for your father,' he says.

'Rachel's with him?'

'I believe so,' says Armand. They are talking to each other in English now, as if, thinks Jeremy, there is no escape from where they are. They stand up and Armand follows Jeremy into the house.

Vikram is alone in the hall when they get there. The front door behind him is open and Jeremy can see a white van parked in the drive outside, its back doors open, where he'd expected to see an ambulance, or a hearse. There is writing on the side of the van and a stretcher by the open doors, low to the ground, with some sort of mechanical cantilever, he supposes, there to raise it. Upstairs, he can hear voices and then Rachel crying out, a gasping cry, and Dhara comforting her, crooning and keening at the same time. He's about to go upstairs, but Vikram rests a hand on his shoulder and he stops himself. You're right, he thinks, I'm better off here. I've said my goodbyes. And then he hears a door slam, and the women's voices are muffled, and he knows he should be with Rachel. He starts to climb the stairs but before he reaches the third step he hears a dull bang of something hard but padded against a wall, and, as he looks up into an unexpected semi-darkness, his view of the landing window is blocked by a man in a black suit holding the end of a long grey rubber bag, bending the bag a little to get it round the curve of the banister, the man on the other end telling him to be careful, they don't want to drop it. At which point Jeremy turns away, ignoring the anxious hands of Armand, running back into the garden, and then down the garden until he comes to the wall, pressing his hands against the wisteria-covered brick until something, a thorn, the uneven, crumbling surface of the brick itself, cuts raggedly into his flesh, aware for the first time this day, in some way he can't account for later, of what death means.

34

RACHEL

Lady Mirabelle left the darkened chamber and the sobbing women around the bed. She lifted her skirts and ran down the stairs, her steel-tipped heels tapping on the marble steps, across the tiles of the echoing hall, against the stone flight that took her down into the cellar. A little light filtered through the cobwebs on the window, just enough for her to see Jerome lift his head as she entered. He was slumped against the wall, his legs stretched out in front. He was wearing britches and a soiled white shirt, open to the waist. When he saw her, he started and she heard the chain move against the straw. She hurried across to him, sank to her knees beside him. She saw him as he had been only days ago, his back still raw from the birch, wisteria blossom in his richly curling blue-black hair. She would never forgive her father for what he had done. She touched his chest with her slim white fingers, stroked the fine, soft fleece she found there. He winced at her touch.

'He's gone,' she said. 'We are free.'

Jerome smiled slowly. He leaned forward until his face was near hers. 'I am not free,' he said. 'I shall never be free.'

She searched in the folds of her skirt until she found what she needed. A key. 'Turn round,' she said.

He remained stock-still. 'If you release me, milady,' he said, in a deep, foreboding voice, 'it is not I but you who shall never be free.'

With a shiver, she reached behind him and turned the key in the lock.

Rachel scrolls down the page but this is all there is. She's relieved in a way. She shouldn't be reading Jeremy's so-called work. Even worse, she shouldn't want more. He must have done this before Thursday, she's sure of that at least. He could never have written it now that their father is dead. But it still makes her sick to see her life, their lives, distorted and dirtied like this. Is this what all writers do, she wonders, take the truth and twist it to suit their nasty, sordid fantasies? This Jerome character even reminds her a little of Denny – the hair, the voice. She can just see Jeremy imagining Denny chained to a cellar wall, unable to fight back. All her love for him reduced to a sad man's sordid fantasy, then sold for money to women who don't know any better, who think this sort of filth is love. Is nothing sacred? She doesn't know her brother, that's what all this comes down to in the end. She thinks she does, she thinks she has finally reached a sort of understanding, and then she reads something like this and she's back to square one. When he stood there at the office door and stared at her as though he'd never seen a woman cry before, and all she wanted was for him to speak to her, anything would have done. Any word at all to make her feel that life would go on. No wonder he's alone, she thinks. But then, so is she. She'll have to watch him when the vicar comes to talk about Daddy this afternoon. Who knows what unlikely stories he'll come out with, given half a chance? He's already told her he doesn't see what the point of a funeral is. He didn't say that when they stuck Mummy's coffin in that poky little Greek church and he was hanging on to Andreas's every word. It's true, though, that a proper funeral is her idea. What an ordeal it will be, she thinks. I wish I believed in something. I don't know if I'll be able to bear it.

She pushes her chair away from the desk. The screen has gone blank and she's trying to remember what she came in here for. All she can think about is her father and where he is. That's what she doesn't grasp about death. That someone isn't here any longer. She'd thought losing Daddy would be like losing Denny, worse perhaps, or perhaps not so bad, but not *different*. Not different in kind. But even when Denny wasn't with her, he was somewhere. And now Daddy's gone, but that's not the word. She remembers that sketch Jeremy had loved so much, about the parrot, and all the words the man had used to describe it. *Late, no more, bereft of life* and so on. For the first time in her life, although the last thing it does is make her laugh – that kind of savage, infantile humour has never made her laugh – she knows what he means. She sees the joke. Gone's not the word, nor passed away. There is no word for it, for the place where her father is. That's what she can't accept. No word. No place. She could bear it if she thought he were somewhere else, it doesn't matter where, another dimension, another universe. Heaven. Even hell. If only she could. If only she could force herself to believe there were some other place than this.

Perhaps the vicar will help after all. She's found herself, these past few days, wandering round the house as if she's looking for something she's misplaced, but can't put her finger on what, and then she's realised she's looking for her father.

That must have been what brought her in here half an hour ago, into the office, to sit at her father's desk, although she didn't know this at the time. Then, yesterday morning, she went into his room and was startled not to see him in his bed, as though she'd actually forgotten he was dead. How is that possible? How is that possible? She'd stood by the window and watched the wind farm and thought: all that energy, all that turning and turning ad infinitum, can't some of it be used to bring him back?

When she closes her eyes, as she is doing now, she can see him. Surely that counts for something? She can see him walk up the drive, slipping his car keys into the front of his brief-case, or flicking through his diary before he leaves the house. She can see him laughing on the phone, or talking to Dhara, or sitting by the fire with one of Jeremy's books in his hands, his glasses sliding down his nose, a tumbler of whisky on the table beside the chair, half asleep. What possessed him, she wondered, to read such dross? She asked him once, although she dreaded the answer would confirm her fear, that he read them to be near to Jeremy, the child he loved most. But what he said was that he read them to understand women. She'd wanted to laugh. She didn't know where to begin to tell him how wrong he was. Jeremy knows nothing about women. If her father had wanted to know about women, he could have asked her. And all the women in his life, because she knew even then he was no saint, to put it mildly, why couldn't he have asked them? All these women buzzing around him like flies around food and what does he do to understand them? He reads the appalling pulp fiction of his nancy-boy son. She'd take the book from his hand and shake him gently by the shoulder until he woke. Time to go to bed, she'd say. He'd finish the whisky first, and slip his bookmark into the novel.

She'd help him upstairs, this was towards the end, hang up his dressing gown, fold back the duvet while he went to the bathroom for a final pee. When he came back, he'd look at her. Sometimes he'd say something: I'd like a little company, or, For old time's sake. Not now, Daddy, she'd say, not now, and he'd sigh and shrug, and she'd wonder later if she'd understood, but she knew she had. She had always understood, she thinks now. Sometimes he'd pucker his lips, like a child, and wait to be kissed.

She's pushing these thoughts away when Jeremy's voice drifts in from outside. He's in the garden, with Armand, as she's learned to call him, both of them chattering away in French. He's still here, after four days. She heard the two of them arguing in the hall the morning after they'd taken Daddy away, and she imagined Jeremy was telling him to go, but she was wrong, as usual. He told her later he was persuading Armand to stay for a few more days, to help them out, he said. I don't know what you were thinking of, she told him, furious, the last thing we need is a guest, but he was adamant. He should be here, he insisted, he's a friend of the family. Which was news to her. Dhara's taken a fancy to him, Rachel's seen her preening and pouring him extra wine, at lunch as well. How quickly she seems to have got over it. Maybe it's an Indian thing: one good long wail and it's over. And that's another thing, she thinks, her eyes still closed. They've been living together, the four of them, with Vikram popping in and out, as though this were some sort of holiday camp. The house is still filled with food and wine her father paid for, bought on his various accounts. There will be some reckoning to do, she thinks. She still hasn't been in touch with Denny.

When she hears the door, she opens her eyes.

'Here you are,' says Jeremy. 'We couldn't find you.'

'I've been sorting things out,' she says. She gestures towards the shelves.

'It's good to keep busy,' he says, although he's done nothing these past few days but wander round the house and garden, talking to Armand, talking to Vikram, drinking too much, avoiding her, she's felt, although she might be wrong. Perhaps she has been avoiding him. The house is so large suddenly, she feels so alone in it. She doesn't know how to talk to him, or anyone else. She has no words for what is happening, and she wonders how on earth he can talk the way he does. She hears him, unstoppable, a flow of sound, utterly meaningless. Sometimes she doesn't even register which language he's speaking. She's never heard so much French, not even in France. In some ways, this makes it easier. She doesn't so much listen as watch, as though by observing him she'll reach some closer understanding. As though, when he speaks, his words mean nothing.

'Your father continued to work from home?' says Armand.

'Not really,' she says. 'He liked to think he did. He was still on the board, right till the end.'

'You worked beside him?'

She shakes her head. 'I haven't worked in the business for years. Not since I married my husband. My ex-husband.'

'Did you miss it?'

'Not at all.' She can tell he's trying to be nice to her, but she isn't in the mood to be nice. She doesn't want him here. There's something clingy about him when he talks to her.

'Rachel prefers horses to plastics,' says Jeremy, as though nothing of importance has happened.

'I think that is true for most people,' says Armand, smiling. 'You must be worried about your horses. I expect they miss you.'

'No,' she says, lying. She is worried sick about her horses, when she forgets her father for a moment and thinks of them. 'I have some very good people working for me at the stables. They're running the show.'

'You have been a devoted daughter,' he says unexpectedly, no longer smiling. 'Your father was a fortunate man, a fortunate man to have you near him.'

She doesn't know what to say. She fights back tears. She refuses to cry in front of this man, this intruder. Jeremy is giving Armand a funny look, as if to warn him. I won't be protected, she thinks, I won't. 'I was lucky to have Daddy,' she says, in the end. She glances at Jeremy, who is watching her, anxious for some reason she can't fathom. 'We both were.'

Armand nods. 'Of course.' He walks across to the shelves, most of which have already been cleared, and picks up a trade journal.

'People don't make things any longer,' he says, thumbing through it. 'Not here in this country. Not in France. It's a shame, I think.'

'Armand sold his printing firm a couple of years ago,' says Jeremy. 'The people who bought it are talking about closing it down, he was telling me earlier today. People don't need printers, typesetters, any longer. It's all computerised these days. It's very sad.' And he's off again, speaking in French, with Armand casting an apologetic look her way. For an instant, against her will, she's glad he's here. She watches them talk in front of her, then closes her eyes a second time, sighs loudly. She wishes they'd go away. After a moment or two, of shuffling feet and whispered French, her wish is granted.

Later that day, an hour before the vicar is due to arrive, she goes back up to her room and looks at the files of letters. She hasn't touched them since Thursday, hasn't wanted to see them before today but she thought she might find something she could mention, some anecdote suitable for the sermon. The letters are the last place to look for a word or two that might be read in church, she's aware of that, yet she can't shake the belief that surely there will be something. Thinking of her father now, all she can see is the last few months, an old man in a bed, as though his entire life had shrunk to nothing behind it. How massive his death is, she thinks, how much it blocks the rest of him out. Perhaps the letters will offer her some way round. She picks up the file marked 1977. What an odd year it had been, with Mummy and Jeremy walking out like that, and Denny walking in. So much of what had happened then remains unclear to her. Why did it all have to end so horribly? Hadn't the four of them been happy enough? She blames her mother still, and then Jeremy. Only her father is blameless, she thinks, or he would be if the evidence weren't here before her, in all these manila files, his constant infidelity. Already he'd started his affair with Dhara, if affair is what it was. She remembers Dhara coming to the house. Such a girl she'd been then, so slim and shy until she got pregnant. Perhaps that was the last straw. If only she could remember the order of things. All she knows is that her father had been so close to her, to Rachel, right through, until Denny came along and he'd stepped back, as though his job was done. She'd never asked him to do that. If anyone had given her the choice, she thinks now, she would have chosen Daddy.

She's flicking through the letters when she comes across one she'd completely forgotten about these past few days. She looks at the address again. Paris. *Septembre 1977*. The letter starts *Mon cher Reginald*, so it's almost certainly from a woman, but the rest of it makes no sense to her at all; not just the language but the writing, spidery and flowery at the same time, how typical of the French, the crumpled paper making it even harder to decipher. Someone had smoothed it out and folded it and put it back in the envelope. Someone must have thought it was worth that effort. The letter that caused it all, she remembers now, the letter of discord. She looks at the signature, but can't make it out. She's been meaning to find someone who can tell her what it says for months now, ever since she found it among her father's papers. She'd have asked Jeremy, but she doesn't want to share this with him, in case it provides him with ammunition he can use against her, against Daddy. And then it occurs to her. Armand is in the house. Armand is French. Armand can tell her what the letter says.

35

JEREMY

Armand is talking to him about some film deal that's brewing, but he can't quite persuade himself to listen. They are seated together in the conservatory, drinking coffee Armand brought with him, in an almost tropical heat. While Armand gestures eagerly, his long arms reaching out from the cradling slump of the garden chair, and reels off strings of figures, potential earnings, sums of money that would be startling at any other moment, in any other place, all that Jeremy can hold in his mind, like one small polished stone in the palm of a cupped hand, is that people shouldn't die in summer. There should be darkness, he thinks, and cold, frost at the window, frost in the bones, contraction. And yet all the people he has lost, if that's the word he wants, if it doesn't smack too much of carelessness, have died in the light of day, the expanding warmth of the summer sun. His mother, Gilberto, his father. What was that poem he used to know by heart, about ice and fire, and death, and which of the two would be worse? But it wasn't a poem about death so much as love, about what love means. He can't remember the details now, but it talked about desire, he's sure of that. It talked about the perils of desire. Yesterday, or the day before, Jeremy's lost track, Armand told him that sales these past few months have soared, gone through the roof, it's phenomenal, awesome, and now there's this interest from a studio. Government funding. German TV, Canal+. E-books have changed the game. Big bucks, he said at one point, with a little ironic twist to his upper lip. These are new phrases, thought Jeremy at the time, additions to Armand's already extensive English repertoire. He's been talking to our American friends while I've been here. People want what you can give them, he said, and Jeremy nodded, half listening. Your time has come. Yours and Nathalie Cray's. For a moment, he wondered who Armand meant.

He remembers this conversation now. It was the day after Dad died – one, two days ago? – when he and Rachel had driven back to the house after seeing the registrar, a thin, neurotic woman in a beige suit who had treated them as if they were lying, as if their father's death were a new sort of scam, and she was on to them. She needed to know Vikram's General Medical Council number, she said. I didn't know he had a number, Jeremy had said, adding unnecessarily, I live in France. I'm afraid I can't proceed with certification without a number, the woman had said, and Rachel had snapped, Oh for God's sake, my father's dead. Outside the office, they'd looked at each other, held each other's eyes, and laughed, for the first time since it had happened – uncomfortably, but nonetheless a laugh, as though, in the end, they'd found a way to share their loss. Wasn't she awful? said Jeremy, and Rachel had said, with a smile, An absolute cunt. Which had reminded them both of their father, and of what Jeremy had said to him, and their mood had separated, darkened. They'd driven home in silence. Back in the house, Armand had said that he should go, that he was intruding on their grief, and Jeremy had insisted he stay; he couldn't bear the thought of being left alone with Rachel and Dhara. No, he said, finally you can tell me why you're here. And so he had talked about sales and some definite interest in a film, or films, a whole series of films, but Jeremy wasn't really listening. And here he is now, talking about film deals again, in a corporate mid-Atlantic English, as though repeating entire conversations from memory. Even his accent has flattened out into a sort of ersatz drawl. Jeremy tries to concentrate. This *matters*, he knows that, and not just to Armand. It must matter to him as well, he must make it matter or he will never be able to go home again. He has been here just over a month, but his life in Paris has never seemed further away. And despite his efforts to follow Armand, he finds himself wriggling in the chair beside him, his knees at the height of his chest, wondering what Jean-Paul is doing, and why he hasn't called, knowing he could have called himself, not knowing why he hasn't. As usual, he supposes, he's to blame. He wishes Armand would go back to speaking French, or his old English at least, not this LA sub-dialect. He's about to suggest they move inside, have a drink before thinking about dinner, when Dhara appears before him like a vengeful child.

'I want to talk to you,' she says.

Armand stands up. 'I'll take a walk around the garden,' he says. 'I need some exercise before we eat.' He rests a hand on Jeremy's shoulder. 'We can talk about this later. I want to show you some figures. I know this is a bad time but I think you'll be as excited as I am.'

'No, there's no need for you to go away,' says Dhara, officious. Armand falls back into the wicker armchair. 'I'm taking him inside.' She looks hard at Jeremy, daring him to resist, then turns round and walks back into the house. Jeremy, startled, follows her.

'We have to talk,' she says when they are both in the sitting room. She has chosen the armchair his father always used and he finds himself slumping onto the sofa his mother would lie on each evening, her drink beside her on a small round table, the light of the television, usually with the sound turned off, flickering in the corner, a book on the cushion, face down.

'Do we?' he says. He doesn't mean to sound hostile, or doesn't think he does, but there it is, that edge of resentment he can't suppress.

'We hardly know each other, I know that,' she says, 'and I know you think there's no reason why you should like me. Well, there is, really. There is one very good reason. Reggie loved me, you see. Your father loved me. You didn't know that because you were never here, but Rachel will tell you, if you ask her. You probably don't believe me. You probably think I'm just the dotty old housekeeper, looking out for herself now that her boss is dead. But Rachel understood what we meant to each other. I'm not sure how much she's ever liked it – not much, I don't think. But I know she understood.'

'I do believe you,' he says. He's sincere. He wishes he had a drink. He adjusts the cushion behind his back.

'I never intended all this to happen,' she says. 'I wanted my own life, like anyone else, a husband, a house, a family of my own and no confusion about all that side of it. But Reggie had other ideas – he kept saying, Dhara, if it works, why fix it? And it did work, in its way. Easier for us both, as well, in some ways.'

'I don't understand.'

'Oh, my family, his family. How would you have felt if you'd come home one day and found yourself with an Indian stepmother?'

'I wouldn't have minded,' he says. 'Anyway, I never did

come home. I was far away, having fun. What I felt wouldn't have mattered.'

'Well, your father didn't think so, but that's by the by,' she says. 'Your mother wouldn't give him a divorce in any case. She said he didn't deserve one after what he'd done. I never really knew your mother, but I can't say I was that fond of her. I know you were close to her. She seems a hard woman from what I've been told. She didn't give Reggie what he wanted, I know that. She left that to others. But it's not for me to judge.' She is silent for a moment. Jeremy sits on the sofa, mouth open, mildly appalled by what he's hearing, less by what she's saying, which he supposes he knew, than by the fact of hearing it from Dhara's lips. Dhara shrugs, continues. 'In any case, by the time she died and he was free to marry me, we'd settled into our routine. There didn't seem to be any point in disrupting everything. I was living here most of the time anyway. Vikkie, thank goodness, was back at home with his grandparents.'

'Vikram, you mean? I thought he was brought up by your parents?'

She smiles. 'He was.'

'I don't understand.'

She shakes her head. 'You haven't noticed, have you?'

'Noticed what?'

'How much Vikkie looks like your father. A bit darker, but still. You have a brother, Jeremy.'

'A brother?'

'Well, a half-brother.'

Jeremy reaches behind his back to pull out the cushion. He puts it on his lap, plays with a corner tassel, his eyes cast down. He doesn't want to look at Dhara for a moment. He's angry with her, but doesn't know why; because she has chosen an inopportune moment, perhaps, or because of what she has said. It could just as easily be the former, he knows that. In some ways the idea that Vikram might be his brother is also thrilling. It is as though he has been blindfolded and twirled against his will in some mad, dangerous party game and then had the blindfold removed. He finds himself in the place he has always known and yet everything, the simplest most domestic thing, is all at once a mystery to him. She might also, of course, be lying. When he's ready, he looks up. 'Why are you telling me this?'

'Well, he may not be the only one, you see.'

'I'm sorry?'

Dhara pulls her blouse down over her breasts in an unexpectedly smug, coquettish way. 'Reggie's written a will, obviously. More than one, to tell you the truth. He had his solicitor come round about six months ago to change the last one, I don't know why. He might have heard from someone, one of his lady friends, I don't know. I never saw his letters. It was just before he started to go downhill, perhaps he knew he didn't have much longer. He wasn't always compos mentis after that, you see. Well, you saw him, didn't you? You saw what he was like. Confused, to say the least. Afterwards he told me he'd thought of everyone, but he wouldn't say what he meant. I didn't push him, it didn't seem right. I didn't want to look like a gold-digger. Isn't that mad, after all we've been through together? It's what other people might think, I suppose. It shouldn't matter at all, but it does, and with Vikkie being a doctor. Being Reggie's doctor. You have to be careful. At first I just thought he meant he'd left me something, and maybe Vikkie too, and that was nice, I thought, and typical of Reggie. But he kept repeating it, with this funny look on his face, and it made me wonder what *everyone* meant.'

'Does Rachel know?'

'About the will? I should think so. Not what's in it though, I don't think. Reggie was very cagey about it. And then I don't think he knew himself.'

'No, not the will. About Vikram?' He'd like to say Vikkie, but can't. It's an intimacy too far, and yet not far enough, from the intimacy he thought he might like, and might still like. He's often wondered what it might mean to have a brother, and to be in love with him. And now he is on the point of finding out. Half-brother; half in love. And does Vikram know? he thinks now. But surely he must. Is that why he's been so sweetly confidential with Jeremy, so giving? With all that talk of seeking and being moved into the light. Because he sees him as a brother?

'Oh yes, dear. She's known for ages. I'm surprised she hasn't told you. But you don't really talk that much, do you? No one does here.'

'No,' he says, 'we don't.' She didn't just not tell me, he thinks. She lied to me. Now why would she do that? Because I've lied to her? He wonders where she is. He hasn't heard her moving around the house since the vicar left, his little book full of notes he'll use to concoct a life out of, lies and half-truths and evasions. These past few days, he's understood something about houses. The last time he lived with others on a daily basis was almost thirty years ago, with Gilberto. Since then his home has grown smaller with each move, as though to exclude that possibility a second time. Now, in the house of his parents, in the house of his failed family, there are four of them, brother and sister, father's lover and, well, Armand, in all his multiplicity of roles, and Jeremy has the sensation that the house is like a doll's house, with a hinged façade, and that some kind of farce is being played out, or

343

tragedy perhaps, inevitable, composed of meetings and sep-
arations, contrived or accidental, for the benefit of someone
none of them will ever know, some malevolent child they will
never see. This is what houses are for. For the mechanics of
intimate terror to play themselves out without even crossing
a threshold. Anything can happen here, he thinks, and maybe
it will. He feels too small, a plaything, and suffocated at the
same time, as though the room, and not only the room, has
shrunk around him.

He thought about all this while the vicar was here, sipping
his tea, smiling in an anxious, benign, occasionally distracted
way. Jeremy had imagined he would know their father, would
tell them what he knew to comfort them, would bring the
dead man back to life. But he was wrong. The vicar had never
met his father apart from the occasional social event, usually
to raise money, as the man admitted, perhaps in the hope of
some small bequest. Rachel wasn't much help either. She sat
there, shredding a paper tissue, lips sealed. Jeremy had found
himself burbling about his childhood, half-formed irrelevant
memories from which his father emerged badly if at all, until
Rachel had angrily interrupted him. He wasn't like that at all,
she kept saying, and the vicar would purse his lips and make
a soothing noise. This must be very hard for you both, he
said. And then, Perhaps you can tell me about his life in
plastics, which brought an involuntary smile to Jeremy's lips;
he didn't dare glance at Rachel. This time, he didn't answer.
It had been Rachel's idea to call the man in, she should have
thought of something useful to say, some neat, revealing anecdote, not just sat there whimpering. They could have asked
Dhara to help them. She would have known what to say.

As soon as the vicar had gone Rachel slunk from the room,
avoiding conversation. She'd stopped at the door for a second

and looked at him. 'Where's Armand?' she'd asked. 'I don't know,' he'd said. 'I think he may have gone for a walk into town.' He hadn't thought it odd at the time; he'd seen it as part of her general policing strategy, as though nothing in the house should happen without her knowing, but later he'd wondered why she'd asked. He hoped she wasn't going to be unpleasant.

'I know you have a soft spot for Vikkie,' says Dhara now, startling his thoughts back into the sitting room, into his nervous, unsatisfactory body on the worn-out sofa. He's been doing a lot of this lately, drifting off while others talk to him. He'd like to think he was working on his current book, in his head at least, but the mere idea of it makes him feel sick with apprehension. This has worsened since Armand's arrival, although most of his thoughts have been elsewhere, on the strangeness of it all. On his father's non-being above everything, and how this has left him an orphan. He'd not understood until three days ago how his father's continuing to live had saved him from this realisation after his mother died. He is parentless. Now there is no one, and nothing, to stand between him, Jeremy Eldritch, and his own death. The safety gate has been removed.

'Yes,' he says. 'I do.'

'He's very fond of you as well, you know,' she says, and, for one absurd, vertiginous moment, hope totters in Jeremy's heart. But that can't be what she means. She's his mother, for God's sake, not his pimp.

'He knows, of course?' Jeremy says. 'About Dad, I mean?'

'Oh yes, dear,' she says, 'he's known for a long time now. 'It seemed only right. I wanted my only son to know who his father was.' She smiles. 'Besides, it isn't something you can keep to yourself, is it? Not if you're a parent.'

'I suppose not,' he says. He stands up, uncomfortable suddenly, choked by the halter and bit of family. Dhara doesn't move as he crosses the room and hurries back to the conservatory. He wants to talk in French, about Paris. He wants to go home to his single room with its cupboard-sized bathroom, to his parquet floor and exquisite window, to the grey-green roofs and the grey-blue sky above them, to the tree in his courtyard, in full leaf, which may or may not be a lime. He wants to be able to sit at his own small table, with his lopsided mattress at his back, four hundred kilometres from here, and to walk the streets of the seventeenth, over the railway tracks and down to the market in Rue de Levis, where there are food shops that smell of cheese and meat, and fruit that tastes of fruit. He wants Jean-Paul to walk in and put a bag of mirabelle plums beside him, and kiss the back of his neck as he squeezes past. He wants Armand to take him home.

But the conservatory is empty. Jeremy is at a loss. He stands beside the chair Armand was sitting in, his hand on the back. And now what shall I do? he thinks. He's about to turn round, go back into the house and pour himself a drink when he hears voices in the garden. Before he has realised what he's doing, he darts back into the shadow of the doorway. A moment later, Rachel and Armand appear round the side of the house. She is holding a letter. They are walking together, deep in conversation, towards a bench in the furthest corner of the garden, the part his mother had let grow wild. He remembers, with a vividness that makes him catch his breath, the two of them sitting there, in the long grass, picking daisies, and his mother showing him how to make a slit in the stem of one daisy and thread the stem of the other daisy through it, one after the other, carefully, don't break the stem, darling, carefully, look, like this. You see? He remembers the chains they made, of daisies, chains that his mother twisted into crowns, and how they walked back into the house together like a queen and prince, hands linked as the daisies were linked, and how the patch of garden they'd sat in was crushed and flattened, and how many daisies his clumsiness had ruined.

36

DENNY

Denny is shaving in a hotel room in Berlin. He is using a disposable razor, the best he could find in the supermarket round the corner from the hotel, having left his electric razor at home, but his throat and chin are already stippled with beads of blood. The hotel towels are white, and it gives him a certain degree of pleasure to examine them after they have mopped the blood up. There's the usual po-faced message on the wall, in German and English, about saving the world by not replacing towels that don't need replacing, which only increases his pleasure at dirtying everything he can find as rapidly and definitively as he can, throwing the towels onto the floor in a sodden heap, kicking them round the foot of the lavvy to be found by the semi-literate Third-World employees of this hotel. He's wearing the dressing gown he's been provided with, also white and bloodied, also destined for the floor. Thank God he's leaving today.

He's been in a filthy mood ever since he arrived, and last night didn't help. He was supposed to be having dinner with a woman he'd met last year, a journalist who'd interviewed him about one of his horses that had done rather well in various gymkhanas. She'd known fuck all about horses, but that hadn't mattered after a few drinks. He'd been looking forward to renewing their acquaintance. He wouldn't have come to Berlin, a city he increasingly dislikes, if she hadn't suggested they have a repeat performance. She'd called off at the last minute, texting him with some excuse about a sick child when he was already sitting in the restaurant, a place she'd originally suggested as convenient for him. It was run by postcard-style Bavarians, and was the kind of place he'd normally cross town to avoid, but he'd already ordered a beer and didn't feel like wandering around in drizzle to find somewhere better. He picked up the menu a second time and tried to concentrate. This was the first he'd heard about children. He consoled himself with the idea that he'd had a lucky escape, although he hadn't thought about the woman beyond a good night's fucking and a fond farewell. He hadn't planned on marriage, let alone adoption. He thinks now and again that he'd have a daughter of – what? – thirty? If Rachel hadn't lost that baby. Now that *was* a lucky escape. Rachel, he said to himself, shaking his head in wonder. Now how did that happen? Her father's money, certainly, but not only that – give yourself a little credit, Denny boy. And the fuss she'd made when he left; he thought she'd never stop crying. This might be the longest journey he's ever undertaken for a one-night stand, he thought as he looked down the list of meat and potatoes in various combinations, a sign of age, perhaps, or the loss of his boyish looks, or merely that he'd exhausted the supply of local totty and needed to cast his net further afield.

When the waitress came back to take his order, pigtails and all, he considered her potential briefly as a replacement for the nookie he'd been denied. She reminded him a little of Rachel: her solid white arms, her height, a general sense of being overlarge. The second time Rachel has come into my head this evening, it struck him. He wondered how she was for a moment, if her business had gone belly up as disastrously as his. What fucking awful times we live in. At least the UK doesn't have the fucking euro round its neck. As the waitress waited, lips pursed, pencil poised over notepad, he decided he'd get more joy from some pay-porn on the flat-screen TV in his room. He ordered something the menu described as a meal for men: pork shank, potato dumplings, a litre of beer. Later, when he went downstairs for a piss, he found himself in a tiny low-ceilinged dance hall filled with pensioners, a live band in lederhosen playing waltzes at the far end of the room. God help me, he said to himself. No wonder they lost the war. Walking back to the hotel, his stomach aching, his head heavy after a second schnapps, he passed beneath the S-Bahn. A group of kids were singing a song he remembered from his youth. That's bloody appropriate, he thought, as a blonde girl he'd happily shag bawled out that she couldn't get no satisfaction.

He was lying on the bed with the remote control in his hand and a box of tissues beside him while two well-built young ladies cavorted on the screen on the opposite wall when his mobile pinged. It might be her, he thought, the journalist's name escaping him, she might have ditched the kid and be looking for some late-night entertainment. But it wasn't. It was his mother. If it hadn't been after midnight he wouldn't have read it, his mother's messages rarely gave him any joy, but it struck him that someone might have snuffed it and that might be worth knowing. It's an ill wind that doesn't blow Denny some good.

He was right. The text – wordy as ever, it must have taken her hours – read: *Thought you should know that Rachel's father died on Thursday. Just found out from Audrey. Quite a shock*

350

although he hasn't been well for some time apparently. Maybe you should pop back. Bygones, etc. Love, Mum xx

He's managed to change his flight, at no small cost. This had better be worth it, he tells himself in the taxi to the airport. His plane is delayed, so he drifts round the duty-free, wishing he hadn't stopped smoking when he sees the sign that says passengers within the EU have no tobacco allowance. That would have been another reason to hate fucking Brussels, he thinks, perversely. He sprays a wrist with some aftershave, which makes him smell like a badger on heat, then decides to buy some perfume for Rachel. He wants to make a good impression on her. He can't recall what type she liked, nor even if she used the stuff; what did she ever smell of, other than horses? They haven't seen each other for more than a decade now, and the last time was hardly a romantic interlude; their lawyers put paid to that. He wanders among the shelves, waiting without success for one of the tight-skirted over-made-up airport girls to approach him and spray him with something, finally going for a perfume he remembers seeing in the bathroom of a rather attractive woman he spent some time with a couple of weekends ago, a little birthday present to himself, seeing that no one else had bothered. It's in a bottle with three fake daisies stuck on the stopper, but he noticed the scent of it on the woman, and then on him, and he sprays some now on his other wrist to remind himself. Sixty-fucking-four, he says to himself, and still up for it, and still, as ever, on the brink of ruin. He rubs his wrists together until the scents are merged, badger and overpriced call girl, rut and cunt. He wonders how Rachel is coping in that great big house, and if that Indian woman is still around the place or if she's thrown herself on some burning pyre, the way they

351

do. He knows how much Rachel loved her father, he'd never stood a chance. Still, buck up, Denny boy. She'll need a shoulder to cry on, he thinks with satisfaction, standing in the queue to pay. There's money in plastic, he reminds himself as he hands over his card. The old man must have left a fucking fortune.

He picks up a car at the airport and drives along familiar roads to the house, the Eldritch family pile. Nice Georgian place, garden all round, high wall. Must be worth a bob or two, even with the market as it is. The first time he saw it he had Rachel beside him, and they were in his dad's BMW, which would have driven this piece of tinny shit – a Daewoo, for Christ's sake! – into the ground. The second time, that same night, her mother was next to him in the other seat and Rachel's weirdo brother was in the back with blood all over his T-shirt, stinking of piss, wrapped in a horse blanket. Funny how some things stick. He was sure the old girl had been up for it, but then she'd gone before he had a chance to find out, run off to Paris or somewhere, then Greece. Her death had come in handy too, but he was still with Rachel then, which helped. Still, he's sure she's got a soft spot for him if she digs down deep enough.

There are three cars parked in the drive, but he finds a space at the side of the house. He's getting out of the car, wrestling with the seatbelt, when he hears a man call his name. He doesn't recognise him at first. It's only when the man walks towards him, his hand held out, that he sees who it is. Jeremy, her whoopsie brother, fatter than he used to be and balding, but then, who isn't? He takes the hand he's offered.

'Denny? It is Denny, isn't it? Well, this is a surprise,' says Jeremy, his voice uncertain, although it's pretty clear to Denny what kind of surprise he is. An unwelcome one. Well, ditto, he thinks. What the fuck is Jeremy doing here, queering my pitch?

'My mother told me about . . . well, you know, your dad,' he says. He looks round the drive and up at the house. 'Same as ever, I see.'

'Rachel isn't here at the moment. I suppose it is Rachel you want to see?'

Well, that's a bloody stupid question. Some people don't improve with age. He wonders briefly what Jeremy has been doing all this time. The last thing he heard he was writing dirty books for frustrated old women, but surely he's found something better to do with his life since then.

'I was in Berlin. On business,' he says, not answering. 'My mother sent me a text.'

'She's still alive?'

Denny doesn't answer this either. 'I don't suppose you know when she'll be back?'

'She shouldn't be too long,' says Jeremy. 'She's gone for a walk.'

'How has she taken it?'

Jeremy shrugs. 'She's coping. Well, I suppose.'

Denny wants to ask Jeremy what he's doing here. Although maybe he'd rather not know. The last thing he needs to hear about is a fatted calf and a deathbed reconciliation. Rachel always said her brother had been cut out of the will, or should have been. One or the other. And here he is, like some bloody vulture, picking at the carcass.

'Was it . . .' Denny pauses, 'painful?'

'Dad's death?' says Jeremy. 'Not terribly, I don't think. We expected it really. It's always a shock though, isn't it? Death.'

We expected it. This isn't looking good. He gives Jeremy's shoulder an awkward pat. 'Condolences,' he says. To his disgust, Jeremy's eyes mist up. For a moment he thinks the other man is going to collapse in his arms. He hasn't flown halfway across Europe for that sort of pansified nonsense. 'There, there,' he says, repeating the pat from a slightly extended distance.

'The worst part is that you find yourself saying the same things over and over again, as though you were reading them from a script,' says Jeremy. 'The death script.'

What in God's name is he talking about, wonders Denny. He's about to get his case out of the car, to make it clear that he's here to stay, for a night at least, when a tall man comes round the corner. Jeremy sees him too, starts gabbling in French. This man also holds out his hand. Denny's had enough of all this bonhomie, but he takes it and lets his hand be shaken. The man's older than he is, late seventies, maybe more. He's big though, not fat, just big, with a cloud of white hair. He reminds Denny of someone – the way he moves, the way he holds his head – but he can't think who.

'My name is Armand,' the man says, 'We've never met. Dennis, I think? I am a friend of the family.' He sighs. 'Here we all are, at this sad time.'

Friend of the family, my arse, thinks Denny. You're no friend of Rachel, that's for sure. She never mentioned you, in twenty years of marriage. What is this? he thinks. Some French farce he's drifted into by mistake? The place is full of faggots and Frogs, and there'll be that Indian woman too, no doubt.

'Denny,' he says. 'It's Denny. No one calls me Dennis.'

'Dennis,' says Rachel. 'You're the last person I expected to see.' She has sneaked up the drive behind him and is standing by the car. The other two must have seen her approaching and said nothing. She's too far away to be hugged or kissed

354

without his moving towards her, and he's not sure he wants to do this. He wants her to fall into his arms, not be trapped against the car door like a loose colt. But that's not how it's going to work this time, he sees that now. He walks towards her, takes her awkwardly in his arms, as much a wrestling hold as a hug. He can feel her stiffen. Oh fuck, he thinks, this isn't going to be as easy as I'd hoped. She's looking better than she did last time, he notices, slimmed down a bit, her haircut changed. He kisses her on the cheek, as close to her mouth as he can get without running the risk she might turn her head away.

'Mum texted me,' he says. 'I came as soon as I could.'

'What do you want?'

He's at a loss. This isn't what he'd expected. She called him Dennis. 'I thought you might want me to be here,' he says.

'I can't imagine why,' she says. Her voice is hard. He steps back so that he can get a better view of her; he's never seen her like this. In the past, she's always looked as though a word from him would change everything, the right word if he could find it. *Sorry* has often been enough, but this time, he senses, *sorry* won't wash. And besides, he has nothing to apologise for. He didn't need to fly across Europe to be here beside her. Who the fuck does she think she is to treat him like this, as though he'd come in on the sole of someone's shoe? He takes her arm. When he feels her resist, he increases the pressure until he's sure it hurts.

'Let's go inside,' he says. 'I need to talk to you.'

'So how has it been for you?' he says. They are sitting in the room her father used to call his office, though he can't have done much in here after he was shuffled off the board. Denny's mother has kept him in touch with the local news, businesses failing, negative equity; just enough information, he's often thought, to keep him out of England, to let him dig his own financial grave somewhere far away from her dirt-dishing coffee-morning cabal of widows and well-heeled divorcees. Most of them dead by now, though, and where has all that money ended up, he wonders. He should have been a gigolo, he's often thought so; he likes older women and what they know, their neediness, and their money, of course. And he has the *physique du rôle* for it still if push comes to shove; no one has ever had cause for complaint about Denny's performance. If he could get Rachel into bed, he thinks now, just for half an hour, for old time's sake, everything would fall into place. She can't have forgotten, surely. She'll come round, he's certain of it, given half the chance. That first time, outside the barn dance, he'd never seen knickers whipped down so fast, never heard so much noise. She loved it, he'd never known anyone like her. Hard to imagine her now, with her legs wide apart and his face between them. Although maybe not. Maybe not hard at all. He risks a sympathetic smile. He's almost there, he'd put money on it. She's lost for words. She's his.

'*How has it been?*' she says after a pause, looking up suddenly and staring into his eyes as though she's never seen him before, with a *Who the fuck are you?* expression. It's the face she had when she called him Dennis. His heart sinks. 'How do *you* think it's been?'

'I mean,' he says rapidly, 'it can't have been easy, I know.' His armchair is too low for him to comfortably reach forward and give her a coaxing touch. She's taken the desk chair and is swivelling slowly from left to right, then back.

'I don't know what you want from me,' she says. 'Or, actually, I think I do.' She laughs, but it isn't a pleasant laugh. 'I don't know why it took me so long to see how you work.

Let's face it, you aren't that difficult to see through. Are you, Denny?'

He doesn't know how to answer this. He isn't sure he's grasped what she means, but he's understood enough to know that neither *yes* nor *no* quite seems to do the job. And to know that he doesn't like it.

'You never answered my last letter, did you, Denny?' she says. 'Or the one before. I suppose you were busy with something. All I wanted was a little advice, but you couldn't be bothered. I wouldn't be surprised if you told me you never even read them.'

She's right. He threw them away as soon as he'd checked there was nothing legal in them. He'd forgotten about them. 'That was years ago,' he says now. When she doesn't answer, but seems to be waiting for him to answer more satisfactorily, he adds: 'I'm sorry.'

'After you left me,' Rachel says, 'I was so sad. I wanted to kill myself. Do you know how that feels, Denny? I used to lie and try to stop breathing so that I'd die. No, not stop breathing exactly, not hold my breath or anything like that, just *not breathe*, like one of those Indian chappies. Just lie there and sort of pause everything, like with a film, you know? With a picture of you in my head. But I couldn't do it. My body wouldn't let me. I'm glad now, but still.' She stands up and walks across to the door. She's going to leave him in here, alone. 'You don't know you did that to me, do you? Or you didn't before today. Do you have any idea of what you do to people? How you leave them? And now you want to know how it's *been* for me?'

A second time, finally humbled, he says it: 'I'm sorry.'

'Go,' she says. 'I hate the sight of you.'

37

JEREMY

'So that was Denny,' says Armand, as the car turns out of the drive.

'Your ex-son-in-law,' says Jeremy.

Armand glances at him sharply. 'My what?'

'Isn't that what you two were talking about earlier? I saw you. She had your letter, didn't she? She wanted to know what it said.'

Armand looks behind him, a pantomime villain. But he has never been that, Jeremy knows. He's the one who has kept the secret, not Armand; kept the secret all these years, the secret his mother shared with him, not knowing what else to do with it, whether to use it as a weapon or a bond. Kept it from the only person who might have had a use for it.

'She doesn't understand a word of French,' says Armand. 'How is that possible? I thought all you English schoolchildren studied French? When you arrived in Paris, I remember, you spoke a perfectly acceptable French, despite your dreadful accent.'

'Armand,' says Jeremy, exasperated. He doesn't mention his degree.

'Yes,' says Armand, with a little shrug, 'she had the letter

I wrote so many years ago to your father. I didn't recognise it at first. My handwriting has changed so much in the past three decades, I hadn't realised. It is so rare these days that I write with a fountain pen. No, more than three.' He sighs. 'Thirty-five years. And yet it seems only yesterday I sat down and wrote that letter. Such a spiteful letter, so filled with hate. I reread it with shame.' He shakes his head. 'I was ashamed for the man I was.'

'Yes, yes,' says Jeremy. 'But how did she react?'

'I was so angry with your mother, that was the truth of it. I lost all sense for a moment. No, no, for more than a moment, for months on end. I'd hoped she would agree to live with me, you remember that I told you this? To leave your father. I would have left Hilary for her, she could have left Reginald, I thought. There was no longer any need for her to stay with him. You were an adult. Your father had lovers, everyone knew that. I thought she would realise how very sad she was, how desperate. How humiliated. We spent a few days together, in London, in a hotel. She never told you, I'm sure of that, she never told anyone, except her last husband, perhaps. It was like the first time, before she ran away from me and took my daughter with her. My only child. Hilary couldn't have children, I didn't think it would matter. It didn't matter. I never wanted children with Hilary. But Vanessa mattered. When she wouldn't have me, I thought I could force her hand, is that the expression? And so I wrote to your father and told him that I was Rachel's father.'

'And Rachel?'

'Do you know that I had never seen her before three days ago?' says Armand. 'All these years, these decades, my daughter, so near to me as the bird flies. I had seen photographs, of course, Vanessa sent them to me — to the office, necessarily.

When she was at school, and later, when she was a young woman. I didn't ask her to. Often I wished she would stop. I cared too much, or I didn't care enough. I was never sure. Hilary found one once, in the . . . what do you call this?' He slides his hand into an imaginary breast pocket. 'The handkerchief pocket of my jacket. She wanted to know who it was; I lied, of course, I don't remember what I said now. She had her suspicions but she never imagined the truth, I don't think. I hope not. She thought I had a mistress, and, of course, I did. I have always had a mistress. You met one once, do you remember? She was a wonderful girl. But she never imagined I was still in love with your mother. That would have hurt her more than I would have wanted. And now, it is all past, your mother and Hilary as well.' He smiles, strokes Jeremy's cheek with the back of his fingers before Jeremy has a chance to move away. 'I have always seen her in you, always. Asleep, you are her.'

So that's what he was doing, thinks Jeremy, that night I woke up and found him in my room. And then, he thinks, my mother lied to me about all this. So many lies. No wonder none of us can tell each other the truth.

'And Rachel?' he says.

'Rachel?'

'How did Rachel react? When you told her?'

Armand smiles again, shakes his head.

'Oh no, Jeremy.'

'What do you mean?' She didn't believe him, he thinks, not at first. By now she'll be in shock.

Armand looks behind him again before speaking.

'Of course I said nothing. How could I tell her? She has just lost her father. How could I tell her that she has never had a father in any way she might understand?'

'You mean she still doesn't know?'

'She must never know, Jeremy.' He spreads his hand. 'Never. You do see this, don't you? What sort of father would I be if I told her?'

'So, when she showed you the letter, what did you say?'

'That it seemed to be a letter from someone your father had dealt with on a matter of business, there were problems with money. She asked why that should have upset your mother so much. I was worried she would ask me to translate it word by word. I had to think quickly. You see, I had no idea the letter still existed. Vanessa never mentioned it. You never said a word that made me think the letter might have been seen by anyone but your father. To be honest, I hoped that even he had not seen it, that it had been lost in the post. As soon as I had posted it, I hoped that it would disappear, sink in the Channel. And then I hoped that it would be forgotten, or thrown away as the work of someone who was crazy, a madman.' He sighed. 'That was what I hoped. And then, no one said anything. Not a word. You never mentioned it. I thought you might, that first time you came to the printing works, do you remember? But I knew from your mother's silence that she had seen it. She was never the same with me after that. That was what I most regretted. That she could no longer respect me for one foolish and petty act.'

'And Rachel believed you?'

'I think so. Yes, I'm sure she did. I told her that, in my experience, money is always a difficult area in a marriage. She seemed to accept that.'

Jeremy nods. 'She would,' he says.

'Rachel's marriage, of course, is over,' says Armand, glancing towards the gate through which Denny's car passed ten minutes ago.

'Judging from the way he drove off, I should say definitely so. Which is quite a relief. I was worried she might fall back into the trap. He spent all the money Mum left her before running off with the stable maid or whatever they're called.'

'Surely Nathalie Cray has written about stable maids somewhere?'

Jeremy finds himself grinning. 'Oddly enough, I don't remember. I'll have to ask her next time I see her.'

'And when will that be?' says Armand. 'Because I would also like to ask her some questions.'

Jeremy shrugs. 'Not now, Armand,' he says.

'I shall be leaving tomorrow,' says Armand.

'Later,' says Jeremy. 'We'll talk about it later. I promise.'

Jeremy leaves Armand and walks into the conservatory. He's planned to find Rachel but is overcome by a sudden weariness and sinks into one of the wicker chairs. Moments later, he's asleep. He wakes up with a start after half an hour. He dreamed that he was in his flat in Paris and that something monstrous was trying to break in through the door. It would enter, he knew, and so he waited to one side of the door, intending to dart out as the monster came in. But the door opened and the monster was too fast for him. The monster was a large woman dressed in grey, with a cowl of some sort over her head. She was covered in cobwebs and filth, her skin was soft and damp, her bosom vast. She caught him by the collar and pulled him back into the room. She grabbed him and pressed him to her, but he was laughing already as he pushed her off. I'm Death, she said. Well, he said, you aren't very convincing, you don't scare me. She looked disappointed. She is a matron in fancy dress. You did your best, he said, to comfort her. If you were the real thing, I'd be scared. But you aren't, you see. I'll know Death when I see her. And now he is sitting in his mother's conservatory, his face on fire from the sun, in a cold sweat. He struggles to his feet.

Rachel is upstairs, standing outside their father's room, her hand on the knob of the door. He can't tell if he's caught her entering or leaving. She doesn't see him at first. When she does, she turns away and walks across to the window.

'I told Denny what I thought about him. I said I hate the sight of him,' she says, not looking at Jeremy. He climbs the last few steps and crosses the landing to stand beside her.

'And do you?'

'Yes,' she says. 'I didn't realise it until I actually saw him sitting there in front of me but, yes, I really do. I loved him so much and now it made me feel sick just to look at him. Incredible, isn't it? I don't know how I put up with him all those years. What a waste of time it was.'

'I'm glad.'

'Are you?' she says.

'I'm sorry, I shouldn't have said that. It's none of my business.'

'That's just it, though, isn't it? In this family. None of it is anyone else's business. I wanted my family to be different. I was determined it wouldn't end up the way we all did. And then I lost the baby.' She stops talking.

'I didn't know you'd lost a baby.'

'Nobody did. I never told you. What would have been the point? Well, Daddy knew, of course, I told Daddy, but he didn't want to talk about it.' She pauses. 'That's something else we're not very good at, isn't it? Talking about it. Asking for help. Explaining things. I used to think it was a blessing.

If it is, it's a mixed one.' She looks at him for the first time. 'Do you have anyone to talk to?'

'Sometimes,' he says. 'Armand, I suppose.'

'Do you talk to him?'

'Not about everything,' he says, immediately ashamed of himself. 'No, not really.'

'Did you talk to Mummy?'

'I wish I had,' he says. 'More than I did, I mean. You always imagine there's going to be time, don't you?' But he hadn't imagined that. He'd known she would die and that so much would be left unsaid when that happened. But it hadn't seemed to matter until it was too late.

'Did they talk, do you think? Before she walked out on him?'

He doesn't like the way she's expressed this, but he lets it pass. 'No, I don't think they did.'

'I sometimes think Daddy didn't know what to say to her.'

'When he wasn't with some other woman, you mean? He could have made more of an effort, perhaps. I think she was bored. Cooking and gardening weren't enough.'

'He told me once he used to read your novels because he thought they could help him understand women,' says Rachel.

'He said that? He actually said that?' Jeremy starts to laugh.

Rachel smiles. She seems surprised, and then relieved, as though some spell has been broken, some evil spell that has held them both in its thrall. 'I wonder, perhaps if you'd started writing them earlier, she'd have stayed with him.'

Jeremy shakes his head. 'I don't think so. She could have left him any time. I'm surprised she didn't do it before she did. Just before she went, she told me she was looking for a flat for herself.' And for me, he thinks. She had Armand in Paris, waiting for her. Why on earth did she send him and not go herself? Was it because of Rachel after all?

364

'You know, I've been so stupid, Jeremy. For years, I thought it was a letter Daddy got that drove her away. I was sure it was from some lover of hers, or some jealous wife. That French letter, do you remember? And I didn't want you to read it, I didn't trust you to tell me the truth. And do you know what it was? Some business about a bill that hadn't been settled. Armand explained it to me this afternoon. All these years, I've blamed Daddy for her going, I thought the letter was the last straw, and I was wrong. It didn't have anything to do with it. I know it was his fault in any case, I'm not that stupid, I know he treated her badly, I know he was unfaithful, but so was she, she treated him badly, all the time. You know she tried to seduce Denny once, before she went? He said she was like a cat on heat. She treated Daddy as though he didn't matter. But I blamed it all on him because of that letter, and I was wrong. All these years, I've been wrong. Such a stupid idea. I knew it wasn't really, but you know how you cling to things? As though they explain everything?' She pauses. 'And I can never make it up to him.' She is crying now, and making no attempt to wipe away her tears. 'I can't bear it. I don't know what I'm going to do.'

Jeremy takes her in his arms and holds her. She is taller than he is, but not by much, and over her shoulder he can see the garden wall, beyond that the sea, the dark clouds low above it as though a storm is approaching, the wind turbines almost still. He fancies he can hear them: a slow deep grinding, like teeth, not human teeth, the metallic teeth of a distant, unoiled cog, or pair of cogs, because a single cog is useless. Weighing one pain against another, one slowly revolving wheel against the next, he will keep his mouth shut, he decides. He will do as Armand has asked him. He will let the engine turn.

38

JEREMY

'I can't do it,' says Jeremy. He and Armand are sitting outside a pub, with the sea less than fifty yards from their table. It is grey and rough, and looks cold, but people are paddling along the edge of it, wincing as pebbles cut into their feet, edging their way from groyne to groyne. 'Not any more.'

'This must be what you call the spirit of Dunkirk,' says Armand, with a shudder. On the table between them is a plate of empty oyster shells and two half-full glasses of stout. Armand has just ordered a second dozen of oysters and two more pints. 'You can't do what?'

'Be Nathalie Cray.'

'Don't worry, my dear,' says Armand. 'No one expects you to recover from this type of shock immediately.'

Jeremy shakes his head. 'No, you don't understand. It's not that. It's just that, well, she's dead. It's got nothing to do with Dad.'

'Who is dead?'

'Nathalie Cray. She's dead and gone. Defunct.'

'Ah.'

'I've tried, honestly I have. I've got a book that's almost

finished, to tell you the truth. *The Chained Gardenia*, I thought I'd call it. But I just can't churn the same old stuff out any more. I'd say my heart's not in it, but that makes it sound as though my heart had been in all the others.'

'I thought it was,' says Armand, sounding hurt. 'Your devoted readers think your heart is in them, every one of them. *Her* heart.'

'Maybe she had more power over me than she does now. I don't know. Whatever she did have, she's lost. I'm sorry, Armand. I'm afraid my devoted readers will have to make do with what they've already had because there ain't gonna be no more.'

'There is talk of a film deal. The Americans I spoke about yesterday are very excited. There's nothing definite, of course, but there never is with these people until something has been signed.'

'Well, look at the backlist. Can't they make films out of all that? I can just see *Love Lashed to the Mast* at the local multiplex.'

Now it is Armand's turn to shake his head.

'They badly want new material. A tie-in with the book we are supposed to be publishing this autumn. The book you're supposed to have completed already.' He looks briefly thoughtful. '*The Chained Gardenia*, did you say? I like it.'

'I never promised to write a book for autumn.'

'Jeremy, dear. Don't be infuriating. You have given me a new book each year for the past how many years now. I naturally assumed that this year would be the same. I am here to encourage you to meet the conditions of the contract I have signed for us.' He gives a rueful smile. 'With my own blood. You would not let me bleed to death?'

'For God's sake, Armand. I never asked you to sign anything

for me. If you'd spoken to me first, months ago, I'd have told you there wasn't going to be any book.'

The oysters and stout arrive. 'You will be coming back to Paris after the funeral, I suppose?' says Armand, tartly, it sounds to Jeremy.

'Of course I will. What would I do here?'

'And what will you do in Paris? Not write, obviously.'

Jeremy pushes the plate away from him. 'Please don't be like this. I know you're disappointed.'

'You have been writing these wonderful books for years now, as regular as clockwork, and finally, after all our work, you have found an audience.'

Jeremy tries not to react to the word *wonderful*. He's irritated now, on two counts. 'Well, actually, I've always had an audience,' he says.

'A real audience. A legitimate audience.'

'They're the same old books. What's changed?'

'Times change. Tastes change. Your time has come.'

'People have always read porn,' says Jeremy. 'They're just allowed to be open about it now.'

'Nathalie Cray is not a pornographer.'

'Oh come on, Armand, surely you don't believe that? You know as well as I do the books are absolute, unadulterated filth. And so politically incorrect I'm surprised we haven't been lynched.' He pauses, picks up an oyster, puts it down. 'My father read them, you know. Rachel told me, and I caught Dhara reading them as well. But I bet you Dad never told her I was the author. He bought them and read them, but he was ashamed of them as well. Ashamed of me, I suppose. Fascinated and ashamed, all at the same time. That's what I've been doing all these years. I've been manufacturing dirty little secrets for people who deserve better. It's time I stopped.'

'You have become a moralist, I see. A petit bourgeois moralist.'

'Don't you dare start quoting Bataille at me.'

'I wouldn't even consider it.' Armand sniffs, then stares out to sea. 'Did you read *Thérèse Philosophe*?'

Jeremy doesn't answer.

'I thought not,' says Armand. 'I'm no longer sure that you know who Bataille is.' Jeremy hears the pronunciation of the name as he is supposed to hear it, as a correction of his own.

Jeremy starts to laugh. 'Well, good. I'm glad.'

'I'm happy to see you're amused.'

'I hope you are happy, Armand. Seriously, I do. It's about time we were all happy.' This time Jeremy picks up an oyster and swallows it. He takes a second one and swallows that, then finishes his first pint of stout, aware of Armand's eyes on him, aware of the cool breeze blowing in from the water and the hairs lifting on his forearms, aware that he is breathing easily for the first time in – what? – days? Months? Something has snapped in him, some taut twined band of tension, snapped and released him. He laughs again. 'You've met Jean-Paul, haven't you?'

'Jean-Paul? Ah yes, your shop-assistant friend.'

'Ouch. That was unworthy of you the first time you said it, Armand, and it still is. Yes, Jean-Paul was a shop assistant once, a long time ago. He isn't now, by the way. In any case, I don't suppose a pornographer deserves much more, do you?'

'I didn't say that.'

'He's in advertising now. He's rather successful. Perhaps that's why he doesn't have as much time for me as he did.'

'Why do you mention Jean-Paul?'

Jeremy stands up, brushes breadcrumbs from his trousers. 'Because I'm going to write a proper novel, about Jean-Paul and me,' he says. 'About the time we spent together. I don't

369

know if I can do it properly, but I mean to try.' He forces his shoulders back as far as they will go, inhales as deeply as he can. 'A proper novel,' he says again, with satisfaction.

Back at the house, Jeremy goes into his father's office, sits down at the desk and turns on the computer. He's not sure what he wants to do, but knows he won't be opening the Nathalie Cray folder. He clicks on his Gmail account. He hasn't seen it since a couple of days before his father died and the inbox is filled with a hundred-plus unread mails for cut-price holidays, Amazon offers, Facebook messages for Nathalie he'll need to look at sooner or later, but not now. Not now. There's an urgent email from Armand announcing his arrival the following day, promising groundbreaking news. Five-, maybe six-figure advances. Film deals. Barriers breaking down. Some book called Fifty Shades of something. Well, thinks Jeremy, I've been there, I've done that. There is nothing that can't wait. He should be telling people what has happened. He wants to let Andreas know. He's about to write to Jean-Paul, but he doesn't know what to say, nor – if he did – how to say it. The last time he spoke to Jean-Paul, a few months before he came back to his family home, in a bar near Gare de Lyon, it was unspoken, shared, time-hardened knowledge that he hated his father. His hatred was a given. And now that's no longer true, it hasn't been true for what feels like weeks, and Jeremy still can't quite account for this. He can't bear the idea that he might have been won round by pity. He's never trusted his capacity for pity. It's always seemed such a passive sentiment, the kind you feel when you see something you can't – or won't – change. It's too attractive an emotion for him, that's the problem. It's a sort of weakness, a gratification.

This is no good, he says to himself. I might not be able to write to him, but at least I can see what he's been doing. He types in the site of the agency Jean-Paul works for, then opens the most recent work. Cosmetics, perfume, sportswear, convenience foods, lingerie, shoes. All the available wealth of the world, thinks Jeremy, clicking on image after image, gleaming and polished and pornographic in its detail. Fifty shades of superfluity. He's getting bored when something stops him, holds his attention.

The door is a normal Parisian street door, the woman wearing a long leather coat, open to reveal a bra and panties, a normal lingerie model. It's the man beside her Jeremy notices. He is bent almost double; otherwise he wouldn't fit into the frame of the photograph. His hair has been bleached blond and is shaved almost to the skull, except for the occasional tuft, coloured brown. He is looking down towards the woman. One of his hands holds a brown and yellow stick but the other arm, with its enormous open hand, is reaching out towards her, reaching down as if to scoop her up. It's a quote from *King Kong*, thinks Jeremy. But it's only a half-quote, because the woman hasn't noticed. She stares out of the photograph, sultry, seductive; buy me, she's saying. It's as though the image were composed of layers, on one of which is the woman, oblivious, and on the other, but not oblivious, the opposite of oblivious, there is the looming, desiring man with the piebald hair and the ungainly, yet elegant legs of a giraffe. There is no way of knowing which layer is the more real, the more authentic, the more needy. But Jeremy knows. This way he will never be hurt, thinks Jeremy, his hand will never be slapped away in horror, or distaste. He will have his other stick somewhere, hidden away somewhere, outside the photograph, in some safe place. The frame is too small for the whole of him. He is older than Jeremy remembers, but not by much. How strange to see him like this, thinks Jeremy. I expected by now that he'd be dead.

'Who's that?'

Vikram is standing behind him.

'Someone I've known for years,' says Jeremy.

'Poor man,' says Vikram. 'I have never seen such an advanced case of acromegaly. It must be very hard for him.'

'Yes,' says Jeremy. 'But there are worse things to be. He lives in Paris, which makes up for a lot.'

'You're homesick?'

Jeremy swivels round to face him. 'Yes, I suppose I am.'

'You will not be staying in England, then?'

'No, I don't think so.'

Vikram looks at the screen behind Jeremy's back.

'He's a friend of yours?'

Jeremy shakes his head. 'He's someone I've seen around. He's very noticeable. The first time I saw him I'd just said goodbye to my mother. Not the last goodbye, although it was almost that as well. The last time we had dinner together in Paris. And then I saw him again, the first time I went to Jean-Paul's flat, when my mother was dying.' He pauses. 'I've seen him a few times since then, in passing. Always near a door, I associate him with doors, and now here he is,' he says, gesturing behind him with his head, 'by a door. Is that cheap, do you think? That kind of thinking? Doors must be difficult for him, but they can be for all of us in the end, don't you think? It's as hard to start something as to end it, sometimes.'

'You are thinking about death,' says Vikram, his voice soft. 'Of course you are.' He fumbles in his pocket. 'I have something for you,' he says, 'for you and for Rachel too, of course, but mostly for you. I found it last night, when I was reading

372

Walt Whitman. I have told you already that I love poetry, I think. We spoke about that poem from the First World War, do you remember? When we misunderstood each other. I think we may have done that too much.' He smiles, then holds out a piece of paper, a leaf from a prescription pad, Jeremy notices. Vikram's handwriting is small and neat, utterly unlike the writing one would expect from a doctor. The paper has a quotation from a poem:

All goes onward and outward, nothing collapses,
And to die is different from what any one supposed, and
*   luckier.*

'You've lost your father too,' says Jeremy. 'I'd forgotten that, Vikram. I shouldn't have. I'm sorry.'

'My mother said she'd spoken to you about the circumstances of my birth. I hope you were not disappointed.'

'I was surprised, I admit that. But, no, not disappointed.' This isn't the time to tell Vikram what else he might have felt for him, and perhaps still does. 'I've always wanted a younger brother.'

Vikram reaches down and pulls Jeremy awkwardly onto his feet to be hugged. 'I am so happy we have found this understanding.' He holds him at arm's length, to see him better, his hands on both Jeremy's shoulders. He's the same height as Jeremy, and stocky, as Jeremy is, but in a good way. One day, if he isn't careful, he will run to fat, as Jeremy has done. They have both inherited their father's build, thinks Jeremy, in the same way that Rachel has inherited Armand's – big-boned, tall. Their mothers have left no trace in them. But that's nonsense. Jeremy is nothing if not his mother's son. Yet there is also his father within him, as his father is within

Vikram. He fights back the urge to thrust his head forward, to kiss his brother full on the mouth.

'Love is what counts,' says Vikram.

Jeremy nods, abashed.

'Who is Jean-Paul?'

'Jean-Paul?'

'You mentioned him before. You were visiting him before your mother died, you said.'

'He's someone I love.' Jeremy smiles, uncomfortable in Vikram's slowly loosening embrace. 'You do know I'm gay, don't you?'

Vikram makes a gesture as if to say, this has no significance. 'Why isn't he here? His place is beside you.'

'We haven't seen each other for a while. I suppose you could define it as a stormy sort of relationship. That's how he'd define it, I'm sure.'

'Does he love you?'

'I don't know.' Jeremy pauses. 'Yes, I think he does. In his way. I'm not an easy person to love.'

'Love is all that counts, for everyone, everywhere. It is our only good, just as death is our only fear. You have it in your own Christian tradition. Agape. Love feast. We must feast on love.' Vikram steps back, breaks contact, as if a thought has just occurred to him. 'I mean this in the metaphorical sense, of course,' he says.

Of course you do, thinks Jeremy. Which is just as well.

39

RACHEL

Rachel waits until Jeremy and Armand have left the house before going back into her father's bedroom. She has been folding his clothes, clothes he hadn't worn for months, but that couldn't be removed while he was there, folding them and putting them into boxes. Shirts with detachable collars, socks that come up to the knees with toes darned by Dhara, she imagines. Long johns. Vests. Waistcoats, some brightly coloured like the kind bookies wear, others designed more soberly for work. Everything washed and ironed and cared for by Dhara. She ought to be here with me now, thinks Rachel, I ought to go and find her and ask her to help me. But something stops her, some sense of ownership, she supposes, although she isn't proud of it. After all, she's never owned Daddy. If anything, he's owned her, body and soul up to Denny, and then again, after Denny had gone. He's been there beside her, in one way or another, since she was born.

She's loved him more than anyone else in her life, she thinks, for the first time without this thought hurting, as she opens a drawer and finds rolled-up ties, dozens of them, placed side by side like brightly wrapped chocolates in a box. He's always loved colour, she says to herself, and she's on the point of tears again as she takes the ties out of the drawer and arranges them on the bed they still have to dismantle and have removed. How sad they look to her suddenly. No one wears ties these days. How sad the whole business is. She can't imagine what anyone would want with all this stuff, and maybe no one will want it, but she would rather be busy than not.

She has always kept herself busy, often to no purpose, but what else is there? Sitting and staring at one's navel like her mother's boyfriend? But that's unfair. She barely knew him. What an awful time that was, and how difficult she must have been. She sees that now. The memory of that awful fight in the car park with Jeremy floods back, carrying with it a small, frail sense of guilt. How easily thoughts of Jeremy and guilt go together, as though she is always doing something wrong, but can't quite work out what it is. Five minutes ago, for example, she should have asked Jeremy in to see if there was anything he might have liked, and now she feels selfish that she didn't, and foolish too, as she thinks about the way she closed the door behind herself, pretending she hadn't seen him until it was safely shut. And then he had been so sweet, and they had held each other with an affection she can't remember having felt for Jeremy since God knows when. Before their mother had died, at least, and probably even longer ago than that. Whole years of time they have wasted between them, as though the world were so full of love they could both afford to be prodigal with it. She had felt herself freeze and then soften, as if she were forgiving him for something. And now she is trying to remember if she has ever seen him wear a tie, and can't.

She pulls open the bottom drawer of the bedside table. There are dozens of those small plastic cups they've been using for pills, and some folded and initialled handkerchiefs, something else that no one uses any more. She bends down, a little grunt at the effort escaping her, and lifts them out, placing them beside the ties on the stripped surface of the bed. Pulling the drawer out a little more, to make sure it's empty, she sees a scrap of pink ribbon. She reaches down to pull it out and discovers that the ribbon is attached to a piece of cardboard, cut to fit the drawer. Curious now, she gets down on her knees to see what the cardboard has been hiding and finds a bundle of letters with the same pink ribbon around them. Her heart sinks, then lifts. She struggles to her feet and then sits back on the bed, as though all the strength in her legs has abruptly drained away, with the letters she wrote to her father in her hand. Pink for a girl, she thinks. Blue for a boy. The ribbon should have been blue.

She is still there half an hour later, although she hasn't been aware of time passing. She remembers when she was pregnant and had only had her father to turn to. She had written the letters she is holding in those few brief months of feeling that her life might matter to someone else, and she had wanted to share that feeling, frightening and thrilling at the same time, with someone who cared. Denny had been so distant, as though he were jealous of the baby before he was even born, although she hadn't known then that it would have been a boy. People didn't, in those days. Perhaps, if Denny had known, he would have been even worse, even more offhand and spiteful with her than he was already. She still remembers how, when she'd told him she was expecting, he'd made her feel both responsible and insignificant, as though she'd left the door open and a neighbour's cat had sneaked into the kitchen – that order of carelessness and unimportance. So who could she have talked to? Her friends? Her friends were Denny's friends. There was Jeremy, of course, but he would never have understood, wrapped up in his own affairs, without a parenting bone in his body as far as she could tell, although she hadn't known about him being gay then. Or had she? She can't remember any longer; it all seems so long ago. She hadn't even considered contacting her mother. The only person left was Daddy. She could have phoned him, but what would she have told him? She didn't know herself. She had written the first letter as a sort of challenge, to hear herself think, she supposes now, sitting on her father's bed in the silent house, to see what on earth she might want to say. He'd written back at once – a lovely, affectionate letter. She still has it in her wardrobe; she has all his letters, still in their envelopes, in a two-pound Black Magic box from a Christmas all those years ago.

And then the letters, almost without her willing it, it seems to her now, had turned into something else. She'd told him how she felt about him, and how much he'd hurt her, and she had continued to send them even when he stopped writing back. And here they were, in her hands: her anger, her accusations, unanswered still.

And she has a flash of memory, she'll never understand when she thinks about it later what might have triggered it, a memory of Jeremy in the garden, sitting cross-legged in his shorts and white shirt buttoned up to the neck, with a smug look on his face as though he's won a prize she's been denied. She sees him open his mouth – to speak, she thinks, but she's wrong – and the glint of spittle on stone as the sunlight catches it. And all her fear comes back to her that he will suffocate before her eyes and she will be left alone. She looks down at the letters in her hands, trembling a little at the shock of it. She tugs at the ribbon and the letters expand in her grasp as if something has been released. How infantile her writing looks, she thinks, as she takes the first letter out from the envelope at the top of the bundle. She starts to read but, almost immediately, decides this isn't, deep down, what she wants to do. She is happy to have found them, that's all. She is happy to discover that he hasn't, as she'd feared so often, destroyed or lost them. She thinks back to that final morning, three days ago now – or is it four? – how quickly time passes, to those moments before her father died, when she forgave him.

She stands up, still holding the letters, and takes them into her room, where all the other letters are, from all the other women in her father's life, no longer hidden underneath her bed or separated into files but spread out over the dressing table where she and Jeremy have left them. She goes back into the room that was once her father's, and picks up an empty box, then fills it with all the letters she has sorted and arranged, all the letters she has pored over these past few weeks, alone and with Jeremy, looking for some elusive truth, or for something that will hurt her, and finding both. Finally, when the surface of the table is clear, she puts her own letters on the top, and picks the box up to carry it down into the garden.

The fire takes no time to catch, but the letters burn best when they are taken out of the envelopes, she discovers, and fed to the flames sheet by sheet. The wind changes more than once and she has to circle the bonfire to avoid the smoke. She doesn't want anyone to find her at first. She doesn't want to have to explain herself to Jeremy or Dhara. Even Vikram has a claim on all this, she thinks. Still, she is doing what her father would have wanted, she's sure of it. The paper curls and crisps and turns bright red along the edges and then black, and finally grey as the ash mounts. But there is always more to feed the flames. She catches glimpses of words, half-words, whole phrases sometimes, endearments and recriminations, my darling, I miss you, you don't know what it's like, you are all my life, next week, he'll never know, your body in mine, yes, no, not a peep. These moments of the letters come back to her, and other moments, but what she feels now is no longer that mixture of shame and curiosity, and growing disappointment, that spurred her on as she read them, with her father still breathing in the adjoining room. She feels released.

She saves her own to last. She crumples and throws the first sheet of the oldest letter onto the heap of soft grey dust at her feet and watches the flame at the heart take a corner of it and spread, greedy, eager, until the whole sheet is burnt, and then the second sheet, and she is deliberately not reading what she wrote as she sees it disappear. The only man she has ever known who understood what it must be like to want a child and to want to protect that child, she thinks, how lucky she was to have him. The second letter, and the third, and they burn along with the others until not even a word of them is left. Everything is consumed.

She is down to the final envelope, which feels bulkier than the rest. She remembers it now, remembers writing it from the hospital after her baby had been taken from her. An awful letter of pain and anger, and some of it, she recalls with a vivid flush of pain, directed at him, at Daddy, who had failed her, she felt then, although she couldn't say why. She reaches into the envelope and, with difficulty, pulls the letter out and sees that there is another letter with it, folded within it. A letter in her father's hand. Three sheets, his handwriting elegant as ever, tightly packed. She starts to read. *My dearest Rachel. I don't know how.*

'That's quite a bonfire.'

She turns round. Vikram is standing beside her, close enough for her to touch him. She didn't hear him approach. How long has he been there, she wonders.

'Yes,' she says. She is blushing.

'Sometimes the best way forward is to free oneself of the past,' he says.

This is the sort of comment that normally annoys her, but today she nods.

'These are your father's letters?'

'Yours too,' she says. 'I should have asked your permission.'

He smiles, then shakes his head.

'That doesn't matter. The letters weren't addressed to me, I don't suppose.'

Is this an accusation? Rachel thinks. And if it is? 'Well, they weren't addressed to me either, if it comes to that,' she says. 'But that didn't stop me reading them.'

'And what did you discover?'

She shrugs. 'Nothing I didn't already know.'

After a moment, Vikram says, 'I've just dropped in to take back all the pills that are left. To dispose of them safely.'

'Oh yes,' she says. 'All that morphine. Before the rest of us can take it and get high?'

'Yes,' he says, smiling back. 'There is always that risk.'

She pauses, looks away, then back at Vikram. 'I'm sorry we haven't always treated you well,' she says. The sun is directly behind his head; it's hard for her to see what his face is doing. He's the same height as her, she notices, or slightly shorter. Solidly built. She can see why Jeremy likes him so much. Her father's genes. She's often wished she were like the others, like her brothers, less gawky. All at once, for no reason apparent to her, she's curious, and no longer embarrassed to have been found. She's done nothing she needs to be ashamed of. When

Vikram tilts his head to one side, a characteristic gesture, she is suddenly blinded by the sun. 'I do want us to be friends,' she says.

'I want that too,' he says. 'I'm sure we can manage it if we try. You and me and Jeremy. I spoke to him yesterday. It was a good conversation, useful. Healing, I want to say, but that is what doctors are trained to say, isn't it? My bedside manner. My mother tells me that she has spoken to him as well.' He touches her arm and then her hand, a light, brief touch, a brushing of fingers. 'I'm sure we can all three of us reach an understanding. As your father – as our father – would have wanted.'

She's holding her father's unread letter in her hand. *I don't know how.* Vikram glances down at it.

'I'm sorry,' he says, 'I interrupted you.'

'That's all right,' she says. 'I've almost finished.'

Her father could have sent her the letter when he wrote it, she thinks, but he chose not to. He chose not to have her read it. She turns back to the bonfire, which has almost died out, and moves the ash with the toe of her shoe until she finds a spark. She feeds the first sheet in, the corner first and then the rest of it, holding it with her hand until it catches and flares up. The paper is old and brittle; it takes no time at all to burn. Before it dies down, she does the same with the second sheet, and then the third.

40

JEREMY

Jeremy is at work. He is sitting in the garden, as far from the house as he can get, with a notebook he bought this morning from a shop in Whitstable. It's a black notebook, unlined, A4-sized or almost, and has an elastic band attached to the cover to keep it shut and safe from prying eyes. He can't have written in a notebook for twenty years and he's glad he bought himself a new fountain pen as well, with cartridges, something he hasn't owned since he was at school and used green ink to be different. He's sucking the end of the pen and wondering what the hell to write. Maybe he should have used his laptop, but he wants to make a break from all his old writing habits, from *her* writing habits. He doesn't want to feel the gin and cachou-scented breath of Nathalie Cray on his neck. He wants to see where his hand will lead him.

Armand left this morning, but has insisted that he will return for the funeral next week. He took the unfinished draft of *The Chained Gardenia* with him, along with a half-promise from Jeremy that he will make an effort to complete it. But first he must see what else he can do, he told Armand this morning, standing beside the car, wishing that Armand would just give up and leave. Dhara has gone back to her own house, Rachel is at the stables for a couple of days, trying to persuade her manager to continue to run the show for another week or two, until the whole business is over. There is the meeting with the solicitor to get through, and decisions to be made about the house, but today none of this is important. Today, in the warmth of the garden his mother made decades ago, on a faded deckchair he remembers from his childhood, with the empty house on the far side of the lawn and the sound of an unidentified bird coming out of the dense, flower-laden tangle of wisteria at his back, he is thinking about Jean-Paul. He could have gone back to Paris with Armand, the solicitor's appointment could have been brought forward, or postponed, it wouldn't have mattered. But he wants to be as distant as he can be from Paris for a few more days, in the hope that this will allow him to see his life there more clearly. He closes his eyes. Moments later, he is asleep.

He wakes up, drenched in sweat, his face burning. He has been asleep in full sunlight for almost three hours. His new pen has leaked on his shirt, his notebook is lying face down on the grass beside his chair. He has had a dream involving Jean-Paul and his mother, arguing in a hotel room about how to roast lamb. Jean-Paul was looking to him for support but Jeremy, despite all his efforts, couldn't make himself heard. Perhaps he was outside the window, hovering above a street, or standing on one of those ledges they always have in silent films, the hero in hazardous balance. He can't remember. He takes a deep breath, vaguely distressed, then struggles to his feet, impeded by the rigid, precarious shifting of the deckchair beneath him. For a moment, he's not sure where he is. And then, falling back into the deckchair, he knows and, at the same time, as though it is this that he has dreamed, he recalls a day with Jean-Paul, a day he'd forgotten about entirely, as though it were today.

They were in a flat they'd briefly stayed in, one autumn, in Sète. The flat was on the first floor, overlooking a canal, with the sea and a cantilever bridge fifty yards to their left as they stood on the narrow balcony that ran the full width of the flat. The only bedroom was an internal room, not much larger than the double bed it held, with, to let in light, an unglazed aperture, high on one wall, onto the living room. The first few nights, they'd loved it, that atavistic sense of entering a hide, or nest, to sleep. They'd burrowed beneath the duvet, like baby hedgehogs, Jean-Paul had said, and Jeremy had wondered why, of all woodland animals, he should have chosen hedgehogs. He can't remember now if that's what had started the row, or if it had been some other small miscomprehension, some failure to align. Jeremy was a worshipper at the cult of perfect understanding; he would fret for hours about what might have been *really* meant by a harmless remark, a glance, suspicion gnawing at his faith in the other, and in himself. But it could just as easily have been some other real or imagined slight. Jeremy is not an easy person to love, he says to himself, remembering Vikram's eyes as he said it, as though his words had confirmed something. Whatever the cause, he and Jean-Paul had begun to argue while they were cooking dinner. They were in the cluttered over-equipped kitchen, Jean-Paul was looking for something he said Jeremy had been the last to use, and wasn't this always the case. But the hedgehog comment had been there as well; it hadn't been forgotten. And yes, that's right, it comes back to him now, he hadn't known the word for hedgehog – *hérisson* – and Jean-Paul had had to translate it for him, and he had remained irrationally annoyed. After all, he can't know every fucking word. And then the corkscrew

385

had gone missing, and Jeremy had been the last to use it at lunch, or so Jean-Paul had said, and he'd snapped back that it hadn't been his idea to open a bottle of wine at lunch. Maybe if they drank less, they'd do more, he'd said, and Jean-Paul had said, Like what? You seemed perfectly happy to snore like a stuck pig on the sofa for most of the afternoon. And so it had gone, from bad to worse, to worst. They weren't unused to this type of skirmish, but this time both of them had said too much. And when the words had hurt enough, or had ceased to hurt enough, Jean-Paul, or Jeremy, he can't remember who, had grabbed a T-shirt from the clothes horse and thrown it across the kitchen. It fell on the stove, on an open flame, where it almost immediately caught fire. Yes, thinks Jeremy now, it was Jean-Paul that started the clothes-burning part of it. The T-shirt was Jeremy's absolute favourite, the Mapplethorpe portrait of Patti Smith from the sleeve of *Horses*. Screaming with rage, he grabbed it from the flame and, when the flame licked up to his hand, ran with it onto the balcony, throwing it to the street below. Haring back into the flat, avoiding Jean-Paul's attempt to stop him with the skill of a quarterback, he whipped a pair of lightweight Bermuda shorts from the clothes horse and held them, tauntingly, over the flame of the cooker. You wouldn't dare, said Jean-Paul, his voice trembling, and this might have been true, but fire caught the hem and before Jeremy had time to react the seersucker had flared into life like a torch. Jean-Paul tore them from his hands and ran, as Jeremy had done, across the flat, hurling them from the balcony with a stifled cry.

By the time they'd finished, half the clothes horse had been stripped, burnt and consigned to the pavement below. They might have continued until the only clothes they had were those they were wearing if Jean-Paul hadn't glanced down when the heat from a flaming pair of underpants reached his skin and seen an old woman staring up at the balcony, both hands raised to her face, surrounded by a heap of blackened rags. Oh my God, he said. His shoulders began to shake. Jeremy saw this from inside the flat, and thought he'd gone mad. He reeled from the shock of it, as though madness had never been so close, had suddenly become manifest and to be feared; as though their behaviour up to that moment, the behaviour of two men in their early forties who were supposed to be in love with each other and had sworn so, a dozen times, that very day, had been the epitome of mental health. He'd reached Jean-Paul on the balcony. The woman below had begun to swear and shake her fist. Vandals, she called them, and then, though how could she know this – from the labels on their clothes? – homosexuals, perverts. Word had got round. Was she a friend of the concierge, they wondered, or the concierge herself? United, despite themselves, by the woman's invective, the two of them had begun to laugh. Later that evening, when the clothes had been gathered up and disposed of, the corkscrew found and used, tears shed and kissed away, Jean-Paul had said that what he saw when he spoke of them as hedgehogs was two small creatures with the warmth and tenderness of themselves turned inwards, each to each, and the prickles turned out against the world.

Jeremy struggles up from the deckchair a second time. Inside the house, he pauses in front of a mirror in the hall and sees his face, three-quarters of it burnt deep red by the sun, already sore. He climbs the stairs and splashes himself with water from the bathroom tap, then takes off his shirt with the ink stain over the heart and stands there, looking at himself in the mirror above the basin. He is old and pale and overweight, but Jean-Paul has also lost his looks, his extraordinary looks, and this doesn't matter, not deeply. They are pale and soft like hedgehogs, he thinks, and they must never turn their backs on each other, or they will do each other damage without even meaning to, because of what they are. He drops his trousers and underpants. He feels like a child, naked in the house of his parents, who could catch him at any moment. He is alone in a place in which he has no right to be alone. Stepping out of his clothes, kicking his shoes from his feet, peeling off damp socks, he turns away from the mirror and walks across the landing into his father's room. Boxes filled with his father's clothes are stacked beside the door, waiting for a charity shop to pick them up, apart from a seersucker jacket that Jeremy has decided to keep, and a dozen ties he will probably never wear, selected for him by Rachel. The hospital bed has been dismantled and taken away and Vikram, with his and Armand's help, has carried the old bed back into the room, this monumental double bed in which his parents must have made love, and his father with Dhara, and with who knows how many other women. He crosses the room and lies on it, at the centre, naked, unmoving, aware of the pulse in his forehead, the beat of his heart. He spreads out his limbs into a star, a stilled turbine.

He could close his eyes and sleep again, he almost does, but he gets up instead and crosses the landing a second time. Rachel's door is closed, but not locked. He opens the door, looks in. Her bed is made, her clothes put away. There is a book on the bedside table, a P.D. James. He will make an effort with Rachel, he decides. She is alone now, or thinks she is. She thinks she has no father, which isn't true, and a half-brother in Vikram, which isn't true either, but that doesn't matter. They are both as true as they need to be. Perhaps they will both have other brothers, and sisters, if what Dhara has hinted is also true. He is amused to find himself enjoying the idea. What an odd family they will finally be.

He goes into his own room now, and puts on a clean shirt and a pair of trousers, slips his feet into sandals. The words of the poem Vikram gave them, about death being luckier than anyone supposed, come back to him. He can't imagine what they might mean. The real luck, he thinks, is to stay alive. Downstairs, he picks up an apple from a bowl in the kitchen and takes it into the study.

The shelf of Nathalie Cray books is by the armchair. He pulls one out and begins to thumb through it. He's tempted to take them out into the garden, the whole damned shelf, and burn them, one by one, as Rachel has done with his father's letters. How hard that must have been for her, he thinks. He could be brave as well, and make a bonfire of the airbrushed witch's work. But then his eye falls on a line or two, and then a scene, and he remembers writing them, and finds himself smiling. Jean-Paul would pick the books up sometimes and read out whole paragraphs until the two of them were weak with laughter. I don't believe this is possible, he would say, and he would pick up a tie, or a belt, from the floor. Now sit on that chair, he'd say, and let's see how long it takes you to work yourself free. He puts the book back where it was. I'll finish the new one, he thinks. I'll finish it, for Armand's sake if for no other reason. I'll find the Nathalie Cray within me one last time. But first there is something else he must do.

Standing up, he crosses to the computer. Someone must have used it earlier in the day, because it is in sleep mode. He fiddles with the mouse, biting into the last part of his apple, the skin on his right cheek taut from the sun, and opens his Gmail account. He writes, pecking at the keys with one finger:

My dearest Jean-Paul,
My father died on Thursday. I need to talk to you. I shall be back in Paris next week.
   I miss you. I love you. Don't give up on me.
   Jeremy

As soon as the email is sent, he realises he is trembling. I might have sunstroke, he thinks. I might be delirious, or hallucinating. He sees himself as he was ten minutes ago, naked in front of the bathroom mirror, his face three-quarters red, one quarter white, and smiles. Is that what I am, he wonders. So bare, so vulnerable, so divided? He sees himself lying naked on the empty double bed, splayed out like a star, a source of infinite energy. Is that what I am? So whole? He sees, in his mind's eye, the discarded notebook and fountain pen in the garden. They were ploys, he knows now, evasions, like the piece he'd started about his mother's lacquered tray, and abandoned. He doesn't need them. He takes a deep breath and opens a new document, entitles it Ice and Fire.
   He types:

There is a story that someone once asked Cocteau what he would do if his house was on fire and he could only take one thing away from it, and Cocteau replied that he would take the fire. Sometimes, I think that Jean-Paul is the fire I would take, and sometimes I think he is the house itself. And so what am I?

This isn't right, he thinks, not yet. He will have to change Jean-Paul's name, certainly, and find some other way in perhaps. Perhaps the first person isn't the way. So many 'I's ahead. Perhaps he should start with the day they met, the party, his smile, the cigarette. There is so much that needs to be said.

But it's a start. And that will do.